Joss Wood loves books and travelling—especially to the wild places of southern Africa and, well, anywhere. She's a wife, a mum to two teenagers and slave to two cats. After a career in local economic development, she now writes full-time. Joss is a member of Romance Writers of America and Romance Writers of South Africa.

Katherine Garbera is the *USA TODAY* bestselling author of more than ninety-five books. Her writing is known for its emotional punch and sizzling sensuality. She lives in the Midlands with the love of her life; her son, who recently graduated university; and a spoiled miniature dachshund. You can find her online at www.katherinegarbera.com and on Facebook, Twitter and Instagram.

Discover more at millsandboon.co.uk

TEMPTATION AT HIS DOOR

JOSS WOOD

HER ONE NIGHT PROPOSAL

KATHERINE GARBERA

MILLS & BOON

First Published in Great Britain 2020
by Mills & Boon, an imprint of HarperCollinsPublishers,
1 London Bridge Street, London, SE1 9GF

Temptation at His Door © 2020 Joss Wood
Her One Night Proposal © 2020 Katherine Garbera

ISBN: 978-0-263-27921-4

0420

MIX
Paper from
responsible sources
FSC® C007454

Printed and bound in Spain
by CPI, Barcelona

TEMPTATION AT HIS DOOR

JOSS WOOD

One

Joa Jones ducked under the red-and-white portico covering the impressive doors to Murphy International, thankful to get out of the snow-tinged rain. She blew into her hands, thinking she was inadequately dressed for Boston in late January.

It had been summer when she left Auckland two days ago. Left what she knew would be her last au pair contract.

In New Zealand she'd been an integral part of the Wilson family, welcomed and loved. They'd suggested she move to London with them but she knew that it was one of those oh-God-what-if-she-says-yes? suggestions. No, moving to London with the Wilsons wasn't an option; their kids were older now and no longer needed a nanny.

Sadly, Joa knew she needed to move on. She could've easily picked up another job in New Zealand but, for the last few months, she'd been unable to ignore the feeling that she was in the wrong country, and in the wrong career.

Returning to Boston was a scary but necessary option. The *only* option.

Joa pushed her fist into her sternum, trying to push her panic down.

Since Iz's death she'd done a load of self-analysis and was now self-aware enough to know that by becoming an au pair, she'd been trying to find the family she'd never had growing up in the foster care system. She was twenty-nine years old and if she wanted a family, she'd have to make her own.

And she was done insinuating herself into other people's lives only to have to say goodbye when the families moved on.

Returning to Boston was her new start, a reset.

She'd take the time to be with her foster sister, Keely, and with Keely's help, Joa could figure out what came next.

Blowing into her hands, Joa looked up and down the street, not seeing Keely. On arriving at Logan International, Joa had received a text message asking her to come directly to Murphy International, the world-renowned auction house situated in central Boston. She and Keely had a meeting with the CEO to discuss the auction of Joa's foster mother's (and Keely's great aunt's) art collection. The collection was one of the best in the world and, on Isabel Mounton-Matthew's death a little over a year ago, Joa and Keely inherited her art, along with a historic house in Boston's moneyed Back Bay neighborhood, a stupendously healthy stock portfolio and various plump bank accounts.

Joa, a child of Boston's foster care system and a teenage runaway, was now an heiress. The mind boggled.

Keely, adopted by Isabel after her parents' deaths when she was little, could've just met with Carrick Murphy on her own; she knew the Murphy brothers from way back and

Joa had given her power of attorney to act on her behalf a week after Iz died. She trusted Keely implicitly.

But Boston was where Joa needed to be, the place where she would—she hoped—figure out her future.

A taxi pulled up and then Joa found her arms full of her curvy, bubbly friend. Keely rained kisses on her face. "It's so amazing to see you, Ju. FaceTime is just not the same."

"It's good to see you too, Keels," Joa quietly told her. And it was.

This woman had welcomed Joa into her house, into her life, and treated her like a sister, a best friend. From the day she'd left the shelter and moved into Isabel's mansion, Keely had shared her clothes, showed her how to apply makeup, coached her through her first date. It was Keely who'd helped her fill in college applications and choose her prom dress.

Most importantly, it was Keely who held her hand as they buried Isabel.

Impulsively and uncharacteristically, Joa reached for Keely again and pulled her into another hug. She was family; the only one she had.

Keely, always happy to hug, rocked her from side to side before pulling back and placing her hands on Joa's cheeks. "You're an ice block! For goodness' sake, let's go in. And what are you wearing?"

Joa looked down at her thin coat, jeans and now-wet trainers. "Not enough, apparently." She followed Keely into an impressive hallway dominated by a wide marble staircase and the familiar smell of beeswax polish.

To the right of the staircase, a sleek woman sat behind an equally smooth desk, waiting for them to approach. Keely pulled off her cashmere coat and draped it over her arm. A security guard stood by the door, another two by the entrances of the viewing rooms. Paintings hung on the walls and massive, tumbling arrangements of flowers spilled from two crystal vases on two plinths on either side of that impressive marble-and-wrought-iron staircase.

Joa, in off-the-rack clothes and shoes and wearing a battered vintage jacket, was in no doubt she'd stepped into another world. In spite of her new inheritance, this was Isabel's world, Keely's world, not hers. Intellectually she knew that she was a now stupendously wealthy woman, but emotionally, she was still that fourteen-year-old runaway, scared and cynical, always looking for the stick behind the carrot. A large part of her was still waiting for someone, anyone, to tell her that Isabel's bequest was a mistake, that a girl from the wrong side of the tracks wasn't allowed to inherit a half share of one of the biggest fortunes in the country.

Joa felt Keely's hand on her back, grounding her.

"It's so good to have you back, darling. How long are you staying?"

"Not sure." Joa moved her rucksack to her other shoulder and shrugged. "My contract in Auckland ended. I think I need to switch directions, find a new career. So I'm staying until I can figure stuff out. Is that okay?"

Keely pretended to think. "Well, I'm not sure if we have room for you at the inn. It's only a turn-of-the-century, fifteen-bedroom house with too many reception rooms, libraries, a ballroom, two dining rooms, a media room and servants' quarters. I'm not quite sure where we'll find a place for you," Keely joked. Looking at her rucksack, she frowned. "Where is your luggage?"

Joa pulled a face. "The airline lost it. I think it's in Kuala Lumpur. I've been told it will be here the day after next."

"Or never."

"That's a distinct possibility," Joa agreed.

Keely's phone rang and she dug in her tote bag to pull it out. She swiped the screen and Joa caught the indistinct outline of a handsome face, a flash of white teeth as the man smiled.

"Hey, where are you?"

Joa started to step away but Keely's hand on her arm kept her in place. Who was this man with the amazing, growly, gorgeous voice? Keely's new boyfriend?

Curious, Joa angled her head and, making sure to keep out of the eye of the camera, took a quick peek at Keely's screen.

Holy crap, cupcake.

Joa looked past the frustration dancing in those mostly green eyes—a light green touched with flecks of blue, gold and jade, the colors of a mother-of-pearl shell—and the annoyance tightening his mouth. Stubble covered a strong jaw and stubborn chin, and his open-collar chambray shirt skimmed broad shoulders, revealing a chest lightly covered with nut-brown hair, the same color as his collar-length, wavy hair. He looked like a fallen angel, someone who could be pretty but wasn't, and was better looking for it.

He rocked the word *masculine* and Joa just knew that his body would match his face. God couldn't be that cruel to team such a sexy face with a body that wasn't as fine. Joa was very certain he had a flat stomach, long legs and a perfect ass.

That was the only scenario that made sense. The butterflies in her stomach flapped their wings in enthusiasm. And appreciation.

When last had she had such a visceral, *sexual* reaction to a man? Last year? Two years ago?

Never might be closer to the truth.

"I've just arrived at Murphy's," Keely replied. "We're running late but I let Carrick know." Keely handed an appointment card to the concierge and motioned Joa to lead them up the steps. "Are you joining us for the meeting?" she asked the hottie on the screen.

"Nah, too much on my plate."

Keely stopped halfway up the stairs and Joa, a step higher, turned around to look down at her. A frown pulled Keely's delicate brows together and concern flashed in her eyes. The man on the other side of the call was someone Keely cared about.

"What's the matter?" Keely demanded.

"Anna's gone."

Joa, knowing they wouldn't be moving until Keely finished her conversation, placed her arms on the railing and looked down into one of the viewing rooms. Murphy staff, dressed in red golf shirts and chinos, carefully lifted a huge painting off the wall.

Keely sounded horrified. "Oh, crap, that's the sixth one you've lost since Lizbeth retired."

Sixth what?

"Tell me something I don't know." The voice muttered, utterly pissed. "She went on a shopping spree."

Keely pulled a face. "What did she buy?"

"Lingerie, designer. Cosmetics, designer. A designer sofa. Various high-end perfumes, shoes, handbags, clothes."

"Wait! Let me guess…all designer."

"Yeah. I single-handedly kept more than a few Boston boutiques in business recently."

"I would not have expected her to do that." Keely placed her hand on her hip. "You have the worst luck in nannies, Ro."

Joa's interest was pricked by the word *nanny*. It was her profession after all. Ah, the conversation was starting to make a little more sense.

And Keely called him Ro…

Keely had to be talking to Ronan Murphy.

Keely had often mentioned him in her frequent, lengthy emails. He was the worldwide director of sales and marketing and Murphy International's chief auctioneer. Keely had known the Murphy family since they were all kids, and she had been a college friend of his wife's.

"I don't need this now. Thandi's parents are on vacation, so they can't help me with the boys and I have a day from hell today."

"I can pick them up from school, spend the afternoon with them and feed them dinner," Keely offered, as generous as ever. "They seemed to enjoy themselves last week."

"Isn't your sister coming in today?" Ronan asked.

"She's here." Keely started to turn the camera toward her and Joa made a slashing motion across her face. Was Keely insane? Joa looked like roadkill.

Keely rolled her eyes but thankfully didn't turn the camera. "Joa won't mind, she loves kids."

She did love kids, but on her first night back in Boston, she wanted to chat with Keely, drink wine, catch up.

Keely ignored Joa's shaking head, her don't-do-it expression. "Consider it done."

Dammit, Keels.

"You are an absolute lifesaver." Joa heard the gratitude in his voice.

"I'll let the school know," Ronan told Keely. "Now I need to start hitting the phones to track down a new nanny."

Boston had some good agencies; he'd pick up someone in a heartbeat. Joa knew this because she'd researched those agencies back in New Zealand, before she'd decided the Wilsons would be her last au pair job.

Keely tipped her head to one side, her bright blue eyes meeting Joa's. "Before you hire someone new, talk to me first. I have an idea."

The temperature of Joa's blood dropped a degree. No way, Joa mouthed. Absolutely not!

"If you are offering to look after the boys on a full-time basis, my answer is yes. Hell, yes."

Keely laughed at Ronan's hopeful statement. "I love you, and your kids, but not that much and not in that way."

So Keely and Ronan weren't romantically or, eek, sexually involved. And why did that make Joa happy? She was, obviously, more tired than she thought.

Keely continued, "But I might have a solution for you. Let me talk to someone and I'll get back to you."

No, she was exhausted and imagining things. Keely couldn't possibly have hired her out on her first day back home. Not even Keely was that bold.

Joa was done with au pairing; she didn't want to drop herself into another family because she couldn't trust herself not to fall back into her bad habit of pretending it was all real.

After Keely said goodbye to Ronan, Joa gave Keely the stink eye. She wasn't interested in becoming Ronan Murphy's nanny, or anybody's nanny. Not today, tomorrow or anytime in the future.

"Do not even think about it!"

"What?" Keely asked, pulling on her butter-wouldn't-melt-in-my-mouth expression. Joa knew her better than anyone and knew a diabolical mind lived under that innocent exterior.

"I don't want to be a nanny again, Keels."

She was done with au pairing, with pretending she was part of a family only to realize that after a year, sometimes two, her families would move on...without her.

Besides, she didn't work for single dads, not anymore. She'd learned her lesson with Liam, then with Johan. Joa knew that single dads were her kryptonite, because she found herself easily believing she was the wife they needed, the mother their children craved.

Liam had met and married someone from his office, someone who adored his kids and was happy to be their full-time mom. The week before their wedding, Joa had gotten her marching orders. And Johan, well, he was gay and had wanted another husband...

If Joa wanted a family, she needed to have one of her own and not appropriate someone else's.

They started to walk up the stairs, Keely's high heels clicking on the expensive marble. Joa could only hope that she wasn't trying to figure out a way to get her to fall in line with her wishes... Keely was a force of nature. Not a gentle breeze or soft summer rain but a Category 5 hurricane or an asteroid strike.

Maybe if she changed the subject Keely would be distracted. It was worth a try.

"I know that Murphy's is going to auction Iz's art collection for us, but I don't understand the reason for this meeting. They have the inventory, they auction it off and then cut the foundation a check. I thought it was a simple process."

"Not exactly," Keely said, guiding Joa down the hallway to her right. "Murphy's has to check provenances to make sure all the items are genuine. Most of Isabel's works have been well documented, but Finn, the younger Murphy brother, found three paintings at Mounton House that we suspect might be lost Homers."

Okay, wow. This was news. "As in Winslow Homer?"

"Mmm. Finn Murphy took one look at them and said we need to establish provenance, which is a pain in the butt. Anyway, the meeting is with Carrick Murphy and Sadie Slade, an art detective. Isn't that a fun career? *Hi, I'm an art detective...*"

Keely continued to talk. "I did some research on Sadie

and she's super smart and, unfairly, as beautiful as she is brainy. She's very much Carrick's type."

Joa rolled her eyes at the speculation in Keely's eyes. Her sister was both lovely and an impossible know-it-all.

Annoyingly, she was often right.

But Keely also had a grasshopper mind and tended to veer off subject. "We were talking about the paintings, Keels."

"Right, we need Sadie to tell us that all three paintings are by Homer. First, because they could raise a lot of money for the foundation but also because I do not want to eat crow."

Joa knew she was exhausted but she kept losing track of this conversation. "Why?"

Keely pouted. "Because snotty Seymour gave me a twenty-minute lecture about managing my expectations. He's the biggest pain in the ass. He's a lawyer's lawyer, a real dot-your-t's-and-cross-your-i's type."

Seymour? Seymour… Right, the lawyer handling Isabel's estate. Joa had met him at the funeral, then at the reading of the will. Grief-stricken, she hadn't paid much attention, and didn't remember much from either occasion.

"Isn't that a good thing in a lawyer?" Joa asked, bemused.

"I suppose," Keely admitted, "but he just annoys the hell out of me."

Joa was curious to find out how he'd managed to elicit such an extreme reaction from her I-bother-men, they-don't-bother-me sister. "What's he ever done to you?"

"He has a stuffy name and it suits him. Seven feet tall, six feet wide, blue eyes, dark blond hair, a long scar on his jawline. His friends call him Dare, an equally stupid name."

Okay, as their lawyer, his looks and a nickname shouldn't

be a factor. Keely had obviously spent a lot of time looking at the face of someone who annoyed her. Interesting.

Keely stopped by a door with a discreet plate stating it was the conference room—thank God!—and Joa prayed that someone behind the expensive door would offer her coffee. And lots of it.

Joa pushed her shoulders back. She was here so she'd attend this meeting but then she'd retreat, leaving Keely to operate in this rarified world of high-priced estate lawyers and world-renowned auctioneers. Her job, her priority, was to redesign her life...

And if that was her plan, and it was a good one, then why did Ronan Murphy's masculine face keep popping onto the big screen of her mind?

Two

Down the passage from the conference room, Ronan Murphy heard the beep of an incoming group message and picked up his cell phone. Seeing the name of the parents' group for his sons' school in West Roxbury, he opened the message and saw it was a reminder about a dance the fundraising committee was hosting at the end of the month. God knew why they needed to raise funds—the school fees he paid should cover everything from buying plutonium for science experiments to European white truffles for staff lunches.

His phone lit up as message after message came in and Ronan recognized some of the profiles as he'd met many of the mothers while doing the school run. He'd also made the mistake of engaging a few of them in conversation. A few casual greetings and some exchanges about the weather morphed into suggestions of playdates for their kids and a heartbeat or two later, blatant offers to buy him coffee, wine or dinner. He'd even had a few offers for some bed-based fun.

They all received his "I appreciate the thought but I'm not currently dating" line and a few told him to call them if he changed his mind. He wouldn't.

His wife was gone but she was still his wife...

Ronan ran his hand over his jaw, ignoring his cramping heart. He couldn't think of Thandi now, he had work to do, a list as long as his arm to get through. And top of his list was finding a new nanny for his boys.

If he cared what anyone thought, he'd be embarrassed by his inability to hold on to a nanny but since he didn't, he wasn't. As Keely recently reminded him, he'd been through six nannies since Lizbeth retired eighteen months ago, with none of them sticking. Mostly because they paid him more attention than they did his kids.

He didn't need their attention and affection, his boys did.

All he wanted was a nanny who didn't hear the Murphy name and immediately think *"ding, ding, ka-ching, rich Boston bachelor."* Four of the six nannies had flirted like crazy, with two being honest and upfront, telling him that sex was also included in the list of services they provided. Three years had passed since Thandi's death, but he still felt married. He didn't cheat: never had, never would.

He'd thought he was safe from further machinations when he hired Anna—she told him she was gay and in a relationship—but her unauthorized usage of his credit card was theft and couldn't be overlooked.

He wanted someone who didn't steal from him, who didn't see him as a potential husband or lover. He just wanted someone dedicated and honest, someone who'd walk into his house and do what he'd asked them to: look after his kids and leave him alone.

Really, was that so much to ask?

Eli, his executive assistant for the last two years, rapped on his door, and stepped into the room when Ronan told him to enter. Ronan closed one eye at Eli's flame orange suit and black tie. Eli was not only a kick-ass assistant, he was also very fashion forward.

Very, very fashion forward.

Ronan closed his eyes and made a show of patting his desk. "Help, where are my sunglasses?"

Eli rolled his eyes, made to look bigger with a hint of eyeliner. "I'll have you know that fire orange is in fashion."

"Where? In prison?" Ronan shot back.

Eli skimmed the folder across his desk and Ronan stopped it tumbling off the edge by slapping his hand on top. Ronan checked Eli's expression and was relieved to see amusement dancing in those faded blue eyes. He frequently gave Eli crap about his clothes but he never wanted to hurt his feelings. Thankfully, Eli seemed to take his comments with a grain of salt.

Ronan leaned back in his chair and placed his feet on the corner of his desk. He linked his hands across his stomach and rested the back of his head on the seat. "I need to find another nanny. Can you call the agencies for me?"

Eli didn't react. "Sure. What happened this time?"

Ronan explained and Eli shook his head. "I'll get on it." He nodded at the folder under Ronan's hand. "That's an updated list from Finn, detailing the contents of Isabel Mounton's collection. It's quite impressive."

Ronan had already read the updated inventory but didn't tell him that. Eli dropped into the chair on the opposite side of his desk and they ran through Ronan's massive to-do list. With Ronan overseeing Murphy International's worldwide publicity campaigns and their many client liaison divisions, there was never a shortage of work.

"Headache?" Eli asked, seeing Ronan rub his temples with his fingertips.

Always. "Yeah. Got any painkillers?"

Eli shook his head. "You used the last of my stash yesterday. I was going to pick up more later."

Dammit. He thought there might be some pain tablets in the executive bathroom off the company gym. But only he, Carrick and Finn had access.

Ronan pushed his chair back and stood up. The sooner he killed his headache, the sooner he could make a dent in his to-do list. He told Eli to contact the nanny placement agencies while he was gone and left his office.

He passed the conference room, deep in thought. How could he balance his work obligations with his kids? Sure, he could work from home in the interim but that wasn't a long-term solution. He needed, dammit, help.

He needed another Lizbeth…

Ronan heard someone calling his name, silently cursed and turned around. He jammed his hands into his olive green chinos, pulling a smile up onto his face. When he realized it was Keely who'd called him, his smile turned genuine.

Keely was one of his favorite people. Frankly, he didn't know what he would've done these past years without her. She was part best friend, part sister, all good.

Keely reached him and Ronan dropped a kiss on her cheek. "Hey, you. Thanks again for helping me out today." Her meeting with Carrick and the art detective must've just ended. "How goes the authentication process?"

Keely pouted. "Slowly. And it looks like only one of the three paintings might be a Homer, the other two aren't good enough."

"That's not a surprise since Finn raised the same concerns when he first saw the paintings at Mounton House."

Keely nodded and, without turning around, reached back, grabbed the sleeve of a leather jacket and tugged her companion forward. "I've been dying for you two to meet. It's ridiculous that you haven't been introduced long before this. Ro, this is Joa."

He'd heard about her, sure, but they'd never crossed paths. When they were younger, it was because Joa was less socially active than Keely and did her own thing. After school, she went out of state for college and as soon as she graduated, she started to travel.

Keely had described Joa—pronounced Ju-ah, he had to remember that—as having some Bengali ancestry, and he'd imagined a woman with straight dark hair and equally dark eyes. Keely mentioned that she was pretty but he'd never expected her beauty to whip his breath away. Keely also failed to inform him that her eyes were the color of moonlight, a pure clear silver, a color beyond description. Ronan had no doubt those eyes would change depending on her mood: would they turn to pewter, to ash gray, to smoke?

Ronan broke their stare and resisted the urge to run his hand across his face. She didn't need to see how much she'd rocked his world, how off-kilter he felt.

But the truth was… God, she was exceptional.

The rational part of his brain made a quick list—high cheekbones, a mouth made for French kissing and black hair, long and straight and thick, tucked behind pretty little ears—but most of his brainpower was engaged in keeping himself from yanking her into his arms.

Desire, hot and foreign, flickered to life. Heat curled down his spine. Ronan swore that if he licked his finger and placed it against his skin, he would sizzle. He'd never, not even with Thandi, had such a visceral reaction to a woman before.

It made him feel a little sick and a lot sad.

Ronan, knowing that he couldn't keep acting like an idiot, told himself to pull it together. He knew how to talk to people, dammit; it was what he did for a living. He slid another smile onto his face and held out his hand.

Joa tipped her head to one side and put her hand in his. Ribbons of pleasure-pain shot through his fingers up his arm. Pleasure because her hand was soft and feminine, pain because he knew this was the only time he'd ever touch her.

He was married; Thandi was the love of his life. Love and loyalty didn't die just because death separated them. Ronan and Joa exchanged polite inanities for a minute and Ronan noticed she seemed to be finding it difficult to break their eye contact.

Good to know this madness wasn't one-sided.

Keely, bumping his arm with her shoulder, interrupted their eye-lock. "I'm so glad I caught you, Ronan. Where were you rushing off to?"

Ronan gave her a blank look. "I was rushing?"

"You stormed past Joa, you didn't even notice her standing there," Keely said.

He hadn't? How was that even possible? And damn, why couldn't he remember where he was going? Oh, that might be because his brain had just been fried by a thousand volts.

"Did you call the agencies to send you a new batch of nannies to interview?" Keely asked him.

Concentrate, Murphy. "No, Eli is working on that now."

Keely grinned at him. "Tell him not to bother, I have another plan. A really good plan."

"What plan?" Ronan asked, his tone wary. He didn't trust Keely's super innocent expression.

"Ro, Joa is going to be your new nanny. She needs something to do while figuring out the next phase of her life, so she might as well look after your monsters while she muses."

Ronan felt like Keely had put a stun gun to his chest and pulled the trigger. Instinctively he knew there was no way he could allow Joa to step into his house; she wouldn't make it three feet in before he kissed her. She was temptation personified.

There was no way she could work for him…

No. Damn. Way.

And, judging by Joa's completely horrified response to Keely's suggestion, she felt the same.

Shock flashed in Joa's bright eyes and annoyance slid across her face. It was obvious that she didn't appreciate Keely's "throw it against the wall, see if it will stick" idea.

Joa held up her hands and nailed Keely with a hard look. "Will you please stop trying to organize my life?"

She asked the question as if Keely was even remotely capable of keeping her nose out of her friends' business. "Joa, you're going to be bored within a week. You'll need something to occupy your time."

"I've been on my own since I was a kid, Keely. I am perfectly able to arrange my own life," Joa replied, her calm tone containing an undercurrent of annoyance. "And I've just come off a long-term contract. I do not want to jump straight back into looking after another set of kids."

Joa's eyes darted to his face and she forced a smile. "I'm sure your children are lovely but I don't need a job right now and I'm looking to do something different."

Fine with him. He couldn't hire Joa, didn't want to hire her.

Ronan rubbed the back of his neck. Before Thandi died he'd been super confident, completely convinced that the world was his oyster, and his lobster and his sushi, too. He made decisions on the fly, trusted his instincts, and easily sailed through any personal or professional storms.

Then Thandi died giving birth to Aron (something he hadn't believed could happen in one of the best hospitals in the Western world) and the world, as he knew it, stopped.

When he'd finally pulled himself out of his soul-stopping grief, he'd acted like the confident and charming man he'd once been. But underneath his PR persona, he was now protective instead of passionate, cautious instead of bold. He constantly scanned his environment, warding off trouble, looking for danger.

And Joa Jones was both. He knew that like he knew his own face.

"He needs help, Joa," Keely insisted.

"As one of the Murphys of Murphy International, I'm pretty sure he possesses enough skills to hire his own nanny, Keely," Joa said, not bothering to hide her irritation.

"Not if you go on his history," Keely snapped back before Ronan could respond. "He's gone through six."

Placing his hand on Keely's shoulder, he squeezed gently. It was time to end this conversation. "Thank you for your concern, Keels, but I'll take it from here."

Keely looked mutinous but Ronan raised his eyebrows, silently insisting that she not push, and she sighed.

"Life would be so much easier if people just did what I suggested," Keely muttered. "I know what I'm doing."

Ronan's mouth twitched with amusement. "Very inconvenient for you that us lesser mortals possess something called free will."

"Very inconvenient," Keely agreed. She adjusted the strap of her bag on her shoulder and nodded to the ladies' room at the end of the hall. "Give me a moment, Joa, and then we'll go home."

"Thank God," Joa muttered when Keely hustled off. "I thought she'd never stop arguing."

Ronan looked down into her exquisite face and itched to

rub his knuckles over her high cheekbone, to slide the pad of his thumb across her sensuous bottom lip.

Wow. What was wrong with him?

Ronan straightened and folded his arms across his chest, pulling his eyes off her lovely face. He searched for something to say—he normally had a million sound bites so why didn't his tongue want to work properly?—and when nothing came to him, Joa tried to break the awkward silence.

"I hope you find a nanny. I'm sure your boys are very sweet."

"You'll meet them this afternoon since Keely offered to look after them."

Joa shook her head. "I've been traveling for days and I'm going to catch up on some sleep, so I'll probably miss their visit. But Keely has mentioned them in her emails. She says they are adorable."

At three and five they *were* adorable. They could also be demanding and challenging. And, occasionally, more than a handful. "Thanks."

Truth was, he did need someone experienced with children. Ronan thought about interviewing another set of nannies and shuddered.

He couldn't think of anything he'd less like to do.

Maybe Joa could be persuaded to change her mind and maybe, if he tried hard, he could ignore the chemistry, could contain his rogue thoughts around stripping her down and taking her to bed.

"Are you sure you're not the in the market for a job?"

"Pretty sure." Joa tucked her long, straight black hair behind her ears.

Right. Fine.

Actually, her refusal was a relief. While he desperately needed help, the last person he needed in his house was someone who made him wonder whether her skin was as smooth as it looked, whether her mouth was sweet or spicy or both.

Ronan rolled his shoulders, uncomfortable with his errant thoughts. His brothers occasionally raised the subject of his dormant sex life, insisting that it was okay to have needs and act on them. Up until today, he'd shrugged off the odd bout of feeling horny. He'd thought that one day, way in the future, when he put enough distance between him and Thandi's death, he'd consider sex again. He'd expected his libido to slowly wake up, giving him time to come to terms with a new reality.

Meeting Joa Jones was like life had placed a defibrillator on his sex drive.

Ronan muttered an F-bomb under his breath.

There was a reason why he avoided sex. He'd never been good at one-night stands or casual flings and the "separating the deed from the emotion" concept. For him, sex was the gateway drug to relationships and he wasn't interested.

Thandi was irreplaceable and his love for her didn't allow room for another woman, another relationship. He didn't care how difficult it was to raise his sons alone, he refused to slide another woman into his wife's place. That wasn't ever going to happen…

He was still married. He might not wear her ring anymore but those ties, those promises of loyalty and fidelity, hadn't been broken by death.

They wouldn't ever be.

Time to get back to work, to walk away from the incredibly lovely, very distracting Joa Jones. He handed her a brief smile. "It was nice meeting you, Joa."

Joa tipped her head to the side and nodded. "You, too, Ronan. I hope you find the au pair you are looking for."

They both knew it wouldn't be her.

Three

She'd had five hours of sleep and it was nearly dinnertime when Joa made her way down to the kitchen on the ground floor of Mounton House. She looked around, saw no sign of Ronan Murphy's boys and nodded, relieved.

"You just missed the boys. They left ten minutes ago," Keely told Joa as she stepped into the room.

Dropping onto the wide window seat, Joa pulled her feet up and wrapped her arms around her knees. After leaving Murphy International she'd been too tired to fight with Keely about her managing ways and, honestly, a bit side winded by her red-hot attraction to Ronan Murphy.

But she knew she couldn't let Keely's bossiness go unchallenged so she tossed Keely a what-the-fudge? glare. "About your suggestion for me to look after Ronan's kids… What the hell were you thinking, Keely?"

Keely put the kettle on the gas stove and reached for two mugs. "Chamomile or peppermint?" She didn't look even remotely chastised by Joa's deep frown.

"Peppermint."

Keely dumped a bag into a bone china mug. "I know you, you'll need to do something soon, Ju. You hate being idle. And Ronan needs a nanny. Where's the problem?"

She loved Keely, she did, but at some point, Keely would have to realize that Joa was no longer a scared, insecure waif from the streets who needed decisions made for her. "And it didn't cross your mind to ask me whether I wanted another au pair job?"

Keely leaned her butt against the counter and crossed her ankles. "I thought you liked being an au pair."

She did. She liked the kids, she liked the unstructured environment, being able to go to work in shorts and flip-flops. But there was a big downside to her job and that was her inability to stop loving the family she was living with and, on more than one occasion, the man of the house.

She was done with being on the periphery of someone else's family.

On her first au pair contract, she'd looked after the five-year-old son of Liam, an Australian gold mining magnate who'd gained custody after a bitter divorce. She'd been Liam's shoulder to cry on, his best friend and, after five months, she was convinced that their friendship was heading toward something real, something deeper. Then Liam had met Angela, fallen head over heels for her and married her within three months of meeting her.

A year later Joa had gone to work for Johan, a German banker who was recently divorced from Hendrik, and she'd looked after the twin daughters they'd adopted from Vietnam. She knew he was gay, but she couldn't stop herself from dreaming that she would become a permanent part of his life...

Johan had been smart enough to recognize her crush and gently suggest she move on, telling her that there was no possibility, ever, of them being more than friends. She'd taken a break and traveled for a while, before accepting a job with the Wilson family. Dave was married, she rationalized; she'd never fall in love with a married man.

She hadn't fallen for Dave; she'd fallen for *all* of them. Annie became a close friend and quickly became a second sister, and their kids were smart, funny and interesting. Joa had loved working for them—not that it felt like work!—and for the first time in her life, she'd felt like part of a functional family unit.

She'd felt secure and safe. And loved. Now, in hindsight, she knew that her attraction to Liam and Johan had been a rationalization for her need to be part of their family, her desire to be loved and needed. She adored her bosses because they were good men and excellent fathers. They put their children first. Something neither her parents nor her foster parents had ever done for her.

On leaving New Zealand, feeling discarded and tossed aside—her fault, not the Wilsons'—Joa knew she couldn't repeat her past mistakes. She needed to switch careers, to find a job or a passion that didn't involve families and kids.

She had two choices: she could come to terms with being single and childless or she could actively look for someone to create a life with, to have children with.

Both scenarios terrified her.

She didn't want to be alone, but neither did she want to risk rejection.

Devil and the deep blue sea…

"Ronan is a good guy who is going through a difficult time, Joa." Keely pulled her back to the present.

"The guy is rich and successful. He can afford to hire the best nanny in the city," Joa argued. Respectfully, his hard time wasn't her problem.

Keely wrinkled her nose. "I don't know what it is with

him but he always, always seems to hire the wrong people. Since Lizbeth, he's been a magnet for bad nannies."

Joa knew there were a lot of weird people out there—she always insisted on a two-week trial period and had left two families when it didn't work out—and not every nanny was Mary Poppins.

But she still wasn't the person for the job.

"I don't want to au pair anymore, Keels. I really want to try something different."

Keely placed her pointed chin in her hand. "Why? You have a master's degree in child psychology and you are so good with kids."

Joa wished she could explain how she insinuated herself into other people's lives. It wasn't healthy and it wasn't… right. And she wasn't doing that anymore.

Especially since Ronan Murphy was exactly the type of guy she was drawn to…

Oh, hell, why was she even attempting to lie to herself? Her other two single bosses were nice men, reasonably attractive, but Ronan had blown her socks off. The man made her tingle, made the moisture disappear from her mouth. She wanted to know how it felt to have his hands on her bare skin, taste his smile, feel those broad shoulders, that wide chest, that hard stomach.

He was hot and sexy and, worst of all, a single dad. If she went to work for him, she gave herself a day before she started fantasizing about becoming his significant other, stepmom to his supposedly adorable boys.

She wouldn't be able to help herself; it was what she *did*.

Not this time.

And not with that man.

Because Joa suspected that if she went to work for Ronan Murphy and once again fell for her single-dad boss, she'd, yet again, end up lost and alone and rejected.

And she didn't know if she'd be able to pick herself up and start again…

When she spoke, her words were soft but laced with emotion. "I can't do it, Keely. Not again."

Keely, because she was perceptive as well as pushy, frowned. "Did something happen at your last job that I should know about?"

Sure, I keep creating a fantasy that never comes true.

"I'd like to do something different, Keels, that's all."

She needed different.

Keely pulled a face. "There's something you're not telling me," she complained, picking up the kettle and pouring hot water into the mugs. She picked up the mugs and walked over to Joa, placing a cup on the built-in table in the corner of the window seat.

There was an enormous amount that Joa wasn't telling Keely. She never discussed her childhood before coming to live with Isabel and Keely, couldn't talk about the isolation and the neglect. She'd been one of the lucky ones. She hadn't been sexually or physically abused, but others, she knew, weren't that fortunate.

But as she'd transitioned from child to teenager, her unusual looks garnered attention not only from lascivious foster fathers but also from her older foster brothers. When her foster father started looking at her in a non-fatherly way, Joa knew she was in trouble. Unable to face another strange house filled with strange people, she'd taken her chances on the streets. She'd lasted three days before landing at Isabel's shelter and, from there, into this wonderful house with Isabel and her great niece, Keely.

Joa had been so lucky. So many girls who chose the streets didn't end up safe. And none of them, of this she was certain, inherited an equal share of one of the largest fortunes in the country. Isabel had given Joa a safe place to stay, an education and, by writing her into her will, life-long financial security. She'd loved Iz intensely, but Isabel had flown in and out of this house and their lives and was never the fully engaged "mom" Joa needed.

Iz had loved being on her own. She'd never needed a husband to make her feel complete. Maybe Iz was onto something. Maybe it was time for Joa to be more like the woman who'd rescued her half a lifetime ago—emotionally independent, sensible and strong.

Isabel had never looked to a man to make her happy and maybe Joa should honor her foster mother by following in her independent footsteps.

Keely cleared her throat and Joa turned her attention back to the present. "It's unlike you to be so intransigent, Ju. Or to refuse to help someone who so obviously needs your help."

She was just trying to protect herself. She was so done with feeling heartsore and miserable, feeling rejected when she walked away from another temporary family.

She couldn't keep hurting herself, borrowing other people's people. She needed to protect herself because, God knew, nobody else would do it for her.

"I'm sorry you're disappointed in me," Joa replied. She *was* sorry, but she wouldn't change her mind about working for Ronan.

Keely covered Joa's hand with hers and released an audible huff of frustration. "I'm not disappointed in you, I'm just confused. And because you are the most private person in the world, I don't understand why you're being stubborn about helping Ronan. You know me inside out, Ju, but even after so many years together, in some ways you're as much a mystery to me as when we first met."

Joa wished, she genuinely did, that she was more open. It wasn't that she didn't trust Keely, she absolutely did, but

Joa was naturally reserved and a little shy. And, for most of her life, she'd lived in an environment where it wasn't always healthy to draw attention to oneself.

It was a hard habit to break.

Seeing the flash of hurt in Keely's eyes tightened Joa's throat. The words weren't easy to say, but she'd push them out; she owed her sister that much. "I'm sorry, Keels, opening up isn't easy for me. But I do love you. You know that, right?"

Keely's eyes lightened and the corners of her wide mouth tipped up. "Of course I know you love me, you goose. I just wish you'd let me inside that head of yours."

Joa wished she could, too. She could offer to try, but she hated making promises she wasn't sure she could keep.

Thinking that it was past time to change the subject, Joa sipped her tea and looked at Keely over the rim of her mug. "So I looked at the list of Iz's possessions to be auctioned off by Murphy International in their spring sale. Is that the final list?"

"Why? Is there something you want to keep? We can withdraw anything at any time," Keely quickly replied.

Joa held up her hand. "I'm happy with your selection, Keels. But as I walked through the house, I noticed that there's still a lot of furniture and stuff left in the house. What are we going to do with it all? And what are we going to do with the house?"

Keely shrugged. "We need to talk about that. And we need to discuss Isabel's foundation. The CEO left a month back and we need to look for someone to run it. It's a full-time job and I can't do it, I'm swamped."

Keely was a speech therapist and loved her work. Joa was happy her practice was thriving. "Now that I am back, maybe I can help out with the foundation, take a little of the load off you."

Keely smiled her appreciation. "That would be awesome, thank you. So, about this house. Do you agree that it's too big for either of us, or even both of us?"

She did. Who needed a fifteen-bedroom house with four reception rooms, two libraries and a ballroom?

"We could sell it…"

Joa pulled a face. "I don't want to live in it, but I don't think I want it to go out of the family, either. Besides, who would buy such a huge house?"

Keely's eyes turned stormy. "Stuffy Seymour says we could convert it into luxury apartments. He has a developer friend who is interested in doing just that."

Joa tipped her head to the side, intrigued by the annoyance she heard in Keely's voice. Keely was the friendliest person she knew—bossy, sure, but she liked people and people liked her back—so Joa couldn't understand her antipathy to Isabel's lawyer. "What on earth did he do to upset you?"

Keely refused to meet Joa's eyes. "I don't know what you mean."

"Keely, you've done nothing but grumble about him since the day you met. From what I can see, he's been professional and he's done a great job of looking after our interests. Yet you seem to be perpetually pissed off with him. Why?"

Keely's shoulders inched upward. "He just annoys me. He's arrogant and bossy and thinks he knows everything about everything."

Pot. Kettle. Lots of black.

Joa swallowed her smile, intrigued by the idea that Keely had finally met a man she couldn't wind around her baby finger. So what was it about Dare Seymour that raised such fury in Keely? Joa couldn't wait to find out. "Let's invite him to dinner."

Keely looked horrified. "What? Why?"

Joa felt laughter in the back of her throat. Payback was *such* fun. "I'd like to thank him for all his hard work."

"He's getting a percentage of Iz's estate for working that hard," Keely complained.

As Dare was one of the most successful lawyers in the city and came from a famous and cash-flush old Boston family, they both knew he didn't need Iz's money. "Keels…"

"I'd prefer to keep it businesslike," Keely muttered.

If Keely really wanted to keep it professional then she wouldn't be squirming in her chair. And why were her cheeks flushed? *Oh, Keely Matthews, what is going through your head?*

Joa made up her mind. "I definitely think he should come to dinner."

Keels drooped her head to the surface of the table and gently banged her forehead against the laminated surface. "Why do you hate me so much?"

"More to the point, why do you hate Dare Seymour?"

"I don't hate him." Keely's reply was muffled. "He just irritates me. I don't know why."

Joa thought it was time that Keely found out. "Tell me what date suits you and I'll set it up."

Keely groaned. "I hate you so much right now."

Joa reached across the table to pat her head. "No, you don't, you love me."

"I can do both. It's a skill I've perfected," Keely mumbled.

After Keely's surprise pronouncement two days before—and after trawling through résumés of nannies, finding problems with all of them—and two days of hell juggling the boys—Ronan thought he should talk to Joa again about the possibility of her coming to work for him as a temporary nanny.

He was *that* desperate.

On the pro side, she had au pair experience and she was immediately available. And Keely, someone he knew and trusted, could vouch for her good character.

If he wasn't attracted to Joa, he wouldn't have hesitated to try and talk her into coming to work for him. But something about her caught his attention in a way that both scared and annoyed him. Yeah, she was beautiful, stunningly so, with her light eyes and warm skin.

And that wide, sensuous mouth made for kissing…

A huge con was that Joa was the first woman to pique his curiosity and interest after Thandi, and if he was smart, which he obviously wasn't, he'd be running in the opposite direction.

But, because dividing his attention between two young boys and his demanding career was freakin' exhausting, he'd texted her last night and asked if she'd pop around to meet him early this morning, before work, to discuss Keely's out-of-the-blue proposal.

Because she was a little early, and he was very late, he was only dressed in exercise shorts and trainers when she walked into his house at eight the next morning. Ronan wished he'd had time for a quick shower after his workout or, at the very least, to toss on a shirt before her arrival, but nope…

Ronan led her into the kitchen area of his great-room-slash-kitchen-slash-living-room. In comparison to him, she looked fresh and feminine, filling the air with her subtle fragrance.

The urge to bury his sweaty face in her neck, to taste those sexy lips, was strong. Ronan closed his eyes. In his gym clothes, if he sported some wood, there would be no way to hide it. He looked past Joa's shoulder to the photograph of Thandi on his fridge and his erection subsided.

Sorry, love. Forgive me.

Ronan rubbed his hand over his jaw, feeling his stubble. He needed to shave, but that wouldn't happen this morning. "Sorry, we're running late."

Joa placed her bag on the granite counter of the center island. "I see that."

Ronan couldn't help noticing how her cranberry-colored silk sweater flowed over her amazing breasts. He swallowed and started to recite mathematical equations in his head. Unlike his brother Finn, Ronan didn't find math a turn-on.

"The kids are still asleep. They wouldn't settle down last night, so I eventually put them into my bed and put on a movie, thinking that would lull them to sleep. No such luck. I also overslept, so it's a bit mad around here," Ronan said. "And I have a crazy day ahead of me."

"How so?" Joa asked, sliding onto a barstool and crossing one long leg over the other. Those legs went on for miles and he'd love to feel them around his hips or, if she was adventurous, around his neck.

Ronan wrenched his mind off what a naked Joa would look like and, needing something to do that hid his reaction to her, turned his back to check the water and coffee beans in his state-of-the-art machine.

Right, she'd asked about his day.

"This time of the year, as we plan the spring sales, every day is crazy. I will be home late tonight. I'm running a specialized sale on sports memorabilia."

As he turned to look at her over his shoulder, he caught the flash of irritation in her eyes and wondered if she thought he'd assumed she'd be available to babysit for him tonight. He wasn't that arrogant.

Ronan turned to face her and gripped the counter behind him. He answered the silent question he saw in her eyes. "Finn, my younger brother, agreed to look after the boys for me tonight. Luckily it's only a small auction, so I should be done by ten."

"I thought you only ran the big sales."

It was a fair observation. As director of global sales and marketing and the company's head auctioneer, he normally didn't bother with the nuts-and-bolts auctions. "Normally I let the junior auctioneers run the smaller sales but my sports guy had a family emergency. I do have other auctioneers but there are some pretty big spenders in the audience. I thought I'd run the sale, connect with them on a guy-to-guy level."

"I'd like to see an auction," she admitted.

If she attended, he wouldn't be able to concentrate. "You're always welcome," he lied, "though I am assuming you will be at the auction for Isabel's collection. It will be one of the biggest auctions any house has conducted. It's been billed as a once-in-a-generation sale. So it's not a big deal or anything," Ronan quipped.

Joa tipped her head to the side. "I presume that you know that Sadie thinks only one of the three paintings might be by Homer?"

Ronan nodded. "If Sadie manages to prove the painting's provenance and if it turns out to be by Homer, it will be the last item auctioned."

Joa had the prettiest frown he'd ever seen. "Do you think it's genuine?"

For her and Keely's sake he hoped it was, but he never, ever gave anyone false hope. And it was important to manage expectations. "I genuinely don't know. Obviously, for your and Keely's sakes, I'd like it to be genuine. But I never emotionally invest in anything that passes through our house. I can appreciate the skill and rarity and beauty but I know we are only temporary guardians of the artwork.

And I refuse to waste my energy worrying whether a piece is genuine. It either is or isn't and I can't change the result."

Instead of pouting, sulking or looking disappointed by his prosaic statement, Joa tipped her head to the side and seemed to give his words some thought. "That's a fair assessment," she eventually told him.

Smart and thoughtful. Damn, his life would be so much easier if she was just another pretty face. Pretty and sexy he could easily ignore, but pretty, sexy and smart was a killer combination.

Joa lifted her hand to fiddle with the clip holding back the sides of her hair. Her extraordinary eyes met his and electricity arced between them.

No! He needed to kill that current. Immediately.

He knew just the way to do that. By being concise and controlled. Businesslike.

So get to the point of this meeting, Murphy. You need a nanny, she is one. Convince her to take the job and work out how to hide your attraction later.

"I need a nanny, desperately. I'm asking you to consider working part-time for me, mostly in the afternoons, until I can find someone else. And, if you do come to work for me, I assure you that nothing will happen between us, Joa."

"Why would you think it would?" Joa demanded. Her back straightened, her mouth tightened and she tapped an index finger on the granite, completely irritated. Good, irritation he could handle...

Ronan needed to push, to make sure there was no wiggle room on this. Nothing could, or would, happen between them. No matter how attracted he was to her, or she was to him. He was still emotionally tangled up with Thandi.

"Look, I know you've been checking me out, that you're attracted to me."

He thought he heard a snort, something that held more

disparagement than amusement. But he couldn't miss the panic in her eyes. "I'm almost thirty years old, and a healthy female who hasn't had sex in a while, and you're a good-looking guy."

But?

"But the world is full of good-looking guys, Murphy, and I can take or leave them."

Now that sounded like a challenge. And Ronan had never backed down from a challenge in his life.

Or was he using her challenge as an excuse?

Either way, knowing he was making a mistake, but unable to stop himself, Ronan moved swiftly to stand next to her, so close he could see the tiny sparks of lightning in her eyes, each individual eyelash and the tiny scar on her top lip. She smelled like moonbeams and mystery and Ronan knew he wouldn't be walking away without tasting her, just once.

Lifting his hand, he brushed his thumb across her bottom lip, waiting for her to pull back. If she did, he would step away.

But Joa surprised him by placing her hand on the bare skin over his heart and when she arched her back and lifted her mouth to reach his, he took her move as the invitation it absolutely was.

Ronan's lips touched hers and his skin sizzled in response. He felt her fingers dig into his chest, the rasp of her nails as he lost himself in the softness of her mouth. Joa sighed and her lips opened and he slid his tongue inside, groaning as he did so. She tasted of coffee and strawberry lip balm, of frustration and fierce desire. It was a combination designed to make his head swim, to cloud his thinking. He couldn't, wouldn't, allow himself to touch her with anything but his mouth. He couldn't take the chance of losing all his control.

In a moment he'd stop kissing her, in just one more moment...

Keeping his hands fisted at his sides, Ronan kissed her for another minute, and then another, fighting his urge to pull her closer, to find out how well her lithe body would fit to his. He was so big and she was so slim but he knew they would be combustible together and that was why they had to stop...

Now. Immediately.

It still took him another minute to release her mouth, to step back. When he did, he turned away to grab the edge of the island, needing something to hang on to.

What in the hell just happened?

Ronan heard Joa's small curse, felt her sliding off the stool to move away from him. He heard her footsteps and turned his head to watch her move to the sink, before reaching for a clean glass on the shelf above her head. The tap ran and she filled her glass, the space between them vibrating with tension. Joa took a long drink of water before turning her back to the sink, resting her glass in the crook of her arm.

Ronan saw Joa's eyes skate down his body and when hers widened he looked down to see his erection tenting his exercise shorts. Well, crap.

Joa closed her eyes and shook her head. "We shouldn't have done that."

"Yeah, not our best move."

He thought he saw disappointment in her eyes, a flicker of hurt. But he had to be wrong; they were barely more than strangers and hardly knew each other.

This was just desire. There was no emotional connection to be had, not with her or anyone else. They'd kissed. Why was he making a mountain out of a couple of grains of sand?

Could it be because he'd never had such a crazy reaction to anybody, ever? Not even to…

No, he couldn't go there.

That would be a betrayal. Shaking his head, he forced the thought away.

He needed to get his morning, and his life, back on track. "You're a sexy woman and yeah, I'm attracted," Ronan conceded. "But—"

"But it's still not going to happen," Joa finished his sentence for him, rolling her eyes. "Damn straight it's not. I prefer my lovers to be excited about taking me to bed, not angry and resentful."

Ouch. But fair.

"So let's admit that there's a mutual attraction that will not be acted on. Agreed?"

Ronan managed a sharp nod and begged his blood to return to his brain.

Joa reached for her bag, pulling it over her shoulder. She looked past him and Ronan turned to see what captured her attention. Damn, it was the photo of Thandi, her hand holding her hat to her head, blue eyes sparkling, and her smile wide.

His heart cracked. Asking Joa to come here had been such a bad idea, one of the worst he'd had. He needed to backtrack, but Joa beat him to it.

"Going back to why I am here…" She gripped the bridge of her nose before forcing her eyes to meet his. "I'm sorry, but no, I can't help you with your boys.

"Best of luck, I hope you find someone suitable." Joa added, walking toward the huge square entrance to the hallway. Then she turned and sent him a tight smile.

"Oh, and if you don't want your female employees lusting after you, then I strongly suggest you put on some clothes when you conduct job interviews, Murphy. Walking around half-naked isn't conducive to keeping the arrangement businesslike and might give potential nannies the wrong impression."

The heels of her boots clicked on the marble floor in his hallway and then he heard his front door opening, then closing. Ronan slumped onto the closest stool. Joa wielded a mean verbal punch. It was just another thing he liked about her.

Crap.

Four

He was late…

Again.

Ronan stepped out of the lift, looked at his watch and grimaced. Thanks to Sam's teacher wanting to talk to him this morning—apparently it was his turn to provide the class with nut-and gluten-free cupcakes on Friday—he was ten minutes late for the Murphy weekly management meeting.

Eli stepped out of their suite of offices, holding out Ronan's favorite cup. Ronan wrapped his fingers around it and took a big sip of coffee before dumping his coat and leather briefcase into Eli's arms.

"You know I hate asking you to do personal stuff for me, but please will you organize cupcakes, free of gluten, dairy, peanut and tree nut, to be delivered to Sam's school on Friday?"

Eli's love of food was reflected in the slight paunch under his lime green shirt. Today, his pants were a sober black. Eli wrinkled his nose. "What's the point of having cupcakes, then?"

"I'm presuming they are trying to avoid a kid being rushed to the hospital in anaphylactic shock," Ronan dryly replied.

Eli sniffed. "The idea offends me."

Ronan smiled. Eli was often dramatic but he was smart and efficient and often caught the balls Ronan dropped.

And he made truly excellent coffee.

Ronan sipped, sighed and gestured for Eli to walk with him. "Anything I need to know before I go into the meeting?"

Eli nodded, his usually merry face sober. "Yeah. As you well know, the Beijing office is holding a sale in Chinese ceramics…"

Ronan nodded. For the last twenty years, rich Chinese citizens were on a mission to bring Chinese art and artifacts back to their country. The French collector who'd decided to liquidate his extensive collection of Asian ceramics and jade through Murphy International was expecting a multi-million-dollar payday.

"…the head auctioneer was rushed to the hospital with a suspected burst appendix. He's currently in ICU."

Ronan grimaced. He liked Wu, a longtime employee of their Beijing office. "Crap. Is he going to be okay?"

"Yeah, he'll be fine. But Mei Lien isn't comfortable asking Chen to run the auction."

Hell, he wasn't comfortable asking Chen to run the auction, either. The younger man was Wu's apprentice, but he had a long way to go. He didn't have the experience to run an auction of such prestige and importance.

"She wants you to run the sale," Eli explained when they reached the conference room. Ronan looked through the glass doors and saw the meeting had already started.

His brother Carrick was standing at the head of the table, his hands holding the back of the chair. Ronan grimaced, remembering that it was his turn to chair the meeting. While Carrick was, technically, the CEO, Ronan and his two brothers ran the company together.

Ronan mouthed a quick sorry to Carrick and turned back to Eli. "Tell Mei Lien that I will call her as soon as I get out of this meeting."

Eli nodded and opened the door for him. Ronan walked into the room and nodded at Carrick, who moved away from the chair. Pulling the chair away from the table, he dropped into the seat and silently thanked Eli for the agenda, complete with handwritten notes, lying on the table in front of him.

"Sorry I'm late."

Finn, his younger brother, leaned forward and rested his forearms on the table. "Problems, Ro? Eli looked a bit frazzled."

Ronan glanced down at the agenda and decided that his Beijing problem needed to be prioritized. And since this wasn't a formal meeting—and the three other people at the table were long-standing and completely trusted employees—he gripped the bridge of his nose and muttered a quiet, heartfelt curse.

Ronan explained that he needed to head to China that night.

"I'll order the company jet to be prepared and have the pilots file a flight plan," Carrick said, as decisive as ever. Carrick knew, as well as Ronan did, that he didn't have a choice; he was needed in Beijing and he needed to leave that night to make tomorrow evening's sale.

He hated to bring his personal life into the office, but this time, he didn't have a choice about that, either. "I'm stuck for childcare," he admitted, frustration coating every word.

"Thandi's parents are still on their three-month Caribbean cruise and I haven't found a new nanny yet."

Carrick winced. "I'd have them in a heartbeat, Ro, but I'm leaving for London in the morning."

Ronan looked at Finn, who shook his head. "I'm going with Carrick, Ro. There's a collection we are looking at."

Ronan groaned. He trusted his brothers with his kids and, more important, Sam and Aron loved spending time with their uncles. There was minimal discipline, forgotten bedtimes and plenty of unhealthy snacks and video games.

"We're looking at his collection and taking him to dinner at Claridges. Beah is joining us."

Finn, as he always did, flinched at the sound of his ex-wife's name. Why those two ever got divorced Ronan had no idea.

Carrick exchanged a look with Marsha, his PA, who was sitting to his left, taking notes. "Can you get hold of Cummings, ask him if we can postpone viewing his collection?"

Paris Cummings was one of the world's most reclusive and elusive collectors. He never allowed anyone to view his collection and only sold pieces from his massive art collection under the direst circumstances. Or when he needed to liquidate some cash to purchase a bigger, or rarer, artwork.

"Cummings? You've got an appointment to see him?" Ronan asked, surprised. "Why didn't I hear about this sooner?"

Carrick lifted one shoulder. "I know Paris from way back. I remember Dad introducing him to me when I was still in high school. He contacted me directly and I roped in Finn. I emailed you."

Ronan hadn't even had time to look at his laptop. Hell, he was dropping balls left, right and center.

Finn picked up where Carrick left off. "He heard about the Vermeer that is part of the Mounton-Matthews collection and he's prepared to sell some of his lesser pieces so he can bid on it. He wants me to evaluate his collection."

Being trusted to sell off some of Cummings's works of art was a coup and Ronan knew how capricious the man could be. If he didn't think Murphy's was paying him enough attention, he'd refuse to meet with them, call up Christie's or Bonhams and move his art through them.

Finn and Carrick missing the appointment with Cummings was not an option. "I'll make a plan for the kids. Maybe I'll just take them to China with me," Ronan said, only half joking.

"You'd still need someone to look after them while you work," Marsha pointed out.

Ronan saw Carrick's lips twitch at her literal response to the joke, but he just nodded at Marsha's earnest expression. "True, Marsha." He saw his brothers' anxiety and sent them all a reassuring smile. "Maybe Keely will take them for me."

"Or Joa. She's an au pair and has experience in looking after kids," Finn suggested. He leaned back and pushed the tips of his fingers together. "Didn't I hear something about Keely suggesting that Joa be your temporary nanny?"

Ronan nodded. "It didn't suit either of us. She's not looking for work right now…"

And he didn't want anyone under his feet, or in his house, who made him feel prickly and uncomfortable and… aware. Sexually aware.

He didn't need to spend his time lusting over his kids' nanny. It was tacky. "I hate getting a stranger to look after them but if I have to, I'll call an agency and get a temporary sitter."

Carrick gestured to the pile of papers in front of him. "Why don't the rest of us carry on with the meeting, Ronan, and you head back to your office and make arrangements for the kids? I can take them tonight but not tomorrow night."

"Ditto," Finn said as Ronan stood up.

Ronan nodded his thanks and picked up his pile of papers. He took the top sheet and handed Eli's handwritten notes to Carrick. "Let me know if there is something you want my input on."

"We'll manage," Carrick said. "Let us know what you need from us."

"Will do." Ronan stood up and pushed his chair back. He sent each of his brothers a quick look, hoping they saw his appreciation. These men had his back, had always been the two pillars propping him up. From Thandi's death to taking the kids when he desperately needed a break, they were there for him.

He couldn't have navigated the past three years without their constant support. He wanted to express his gratitude, but this wasn't the time or place.

So, because he found it difficult to be vulnerable, he swallowed the words down and hoped they knew how grateful he was that his brothers were his two best friends.

One day, he'd find the guts to say thank-you.

"I wish I could help you, Ro, but I'm out of town, at a conference in Miami. But Joa is at home and I'm sure she'll help you out. If she can't, I'll come home."

After speaking to Keely, Ronan knew Joa was his last shot before hiring a sitter from an agency, something he didn't want to do. Oh, he knew the sitter would be professional and come highly recommended, but he hated the idea of leaving his kids with someone he didn't know.

Leaving his kids with Joa—the woman he hadn't been able to stop thinking about—was still better than leaving them with someone he'd never met before.

Ronan ran up the stone steps to the front door of Mounton House. Ronan had visited before, with his stepmom, Raeni, and remembered Raeni pointing out the massive staircase, the exquisite moldings, glimmering chandeliers and carved mahogany paneling. He'd been ten and thought that the huge hall would make an excellent bowling alley and the staircase would be great to slide down.

While he waited for Joa to respond to the pealing doorbell, he shifted his attention from his lack of babysitters to wondering what Keely and Joa intended to do with the enormous mansion. Others like it had been turned into apartments and he supposed that was an option; it really was too big for a modern-day family. Ronan glanced at his watch, tapped his foot impatiently and rocked on his heels. After hitting the doorbell again and getting no response after five minutes, he called Keely again.

"She's not here," Ronan told her. "Any idea where I can find her?"

"She's there. She's probably doing yoga in the ballroom and zoned out. I can scream at her and she doesn't respond. There's a keypad to the left of the door, do you see it?" Keely said.

Ronan's eyes flicked over the door and he saw the discreet panel. "Yeah?"

Keely gave him the code. "The ballroom is at the end of the hallway, toward the back of the house," Keely told him. "Go hunt her down."

Ronan thanked her, punched in the code and pushed open the heavy door. In the hallway he inhaled the smell of beeswax polish and fresh flowers and looked at the massive walls sporting faded squares and rectangles where art pieces, up until a couple of months back, graced the walls. Those paintings, along with dozens of others, were now in the Murphy International vaults, or out getting cleaned or reframed.

Ronan heard his footsteps echoing in the huge space and took a moment to admire the hand-carved staircase. His ten-year-old self had liked the idea of sliding down the banister—and the man he'd been before Thandi's death probably would've tried it.

Finn, his daredevil brother, wouldn't hesitate.

Ronan rather missed throwing caution to the wind, but then he thought about his boys and remembered that they only had one parent and that he couldn't take any unnecessary risks.

So he admired the intricate carving, the skill of the carpenters and the quality of the Italian marble before striding down the wide hallway, peeking into rooms as he walked past open doors. He'd grown up in a house full of antiques and while he preferred modern furniture and art, he still appreciated the workmanship and history of the eighteenth-century Chippendale table, the solid silver Georgian candelabras and a five-foot Ming vase.

As he walked deeper into the house, Ronan heard the faint sounds of music drifting down the hallway and knew he was getting closer. The music wasn't what he expected from a yoga session; it was heavy rock, with long guitar riffs occasionally punctuated by a deep, thirty-cigarettes-a-day voice.

It was loud, rough, sexy music. The type of music he'd once loved and never listened to anymore.

Ronan saw the half-open door and pushed it with his foot, his heart slamming against his ribs as he watched Joa place one hand on the floor and extend her leg up so she was practically doing splits, standing up. God, those legs…

He knew they were shapely but the Lycra fitted her like

a second skin. Joa, still unaware of his presence, dropped her leg and effortlessly slid into another pose. Keeping her hands on the floor, she tucked her knees behind her elbows and, without a hint of strain, balanced only on her hands. Then she moved her bent knees to the side and held the pose.

And he'd thought he had decent core muscles.

"Crane pose."

Ronan, fascinated at how she was moving her body, took a moment to realize she had spoken. He blinked once, then twice.

He shot an uneasy look down the hall, thinking he should explain why he was in her house. "Keely gave me the code. She said you were here."

Joa pulled one leg up to her chest and let her other leg extend behind her.

Ronan shook his head. "How the hell do you do that?" he asked, stepping into the room.

Joa lifted her head to look at him. "Practice."

Dropping her legs to the floor, she released her arms to stretch out into one of the few yoga poses he could name. "That's the child pose."

Joa's bare shoulders shook with what he presumed was amusement. "Very good. You do yoga?"

"Uh, no." Thandi had, for a few months in between her pregnancies, but she'd never gotten beyond the basics.

"It's great for stress relief."

But her outfit wasn't. Her exercise pants had sheer cutouts in the thighs and calves and her matching top, ending just beneath her breasts, and showing off a tight, super flat stomach, had the same sheer cutout bridging her breasts. Beneath the black Lycra and sheer material was creamy, rich skin.

She'd pulled her hair up into a pile on top of her head and she wore no makeup. She didn't need it.

God, she was beautiful.

Joa walked, her bare feet not making a sound, across the big room to pick up her phone off the small table tucked into the corner of the room. She tapped the screen, the music abruptly stopped and silence dropped into the space between them.

Joa picked up a bottle of water and walked back to him, her light eyes on him while she sipped. "Why are you here, Ronan?"

He couldn't remember. All he could think about was slapping his mouth onto hers and rolling that Lycra down her hips and the top up and over her breasts, revealing all that skin to his appreciative eyes. Conscious that his pants were tight and that air felt scarce, he pulled the water bottle out of her grasp and took a long, reviving sip.

The cold water didn't help him at all. He still wanted her.

Crap. Dammit. Hell.

"Ronan?"

Ronan handed the water bottle back and scrubbed his face, wishing he could dispel the image of those long, strong, supple legs wrapped around his hips, her nipple in his mouth. He held up his hand. "Give me a minute."

"Are you okay?"

Ronan shook his head. No, he was drowning under a tidal wave of lust, looking for air as desire swamped him. He hadn't felt like this for years, if ever. He'd loved Thandi with every fiber of his being but he'd never felt such instantaneous, heart-stopping lust. Never, not even with the wife he still loved and still mourned.

The wife who wasn't here…

Ronan pushed back his grief and his guilt at feeling the way he did, focusing his attention on why he was here, what he needed. He wanted more than anything to leave the room, to walk away from Joa with her light eyes and milky skin and bendy, amazing body. But unfortunately, he needed her help.

"I need a favor," he muttered, noticing that his voice sounded rough. From desire or irritation? Or a combination of both?

Joa didn't respond except to raise her already arched eyebrows higher.

Dammit, he hated asking for help, especially from a woman whom he needed to avoid, but he was, as his English stepmom used to say, in a pickle. "I need someone to look after the boys, tonight and tomorrow night."

Joa lifted her bottle to her lips and frowned. She shook the bottle and then he realized that he'd finished her water. He gestured to the empty bottle. "Sorry."

"I can get more," Joa replied. "Why are you asking *me* to look after your boys?"

"My brothers are going to London to meet with a cantankerous, reclusive collector, and Tanna, my sister, has also gone back to the UK. I haven't found another nanny yet and Keely is—"

"Out of town."

Ronan jammed his bunched fists into the pockets of his beige chinos. "Yeah. I'm stuck. I mean, I could hire a babysitter but I don't like strangers around my kids, in my house."

Joa cocked her head. "Where are you going?"

"China. I need to run a sale in Beijing."

"Chinese ceramics and an incredible collection of carved jade."

It was Ronan's turn to lift his eyebrows. "And you know that how?"

A touch of pink hit Joa's cheekbones. "I might've visited your website."

Ah. "My senior auctioneer is in the hospital and the head of the Beijing office isn't confident in his apprentice."

Joa tipped her head to the side at the same time as she placed her right foot on the inside of her left thigh. The odd pose took nothing away from her beauty.

A small frown appeared on Joa's forehead. "I'm sorry, are you trying to tell me that they want you to run the sale?"

Ronan nodded.

"But you're American. Do you use an interpreter?"

"No, I manage since I speak close to fluent Mandarin."

Joa's mouth dropped open. "Really?"

"My stepmom insisted that we learn another language. My brother Finn, being the intellectual overachiever that he is, learned a whole bunch. I think he's fluent in six or seven, and able to converse in three or four more," Ronan explained. "I chose to go with one, thinking I'd choose Mandarin because it was really hard and maybe Raeni would let me give it up in a few weeks because I wasn't making any progress."

Amusement flashed in Joa's eyes. "Except that she wouldn't let you quit."

"And I wasn't as bad at it as I thought I'd be. Then I spent a year at the Beijing office when I left college." Ronan shrugged, thinking they were way off subject. "Anyway, I'm going to run the auction but I need someone to stay with my boys."

"Me?"

"If you're willing."

"And if I don't say yes?"

Ronan rubbed the back of his neck. He was stuck but he wasn't going to beg. "Look, if it doesn't suit you, I'll call an agency, ask for an emergency sitter. It's not something I want to do, but I'm out of options. This sale will be one of the biggest of the year and many influential billionaires are expected to attend. Handing them an inexperienced auctioneer would offend them and our clients will feel like they are not important enough to rate a decent auctioneer. It would be a snub Murphy International might not recover from."

Joa bit the inside of her lip and Ronan waited for her response. "Two nights?" Joa asked, tapping the empty bottle against her thigh.

"Tonight and tomorrow night," Ronan said, hope building.

Joa's chest rose and fell in a movement that suggested agitation. Or resignation. He didn't care, as long as he got a yes.

"Okay. I'll do it."

Ronan felt his stomach unravel and his lungs release the air he'd been holding. *"Thank you."*

"But just for two nights, Murphy. I'm done with au pairing. I'm trying to find a new direction, a new path to follow."

He didn't care what she did with the rest of her life, he just needed her for the next forty-eight hours. But he did need to find a new nanny soon; this situation was bordering on ridiculous.

"I'm so grateful." And he really was. Ronan twisted his wrist, looked at his watch and gestured to the door. "Is there any chance that you could leave with me now? I need to show you the house, then we need to collect the kids from school and introduce you to the staff there so they'll let you collect the kids tomorrow."

Joa gestured to her bare feet and skimpy gym outfit. "Can I shower and change first? And I need to pack a bag."

Now that he had her agreement, Ronan was loath to let

her out of his sight in case she changed her mind. But if he bundled her out the door and into his car just as she was, he'd look like a raving idiot.

"Okay. I'll wait—" he looked around the empty room and lifted his hands "—where?"

"In the kitchen," Joa replied, walking toward the door. "There's a coffee machine, help yourself. Or maybe you should have a cup of chamomile tea. You're looking a bit stressed."

She had no idea.

Five

Joa was pretty sure that at one time, Ronan's house in West Roxbury had been a designer showcase. His low-slung couches and carefully chosen furniture screamed Nordic minimalism, the bold art giving the eyes a break from the very white double-volume walls.

Joa stood in the great room off the hall—a long and wide room that held a sitting room on one side and a well-designed kitchen on the other with a huge island and a white wood dining table splitting the two spaces—and the huge windows provided views of what was once a landscaped but was now a neglected and denuded garden. Joa wrapped her arms around her body and turned in a slow circle in the huge room. Sadness could sometimes be a tangible thing.

Joa's throat tightened at the image of Ronan's stunning wife in a silver frame on the dusty surface of the Steinway piano. She was cuddling her toddler—Sam?—her huge stomach telling the world that she was about to birth another child, her wide smile tender and her eyes full of happiness.

This was still her house, in so many ways. There was a massive portrait of her immediately catching attention as one stepped into the hall. There was a wedding photograph of her and Ronan on the hall table. A Hermes scarf, pink and gray, hung off the coatrack, as well as a gray felt hat adorned with scarlet flowers.

To Joa, it felt like Thandi had stepped out to run an errand, or that she was upstairs. This was still, in every way that counted, her house.

But there were hints of Ronan, too: a tie on the granite counter, cell phone chargers, a shopping list in what had to be his scrawl on the fridge. And, of course, signs that kids lived here. There was a small shoe under the leather sofa, a green glove on the floor, die-cast metal cars on the Persian carpet.

A massive train set crisscrossed the corner of the room and toys of all description were tossed into boxes, into corners, piled up on chairs.

Yep, this house was chaos. Yet she still preferred chaos to clinical sterility.

Joa turned at the sound of footsteps and her breath caught when Ronan strode into the room, pulling a small suitcase with a laptop bag resting on top. He'd changed into a light gray suit, a pale mint green shirt underneath the designer jacket.

Stepping into the great room, Ronan glanced at his watch and grimaced. "We have so much to talk about and minimal time."

Joa perched on the arm of one of his long and wide sofas. She crossed her legs and linked her hands around her knee. "On a scale of one to ten, how upset are your boys going to be having a stranger look after them?"

Ronan rubbed the back of his neck and Joa saw the worry in his green-gold-blue eyes. "I'm hoping they'll be fine and they'll feel better if we pick them up from school together. Sam is stoic, he's a mature kid, but Aron might get a bit weepy."

Ronan walked across the room to the double-door fridge and pulled out a bottle of water. He waved it in Joa's direction. "Still or sparkling?"

"Sparkling." Joa joined him at the granite center island and slid onto a barstool, perfectly content to watch the tall, rangy, ripped-as-hell Ronan move around his messy kitchen. God, she was so attracted to him. Really, what warm-blooded woman wouldn't be? Thank God she was only going to be his nanny for two nights; more would be impossible.

Joa refused to put herself in the position of having and losing a family again. It hurt too damn much.

It was like putting yourself into a story where you didn't belong, singing a hymn when you should be chanting, painting with oils when you should be sketching with pencils.

She had money, she had time, she had choices. She had so much more than she, a child from the wrong side of the tracks, had ever expected. She owed it to Isabel, to herself, to find her niche, to write her own story, her own song, to live her own life instead of hijacking someone else's.

She was helping Ronan out; she would be out of his life within forty-eight hours, and then he would just be a memory. It didn't matter that she was brutally attracted to him and he kissed like a dream; she was not going to allow herself to indulge in the smallest fantasies around him.

She was all about reality now…

Ronan picked up her water bottle and dashed the liquid into a glass before pushing it across the granite surface in her direction. "We need to leave in fifteen minutes, so let's use that time to go over the ground rules."

"Sure."

Thankful for his businesslike tone, Joa listened as he ran through his dos and don'ts, all of which were pretty standard. Then Ronan pointed to a round light in the ceiling. "I have cameras everywhere so I can see what's going on. All the time."

Joa narrowed her eyes. "Define everywhere? My bedroom, my bathroom?" And that reminded her… "Where am I sleeping, by the way?"

Ronan pushed his hand through his hair. "The boys share a room on the top floor, next to mine. But the guest suite is a floor down. The nanny usually stays there."

Joa shook her head. "I won't hear them if there's a problem."

Ronan took a long sip of his water. "There's an iPad next to your bed. Switch it on and you can see and hear what they are up to. If the boys are upstairs and you are down here, you can carry the iPad and check up on them."

Handy in a place as big as this but he didn't answer her question. "Do my bed and bathroom contain cameras?"

"No, of course not."

Ronan drained his glass and picked up her half-full glass and took them through to what she assumed was a utility room. "We need to go." Ronan told her when he returned, looking reluctant.

Joa sensed how difficult it was for Ronan to leave his sons with her. Sure, Keely had vouched for her and she had nannying experience but she was still a stranger and he wasn't just leaving the city, he was going halfway across the world. If anything went wrong, he'd be nearly seven thousand miles away.

She saw him hesitate and knew he was second-guessing

himself. Knowing that he was on the point of calling off his trip—she could see it on his face—she stepped over to him and placed her hand on his strong forearm, feeling his heat despite his shirt and jacket.

"They'll be fine, Ronan, I promise."

Ronan handed her a look that was long on disbelief and short on confidence. "You can't promise that," he muttered.

Okay, he was splitting hairs, but she got it. "True. Okay, how about this? I will do everything in my power to keep your boys safe. Everything I possibly can."

Ronan stared at her for a long time and Joa knew that she couldn't break the eye contact. If she did, he'd call off his trip. After what seemed like a millennium passing, his shoulders dropped and his face relaxed. He managed a small smile. "I'm being ridiculous, aren't I?"

Oh, that self-deprecating smile was too charming and too sexy for words. It made him seem years younger and very approachable. Joa smiled. "A little. But you're their dad. It's allowed."

"Sometimes I think I've made it into an art form. But I am so damn scared that something will—" He stopped abruptly, his words drying out. Joa waited, hoping he'd finish his sentence but he just shook his head, as if irritated with himself. "Ignore me, I'm rambling. Let's go."

Ronan took her hand and linked her fingers in his, his other hand reaching for his suitcase. As he pulled her and the suitcase toward the front door, Joa was conscious of his strength, the way his big hand enveloped hers, his palm and fingers dwarfing hers. In his hand, hers felt small and feminine and, yeah, safe.

And were those tingles she felt skittering up her arm? Yep, she thought they just might be.

In the hallway, Ronan stopped at the front door and looked down at their linked hands. He pulled his hand from hers and smiled wryly. "Sorry, force of habit. I'm constantly grabbing a child's hand."

Joa felt a vicious stab of disappointment, mortified that while she was thinking of him in terms of being a sexy man, he equated her with being a child.

Joa folded her arms and waited for him to open his front door. "I'm not a child, Murphy." She couldn't help the comment, knew that she was poking a bear with a stick, but she needed him to see her as a woman.

Stepping into the cold wind of a late January day, Ronan pulled the door shut behind him and sent her an inscrutable look. "Trust me, I noticed."

And what, Joa wondered as he led her over to his white Land Rover sitting in the driveway, did that mean?

On her second night of babysitting duty, Joa made herself a plate of nachos and poured herself a glass of red wine. She was just about to sit down in the media room to watch reruns of *Downton Abbey* when she heard the doorbell ring.

Taking a slug of wine—and hoping that the strident doorbell didn't wake Aron who'd refused to go to sleep without three stories, a cuddle and a monster-under-the-bed check—she placed her nachos on the coffee table and headed to the hall.

In yoga pants, a slouchy sweatshirt and comfy socks, she wasn't dressed for receiving visitors. Then again, she wasn't expecting company and anyone who made house calls so late without advance notice was just plain rude.

Joa looked at Ronan's iPad, clicked on the screen showing the view of the front door and saw Keely standing on the steps, accompanied by a tall man built like a lumberjack, his back to the camera. What was Keely doing here at this time of night?

Joa hurried to the hallway, yanked open the door and

gasped at the frigid air. Looking past her guests onto the dark driveway, she saw that it was snowing.

Again.

Joa reached out and grabbed Keely's arm, tugging her into the hallway. The Armani-wearing lumberjack followed her inside. In the brightly lit hall, Joa immediately recognized that masculine face: Dare Seymour, the man she had yet to invite over to Mounton House for a casual meal.

"Hi, Dare, Keely. What are you guys doing here?" Joa asked, shutting the door behind him.

Keely unwound the scarf from around her neck and shrugged out of her coat. Dare took her coat, hat and scarf and hung her garments next to his on the coat rack by the door. Without asking, he plucked her gloves from her hands and tucked them into the outside pocket of her coat. His movements were economical and easy, as was the kiss he dropped on Joa's cheek. "Hi, Joa. It's been a long time."

"Hi back," Joa said, her eyes darting from his implacable face to Keely's stormy expression. Oh, God, what were these two arguing about now?

"Sorry to disturb you." Dare said, pushing back his jacket to slide his hands into the pockets of his suit pants. "I did tell Killer that this could wait until tomorrow but she insisted on getting the issue settled now."

What issue? And Dare called Keely Killer? Did he have a death wish?

"Do not call me by that ridiculous name," Keely said, obviously irritated.

"Why do you call her that?" Joa asked him, as she led them through to the great room and gestured for them to take a seat.

Dare waited for Keely to sit down before taking the seat next to her on the big sofa, stretching out long, muscled legs. The guy had to be six foot five plus and he sucked up space. With his dark blond hair and masculine features, he looked like Thor.

"I call her that because she reminds me of one of those feisty Jack Russell dogs who think they are a lot bigger and scarier than they actually are."

Oh, God, Joa shouldn't laugh, she really shouldn't…

When Keely sent her a fulminating, you're-dead-to-me look, Joa realized she hadn't managed to hide her amusement. She winced and shrugged. Unfortunately, Dare's characterization was spot-on.

But she'd rather die than admit that to Keely.

"Can I offer you something to drink? I've just opened a bottle of merlot."

"I can't stay," Dare said, shaking his head.

"Hot date?" Keely asked, in a super sweet, sarcastic voice.

"As a matter of fact, I do," Dare smoothly replied.

Keely opened her mouth to say something, then flushed and snapped her teeth shut. Keely turned her head away from Dare and stared out of the floor-to-ceiling windows at Ronan's tree-filled backyard, where snow gathered on the bare branches.

Dare stared at Keely's profile, exasperation on his face. Wanting to avoid blood on Ronan's furniture, Joa sat down on the chair opposite them and leaned her forearms on her knees. "So, what's up? What did you come to talk to me about?"

Dare rested his arm on the sofa behind Keely's head. Joa noticed Keely stiffen, then relax fractionally, as if unable to help the back of her head brushing his wrist. Awareness jumped in and out of Dare's eyes and Joa knew that if she got up and left, that sofa might see some action.

Of the "I don't like you but I'm going to kiss the hell out of you" variety.

"I received a letter from a film director this afternoon. He's arriving in Boston at the end of this week to start filming a turn-of-the-century horror." Dare said.

Joa wrinkled her nose. She liked action movies with sexy heroes but horror films gave her nightmares. And how did any of this concern her?

"Isabel rented Mounton House to him shortly before she died," Dare said. "He paid her an extraordinary amount of money to rent the mansion and its furnishings for the film. According to the correspondence between him and Isabel he forwarded to me this afternoon, Isabel was planning on spending the next three months at her villa in the south of France."

She'd forgotten that she and Keely owned a French villa.

Joa looked from Dare to Keely. "And this arrangement is binding?"

Dare nodded. "I saw the contract. She accepted his money and his entire crew is already in the city. If you two don't agree, he can sue the estate for monies paid, for breach of contract and for loss of profits."

"That's absurd," Keely muttered.

"I never said he would win, I said he could sue. And that would garner some press attention since he's very well-known and influential—"

"As a director of horror films?" Keely scoffed. "Sure he is."

Dare ignored her. "My point is that you do not need bad PR, as the publicity for the auction is starting to gather traction. And this would be bad PR."

Joa looked at Keely, still staring out the window, her expression stubborn. Joa knew that Keely hated the idea of strangers in their house. She'd even objected to Isabel's open houses and tours, thinking they were a security risk. "You're not keen on the idea, are you, Keels?"

Keely eventually looked at her. "No, I hate the idea of strange people in our house, touching our stuff. While the most treasured items have been moved to the storage facility at Murphy International, there are still some very valuable items there. And if someone stole something, we'd never know because there's so much."

"We have an inventory from the estate, and Derek has agreed to employ security and to put systems in place to negate any theft and damages." Dare said. "I will review those arrangements and if I'm not satisfied, I will insist on more security."

"They can't guarantee that nothing will be stolen or damaged, can they?" Keely demanded.

Dare shook his head. "There aren't any guarantees in life, Keely." He thought for a moment. "Maybe we should hire an additional security company I trust and we'll pass on the cost to the production company."

"That's a good idea, Dare, thank you," Joa said.

Joa widened her eyes at Keely, silently reminding her to use her manners. Keely wrinkled her nose and her next words sounded like they'd been pulled out from under a fifty-ton boulder. "Good idea."

"I have them occasionally," Dare dryly responded. Dare turned his attention back to Joa. "Another thing… Most of their filming will take place at night because it's a horror film. That means that you'll both have to move out."

Oh, that wasn't good.

Keely scooted to the edge of her seat and placed her elbows on her knees. "I'm actually heading to Florida for a month to work with a special needs school down there, so I was leaving for a while anyway. But you'd have to move out, Joa."

Dammit. She rather liked her massive four-poster bed,

doing yoga in the ballroom, sitting in Iz's library amongst her books.

Joa looked at Dare. "Do I have to? Can't I stay there and keep out of the way?"

Dare shook his head. "They've been promised an empty house and that's what you'll have to give them."

Joa quietly cursed. "When do I have to leave?"

"Mid next week," Dare said, spreading his hands in an apologetic gesture. He stood up and looked down at them from his great height. "So, are you agreeing to let the house?"

Joa raised her eyebrows. "Do we have a choice?"

"You always have a choice," Dare replied.

"I suppose we have to honor Isabel's arrangement with him. Where will you go, Joa?" Keely asked her, looking worried.

Joa had a healthy bank account and she could afford to hire an apartment or move into a hotel for a few months. "I'll be fine, Keels. And I agree, I think we should abide by the contract Iz signed, as inconvenient as it is."

"Okay, then. But I'm not happy," Keely muttered.

Joa smiled. "Yep, I'm getting that vibe."

Dare glanced at his watch and pulled a face. "Let's go, Killer, I'm tired. I want a drink and some food."

"And to join your hot date," Keely added, her tone dark.

"Exactly so," Dare agreed, his tone genial.

Confusion and annoyance flashed across Keely's face. Joa suspected that Keely might not like Dare Seymour but she didn't like the idea of him dating anyone else, either.

Now wasn't that interesting…

But as much as Joa would like to focus on the weird vibe between Keely and their sexy lawyer—really, between the Murphy brothers and Dare Seymour, Boston was looking pretty fine these days—Joa needed to think about where she was going to live for the next three months.

She heard a thump coming from the hall and frowned. Jumping to her feet, she rushed across the room but Dare's long stride beat her to the hall and she was grateful for his large presence. Had she locked the front door behind Dare and Keely? Who was in the house?

She had two young boys upstairs, and she had to get to them...

Joa darted around Dare to get to the staircase and skidded to a stop when she saw Ronan standing by the hall table, dropping his keys into the flat, ceramic dish on the hall table.

She blinked, shook her head and blinked again. He was only due back sometime in the morning...

Joa put her hand on her heart and sucked in the sight of him. He wore dark black chinos and a mulberry-colored sweater under a thigh-length leather coat, and he looked hot.

If Dare was Thor then Ronan could easily play a not-quite-so-perfect Superman...

Come on, Joa, you can't keep staring at him, acting like he's a salted caramel ice cream you can't wait to taste. Say something, dammit.

"Um...hi? You're home early."

"Yeah. Some lots were withdrawn from the sale so the auction finished earlier than I expected."

Ronan's eyes darted from her to Keely to Dare, obviously curious as to why they were in his house this late. After hanging up his leather coat, he pushed the sleeves of his sweater up his arms, shook Dare's hand and dropped a kiss on Keely's cheek.

Joa rocked on her feet and wondered if he'd kiss her, too. She wanted him to but also didn't. Mostly because a casual kiss just might turn combustible...

She so wanted his lips on hers again, his tongue in her mouth.

"Ju. All good? Are the kids asleep?"

Joa, jerked out of her sexual haze by the casual use of her name, just nodded. She cleared her throat and tried to be the adult she was reputed to be. "All good, and yeah, they are fast asleep."

"Any problems?" Ronan asked.

Strangely, there hadn't been. The boys had been remarkably accepting of her presence in their house.

Ronan pushed his hand through his hair. "I'm just going to check on my kids and then we can have a drink."

Dare shook his head. "Keely and I were just leaving, Ronan. We popped around to give Joa a heads-up about an upcoming change to her circumstances."

Ronan shot her a concerned look. "Problem?"

Joa quickly shook her head. "No, nothing insurmountable." She walked over to the coatrack and picked Keely's coat off the hook, pushing it into her sister's arms.

"When do you leave for Florida?" she asked, keeping one eye on Ronan's back as he jogged up the stairs.

"Not for a day or two," Keely said. "I'll be going back and forward for the next couple of months. But I'll catch up with you in the morning and we can talk."

"Sure," Joa replied. She looked up, and up, into Dare's face. "Thanks for stopping by, Dare. When Keely gets back from Florida, you should come for dinner."

"I'd like that, thank you." Dare bent down to kiss her cheek. Keeping his head close to hers, he dropped his voice but not enough to keep his words from reaching Keely. Which was, Joa realized, his intention. "But, please, can you cook? I'm terrified Killer will slip something into my food."

"It's a distinct possibility," Keely said, pulling on her gloves. "Especially if you keep using that stupid nickname."

Joa shut the door behind them, leaving them to bicker. She looked at Ronan's suitcase and laptop bag and sent an anxious glance up the stairs. He was home, so she should head back to Mounton House.

Ronan's footsteps on the stairs had her looking up and she immediately noticed he'd changed into straight-legged track pants and a tight-fitting Henley, sleeves pushed up his strong forearms. Instead of six-hundred-dollar loafers, he wore thick socks.

This was what he'd look like on a normal night at home, a man at ease in his space. For the rest of her life, she'd remember him looking like this, sexy and rumpled and a little stressed.

Before she could say anything, Ronan's phone rang and he pulled it out of his pocket. Joa was surprised when he placed it on speakerphone.

"Hey, Carrick. How's London?"

"Wet, as always. I had a meeting with Beah this afternoon."

Now that was a name she hadn't heard in a while. Beah, she remembered, was Finn Murphy's ex-wife but she was also one of Keely's closest friends. She also, if she could trust her memory, worked for Murphy International out of their London offices.

"Everything okay?" Ronan asked Carrick.

"Sure. I had some time earlier so I went through Isabel's inventory with Beah and she has a fair idea of which art collectors will be interested in the Mounton sale."

"Thanks. That takes some pressure off me."

"Is Beah still joining you and Finn for dinner with Cummings?" Ronan asked.

"Mmm. Hopefully it won't be as awkward as I'm imagining it to be."

"Um…have you seen Sadie at all?" Carrick then asked and to Joa, he sounded, strangely, hesitant. It wasn't a trait she associated with the Murphy brothers.

Joa's pulse skyrocketed at Ronan's smile and the amusement lightening his incredible eyes. "Well, no. Since I've been in China for the best part of two days. Why are you asking about our art detective? Do you not have her number?"

"Of course I do. She's not answering." Carrick tersely replied.

Ronan grinned at Joa. "Maybe she's on a date."

Carrick's only answer was a muffled growl.

"Or maybe she isn't as attracted to you as you are to her." Ronan teased.

"I…what… I've got to go. If you speak to her, tell her I'm looking for her. No, don't bother…*dammit*."

Joa smiled at the mischief in Ronan's eyes.

"You're sounding a bit unhinged, dude." Ronan said, sounding smug. When Carrick abruptly disconnected the call, Ronan laughed.

Joa cocked her head. "Why were you hassling Carrick about Sadie?"

"Because something is brewing between them and it's my brotherly duty to give him crap about it."

Man, smiling upped his sexy factor by a thousand percent and Joa's stomach did backflips. And then a double twist. She needed to go. Before she did something really stupid.

Like throw herself at him.

Bite the bullet, Jones. "I'll call a taxi and I'll be out of here in fifteen minutes."

Ronan frowned at her. "That's not necessary. It's freezing out and it's late. Go home in the morning."

Joa pulled the inside of her right cheek between her teeth. Should she stay or go? She looked out the window, saw the wind had picked up and the snow was swirling. The weather was dreadful and it was a fine excuse to stay…

She really shouldn't stay…

"Okay. Thank you."

An awkward silence fell between them, which Ronan eventually broke with a wry smile. "I need a huge glass of wine and some food. Any ideas?"

"I made the kids a rice-and-fish dish, and there's some left over. I also made spicy nachos for myself. You can share."

"Nachos sounds perfect," Ronan said. "Wine sounds better. Let's go…"

Said the sexy spider to the fly…

Six

Beah Jenkinson exited the black taxi at the swanky entrance to Claridge's, grateful for her long black vintage cashmere coat. After paying the taxi driver, she tucked her designer clutch bag under her arm and sucked in a deep breath. She could do this, she *had* to do this…

It was only dinner with one of the most important and elusive collectors in the world.

And her ex-brother-in-law Carrick and her ex-husband, Finn.

Who also happened to be two of her three bosses.

Not a big deal.

Liar. It was *such* a big deal…

Beah handed a black frocked doorman a smile and walked up to the doors of the impressive hotel. Allowing her coat to swing open, she resisted the urge to check her reflection in the glass doors, to reassure herself that her off-the-shoulder, tight-fitting, cobalt blue cocktail dress with its ruffled hem was suitable.

She looked perfectly fine. She was thirty years old, a woman confident in her body and her looks. She had an amazing career, a wonderful life.

She was not the insecure girl she'd been when she met and married Finn Murphy the best part of a decade ago.

She'd been twenty-one and working as an intern at Murphy International when she met the brilliant Finn and she'd been entranced by his quick brain and his encyclopedic knowledge of art and history. Within a week they were sleeping together; within a month they were engaged. They married in Vegas on the three-month anniversary of the day they met.

After a visit to the ladies' room and a conversation with her best friend, Beah walked in the direction of Davies and Brook, Claridge's brand-new restaurant, Beah admitted that she'd gone into her relationship with Finn, and her marriage, with a cruise ship's worth of baggage. Her mother had passed away just a year before, after a six-year battle fighting cancer. Her dad, her hero and the first true love of her life, had left them both around the time she started getting ill, and it was a betrayal Beah had never come to terms with.

Maybe she'd thought that marrying Finn would close the holes in her heart, would give her the security she craved, but she'd failed to recognize the fact that she'd married the most emotionally independent and unavailable man she'd ever met. Finn wasn't a talker and he struggled with her bouts of emotion and her need for reassurance. He'd started to pull away and she'd responded by trying to pull him closer.

He'd told her that her constant demands about where he was and what he was doing, and her incessant pleas to give up his adventure sports smothered him. Having lost both her parents, one to illness and one to abandonment, Beah had lived in agony, thinking Finn would be next to leave.

After an excruciating year, Finn had asked for a divorce, telling her he loved her but he couldn't live with her insecurities.

Admittedly, the divorce had been the catalyst for Beah to change her life. It was a point of pride that eight years later, Beah was now as, or more, independent than Finn and she barely recognized the girl she'd been when she married him.

Taking the opportunity Carrick offered her to be a client liaison in London, she'd crossed the Atlantic and was now Head of Client Advisory, reporting directly to Ronan. As an advisor for both buyers and sellers, she helped the company's most important clients with the formation of, and the disposal of, important collections.

As for her and Finn, well, they communicated when they needed to, via very brief and pointed emails. Working for the same company, they'd run into each other over the years but they both made a concerted effort to avoid each other as much as possible.

But Paris Cummings was an important collector, one she'd been pursuing for years, and she had to attend this dinner, had to join the two Murphy brothers in their attempt to woo the stubborn collector to their side of the fence.

And that meant sitting at the same table as her ex-husband, pretending that all was well.

All *was* well… It had to be.

At the entrance to Davies and Brook, Beah smiled at the maître d' and gladly surrendered her coat. Resisting the urge to check that no fire-red curls had escaped her smooth chignon, she looked over the exquisitely decorated dining room, her eyes immediately going to the best table in the room.

As if he could feel her eyes on his dark blond head, Finn jerked his head up and their gazes clashed and connected. Beah's feet were glued to the floor; she was unable to pull her eyes off his masculine, oh-so-handsome face. A short, tidy beard covered his cheeks and jaw, his hair was overlong and could do with a trim, and his shoulders were wide in that designer suit tailored for his tall frame.

Finn pushed to his feet, unfurling his long and muscled body. He wore a black shirt without a tie and his eyes—a light, light green—remained on her with laser-like intensity.

He used to look at her like that while they were making love, as he was about to slide into her. Like she was a puzzle he didn't understand but needed to complete…

"Ms. Jenkinson? Ma'am?"

Beah heard her name being called from a place far away and she wrenched her eyes off Finn onto the concerned face of the maître d'.

"The Mr. Murphys are expecting you and, I'm sure, delighted to have you join them." He gestured her to precede him.

Beah forced herself to cross the room, her face impassive. Yeah, she could pretty much guarantee that Finn Murphy was *not* delighted to see her.

Just as she wasn't thrilled to see him…

It was both strange and nice to come home to a gorgeous, sexy, sweet-smelling woman after an exhausting business trip, Ronan thought as he inspected the bottle of red wine Joa left on the kitchen counter. Although he had a rack of wine in the corner holding better and more expensive bottles, and an extensive collection in the state-of-the-art cellar in his basement, she'd brought her own, a decent red, and he appreciated the gesture.

He helped himself to a glass and watched as Joa assembled a plate of nachos for him. Judging by the smells wafting his way, he knew that she'd used proper Mexican ingredients, from chipotle seasoning in the ground beef to refried beans. He was hungry and had he been asked what he wanted to eat, ground beef nachos wouldn't have crossed his mind, but seeing the ingredients hitting the plate, his mouth started to water.

It had been well over three years since a woman had prepared a meal for him in his own house and it felt both weird and wrong, but he was too exhausted to care. He just wanted some food, a little conversation and the soothing properties of a good merlot.

He didn't need to overanalyze every damn thing. And he couldn't help noticing how unbelievably sexy Joa was—despite her messy hair, her skin devoid of any makeup and clothes that completely hid her amazing curves. He dismissed his thoughts as a normal straight man's reaction to having an Indian goddess look-alike in his kitchen.

"You wear glasses."

Joa's head shot up and she touched the frame of her delicate gold-rimmed glasses with three fingers. "I usually wear contacts but my eyes get scratchy, so I take them out and shove these on."

It was nice to know that she wasn't completely perfect. Ronan gestured to the plate. "Aren't you eating?"

"Mine is in the media room. I was about to eat when Keely and Dare arrived."

Ronan nodded and slid off his barstool. Within a minute he'd collected her plate and glass of wine and placed both on the island. Joa smiled her thanks as she scattered sliced jalapenos over his nachos.

Ronan resumed his seat at the counter and placed his arms on the granite. "So what's your change of circumstances?"

Frustration and worry crossed Joa's face and flashed in her eyes. She turned to take the cheese out of the fridge and Ronan saw the tension in her stiff back, in the way she held her head. When she finally turned around, she flashed him a quick, back-off smile. She held up two blocks of cheese. "Monterey Jack or cheddar?"

Was that a trick question? "Both?"

"Your arteries just let out a massive groan."

"I work out every day, so my arteries are just fine."

Joa shrugged. "It's your heart attack."

"I'd be very happy for you to give me CPR."

Ronan heard his flirty words, surprised at his sex-tinged tone. What the hell? He was flirting? Hell, he'd thought his ability to do that had died with Thandi. It should've died with Thandi!

Guilt, hot and sour, washed over him and he took a large sip of his wine. He risked looking at Joa and noticed that she was giving the grating of his cheese far more attention than it deserved. Her extraordinary cheekbones were slightly tinged with pink. He dropped his gaze lower and immediately noticed that her nipples were hard and pointy beneath her loose sweatshirt and that her breathing was ever so slightly erratic.

Jeez, she was as turned on as he was. Dammit, this wasn't good.

At all.

Needing to reset their conversation, Ronan cleared his throat. "How were the monsters today?"

Joa's head flew up, all sexual awareness gone. Her eyes sparkled with amusement. "Man, they are too cute. Aron is a riot—the kid has a wicked sense of humor for a three-year-old."

Aron was more like him when he was younger while Sam was more studious. And serious. "He is funny." Then her words sank in and he grimaced. "Oh, God, what did he say?"

Joa grinned. "On the drive home, I asked them to tell me some of your rules and I got the standard responses... pick up your toys, say please and thank-you." Joa's grin was wide and infectious and he couldn't stop his lips from curving upward, even though she had yet to come to the punch line. "Then Aron informed me that only Daddy is allowed to say goddammit, *goddammit*."

Ronan laughed. "At least he didn't tell you that he wasn't allowed to pick his nose or worse."

Joa slid both their plates under the hot grill before turning back to look him in the eye. "Oh, he told me those, too."

Ronan groaned. "That kid has no filter."

"He's super cute, though." Joa picked up her glass of wine and swirled the red liquid around. She looked deep in thought and when he could look into her eyes again, he noticed her laughter had faded.

"Sam is quieter, more anxious."

Ronan straightened and frowned. "What do you mean?"

Joa placed the plates on the counter. She switched off the grill and took her seat opposite him. "When we got home, Sam asked me, twice, whether you had landed safely. I went online, showed him the website where you can track your plane via radar and found your jet. He kept checking it until you called and told him that you were safe on the ground. I don't need my psychology degree to tell me that he's scared to lose another parent, that's obvious."

Joa scooped up some meat with a piece of tortilla and popped it into her mouth, keeping her eyes on him. He didn't want to talk about his kids or his dead wife. Hell, he wasn't sure he wanted to eat, unless it was to devour her. He reminded himself that he was hungry, and forked food into his mouth. It was delicious and they ate in silence for a few minutes. "This is great, thank you."

"Pleasure," Joa calmly replied, meeting his eyes. Attraction and hot, molten desire flared and Ronan wasn't sure who made the first move, him or her, but one minute he was eating, the next she was standing between his legs, her cool hands on his cheeks. Then, somehow, again without his knowledge, his hands ended up gripping her hips and his arms banded around her tiny waist, pulling her so that her breasts pushed into his chest, his thighs caging her in. He inhaled her scent and relished the feel of feminine curves, female comfort.

Then he made the mistake of dipping his head to place his lips against that small, butterfly-shaped birthmark on her collarbone…

God, she was so soft, her skin so smooth. He shouldn't be doing this, it was wrong, but he couldn't help himself, it had been so long since he'd held a woman, heard the hitch of her breath, sensed the delicious tension in her body. Should he advance, should he retreat?

Ronan was still trying to make up his mind, resist temptation, when Joa's tongue touched the cord in his neck, and electricity, hot and powerful, danced over his skin. If this was wrong, why did having her in his arms—her lithe, fragrant body pressed against his—feel so damn right?

He couldn't help it but he needed to taste her, to feed on the essence of her, so Ronan turned his head to capture her mouth. He knew how to kiss her—he'd relived their previous kiss a hundred times—but then Joa opened her mouth. His tongue slid against hers and the world stopped. Time ceased to exist as he explored her mouth, his hands running up her back and cupping her butt. His erection pushed against the barrier of his pants and he wished she'd drop her hands from his shoulders to free him, desperately needing her hot hands on his shaft.

Ronan felt dizzy and sideswiped but his body knew exactly what to do, how to please her. Sliding his hand up and under her sweatshirt, he encountered her bare breast, her nipple a tight bud. Rubbing his thumb across her, he heard her muffled moan and she arched her back in a silent plea for more. Ronan hitched up her sweatshirt and looked down at her breast, small but perfect with its dark, merlot-colored nipple. So sweet, so rich.

He ducked his head to kiss her, to pull her against the roof of his mouth, and when her hand pushed between their bodies to hold him, he groaned against her skin.

It had been so long and he knew that it wouldn't take much for him to climax. Damn, this was so much better than those lonely, sad, solo efforts in the shower.

But pleasure was so much better shared, so Ronan ran the backs of his knuckles down her abdomen, flirting with her mound. When Joa pushed his hand underneath the band of her yoga pants, he only encountered a small patch of hair—no bra and no panties, so hot!—and feminine heat. Ronan captured her chin in his free hand and pulled her mouth back to his, awash with sensations.

His hand in her pants, her hand on his shaft... Her mouth was warm and wonderful.

He'd just touch her a little, maybe get her off, and then he'd stop. He wasn't going to make love to her, he couldn't... He'd stop, he *would*.

Then Joa yanked his pants down, just far enough for her to have unfettered access and Ronan knew that this was a battle he wouldn't win, a war where he was uninterested in victory.

He wanted this, he wanted her...

To hell with it...

Ronan gripped Joa's hips and surged upward, easily lifting her. Her legs banded around his hips and she nipped at his mouth as he carried her across the room to lay her on the cushions of the closest sofa. He placed his hands on either side of her head, staring down into those passion-fogged eyes.

"Do you want this?" he demanded, his voice rough with passion. Joa stared up at him, her eyes on his mouth, filled with do-me-now. But he needed to hear the words…

"Do. You. Want. This?"

Joa didn't pretend to be coy, didn't hesitate. "More than I want my next breath. Come here and kiss me, Murphy."

In a minute. He still had something to say, if he could get the words to roll off his tongue. "It's been a while, Ju, and I'm not going to last."

Joa licked her top lip and smiled. "That's okay, I don't think I will, either." She pushed herself up to rest on her elbows. "You done talking yet, Ronan?"

Hell, yes. Besides, the conversation he most wanted to have with her was silent but powerful. Ronan stood up and reached behind his head to pull his shirt over his head. Joa watched, appreciation on her face. "Ooh, nice chest."

His mouth twitched with amusement. Keeping his eyes on hers, he pushed his pants down his hips and allowed the fabric to fall, toeing off his socks. It had been an age since he'd been naked in front of a woman but seeing the lust and admiration on her face made him feel ten feet tall, ripped as hell. He felt like himself again.

Not the boys' dad, or a widower or a Murphy, but Ronan.

Joa's appreciative eyes danced over his body and his hands itched to make her his. "Strip, Ju."

Joa, not breaking eye contact—God, how sexy was that?—pulled her sweatshirt off and leaned back on her elbows, her pretty breasts on display. It was his turn to look, admire, salivate. Man, he wished he had ten mouths, twenty hands—there were so many places he wanted to touch, so much he wanted to do to her.

But this would only happen once and he had to prioritize, dammit.

Ronan bent and pulled her yoga pants down her hips. He threw her pants over the back of the couch, entranced by her elegant arms, her tiny waist, the curve of her hip. Her legs were long and mouth-watering and he couldn't wait to have them wrapped around his hips.

Feeling the sexual heat, he dipped a finger between her feminine folds and sighed when his fingers came away wet. She wanted him, proof positive.

He muttered a dark curse, resisting the urge to plunge and plunder.

Joa sat up and dragged the tip of her index finger over his steel hard shaft, swiping her thumb over his sensitive tip. "I'm clean and I'm on the pill. I'm presuming you are clean, too?"

He nodded, unable to speak.

Joa met his eyes and he fell into that vat of molten silver. "You can take the time to find a condom. I won't change my mind, I promise, or you can just come on home."

Choosing door number two—*thank you, Jesus*—Ronan dropped his big body to cover hers, his tip probing her entrance. Joa bent her knee to rub his hip and then her legs wound around his waist, crossing at the ankles. She was beyond anything he'd imagined...

Joa tipped her hips and rubbed herself against him and he knew he was way past coherent thought, that he couldn't stop if he wanted to.

He didn't want to...

Ronan felt her walls clench around him, felt her every shudder, every sigh. Her words made no sense; then again, neither did his. Pleasure was their only goal, giving and receiving.

He pumped, she rose to meet him, she kissed the side of his neck, he sucked on that butterfly birthmark. Her nails pushed into his butt cheeks and he welcomed the sting, the sexy pain. He slid a hand under her, adjusted his position to go deeper and Joa gasped, releasing a little scream.

He surged, she rose…

And the world shattered.

Seven

AWKWARD.

In capital letters.

Joa pulled down the throw lying over the back of the sofa and dragged it up her still pulsating body. She darted another look at Ronan.

His face was granite hard and his mouth, so soft and sensuous earlier, was compressed into a hard line.

She didn't need her advanced psychology degree to know that he was feeling guilty, regretful and, yeah, pissed.

At himself? At her? Who knew?

Ronan stared up at the ceiling as Joa stood up and yanked on her clothes. When she was dressed, she pushed her hands through her hair, which fell down her back in what she was sure had to be a tangled bird's nest because she'd lost her hair band. With her back to Ronan, she touched her lips, remembering his kiss, his passion-soaked eyes, his gentle touch.

It had been the best sex of her life.

Sex he obviously and immediately regretted. And because he did, so did she.

Joa looked over to the piano, to the silver frame containing the large photograph of Ronan's wife. Thandi was laughing at the camera, her smile wide and full of joy. Sam stood at her side and she had her hand on her massive belly, in that age-old gesture of connection.

Thandi had watched them make love. Sort of…

Joa covered her mouth with her hand, feeling a little sick. Oh, rationally she knew the woman had died a while ago, but Ronan's reaction made it feel like they'd had a quickie on the couch while she was out of the room.

It made no sense but she definitely felt like the other woman.

Thandi was everywhere in this house. There was a note to Ronan in her handwriting on the fridge—something along the lines of Thandi wishing her pregnancy to be over so that Ronan could start treating her like a sex object again—and her designer scarf still hung on the coatrack. There were photos of her pinned to the fridge by magnets, in frames and on the walls of the halls.

Joa wrenched her eyes off Thandi's face and stared at her bare toes, ridiculously angry with herself. She'd done it again, thrown herself at an unavailable man. Okay, she hadn't been thinking of Ronan in terms of his family and wanting to be part of their close-knit circle of three but she'd stepped over a line she'd never crossed before: she'd slept with a man who wasn't only emotionally unavailable but also completely in love with his dead wife.

How messed up was that?

Feeling a little sick and a lot sad, Joa picked up her shoes and ran up the first flight of steps to her room. After using the facilities, she looked at herself in the mirror above the basin and stared into her sex-fogged eyes. It was just sex, she told herself, nothing more.

You aren't working for him, staying with him, looking after his kids on an ongoing basis. You were always going to leave in the morning...

If only the sex hadn't been so mind-blowing. She wasn't an idiot; she'd realized, possibly from the first time they met, that they were attracted to each other, that something was bubbling between them. But this was more than a bubble; this was full-blown chemistry.

And if she didn't leave, if they kept connecting, sleeping together, it would blow up in their faces. Because she'd always feel like the other woman with Ronan.

She wasn't doing this to herself again; she wasn't going to look for happiness and fulfillment when there was none to be had.

Thandi might be dead, but Ronan was still very, very married.

Time to go, Jones. And she'd never be back.

Nobody knew how difficult it was to date after losing the love of your life. It was intensely hard. Not only did he feel like he was betraying Thandi's memory, Ronan felt like he was cracking open the door to a world he'd closed off, a world he no longer had access to.

Even if he hadn't had sex with Joa—sex, such a tame word for what they'd shared!—he'd still opened to her; their conversation had flowed easily and smoothly. He'd felt completely comfortable with someone other than the person he'd originally planned on spending his life with.

It felt both wrong and right, crazy and desperate. Ronan rubbed his hands over his face, staring at the note Thandi had left on the fridge, days before she went into labor. She'd been grumbling about feeling fat, uncomfortable and horny.

She'd been desperate to meet their second son and neither of them imagined, not for one minute, that a half hour after he placed Aron in her arms, she'd be rushed into emergency surgery and be gone.

It was so freaking unfair.

They said that life went on, that he would, at some point, need love, companionship and intimacy. And sex. He'd done without it for so long and had been, *was*, comfortable in his self-imposed, lonely state because if you didn't get close to anybody, you could avoid the pain of losing them. Up until tonight, he'd avoided one-night stands, casual flings, brief affairs. He knew that people, his brothers and his friends, didn't understand, but in his head, he was still married, and any of the above would be cheating on his wife…

Ronan picked his still half-full wine glass and took a large sip.

The problem was that while by his own definition he'd cheated on Thandi, he didn't feel as guilty as he should. He'd had fast and furious and fantastic sex with a woman who wasn't his wife and he was…

Hell, how could he articulate this?

He felt damn good, relaxed and, yeah, maybe even a little happy. He should be racked with guilt, feeling like scum on a shoe, but he didn't…

If anything, he felt guilty for *not* feeling guilty. What did that mean? What did any of it mean? Was he just so damn happy not to be sexually frustrated that he was pushing aside his guilt so he could hold on to this postorgasmic glow? All he knew for sure was that he wanted Joa again…

And again.

Ronan turned at the sound of her heels on his flooring and his heart dropped when he saw Joa standing in the doorway, holding a large leather bag, her tote bag over her shoulder. She'd brushed her hair, slicked gloss over her lips and changed into tight-fitting jeans, knee-high boots and a cream cable-knit sweater.

"I've called for a ride. It should be here any minute," Joa said, meeting his eyes.

He started to make the offer to take her home but then he remembered that the boys were upstairs, that he couldn't leave them alone. "You don't need to go."

As he said the words, he knew they were a lie. He did need her to leave because he couldn't think straight when she was around. He'd be distracted by her lovely skin and her expressive eyes, his thoughts constantly returning to how she looked naked and all the things he wanted to do to her. She needed to leave so he could *think*, so he could put this entire crazy night into perspective.

Joa's eyes drilled right through him. "We both know it's better if I do, Ronan." She bit her bottom lip and the fingers gripping the straps of her bag turned white. She nodded to the couch. "We both know that was a one-off thing, something inexplicable. And that it won't ever be repeated…"

Well…

Damn.

Ronan folded his arms and silently cursed when he heard a car horn announcing Joa's ride was here. Fighting the urge to go to her, to carry her up the stairs and into his bed, he planted his feet and hoped none of his confusion was reflected in his eyes or on his face. This situation was weird enough, complicated enough without letting Joa see how much she affected him.

Joa looked behind her and took a step back. "Will you tell the boys I had to leave, that I had fun with them?"

"Joa…"

He wasn't sure what he was about to say but it didn't

matter because she'd stepped out of sight. *Do not go after her, Murphy, don't you damn well dare!*

Ronan heard his front door open and close and closed his eyes, pushing his toes into the flooring. He heard the slam of a car door and only when he heard the vehicle pulling away did he release the breath he was holding, allow his arms to fall to his side.

Spinning around, Ronan grabbed his wine glass, drained the contents and then lifted Joa's glass to his lips and drank that, too.

Sometimes, there was only one decent way to get out of your head. And that was to get off your head.

Finn missed his brother.

Well, he missed the guy Ronan used to be. That fun-loving, impetuous, try-anything-once guy he'd been before Thandi died. Finn had loved his sister-in-law, they all had, but a little of Thandi's fearful attitude had rubbed off on Ronan in the years they were married, and her death had made him doubly cautious.

He was not going to like what Finn had to tell him. Finn knew how this conversation would go... He'd tell Ronan what he intended to do, Ronan would flip his lid, forbid him to do it and Finn would dig in his heels, reminding Ronan that he was an adult and could do anything he damn well pleased.

Thandi had hated Finn's adrenaline-chasing adventures and had nagged him about being careful, about the risks he was taking, frequently telling him that the family would fall apart if he died doing something stupid.

How ironic that it was Thandi who'd died giving birth, something that billions of women did all the time.

Finn leaned his shoulder into the door frame of Ronan's office and rubbed the back of his neck. In the days and months after Thandi's death, he and Carrick had taken turns spending the night at Ronan's, making sure the boys were fed and bathed and put to bed. Once that was done, they sat with their brother while he cried, stared into space or drank himself into oblivion. It was during one of those drunken rages that Ronan demanded he promise to give up adventure sports, to stop taking risks with his life.

Unable to give his brother what he wanted, Finn had compromised and told Ronan he'd always tell him when he was about to do something dangerous and it was a promise he now deeply regretted.

Ronan would hear him out, give him a thousand words and ask if there was anything he could do or say to change his mind. He'd say no and Ronan would retreat, his disapproval obvious.

Ronan took Finn's need for speed, his chasing of bigger and better thrills, as a personal affront. For Finn, it was a way to burn off stress, to get out of his head.

Some people drank, some did drugs, some screwed their frustrations away but Finn chased adrenaline. And tried, very hard, not to die while he was doing it.

So far he'd been successful.

Well, he might as well get this over with…

Finn knocked on the door frame to Ronan's office and, when his brother raised his head, instantly realized that Ronan was nursing a hell of a hangover. At one point Finn and Carrick had been worried about Ronan's fondness for drowning his grief in a bottle of Jack, but after six months, he'd cut down on his consumption of alcohol and started to be the father his boys needed. Within the year, he was back to being the social drinker they all were.

Finn stepped into his office and, because he could, raised his voice. "Hey, bro! How was the auction?"

Ronan leaned back in his chair and held up his hand. "Not so loud, dammit."

Finn grinned and dropped into the chair on the opposite side of his desk. "You look like crap."

"I feel like crap."

Ronan's honest reply surprised Finn. Wondering what had sent him to the bottle, he scrolled through his computer-like memory, searching for a reason Ronan needed to drown his sorrows. It wasn't the anniversary of his wedding or Thandi's death, it wasn't her birthday. Sam and Aron were fine and Carrick was in his office down the hall, some of his attention on work but most of it on Sadie, the attractive art detective. Finn knew they were sleeping together, that much was obvious, but he suspected that his oldest brother wasn't managing to keep their affair surface based.

Finn was sure Carrick was, as millennials liked to say, catching feelings.

Apart from Carrick's love life, it was, as far as he knew, just a normal day at the beginning of February in cold and wet Boston. "How was the Beijing auction?" Finn asked, placing his ankle on his opposite knee.

"Some lots were pulled but the five-hundred-year-old Ming vase made bank."

"Did it break the record?"

Ronan managed a smile. "It *shattered* the record by a million five."

"Nice." Finn grinned. "Did your Mandarin pass muster?"

"Mostly. If I need a lesson in humility, speaking Chinese is a good way to get it." Ronan rubbed his forehead. "Those damn words that sound the same—"

"—homophones—"

Ronan pointed a finger at him and nodded. "Those. I swear they invented them to confuse us foreigners."

"It's all about the tone," Finn told him but knew he was speaking to a brick wall. Ronan was competent but he wasn't a natural linguist. He wasn't like Finn, who was fascinated by language, words and puzzles.

Finn tended to absorb too much information too quickly, and when that happened, he found the easiest way to slow down was to do something that took him totally out of his big brain. Since his teens adventure sports were his way to blow off a whole bunch of steam.

Talking of...

"Don't freak—" Ronan would freak, of course he would "—but I'm going to Colorado this weekend."

Ronan shot him a hell-no look. "Heli-skiing? Black diamond runs?"

Not this time but he'd do both before winter ended. "Ice climbing."

"What the hell is ice climbing?" Ronan demanded.

"We climb ice formations such as frozen waterfalls, using axes and other specialized climbing equipment."

Finn saw Ronan's jaw clench. "And have you tried this before?"

Yeah, sort of. But he wasn't about to admit that to his highly overprotective brother. "Sure."

"Liar." Ronan put his elbows on his desk and his head between his hands. "You're giving me a headache, Finn."

"You had a headache when I walked in," Finn said, rising to his feet. If that was all the grief he was going to get, he'd take it. He really wasn't in the mood for a lecture. But he couldn't help wondering what had put his brother in a foul mood and sent him to the bottle.

Finn was nearly at the door when Ronan spoke again. "I heard you saw Beah in London."

Finn tensed, as he always did when he heard his ex-wife's name. A stupid reaction since Beah was as much a part of Murphy's as he was.

"Yeah."

Ronan raised his eyebrows. "And?"

What did Ronan want him to say? That seeing Beah was both pleasure and pain, that sitting across the table from her was an exercise in torture when all he wanted to do was take her to bed?

Later, he'd acted on that impulse and he and Beah did get up close, personal and very, very naked. Making love to Beah had been better than he remembered.

Then again, they'd always been good in bed; naked they were fine, but when they dressed, they argued about everything.

Finn shrugged. "We didn't kill each other."

Then Finn remembered Beah had agreed to help organize a mutual friend's wedding. He sighed. By the time Ben and Piper exchanged vows, there was a healthy chance one or both of them would end up dead or wounded. Or worse.

He had no intention of explaining any of that to Ronan so Finn changed the subject. "Cummings agreed to move his collection through us and is working with Beah."

"Yeah, she told me. She also has a couple of clients in Asia who are interested in Isabel's Vermeer and the possible Homer—"

"It is a Homer, trust me."

"You might be right but unfortunately, your gut instinct isn't proof," Ronan responded, his tone dry.

Because Isabel's collection was such an important sale, Beah would be flying into Boston to attend their in-house meetings to discuss interest and values and possible buyers. During that time, she'd also help him organize the wedding.

He was both excited and terrified at the thought of having his gorgeous, arty, fiercely intelligent wife back in Boston.

Ex-wife. Whatever.

Finn glanced at his watch and saw that he was running late. "I have to get over to Mounton House. I need to do another sweep of the premises, make sure that I haven't missed anything important before the film crew moves in."

Ronan's frown was part pain, mostly curiosity. "What film crew?"

"Apparently Isabel rented the house to a film crew for a couple weeks, or months. Not sure how long… Anyway, they are moving in next week."

"Keely and Joa are going to hate sharing their house with a lot of people," Ronan said.

"They have to move out, that's part of the deal. Keely went to Florida. I'm not sure what Joa is going to do," Finn explained.

Ronan straightened his spine, his eyes turning the color of dangerous ice. "Joa is moving out?"

Was he not speaking English? That was what he'd said. "Apparently."

Ronan pushed his chair back and stood up, picking up his phone and wallet off his desk. "You said that you are heading over there?"

"Yeah."

"Good, you can give me a ride," Ronan stated, his words clipped.

Finn stared at Ronan's back as he strode past, his expression furious. Finn thought he heard something along the lines of Joa being an impossible woman and driving him crazy and suddenly he had the answer to his earlier question.

Ronan had hit the bottle because of a woman. A woman who wasn't his dead wife.

Finn couldn't be happier. He was also ecstatic because he'd managed to have a conversation with Ronan that didn't include "death wish" and "reckless."

It was turning out to be a decent day.

Eight

Joa was sitting cross-legged on her massive double bed, her laptop on her lap, searching for rental properties when she heard large feet hitting the stairs and stopping on the landing just outside her room. Since her bedroom was on the third floor, she knew that whoever was up here was either lost—an easy feat in a house the size of Mounton House—or looking for her.

"Joa!"

Yep, that was Ronan.

Joa, because she was a girl and he was fantastically good-looking, glanced toward the French-styled, freestanding mirror to the right of her bed and wished she'd done something other than shove her hair into a messy bun, that she'd thought to put on some makeup, some lipstick.

Thanks to reliving her best sexual encounter into the early hours of this morning—again!—she'd also had minimal sleep. Frankly, she looked like a corpse.

And, yet again, she was dressed in leggings and a bulky

thigh-length sweater. One of these days she would have to show Murphy that she did own some decent clothes.

Ronan appeared in her doorway, a long cashmere coat covering his dark gray suit. His tie was pulled away from his collar and he looked like he'd had, if that was possible, even less sleep than her.

Joa put her laptop on the bed beside her and bent her knees, wrapping her arms around her legs. She tipped her head back. "Ronan? What are you doing here? And how did you get in?"

"Finn is downstairs. Keely gave us both the code," Ronan replied, pushing his coat back to jam his hands into the pockets of his pants. He looked around her room and winced. "God, it looks like a rainbow exploded in here."

Joa looked around, silently admitting that the room was a crazy combination of color: reds and oranges and pinks, a bright blue carpet and purple velvet drapes. When she first arrived at Mounton House as a teenager, this room, one of the smallest bedrooms in the house, was the only one furnished on the third floor—all the luxurious, stunningly decorated bedrooms were a floor down—and she'd liked the idea of having advance warning of anyone coming up the stairs. While she instinctively liked Isabel, trust took a lot longer and some habits took a long time to die.

As for the colors, well, she'd been happy to have a soft bed and heat, to be in a safe place, and the decor hadn't mattered. It still didn't.

This was her bolt-hole, a link to Isabel and she was used to the crazy color scheme. "Did you really drive over here to talk to me about my decor choices? And it's not that bad."

"It's awful." Ronan shuddered again. "But I do, admittedly, have a hangover."

The hangover explained his bloodshot eyes, his pale complexion. Joa dropped her knees and swung her legs off the bed and stood up.

"Why is Finn here?" Joa asked, her hand on her shabby chic bedside table. Actually, it was more shabby than chic and probably used by dozens of live-in servants over the past century.

"He's checking to see make sure he hasn't missed something incredibly special or valuable before the movie crew moves in."

"Like a Fabergé egg or a first-edition Charles Dickens?"

Ronan lifted one shoulder in an elegant shrug. "It wouldn't surprise either of us and you're closer to the mark than you realize. Back in the eighties, Isabel tossed a first-edition *Pride and Prejudice* onto Raeni's desk—"

Pride was one of her favorite books. And Isabel once owned a first edition of the famous romance? Wow. "Really?"

"Yeah. During that visit to Murphy's, Isabel also pulled a Warhol sketch and a Fabergé snuffbox out of her bag. She sold all three objects for record-breaking prices and used the money to establish her foundation."

Ronan stared at her face and Joa resisted the urge to check whether she had strawberry jam on her lips or sleep in her eyes.

"What?" she eventually asked when the silence stretched out.

"You look a little like Raeni. Like you, she was a stunning combination of Anglo and Indian genes."

Joa wasn't sure how to respond to his factual compliment. His voice was so bland but his eyes told her that he was remembering their red-hot encounter on his sofa, how they fell apart in each other's arms.

But remembering the way he kissed and the heat they

generated wasn't helpful; it had been a one-time thing and wouldn't happen again.

She didn't think...

Annoyed with her lack of willpower—what was it about this man who just had to look at her to have her panting?— Joa pushed her shoulders back and arched her eyebrows. "So Finn is downstairs hunting for any overlooked treasures but that doesn't explain your presence in my bedroom at—" she glanced at her watch "—nine forty-five on a Thursday morning."

"Why didn't you tell me that you had to move out of this house?"

Well, that was a question she hadn't been expecting but it was an easy one to answer. "Because I was under no obligation to?"

Ronan's eyes flashed with irritation. "Where are you going to go?"

She wasn't sure yet, unable to decide between a furnished apartment or taking a suite at the Forrester-Grantham for a few months. She didn't want to do either: hotels were impersonal and apartments were lonely. While she liked to be able to retreat when she felt like she needed some solitude, she liked knowing that people were in the house, that she wasn't completely alone.

She hadn't been truly alone since she spent those few terrifying nights on the cold streets of Boston nearly fifteen years ago. She'd never felt so scared, so utterly vulnerable. She'd come a long way but she still hated the idea of complete solitude.

But Keely had left Boston and Joa had no friends in the city. She'd simply have to suck it up. Maybe a hotel would be better; if the silence and loneliness overwhelmed her, she could head down to the bar or sit in the lobby.

She didn't need to talk to anyone or interact, she just

needed to feel safe. It wouldn't be fun, precisely, but she'd be okay. "I think I'll take a suite at a hotel," Joa told Ronan, even though her plans shouldn't concern him at all.

"That will be as expensive as hell."

Thanks to Isabel, she could live out of a hotel for the rest of her life and still have enough cash to buy a Caribbean island. Or two. She was one of the wealthiest women in Boston, a weird and strange reality. "I can afford it."

"Maybe. But it's not something you really want to do."

Joa jerked her head up, surprised that he'd picked up on her reluctance. Damn, but the man was more perceptive than she gave him credit for. "How did you come to that conclusion?"

"You have the most expressive eyes in the world," Ronan replied. "And I'm good at reading body language—it's part of what makes me a good auctioneer."

Man, she really needed to work on her poker face. She didn't need him to see her thoughts, especially the ones she had about stripping him naked and exploring that rangy, muscular body.

Ronan walked over to the window and leaned his shoulder into the windowpane, looking down at the snow-covered garden below her window.

"Come home with me."

Joa frowned, not sure that she'd heard him right. Her heart rate shot up and her stomach whirled and swirled. "Sorry, what?"

Ronan continued to stare down at the drifts of snow. "Come back to West Roxbury. Move in with me…us."

Uh…

Joa didn't know what to say. What was he proposing? Or did he just feel sorry for the poor little temporarily homeless rich girl? Realizing that her knees were the consistency of jelly, Joa sat down on the edge of the bed.

Ronan finally turned around, resting his butt on the wide wooden windowsill, stretching out his long legs. "I need a nanny, you need a place to stay. Help me out with the kids in the afternoon and, occasionally, some evenings. I'll pay you."

"I don't need your money, Murphy," Joa replied, irritated.

"But you do need a place to stay and I do need help," Ronan stated, his eyes steady on her face. "The boys were devastated to find you gone. From the moment they woke up it's been Ju this and Ju that."

His boys were lovely but... "I don't want to be a nanny, Ronan."

In fact, she thought she might like to become more involved in Isabel's foundation. With Keely out of town, she'd started dropping in and was fascinated by the work the foundation did with various shelters, hospices and underfunded schools and she was touched by the impact Isabel's money made.

But moving in with Ronan was not a good idea; she knew this. Before the Wilsons, she'd stood on the outside of a family circle, looking in and longing to be a part of their world. Then, with her family in Auckland, she'd felt part of that inner circle and she'd loved it. But life moved the goalposts and showed her there was no place for her long-term.

Having what she most wanted, a family, and then losing it, had carved a chunk out of her soul. She wouldn't do that to herself again. It hurt too damn much.

"It's not a long-term solution, Joa, not for me, or for you. But it will serve both our needs in the short term. It'll give you a place to stay that's not an impersonal hotel and something to occupy your time while you decide on the new direction you want to take. And it will give me time to find a decent, long-term nanny."

He made the whole notion sound so damn reasonable. And it would be, if they hadn't nearly set his couch on fire last night. "We made love last night…"

"So?"

Joa widened her eyes and her hands in a you've-got-to-be-kidding-me gesture.

Ronan looked down at his feet before lifting his head to look at her. "I admit, that took me by surprise. But, if you agree to work for me, for us, it won't happen again.

"Look, last night was an aberration. It had been a while and I got a little carried away but I won't let it happen again," he added.

He looked so damn sincere, sounded so determined. He really believed what he was saying. Well, hell.

"It shouldn't have happened last night. My boys were upstairs and had I been thinking straight, I would not have let it go so far, so quickly."

He looked like he was expecting a response but Joa had no idea what to say. She was both relieved and disappointed, annoyed and thankful for his matter-of-fact approach to their out-of-control, wildfire encounter.

"Uh-huh."

"So, is that a yes, a no? A go-straight-to-hell?"

Joa quickly tallied up the pros and cons in her head. She didn't want to be alone; she didn't want to go to a hotel or to a furnished apartment. She really enjoyed Aron and Sam and it wasn't like she was committing herself to a long-term contract. She had to temporarily leave Mounton House, he needed time to find his forever nanny.

All pros.

On the con side, she still wanted to sleep with him. Like, desperately. He, on the other hand, seemed completely un-fazed by their explosive sexual encounter.

And that pissed her off. Joa knew she needed to be sensible, that Ronan could mess with her head, mess with her plans. She was so attracted to him, a hundred times more so than she had been to any of her previous bosses. Looking back, and comparing what she felt for Ronan to those tepid feelings for Liam and Johan so long ago, she realized that she hadn't been physically attracted to any of those men.

Sure, it hurt when she left their employ and she mourned the dream of being part of a family, but her feelings had little, if anything at all, to do with the individual men.

Ronan was different. She liked his boys, sure, but she wasn't thinking "family" with him.

She was just thinking about having him, in any way she could get him. Preferably naked. And that was bad, very, very bad indeed.

She had to be sensible, she had to protect herself and her battered and bruised heart. Gathering her courage to say no, when she desperately wanted to say yes, Joa shook her head. "I'm sorry, Ronan. I don't think it's a good idea."

"Why not? Because you think I'll hit on you?"

No, because she was terrified that he wouldn't.

Joa told herself, once again, that while she might be strong enough to resist Ronan Murphy, she couldn't resist the voice message, sent from Ronan's phone, from his oh-so-serious older son.

She might have issues with Sam's dad but she refused to allow the little boy to think she didn't like him.

Stepping up to Ronan's front door, Joa rang the doorbell, stamping her feet and blowing air into her hands as she cursed the icy, snow-tinged wind. Would winter ever end?

Joa heard footsteps and told her excited heart, and ovaries, to calm the hell down. She'd seen Ronan the day before yesterday; there was no need to act like a teenager at a K-pop concert.

The door whipped open and Joa caught her breath, her words deserting her as she drank Ronan in. He was dressed in jeans and an untucked button-down shirt, and stubble covered his jaw. He still looked tired and harassed and so damn sexy.

"Joa. What are you doing here?"

Joa started to reply but a shiver racked her from head to foot and then she felt Ronan tugging her inside his warm house. "Man, you're an ice block. How long were you standing out there?"

Joa shook her head. "Not long. Stupid weather. I hate the cold."

"I can tell," Ronan replied, unwinding her scarf so that he could see her face. He smiled and pushed her knitted cap off her forehead. "There you are."

"Hi," Joa said, suddenly tongue-tied. Where had all her words gone?"

"Hi back," Ronan said, stepping away from her. "So, this is a surprise. I didn't expect to see you again."

"I didn't expect to be here but then I got a voice message from your phone." Joa pushed her hand into her coat pocket to pull out her phone and waved it at him.

Confusion passed over Ronan's face. "I didn't send you a voice message."

"I know." Joa pushed buttons and held up the phone. Sam's serious voice filled the space between them.

"Joa, this is Samuel McKenzie Murphy. My dad said that you can't be our nanny but he couldn't tell us why. We like you and we thought you liked us. So, anyway, me and Aron were just wondering what we did wrong."

Ronan tipped his head back and stared at the ceiling. When he dropped his head again, Joa shrugged. "I couldn't let them think that I didn't like them. I do, very much…"

Joa took a deep breath and, before she could change her

mind, released the words in a heated rush. "If you haven't made another plan for them, I'll do it. I'll look after them."

Ronan's mouth dropped open. "You will?"

"Yeah."

"Why?"

God, she didn't know. Because she liked being around people and living alone sucked? Because she missed her sister and she didn't know anyone else in Boston and she'd had the most fun with Ronan's kids? Because, while she could help out at the foundation, she wasn't employed there and there was only so much she could do?

Because she really, really wanted to spend time with Ronan Murphy?

"Am I too late? Did you find someone else?"

"No. Not yet…" Ronan rubbed his jaw, his expression still bemused. "I can't believe you are here."

Yeah, she couldn't, either. Ronan took a step toward her and lifted his hand to cup her cheek. His thumb skimmed her cheekbone and Joa sucked in a big gulp of air, leaning into his touch. This was temporary, she reminded herself, she would not dream for more.

Besides, Ronan was still in love with his wife. Great sex was just great sex, it didn't translate into there being a space for Joa in his heart. There never would be.

Joa took a step back and Ronan's hand fell to his side. Best to start as she meant to go on. Joa fiddled with her earring. "I'll also look for a long-term nanny for you."

"You will?"

Joa nodded. She'd thought about this. "Part of your problem is that it's *you* who is looking and *you* are doing the interview."

Ronan looked puzzled, so Joa explained that his famous name was, in this instance, a stumbling block. "If I take on the task, I will say that I am looking for a nanny for a client who has two small children, and you will remain anonymous until we find a couple of solid, genuine candidates. That will weed out all the ones who won't suit you or the boys."

"That might work."

Of course it would work. "And until I find you your paragon of nannyhood, I will look after the boys for you."

"You will?"

"Sure, they'll keep me busy while I look for my life's purpose."

"It's gone missing?" Ronan drolly asked and she saw a hint of the man Keely once called the greatest tease in America.

"Temporarily, I hope," Joa replied. She sucked in air and rolled her shoulders to release the tension gathered there. "So let's forget what happened between us—" hah! As if she could! "—and start fresh." She held out her hand. "Friends?"

Ronan arched his brows and looked down at her outstretched hand. Eventually, a million years later, he gripped her hand in his and pumped it once, hard.

"Yeah, something like that. Let's go find the boys. They are in the playroom."

What did he mean by that cryptic sentence? Joa followed him up the stairs, ignoring the photos of Thandi on the wall, looking so gracious and lovely and in love with her husband, her boys and her life. "I'll look after your boys, Thandi. I'll do my best, but only temporarily," she added, her words an indistinguishable murmur.

Ronan stopped abruptly to look back at her, and Joa put her hand on his back to stop herself from crashing into him. Beneath his shirt, she could feel hard muscle, feel his heat. She dropped her hand and surreptitiously wiped her clammy hand on the seat of her pants. "Sorry, talking to myself."

Ronan flashed her a smile. "You do that often?"

Joa flashed what she hoped was a cheerful smile. "How else would I get expert advice?"

Ronan laughed. "Fair point."

"Nice dress," Keely commented, holding out a glass of champagne.

Joa gestured to Sam and Aron, playing on the carpet by her feet, and shook her head. "Can't, I'm working."

"It's a party, Ju. Ronan won't have a problem with you having a drink."

Joa took the glass and put it on the table next to her elbow. She looked around the room filled with Carrick's guests, people who obviously knew the Murphy family well.

Tanna, the youngest Murphy sibling, was back in Boston and, judging by the heated exchanges between her and Levi Brogan, very much in love. In fact, between Tanna and Levi and Carrick and Sadie's hot looks, Joa was very impressed that the walls and drapes were still fire free.

"I'm not sure why I was invited tonight. I'm just helping Ronan out with the boys, trying to find him a nanny. I'm not part of your social circle."

"Social circle? It's a party with some friends, Ju. You are my sister and you're also Isabel's heir. And a Murphy client. And I've been friends with the Murphy brothers since we were kids. And Beah, Finn's ex-wife, is my best friend."

Joa cocked her head to the side. "How is she? I haven't seen her for, man, ten years?"

"She's good. She still works for Murphy's, but out of their London offices. She's their head of client liaison."

Joa wrinkled her nose. "Which means what?"

"She's the link between Murphy International and the client, advising them on what art to buy, what art to sell, what they should pay or sell the art for. She's really good at it, too. Her clients include Russian oligarchs, Arab princes, Asian billionaires."

"And she still works with Finn?" Joa asked, intrigued.

Keely rocked her hand from side to side. "Not really. She reports to Ronan. If she needs some information from Finn on provenance or history, they communicate by email."

Joa wanted to ask what went wrong with their marriage, but it had nothing to do with her.

"That really is a great dress." And because Keely changed the subject, she presumed she didn't want to gossip about Beah or Finn, either.

Joa looked down at the pretty, sunshine-yellow floral lace dress. It was shorter than the dresses she normally wore, the fabric sweeping from spaghetti straps into a V-neckline and from there into a fitted bodice. The flirty miniskirt ended midthigh, with a scalloped hem.

"The person who chose it really has excellent taste," Keely said, her tone completely serious.

"The person who chose it could've made sure it was an inch or four longer," Joa grumbled.

Ronan had issued the invitation earlier this morning, asking her to accompany him and the boys to Carrick's house for a cocktail party to celebrate Tanna's return to Boston. Keely, because she had the afternoon off, had been dispatched to find Joa a suitable dress. The yellow dress was the only one of the three that fit her properly.

"Thanks for helping me out," Joa said, squeezing Keely's arm. "By the way, I'm sending through a requisition for funding from the foundation to you. Can you approve it as a matter of urgency?"

"For what?" Keely asked.

Joa explained that she'd spent the morning talking through the renovations needed on a halfway house in East Boston with the house's director, who needed financial help from Isabel's foundation. With Keely being tied up in Florida, Joa had stepped up and taken over some of the decision-making for the foundation. They really needed to find a new CEO soon. And she needed to find Ronan a nanny. When she met those two goals, she'd turn her attention to finding her own purpose in life.

"Sure. Thanks for taking over some of the foundation work, Ju. Between trying to sort out the estate and my speech therapy practice, the foundation has taken a back seat."

Joa didn't mind; someone had to evaluate the requests for funding, to make sure they weren't being scammed. And surprisingly, she'd found herself enjoying the work. She looked down at the floor and saw Aron's yawn; the small boy was fighting sleep. Crouching on her stilettos, she scooped him up and placed him on her hip. Then she dropped to her haunches again, balancing on her spiky heels to look at Sam. "Are you tired, honey?"

Sam shook his head but his tired eyes gave him away.

Sam yawned and Joa stood up, Aron's face in her neck. Holding out her hand to Sam, she walked across the room to where Ronan was standing, talking to his brother Finn and Levi, Tanna's fiancé. Tanna and Levi had announced their engagement earlier, and the guests were also told that Sadie, Murphy International's art detective, was pregnant with Carrick's baby.

It had been quite a night.

The men stopped talking as she approached. Joa handed them each a smile before looking at Ronan. "The kids are exhausted. If it's okay with you, I'll take them home, uh, back to your place. Maybe you can get a lift or call a ride?"

Ronan placed his hand on Aron's back. "Let me take him."

Joa shook her head. "He's fast asleep, let him be. If you can help me get them strapped into their car seats, I'll get them settled in their own beds at home."

She had to stop using that word. Ronan's house was not her home.

"Let's take them upstairs." Ronan saw the skepticism on her face and smiled. "After Thandi died, we moved back here for a few months and they often stay with Carrick. We'll put them down in my old room and Sam will be asleep in ten minutes."

"Really, Ronan, I can take them home—"

Again? Had she not just had this conversation with herself?

Ronan placed his hand on her hand and turned her away from Finn and Levi. "We'll get them settled and later, we'll take them *home*, together."

His tone suggested that she not argue, so Joa sighed, then nodded. Ronan picked up Sam and led Joa into the hallway and up the fantastic hundred-year-old staircase. Joa passed huge paintings on the wall, taking a moment to slide her free hand across the satiny wooden banister.

"Your family seems nice," Joa said as they hit the landing of the first floor. Ronan turned right and looked over his shoulder to send her a smile.

"They are nice. And I'm really happy that my boys are going to have a cousin to play with."

"Apparently, you were right about something sparking between Carrick and Sadie."

"It was pretty difficult to miss since they've only had eyes for each other since the day they met. I knew for sure when he got all flustered when I teased him about her that night I returned from China."

The night they made love. The memories of that night were etched into her brain. Joa followed him into a room with two sets of bunk beds. The walls were lined with a bookcase filled with books for kids and teens. Another set of shelves held a bunch of boxes containing cars and toy soldiers and board games. The beds were covered in brightly colored linen. It was a perfect playroom for two little boys.

"Nice room," Joa commented.

Ronan looked around and smiled. "This was the room Carrick, Finn and I shared from the time we were little until way into our teens."

"You lived here?"

Ronan nodded. "All of my life until I got married. This was our family home."

Joa looked at Sam and saw that he was fighting sleep. "Just put both of them into the bottom bed, it'll be easier to haul them out when we leave," Ronan suggested.

Joa bent over and gently placed Aron on the bed, pushing him over to make room for Sam. Stepping back, she allowed Ronan the space to do the same, and when he straightened, he looked at her. Joa sucked in her breath, astonished at the desire in his eyes. It danced between them, hot and tempting, and Joa felt that delicious, sexual heat sweep through, her skin buzzing and her stomach jumping.

Ronan flushed and, grabbing her hand, pulled her out of the room into the dim hallway, spinning her around so that her back rested against the wall next to the door. He placed his hand on the wall next to her head and when he leaned in close, she tasted his breath, whiskey and toothpaste. Warmth rolled through her system and fireworks erupted on her skin.

"Ronan?" Joa murmured his name because she liked the sound on her lips.

"Mmm?"

"Please tell me you are going to kiss me," Joa whispered, entranced by the desire in his green-gold-blue eyes.

"In a minute." Ronan's other hand landed on her hip, trailed around, down her butt and up and under her skirt. He gripped her thigh, his big hand under her butt cheek, his fingertips on the inside of her thigh.

"This dress is dangerous," he growled. "Do not bend over in it."

"And what would you do if I did?" Joa teased, loving his sexy growl.

"Something like this…"

Ronan's mouth covered hers and his tongue slid into her mouth, twisting around hers in a kiss that was as desperate as it was hungry. His fingers on her leg inched closer to her happy place and his other hand covered her breast, kneading her nipple into a hard point.

His kiss deepened, became more ferocious, more demanding, and Joa forgot where she was, forgot that there was a house full of Ronan's happy relatives below her. She was consumed by his kiss, hankering for more.

For everything…

"Ro? Where are you?" Tanna's voice drifted up the stairs and Ronan pulled back, with all the tension of a stretched rubber band.

He stared at Joa, his eyes intense in the shadows of the hallway.

"Ro? Carrick wants to make a speech. We're all waiting for you, brother."

Ronan's hands left her and he stepped back, rubbing his hands over his face. He hauled in a deep breath, keeping his eyes on Joa as he responded to his sister. "Yeah, Tan,

I'll be there in a second. I'm just getting the boys settled. Give me five and I'll join the family downstairs."

His words hit Joa with all the force of a meteor strike. His family was downstairs, his family was sleeping in the room next to them. *His* friends, *his* people.

People she had no connection to…

His family.

Joa heard Sam's call for Ronan and she forced a smile onto her face. Pointing to the stairs, she gestured for him to go. "I'll see what Sam needs, you go on down. Your family—" her voice hitched on the word and she hoped Ronan didn't hear it "—is waiting for you."

Nine

Organizing a last-minute date had never been a problem for Ronan, and even though seven years had passed since he last invited a woman to dinner, for a drink, it was as easy as it had ever been.

Janie was a divorcée he'd met at the kids' school and they'd become friends, mostly because she was the least obvious and in-your-face of the mommy crew. She'd let him know she was interested in seeing him outside of school hours, and now that he had both a nanny and a new attitude toward sex and dating, he could explore his options.

Making love with Joa had released the cork holding all his sexual impulses at bay, and in the week since that happened, he'd had a lot of time to process their coupling and the ramifications of that life-changing encounter.

Sex, as his brothers had been telling him, was a natural and normal urge and Ronan finally accepted the idea that he could…well, indulge. In his desperation to honor his wife and his marriage, he'd sublimated all those urges, bundling sex and love and marriage together. Sleeping with Joa had made him realize something he'd long forgotten: sex wasn't love and didn't need to be.

Sex was sex and he could share the physical experience with a woman other than Thandi, understanding that love and marriage belonged to her. And always would.

She wasn't here; their marriage was, on a physical level, over. He would always think of her as his wife but sleeping with someone else wasn't cheating on her…

He was sure it wasn't.

Ronan looked at the cool blonde sitting opposite him, felt a surge of panic and quickly reminded himself there was nothing wrong with sharing a meal with a nice woman. He was entitled to have a social life.

He couldn't sleep with or date Joa; she was his employee, at least temporarily. So he was going with plan B…

Ronan watched Janie's mouth move and nodded, hoping he was giving the right response. Since sitting down in this small, intimate West Roxbury restaurant, she hadn't stopped talking and he'd lost track of her conversation ten minutes ago. God, for all he knew, he could've agreed to a holiday in Saint Bart's or to buy her a house.

He really should concentrate.

"I insisted that Pasco be given extra reading lessons so he didn't become bored."

Ronan looked down at his perfectly baked fish and hoped Janie would, and could, discuss something other than her kids. This was his first date in so long and he would prefer to discuss something other than child-rearing.

He wanted to flirt, to laugh, to see if there was a chance of ending the evening with a bang… Ronan pushed away the image of Joa's perfect breasts, those responsive nipples, the citrus tang to her skin. Two kisses and one couch-based coupling and he couldn't stop thinking about her…

"And Michael is an amazing natural athlete. I have enrolled him with a private tennis coach…"

Blah-blah, yada yada. Ronan took a bite of his fish, keeping his eyes on her pale blue eyes, wishing he was looking into a pair of mysterious silver eyes instead.

Joa again. Ronan mentally threw his hands up in the air and reluctantly accepted that not thinking about Joa was an impossibility…

Janie was pale while Joa was darker, her skin a rich light brown with peach undertones. Janie's hair was short, streaked with various shades of blonde. Joa's was a straight, luscious fall, as dark as a sable coat.

Ronan looked down at his fish, thinking it tasted like sawdust in his mouth. Janie was just picking at the salad she'd ordered as a main course, taking tiny bites between long, overenthusiastic sentences.

He didn't want to be here; this wasn't any fun. And, let's be honest here, he didn't want to sleep with Janie, he didn't want to sleep with women in general.

He just wanted to sleep with Joa again…

But Joa, now working for him as his nanny, was completely off-limits. So if he wanted sex, he'd have to give Janie some sort of hint that he was interested…

Problem was that he wasn't interested.

Janie dabbed her mouth with her linen napkin and carefully placed it to the side of her plate. She leaned back in her chair and looked at him for a minute, maybe longer.

"You're not having any fun." Janie verbalized his earlier thought, breaking the tense silence.

"Uh…" Ronan inwardly cursed and wondered how to edge his way out of this conversational minefield.

Attempting to change the subject, he gestured to her plate. "You've hardly eaten anything. Would you like to order something else?"

Janie shook her head. "And spend another hour trying to rack my brains to come up with something to talk about? No, thanks. I tried to connect with you over our boys, the school, parenting in general, but you didn't engage with me at all."

That was because he was on a date, and he didn't want to talk about his kids. He was a father twenty-four seven; he wanted a break.

And they hadn't connected because he'd spent most of their time together thinking about Ju…

Crap.

Ronan pushed his plate away and took a large sip of his wine.

"Would you like to go?" he quietly asked her.

"No, but I know you do," Janie said, her voice soft but pride flashing in her eyes. She pushed her chair back and stood up. "Why don't you settle the bill while I visit the ladies' room?"

Ronan followed her to her feet and watched her walk away. The maître d' immediately approached him, concern on his face. "Mr. Murphy, are you leaving? Has the food displeased you?"

Ronan placed his hand on the elderly man's shoulder. "No, John, not at all. The service and meal were impeccable, as always."

Ronan exchanged casual conversation with John until Janie returned. Ronan flashed John a smile. "I'll see you again, John."

Sympathy flashed in the older man's eyes. "Thank you for joining us tonight, Mr. Murphy, madam."

"Add a good tip to the bill, John," Ronan told him, knowing that the restaurant had his credit card details on file.

John nodded gravely, murmured a quiet thank-you, but Ronan caught the flash of mischief in his eyes and sighed.

He was about to make a decent contribution to John's bank account this month. Ronan placed his fingers on Janie's back to guide her to the door.

"Have a good evening, sir," John said, whipping in front of them to open the door.

He would. If he could get back to Joa.

Ronan tipped his face to the stars and shook his head. He had a dead wife, a failed date on his arm and he was thinking about his sons' nanny.

He was all kinds of messed up.

Joa heard the slam of the front door and the ping of Ronan's keys hitting the ceramic plate on the hall table. Sitting on the multicolored Persian carpet in the great room, she looked up as his big frame blocked out the light coming from the delicate French-inspired chandelier hanging in the double-volume hallway.

Being tall, he was a natural clotheshorse and she approved of his outfit of dark jeans, a checked brown-and-blue shirt worn under a flecked cream sweater, topped off by a well-worn but obviously expensive leather bomber jacket.

What she didn't approve of was the fact that he was dating.

Ronan Murphy was still in love with his wife and men who were still head over heels for their dead wives didn't date. Or shouldn't date.

Then again, neither should they have hot sex on the sofa.

Joa pushed a loose strand of hair behind her ear and looked up at him as he shrugged out of his jacket, throwing it onto the back of the nearest chair.

"You're home early," she commented, pulling her finger off the paper plate in her hand. She had glue everywhere, on her fingers, on her loose-fitting flannel pants, in her hair. "How was dinner?"

"Interminable," Ronan replied, resting his hand on the back of the sofa opposite her. He looked at the mess on his floor—paints, glue, colored paper and markers scattered across the carpet—and frowned. "What are you doing?"

Ah, she'd been waiting for him to ask. "Do you recall hearing anything about the boys needing animal masks for Zoo Day?"

"What the hell is Zoo Day?"

"It's been in their communication book, on and off, for about a month now."

"Uh, I tend to forget to check that."

She'd realized that. "And because you didn't, I was reminded by them both, just after supper, that they needed masks. Aron demanded a chimpanzee mask and Sam, a tiger."

Ronan pulled a face. "I could just go and buy them one."

Joa shook her head. "That's not the way it works. It has to be homemade and the kids should've helped to make it."

Ronan sat down on the edge of the sofa and rested his forearms on his knees. "Dammit, sorry." He looked at the mess and picked up a paper plate she'd painted with orange, white and black stripes.

Ronan pointed to the mess surrounding her. "Do you need some help?"

Well, yes. Or she'd be here until dawn. Not giving Ronan time to rescind his offer, she handed him a piece of paper and a pair of scissors. It was the template for Aron's monkey mask. "Cut this out."

Ronan took the paper and scissors and without saying another word, began to cut. Joa glanced at the expensive watch on Ronan's strong wrist, surprised to see that it was only nine thirty. She wasn't going to ask why he was home so early; who he dated and what he did had nothing to do with her. They'd just had a one-night stand and it would never be repeated…

"That was a quick date."

Inquisitive much, Joa?

Ronan didn't lift his eyes off his task. "Yeah. We ended it earlier than expected."

"Oh."

Oh *was good,* oh *was noncommittal.* Oh *wasn't nosy. Good job, Joa.*

"Why did it end earlier than expected?"

Bad job, Joa.

Ronan's lovely eyes slammed into hers. "She was as boring as hell."

Joa winced, partly in sympathy for the unknown woman, partly because she wondered if he found Joa equally boring. After all, she was sitting in PJ pants and a tank top, bare feet, cross-legged on his carpet, making a kid's mask. Sophisticated she was not.

"She wouldn't stop talking about kids, hers and mine." Ronan rested the paper plate on his knee and pushed an agitated hand through his thick hair. He had lovely hair, nut-brown and glossy, with a wave to it that wouldn't be tamed. "I love the monsters, but I could've done with talking about something else, anything else."

"Art?" Joa teased him.

"Sure. Baseball, climate change, books, history…"

"Ancient or modern?"

"More modern than ancient, although I am partial to those bloodthirsty Vikings and randy Romans."

Joa smiled. "I've always been fascinated by the Russian Revolution."

Ronan resumed his task of cutting out the monkey face and Joa resisted the urge to rip it out of his hand and get it done. She didn't need perfection, just a rough outline. "Speed it up, Murphy, I don't want to be doing this all night."

"Bossy as well as beautiful," Ronan murmured. Joa felt her face heat and slowly raised her eyes to look at him, both frustrated and relieved when he kept his eyes on directing the scissors around the monkey's ear. Dammit, he shouldn't say things like that, sexy things.

Things that made her remember the feel of his hard muscles under her hands, the crisp hair on his chest, the rougher hair on his...

For crying in a rusty bucket, Jones! Get your mind out of the bedroom...

"What got you interested in the Russians and their revolution?"

"Don't all little girls want to be princesses?" Joa blithely replied.

"That family didn't come to a gracious end."

"Sure, but their lives, before the revolution, were amazing. To a kid who grew up hard, they lived a fairy tale. Well, up until they were shot."

Ronan cocked his head to the side, all his attention on her. "You grew up hard?"

Dammit, how had she let that slip? She never, ever, not even with Keely, spoke about her past. What was the point of telling people that she was put into the foster system through sheer neglect, that she had no idea whether her druggie, far-too-young mother was alive or dead, that she'd been relying on herself for, well, all of her life? She loathed pity and she'd learned that sympathy didn't change a damn thing...

Her past was over, she was no longer a child and she didn't want to think about it anymore.

"I *grew* up," Joa replied, her voice tight.

"Where are your parents? Do you have siblings?" Ronan asked.

Joa tensed. "I grew up in the foster system," she reluctantly admitted, hoping he didn't press her for more information.

Ronan's expression held empathy but no pity. Thank God. "You don't like talking about your past, do you?"

"Do you?" Joa countered. "You lost your parents when you were young. Do you like talking about them?"

"I don't mind, actually. My parents were great, and it was a long time ago."

Good for him. Joa wanted to know more about them, but if she pried into his past, that would give him the excuse to pry into hers. Not happening.

Needing to change the subject, she returned to the subject of the Romanovs. "I'm not good at art and furniture but I have read quite a few books about Carl Fabergé." The imperial jeweler was an incredible goldsmith and produced some amazing works in gold and jewels. "He was so talented."

"That he was," Ronan agreed. "My father sold a Fabergé egg once."

"Really?"

Ronan looked at his monkey mask and handed it over. Joa handed it straight back. "Cut out the eyes, the mouth and the nose."

Ronan pulled a face and picked up the scissors again.

"What egg was it?" Joa asked.

"The Bay Tree egg. Nephrite leaves, white enamel flowers, diamonds, rubies, pearls. Lots and lots of diamonds.

The surprise is a feathered bird that appears, flaps its wings and sings."

"Did you see it?" Joa asked, fascinated.

"It was before my time." Ronan looked regretful. "I saw photos of it."

"Wow. How does it feel to have had all these wonderful treasures pass through your hands?"

"Privileged, I guess, is the best word. Blessed."

Joa turned her head to the right and looked at the framed photograph of Thandi and her boys. "Do you see Sam and Aron going into the business, as well?"

"Carrick, Finn and I discussed this, just the other day, actually. We were talking about Carrick's baby and we agreed that if our kids want to join the business, if they are passionate about what we do, then we'll let them, agreeing that they would start at the bottom and work their way up. Kind of like we did. Well, not Carrick, but only because he was the oldest and someone had to jump right in when our parents died, but Finn and I had to prove our worth. But if our kids want to become lawyers or doctors or pilots, that's their choice."

Joa thought back to earlier when she'd caught Aron climbing up the double-door fridge to get into the snack cupboard. "I think Aron might become a stuntman."

"I think he might end up in jail," Ronan muttered. "He's his uncle all over again. Always chasing the next thrill, the next challenge."

"Carrick or Finn?"

"Finn." Ronan slid off the sofa to sit on the carpet, stretching his long legs and leaning back against the sofa. "Finn is going ice climbing!"

"Like waterfalls and stuff?"

"Yeah, that. Have you ever heard of anything that crazy?" Ronan demanded, looking completely irritated.

"Base jumping? Spelunking?"

Ronan reached over and tugged the strand of hair that had fallen out of her messy knot. "Don't be facetious. And he's done both."

Joa attached the last strand of wire to the plate—whiskers for the tiger—and looked at her creation. It would have to do. "Why are you so against Finn ice climbing?"

"It's dangerous."

"So is driving a car or flying an airplane or riding a motorbike," Joa pointed out, dipping her paintbrush into gray paint to color Aron's mask.

"Our friend Levi just broke his leg dirt bike riding," Ronan stated.

"Accidents happen." Joa shrugged. "And it is his life."

Ronan stared down at Sam's mask, his fingers tightening on the paper plate. "I can't lose anyone else. It would kill me, Ju."

"Is that why you don't date, why you refuse to look for love again?" Joa quietly asked.

"Yeah, it's a big part of it."

"What's the rest of it?" Joa asked, her hand shaky as she painted the mask.

"I'm still in love with my wife."

That wasn't news. Joa forced herself to look up into his eyes and was startled at the maelstrom of pain, confusion and irritation she saw in those deep green-blue depths.

Joa wanted to hug all his pain away. She felt herself leaning into him and then remembered she wasn't doing this again, she wasn't going to fall into his life and pretend it was hers.

It wasn't and it never could be.

"Learning to live again is hard, Ju."

Joa couldn't resist. She turned, rested her forehead on his shoulder and placed her hand on his hard thigh.

The muscles under her palm flexed, tightened, but she didn't react.

What could she say? She was the very last person in the world qualified to give advice.

Ten

With ample warning that Joa had an important meeting at Isabel's foundation—a discussion with the board to look over the résumés for the new CEO of the organization—Ronan had asked Tanna, his sister, to collect the boys from school. It felt strange to have the afternoon off and to drive back to the house without the chattering boys in the car.

But the silence did give Joa time to think.

The candidates for the CEO position were, like the candidates for Ronan's nanny, just not right. Oh, they were all very qualified and very slick, but none of them possessed the amount of enthusiasm Joa felt was needed to run Isabel's beloved organization.

Like so many of the au pairs she'd interviewed, she felt they were all there for the paycheck.

For the boys, she wanted a nanny who would get down and dirty, who'd paint and play and talk to Sam and Aron, someone who'd interact on their level. For the CEO, she wanted someone who cared less about the glitzy benefits of the fund-raising parties and more about the people she, or he, would be ultimately helping. She wanted someone who would paint a room and serve food in a shelter, who'd stack books in a library, who'd visit the disaster-ravaged areas they funded. Good help, Joa was coming to realize, was very hard to find.

She whipped into the driveway to Ronan's house, noticing an unfamiliar car parked in her space. Pulling off to the side, she hurried up the steps, slipping her key into the lock and stepping into the warm hall. Calling out a hello, she dumped her coat and bag on the hall table, and walked into the hallway to see Tanna standing by the window of the great room. Ronan's half-sister was tiny compared to her big, burly brothers, and, like Joa, was a complicated mix of different cultures.

"Hey, Tanna. Sorry I'm late."

Tanna turned and smiled. "No worries. I took the afternoon off and I love spending time with the mini-monsters."

"Where are they?"

Tanna used her coffee cup to gesture to the garden outside, still covered with snow. Joa saw the boys crouched by a rock formation, fascinated by whatever an older woman was telling them.

Joa frowned. "Who is that?"

"Abigail Houseman," Tanna replied. "She said she had an interview with you about the nanny position?"

Joa thought for a minute and then winced. "Damn, I totally forgot about her."

She'd made the appointment weeks ago, when she first came to help Ronan out. Abigail, she now remembered, had been on a walking tour in Scotland and could only be interviewed when she returned. They'd agreed that if Joa found someone suitable, she'd email Abigail to cancel the appointment.

"What on earth are they doing?" Joa asked, confused by the boys' interest in a set of rocks.

Tanna laughed. "Abigail is giving them a history of gnomes in Boston. Apparently, gnomes live in boys' gardens and fairies in girls' gardens," Tanna said, with a completely straight face.

Well, that made sense.

Joa's lips twitched with amusement. "And the boys are buying it?"

"Aron is lapping it up, Sam suspects it's rubbish but he's enjoying the story." Tanna turned away from the window and headed toward the kitchen area, asking Joa if she wanted coffee.

Joa said yes and watched the boys for a few minutes more. Abigail looked to be in her midfifties, fit and slim. She wore her blond hair in a bob and was naturally attractive. Best of all, her attention was fully on the boys.

Aron had her hand in his and Sam's normally reticent expression wasn't anywhere to be seen. Joa instinctively knew they liked her.

Turning back to Tanna, Joa joined her in the kitchen and sat down on one of the stools at the island. "What do you think of her?" Joa asked.

Tanna thought for a minute.

"I really like her. She's easy to talk to, seems completely unfussy. The boys took to her immediately." Tanna pushed her cup toward Joa and her lips curved into a rueful smile. "I kind of interviewed her. I hope you don't mind."

She really didn't. The boys were Tanna's nephews and Joa appreciated a second opinion.

"She's fifty-nine, her husband died two or three years ago. No kids but she's taught grade school for thirty years and gave up work to nurse her husband who died of cancer." Tanna explained.

Joa felt a spurt of sympathy and asked Tanna to continue. "She's not looking for a live-in position as she has a house ten minutes away but she's not averse to spending the occasional night here if Ronan needs to travel for work."

"Did she say why she was looking for a job?"

"She simply loves kids and she's bored. She's traveled a bit since her husband died but, as she said, she's not the sitting-at-home-knitting or lunching-with-her-friends type. She doesn't want to go back into full-time teaching and she thought that a part-time job might suit her better."

Tanna's shoulders lifted and fell. "Honestly, Joa, I think she's perfect."

Oh, she sounded like she was. Of course, Joa would grill her again before she recommended her to Ronan but Abigail did sound perfect.

Dammit, dammit, dammit.

Joa didn't want Abigail to be perfect; she didn't want to find Ronan his forever nanny because then Joa would be obsolete. She'd have to move on.

She'd lose her family.

No, dammit! Joa scrubbed her face with her hands, reminding herself that she was repeating past mistakes, that she didn't have a family, that this was a temporary position. She *had* to move on. She had to find her own spot of sunshine, her own place to stand. It wasn't here, in this house, with those boys and that man.

"So are you going to tell Ronan about her?" Tanna asked.

Joa pushed her coffee away and stood up. "I suppose I have to, don't I?"

Joa turned away and didn't see Tanna's satisfied smile.

Joa walked down the hallway of Murphy International, feeling out of place in her skinny jeans tucked into flat knee-high boots and a thick hooded sweatshirt worn under a quilted puffer jacket. The other women darting in and out of offices wore form-fitting dresses in bold colors, with neutral or skin-tone stilettos. But Joa had spent the morning at the halfway house, going over plans for the renovation, and she'd spent most of that time outside. Dresses and heels were pretty but impractical.

Office dresses and heels had never been her thing anyway. She doubted they ever would be. She liked wearing flip-flops and sneakers, shorts and jeans. She couldn't imagine dressing up and slapping on makeup; she far preferred to get her hands dirty, whether it was looking after kids or climbing up ladders to inspect roofs.

Earlier, and still without telling Ronan about Abigail, she'd dropped off the boys at their school and headed to Isabel's foundation, joining the staff meeting already in progress. Thirty minutes in and they were still on the first item on the agenda. Joa made an executive, and easy, decision to move them along. By item number five she was chairing the meeting and afterward, the acting CEO told her that they'd achieved more in an hour than they had all week. They needed direction, Joa realized, someone to make decisions and to provide leadership.

She thought she just might be that person. She was passionate about the foundation, about the work they did, and she felt supremely comfortable in the role of CEO. But she wasn't qualified. She didn't have the business, accounting or management background, or any of the qualifications the board required.

But damn, it was fun. Running the foundation was something she could see herself doing for a long, long time… possibly for the rest of her life.

"Ju."

Joa jumped a foot high and slapped her hand on her heart. Catching her breath, she saw Ronan standing in the doorway to his office, arms folded across his chest, biceps bulging under his cream shirt, amusement dancing in his eyes.

"Holy crap. You scared me."

"You were a million miles away. What on earth were you thinking about?"

She might as well tell him and he'd confirm that she didn't have a hope in hell of getting the CEO position if she applied. Maybe he could help her find a way to still be involved with the foundation, to work with the new CEO, maybe as a consultant? She respected Ronan's sharp brain; she was sure he could help her figure it out.

"I was thinking about Isabel's foundation and how much I would like to run it," Joa admitted.

"What, as the new CEO?"

Joa nodded. "Crazy, isn't it? I'm not qualified, I don't have a business degree or know anything about accounting. And Keels is the one who can schmooze with donors—she can get blood from a rock. I'm not good at that. I feel out of place and tongue-tied at fund-raisers, very much like the girl from the wrong side of the tracks."

She waited for Ronan to speak but when he didn't, she jammed her hands in the pockets of her jacket and tried not to let the disappointment show on her face. His non-answer was an answer in itself. She wasn't suitable for the position. It was obvious…

"So why did you ask me to come down here?"

"We'll get to that in a minute," Ronan replied, his posture indolent but his eyes as sharp as razors. "We're still discussing the open CEO position at the foundation."

"Well, I was. You weren't saying anything," Joa pointed out, a little peeved.

"I was thinking."

"And?" Joa demanded, wondering if she could slap a response out of him.

"I think you need to get over yourself," Ronan said, his tone and words blunt. "You're finding reasons why you can't take the position and you're missing the most obvious reason why you can."

"Sorry?"

"A, you can talk to anyone. You are one of the wealthiest women on the East Coast. People don't give a rat's ass where you or your money came from. The only person who seems to have an issue with that is you."

Wow. *Ouch.*

"B, so you don't have a business or accounting degree, but you have a brain behind that gorgeous face and great instincts. You can hire people to look over a contract, to dissect balance sheets, but finding someone who is as passionate as you would be impossible."

"But the board makes the decision…"

"Do you really think the board is going to vote against you and Keely, the two most powerful trustees? Tell your sister you want to do this and she'll persuade, possibly bully, everyone else to support you." Ronan skimmed his knuckle over her cheekbone. "Can I ask one favor, though?"

Joa blinked, trying to make sense of what he'd just said. He hadn't dismissed her; in fact, he seemed to take her suitability for the job as a given. She had his unqualified support and, while she didn't need it, it was wonderful to have.

Empowering, heart-warming…

Joa remembered that he'd asked her for a favor. "Yeah, sorry, what do you need?"

"Before you join the foundation on a full-time basis, can you please, please find me a nanny?"

Oh, she had… She just hadn't had a moment to tell him about Abigail. And a part of her still didn't want to. She still wanted to be involved in the boys' lives, be able to pick them up from school, play Legos on the carpet, take them skating at Frog Pond.

She wanted to run the foundation, but she still wanted the boys. And Ronan, she wanted him most of all…

Joa's gaze met his and she watched as desire, hot and heavy, turned his eyes to a deep gold-green. Ronan's eyes dropped to her mouth and Joa shifted on her feet, her blood heating by a degree. He wanted her; she knew that. On the floor, up against the wall, anyway he could take her…

Oh, God, she wanted him, too. She wanted him in a big bed, rolling around, a tangle of hands and limbs and feet and tongues, creating sparks and mind-numbing pleasure.

Joa, feeling a little shaky, placed her hand against the wall because her knees had turned to mush and her brain to slush.

This man could send her from nanny to naughty in five seconds flat.

Not, on any planet, a good thing.

Joa swallowed, closed her eyes and counted to ten. Then she counted to twenty, telling herself she had to get it together. She was in his employ. She shouldn't be having naughty-but-nice thoughts about him.

But dammit, he looked like a sports model—six foot three of defined muscles topped by a masculine face. How could she *not* want to jump him?

Joa gripped the strap of her bag and held on for dear life. Dimly remembering where they were, she gave herself a mental slap and hauled in some air. She'd tell him about Abigail later. "So, was there a reason you called me down here?"

Ronan took a minute to make sense of her words and he eventually nodded, excitement replacing lust. "Oh, right! Yeah, there's something I want to show you."

Joa couldn't work out what he could possibly want to show her at his place of work. Their only connection, apart from their take-me-hard attraction, was the boys and the sale of Iz's collection. She wasn't an art buff and knew nothing about antiques.

"Okay." Joa shrugged.

Ronan threaded his fingers in hers, pulling her toward the bank of elevators at the end of the hall. He keyed in a code on the far right and when they stepped inside, Joa realized the elevator was smaller than normal and couldn't take more than two people, maybe three.

"Where are we going?"

"A secure storage room in the basement," Ronan explained. "It's where we store our most valuable works."

She was still in the dark. "Why are we going there?"

Ronan ran his knuckle over her cheekbone, his abalone-shell eyes glinting with an emotion she couldn't quite read. Tenderness? Excitement? A mixture of both? "You'll see."

The elevator opened into a small vestibule and was guarded by a solid, opaque door. Ronan keyed in another code and the door opened. They walked into a massive storage room filled with shelves. In the center of the room was a long table and on it, packages in bubble wrap.

Joa glanced around, saw the cameras on each corner and raised her eyebrows at the security. "I feel like a hundred eyes are watching me."

"Not quite a hundred but, yes, this room is constantly monitored by our security team. Finn, Carrick and I are the only people allowed down here on our own and if someone needs to retrieve an item from storage they are accompanied by the head of our security. Everything that happens in this room is recorded from every angle."

Joa resisted the urge to wave at the nearest camera.

Ronan walked across the room to a panel on a monitor

on the wall and Joa looked over his shoulder to see herself looking over his shoulder in the screen.

It was weird seeing what the security team was seeing…

Ronan pushed a button on the intercom next to the screen and when he spoke, his voice was strong and commanding. "Please cut the camera and audio feed to this room."

There wasn't a response but the screen was replaced with snow. Ronan walked over to the table and Joa followed him, dropping her bag onto a stool he pulled out from the table.

She looked back at the fuzzy screen. "You can cut the feed?"

Ronan nodded. "The art and auction world is highly sensitive and sometimes Carrick, Finn and I, or a combination of all three, have conversations down here that are highly confidential. We are the only ones who have the authority to order security to shut down the cameras and audio."

Joa sent him a small smile. "Are you going to tell me some sensitive company secrets? Please don't, I can't cope with the pressure."

Ronan grinned. "Nope, sorry. But I'm not sure if I'm going to be able to keep my hands off you and I'd prefer not to have witnesses while I kiss you stupid."

Joa's mouth fell open and it took her ten seconds, maybe twenty, for her to come up with a response. "Putting aside the fact that any sort of physical contact between us is not a good idea, and we agreed it wouldn't happen, you could've just taken me into your office and kissed me there. Why did you bring me to the bowels of the building?"

Ronan rested his forearms on the table and nodded to the cardboard boxes, openly amused. "Because of those?"

"I don't understand."

Ronan reached for a roughly shaped square and handed it to her. "Here, unwrap it."

Joa, still trying to understand Ronan's rather prosaic

statement about kissing her, took the parcel and peeled the plastic away to reveal a photo frame.

Joa felt her breath hitch. The frame was square with bracket corners and a deep, vibrant royal blue. Each corner held a fleur-de-lis constructed from what could only be big, fat diamonds. In the middle was an oval cut out, framed in more diamonds.

It was obviously expensive, terrifyingly rare and undeniably breathtaking.

Ronan ran the tip of his finger along the edge of the frame. "So, as I'm sure you know, Carl Fabergé, along with his brother Agathon, took over their father's jewelry business. They couldn't manage all their commissions themselves, so they employed goldsmiths who managed their own workshops. Those goldsmiths produced a lot of items under Fabergé's name. This was made by a guy called Michael Perkhin."

"It's exquisite." Joa couldn't take her eyes off the frame, fascinated by the intricate detail.

Ronan gently removed the frame from her hand and gave her another parcel. "A world-renowned collector decided to thin out his collection of Fabergé and wants us to sell these items for him."

"Why would he want to sell something as beautiful as this?" she asked, holding up an earthenware container partly covered by silver scrolls and flowers. She found the silver lid and placed it on top of the bulbous container. "I don't even know what this is?"

"It's a ceramic tobacco humidor. It's special because it's by Fabergé himself and has the imperial seal."

Joa stepped away from the table and held up her hands. "I'm scared to touch it."

"Don't be. It's only worth more than three hundred thousand dollars."

Joa squealed and took another step back. "I'm not touching another thing!"

Ronan smiled and quickly unwrapped another parcel, sliding the tiny object into his hand before she could see what it was. Ronan clenched his fist and told her to hold out her palm. When she did, Ronan dropped the small object into her hand and Joa gasped at the miniature egg, festooned with diamonds and rubies, and edged with gold. It was designed to be worn as a pendant.

"Circa early 1900, marked as Fabergé, but accredited to one of his more experienced goldsmiths."

Joa examined the egg, running the tip of her finger on the bands of diamonds. "This takes my breath away."

Ronan took the pendant from her and placed it back in its box. "There's been a rumor circulating that one of the imperial eggs might be coming up for sale. We think that's why this collector is moving these items on, and if it does come up, he wants to liquidate some cash to bid on that egg."

"What would an egg be worth?" Joa asked.

"However much a collector would be prepared to pay for it," Ronan replied. "Ten, fifteen, thirty million? More? We won't know until it comes up for sale."

Joa spent the next twenty minutes inspecting each of the twenty lots, completely intrigued by the artistry of the objects. She took the loupe Ronan handed her and examined the diamonds, the emeralds, the fine detailing in the enamel. Then she went back and looked at some of the items again.

"I used to read about the Romanovs and the royal court, and about Rasputin and Fabergé. This world, for most of my fourteenth year, was my escape. I spent many hours imagining that I was an aristocratic Russian with a powerful father and a loving mother, cossetted and protected."

She sent Ronan a quick smile. "I didn't have a great childhood. I spent most of my life in the system. Then I was a teen runaway."

Joa felt Ronan's hand on her back, but she couldn't look at him. She didn't want to see the pity in his eyes. "I find it so strange that I landed with Isabel, who surrounded herself with all the trappings of a wealthy, artsy world. That I'm standing here, looking at these objects, some of which I could, maybe, afford to buy."

Ronan walked around the table and placed his back to the table to face her. "How did you end up in foster care?"

She'd opened the door. She couldn't slam it in his face. She wanted to keep her past private, but she also wanted to tell him, show him who she really was. "Young, addicted-to-meth mother, father unknown. She tried to keep me. I have some very vague memories of bouncing between her and the system."

"Your dad?"

She shrugged. "I don't know who he was. She probably didn't, either. But he had to be of Indian descent because my mom was a blue-eyed blonde."

Ronan picked up a strand of her hair and rubbed it between his fingers. "How did you end up with Isabel?"

Joa picked up the egg pendant again and rolled it around her hand, focusing on the massive ruby at the bottom of the egg. "A foster mother who worked nights, a foster father who was losing the battle to keep his hands off me. I used to put a chair under the doorknob. One day I came home from school and the chair was gone and the lock to my bedroom was broken. I knew I had to get out."

She saw the anger in his face and it warmed her that he could feel rage on behalf of her teenage self. "I ended up at the shelter Iz funded, and she found me there. Two days later I was living with her and Keely. For the longest time, I thought of myself as Princess Anastasia, someone who'd escaped death." She shrugged. "I had an active imagination."

Ronan linked her hand in his. "I think you are amazingly brave. And incredibly resilient."

Joa finally lifted her eyes to his, grateful not to see any pity. "Thank you for not uttering any platitudes," she murmured.

"Yeah, I hate pity, too."

Of all the people who'd understand, Ronan would do it best. He seemed to accept that her past was in the past, unable to be changed.

It simply was…

Joa placed the pendant on the table and stepped up to him, wrapping her arms around his hard waist. She rested her forehead on his chest. "There's no point in looking back, Ro. It's not a pretty picture, so that's why I don't."

Ronan gathered her close. "I get it, Ju. I do. But I am sorry you went through that."

Joa snuggled in, happy to be held. It wouldn't last and, in a few weeks, she'd move on. But right now, he was here, solid and stable.

Ronan dropped a kiss into her hair. "Did you ever look at the list of items from Isabel's collection that are going to auction?" he asked, his deep voice warm in her ear.

Joa shrugged as she pulled back. "Sort of." It had been a long list and she'd been busy. "Why?"

"Isabel did own a miniature Fabergé pendant egg."

Joa pulled back and frowned at him, not sure if he was pulling her leg. "You're kidding!"

"It's silver, covered with gray guilloche enamel. Studded with diamonds. Circa 1910. Do you want to see it?"

"Hell, yes!"

Eleven

Later that night, Ronan jogged up the stairs to his third-floor master suite, feeling a hundred and four instead of thirty-four. It had been a long day and, thanks to spending two hours in the vault going through Isabel's treasures with Joa, he'd had to work late to catch up with reports, market research and various publicity campaigns.

It was now past eleven, the boys had been in bed for hours and Joa had retired to her suite shortly after dinner. She'd been quiet for most of the evening, pushing food around her plate, a million miles away. He knew the day had taken an emotional toll on her. He understood how difficult it was to open up, to talk about the past.

She was trying to plot her future, was dealing with her past and how best to protect Isabel's legacy. He remembered Isabel as being acerbic and imperious but he'd always feel grateful toward her for giving Joa a home, for allowing her to feel safe. Every time he considered Joa,

young and alone on the mean streets of Boston, his heart
sputtered and stuttered.

The thought of an adult man entering her room and
sexually assaulting her made him want to punch a wall. At
various times over the past few hours he'd thought about
checking in on her but he knew, better than most, that sometimes the kindest thing you could do was give people the
space to be alone, allow them to work through their own
issues in their own way.

So he was surprised to see Joa standing in the doorway to her guest suite, obviously wanting to speak to him.
It was obvious she'd been doing yoga, maybe in his gym
downstairs or in the living room area of her suite, because
she was dressed in matching white skin-tight pants and a
crop top and her skin glowed from exercise.

His cock, polite as always, rose to the occasion.

Stand down, dude, she's had a hard day.

Right then, Ronan realized he didn't want her to leave,
not now, not next week, not ever. She fitted in his life, in
his boys' lives; she made it better, brighter…

He liked her and, given some time, he might even come
to feel more for her. The thought no longer scared him as
it once had.

Serious food for thought…

"Ronan?"

Joa calling his name jerked him back to the present, to
the fact that he was standing in the hallway, looking like
an idiot. He rubbed his jaw and took a deep breath. "Yeah,
sorry, I zoned out. What's up?"

Joa leaned her shoulder into the door frame and crossed
one bare foot over the other. Her feet were long and delicate and tipped with fire red nail polish.

Sexy feet…

"If I wanted to, could I withdraw Isabel's egg pendant from the sale?"

Ronan nodded. "Sure, with Keely's approval. Are you thinking about doing that?"

She'd held on to the silver pendant egg the whole time they were looking at the more expensive items in Isabel's collection, like the Modigliani, the Degas sketch, the Vermeer. She'd appreciated Isabel's treasures but it was obvious that she adored the egg pendant. It resonated with her as a concrete link between her past and her real-life fairy godmother.

"I'm not sure." Joa bit the corner of her lip. "I'd like to, but I also feel like I should allow the pendant to be sold. It'll raise a lot of money."

"Honey, it might raise twenty-five thousand dollars, maybe more. Say it raised fifty thousand, a hundred thousand. That's a drop in the ocean compared to the many, many millions that will be raised overall. You could make a donation for the equivalent amount, if you wanted to.

"I heard you're pretty wealthy now," he added, teasing her. He liked the fact that she didn't take her wealth for granted. Or flash her cash around.

Finally, a smile hit her lips and her eyes. "Yeah, okay. I'll talk to Keely about pulling it."

Oh, Keely would be fine with it but, on the very slim chance that Keely objected, Ronan would buy the egg himself to ensure that Joa took ownership of that pendant.

"Do that, let me know what she says. Then send me an official email, pulling the pendant from the sale," Ronan said, trying to sound professional. Really hard when she was dressed in next to nothing and all he wanted was to pull those clothes off her...

"Ro?"

"Yeah?" His voice sounded rough, laced with sex. He wondered if she noticed.

Joa's eyes were big, round and full of emotion. "This sounds really strange, but when we hugged this afternoon, it was really nice. Can you, I mean, will you…"

She was asking him to hug her? She had to be kidding. "No."

At his sharp retort, the hot blush of mortification hit her skin, turning her face red. She immediately dropped her eyes and took a hasty step back, her hand on the door, ready to slam it in his face.

Smooth, Murphy. Not.

Ronan moved quickly to catch the door, staring down at the top of her head. She turned away from him, shoulders back and her spine ramrod straight. Now she was pissed.

He needed to explain and quickly. "I can't hug you, Ju. Because if I do, I'm going to strip you, taste every inch of you and then make you mine."

Joa turned slowly and he saw the rapid rise and fall of her chest, desire in her eyes. She lifted one shoulder, attempting to be casual. "Okay. I'll settle for that…"

Ronan shoved his hands into his hair, tugging at the roots, trying to keep his cool. He needed his hands on her, his mouth on hers but first he had to make sure…

"Are you telling me that you want me, too?"

Okay, maybe he needed a little reassurance, to know she wanted him as much, but nobody needed to know that fact but him.

Joa didn't answer and he felt his stomach sink to his toes, disappointment rolling over him. Then Joa crossed her arms at her chest and gripped the edges of her exercise top, pulling it up and over her head, revealing her oh-so-very-pretty breasts with their tight, dark buds to his appreciative gaze.

He clenched his fists to keep from going to her, wanting to see what she'd do next.

She didn't disappoint. Pushing her thumbs beneath the fabric at her hips and pushing her pants down her thighs, kicking the fabric away. Standing in a tiny pair of silky white bikini panties, she hesitated a moment before pushing the scrap of fabric down her hips. Her fantastic eyes slammed into his.

"Does me being naked count as a yes?"

He tried to speak but his tongue, for the first time ever, was unable to form the words. Okay, well, then, he'd get his point across in another way, too.

Ronan lifted his hand and his fingers skated across her collarbone, down her chest. Ignoring her pointed nipple, he cupped her breast, lifting and tasting that smooth skin. He felt her back arch, trying to urge him to suck her, but his lips just curved across her skin. No, he was in charge here. He'd give her what she wanted, eventually, but he wanted to draw her pleasure out, tease and tantalize.

And be teased and tantalized.

Ronan placed his flat palm on her chest and gently pushed her backward so the back of her knees hit the bed, and she sat down. Keeping his hand on her chest he gently pushed so she was lying back, looking up at him, flashes of lightning in her silver eyes.

Ronan clasped her wrists and placed them above her head and Joa arched her back and lifted her hips. He liked that she wasn't self-conscious around him—she didn't need to be—and that she approached lovemaking as a natural, sensual act, nothing to be ashamed of. She might be skittish about commitment and have little experience of family life but she was a woman who liked pleasure.

And he intended to pleasure the hell out of her.

Keeping his clothes on—if he stripped he wouldn't be

able to resist slipping inside her—he placed a hand on the bed covers next to her shoulder and loomed over her, taking in her perfect breasts, her flat stomach, the gentle curve of her hips and legs. Then his free hand followed his eyes, exploring the femininity of her shoulder, her narrow rib cage, and spent some time exploring her belly button. He spent endless minutes teasing her nipples, rolling them between his thumb and fingers, plucking them into even harder points. He wanted to kiss her, to give his mouth what his hands were enjoying, but if he did, this would be over in a matter of minutes.

He was on a knife-edge, his cock hard and straining against the fabric of his pants.

"Please, Ro."

Joa's slim legs fell open and he looked down, sighing. She was very pretty down there. He trailed a finger between her lips, heat rolling through him as he realized how ready she was for him. Dipping into her, pushing inside with just one finger, told him she was a flick or a slide or a kiss away from coming. Or even a word.

And if he gave her this, then he could start the delicious game all over again, building her up. Of course, there was the possibility that he would go off his head with need but it was a chance he was willing to take.

Ronan withdrew his finger and painted the inside of her thigh with her juices. Joa moaned her dissatisfaction and lifted her hips, wanting more, wanting everything.

"Ronan, I'm so close. Don't stop touching me."

Ronan pushed himself up so his face was above hers, enjoying the flush on her cheeks, the rapid pulse beating in her throat.

He did *that*. He made her hot and made her thrum, made her look like a wild woman. He was in his midthirties but he'd never felt more like a man than he did when he loved this amazing woman.

"What do you need, Ju?"

Those eyes drilled into him. "You, dammit. Now."

Ronan fumbled with the button on his pants, with his zipper. He wouldn't enter her, definitely wouldn't let himself come; he wanted this to last all night, but he could torture them both, just a little more.

Still only using one hand, and with Joa's fumbling help, he pushed his pants down and Joa pulled his shirt up and over his head. Ronan rubbed his cock over her and Joa release a soft series of *ohhhh*s and *Ro*'s.

Her voice sounded like an ocean breeze and her scent was an orchard of apple trees.

And when he pushed into her, she felt like home.

He'd pull out, he would, in a minute—there were still things he wanted to do to her—but for now, he'd allow himself to sink, to fall.

Resting his elbows on either side of her head, he brushed his thumbs over her cheekbones, rested his forehead on hers. This—being here, with Joa—was both heaven and hell. Heaven because they fit together so well; hell because he'd thought this part of his life was over forever.

Not wanting his mind to send him down that path, he dropped his head to kiss Joa's sensual mouth, all thoughts of right and wrong, past and future dissolving.

There was only now, and the present was perfect.

Ronan pushed his hand under Joa's butt, lifted her hips and slid in a little deeper. This was as close as he could get, as far as he could go.

Feeling that familiar buildup at the base of his spine, in his balls, he gritted his teeth, telling himself that if he wanted to tease her, *them*, some more, he needed to pull out, to pull back.

"I love this, Ronan. I love your body. I love what you do to me."

Her words were softly spoken but she lit the fuse allowing his self-control to detonate. With an animal-like roar, something he never recalled himself doing, ever, Ronan slammed into her, a voice telling him to be gentle, to take it easy. But he couldn't, he needed to brand her, to mark her as his. Then Ronan realized her nails were pushing into his butt and she was lifting her hips to meet him, seemingly as desperate for him as he was for her. Wanting to test his theory, he slowed down, but Joa was having none of it. She jerked her hips up, taking what she needed, pushing up and into him, harder and faster.

Amazed by her passion, blown away by her need, he allowed her to control the rhythm and when he felt her ripple, when her channel clenched him, he started to move, long, sure strokes that were designed to maximize pleasure, to wring every drop from them both.

From far away he heard her scream, felt her blow apart, but then he was consumed by his own big bang, his own cosmic collision.

Pleasure, hot, fast and overwhelming, consumed him, and as he fell into that black hole of deliciousness, he felt Joa's second orgasm setting his nerve endings alight.

His head ripped from his shoulders and his heart blew out of his chest.

It took a long time for Ronan to search for his missing body parts, longer still for him to patch himself back together again.

Joa shot up in bed, felt the cool air on her chest and looked down, shocked to notice she was naked. Lunging sideways, she whipped her phone off her bedside table and forced her eyes to focus on the screen.

It was nine twenty…

Crap, crap, crap.

Joa checked her alarm, saw that it had been turned off and silently cursed the very absent Ronan. She'd fallen asleep in his arms—somewhere around three thirty, after three bouts of lovemaking, twice in this enormous bed, the last in the shower—her head on his chest, her hand on his stomach, her knee nestled between his legs.

She'd felt warm and happy and safe and sated.

Well loved and well used, in the best way possible.

Joa slipped out of bed and stretched, placing her hands on the floor and arching her back. Sex, she decided, was as good as yoga for stretching her muscles, for flooding her system with endorphins.

Walking her hands out, she twisted her head to the side, elongating her neck. And on the floor, half under her bed, was Ronan's shirt. After a few more stretches, she picked it up and slipped it over her head, pushing her arms down and smiling when the cuffs fell over her hands. She rolled back the sleeves and sniffed the collar, the scent of him warming her from tip to toe.

She'd amble downstairs, make some coffee and then come back up for a shower. Then she needed to go to the foundation offices to peruse some paperwork, and later this afternoon, she'd collect the boys from school. Maybe she could take them ice-skating on Frog Pond.

Joa walked down the stairs, trying to ignore the family photographs on the wall. It felt, yeah, *weird*, to be walking around half-naked in Ronan's house. Shrugging off her unease, she hit the bottom of the stairs in the hallway and deliberately didn't glance at the massive portrait of Thandi hanging on the wall to her right.

If she looked, she'd lose these wonderful morning-after tingles. She'd loved being with Ronan and loving him, and she wanted to hold on to those magical sparks still danc-ing across her skin.

Heading straight for the coffee maker in the kitchen, Joa popped a pod into the machine and shoved a mug under the spout. She hit the button and turned to open the fridge. And there, at eye level, was that damn note from Thandi to Ronan that Joa had read a million times.

Joa looked at the feminine handwriting, feeling her heart constricting. There were other notes under that one and, despite knowing she shouldn't, Joa pulled them out from under the magnet keeping them attached to the fridge.

Welcome home, honey. You've been in my thoughts. (But mostly in my sexual fantasies.)

Ro, I'll love you forever.

Kick ass at the auction, babe. We'll celebrate your re-cord-breaking sales with bed-breaking sex.

There were more, but Joa had read enough. Replacing the notes, she felt her stomach lurch. She slapped her hand to her mouth, dry heaving. She slid down the fridge and wrapped her arms around her stomach, tears running down her face.

She was such a fool. A colossal idiot.

She'd fallen in love with another unavailable man.

Resting her forehead on her knees, Joa cursed her tears, mortified and disappointed with herself. She'd returned home to Boston with a clear vision, a plan to get her life on track. She hadn't planned on taking on more au pair work, determined to stop feeding her need to be part of a family by inserting herself into someone else's life.

She remembered thinking that she had money and a place to live and that she could afford to take the time to write the pages in this next chapter of her life. She'd planned on taking some time to chart a path forward...

But what had she done? She'd repeated past mistakes by

not only taking another au pair job but also falling in love with, and sleeping with, her boss.

And this time she wasn't projecting, imagining, constructing a reality that wasn't there. She was irrevocably, comprehensively, forever in love with Ronan. She also loved his gorgeous sons.

But it was the man who rocked her world, who spun her around, who flipped her inside out. She loved his body, enjoyed his wicked sense of humor, his sharp brain and his easygoing-until-he-wasn't personality. She respected his devotion to his boys and his loyalty to his wife.

His *wife*...

Joa's groan pierced the early-morning stillness of the house as reality, hard and hot and vicious, hit her. Ronan was still married in his heart, and probably always would be. Joa was the classic other woman, providing something Thandi couldn't, but there was no doubt that Thandi held his heart. Ronan would never love Joa as he did Thandi.

The evidence to back up that statement was everywhere. Gorgeous Thandi, a dedicated mother, was said to have been his best friend. Ronan still called her his wife, not his late wife, and the massive portrait of her by the front door announced to anybody who stepped in this house that she was still mistress here.

Her presence was freakin' everywhere. Fact: there wasn't room for anyone else in Ronan's life or his heart.

Ignoring the tears rolling down her face, Joa pushed herself to her feet and, carrying a heart as heavy as lead, made her way back up the stairs to the guest bedroom. She'd been so overwhelmed by Ronan last night she hadn't thought about where they'd made love but now it didn't escape her attention that they'd made love in the guest bedroom, she being the *guest*. She'd never even seen his bedroom, had no idea what was behind that perpetually closed door.

Joa walked into the en suite bathroom to flip on the taps to the shower. When the water was as hot as she could stand, she stepped into the glass cubicle, pushing away the images of Ronan's head between her thighs, taking her up against the wet tiles while she writhed and screamed.

She'd never seen his bathroom or his bedroom because those were spaces he'd shared with Thandi, hallowed ground.

She got it, she did. She understood that he didn't want those memories tainted, but it still hurt, dammit. It made her feel second best, less than. Joa would never be able to step into Thandi's shoes…

She was a girl from the wrong side of the tracks. She'd never felt like she belonged anywhere and she certainly didn't belong in this house, Thandi's house. Even if Ronan offered the opportunity to try, Joa would never measure up.

Scrubbing the scent of Ronan off her skin, Joa pushed down her tears and forced herself to think.

She had to stop feeling sorry for herself and make a plan… She needed to look after herself because she was the only one who could.

She needed to extricate herself from this house, causing the minimum of disruption to both Ronan and the boys. And she already had the perfect excuse to do that—she'd found Ronan's forever nanny. She just needed to set up the introduction. Abigail was kind, generous and suitable, and her presence in the house meant that Joa could move on.

While she was being honest with herself, she should accept that running the foundation as the CEO was just another pipe dream. Like Ronan, it was something she wanted but couldn't have. She wasn't qualified. Maybe she'd go back to au pairing, maybe not, but she knew that she had to leave Boston. She couldn't stay in this city; it would be too hard.

Luckily, she had time and she had money. She could figure out what she wanted from life as easily in Morocco or Monte Carlo as she could here.

She would drop out of Ronan's and the boys' lives, and soon she'd be nothing more than a pleasant memory. If she gave Abigail's name to Ronan, he would hire her—there was no reason for him not to—and they'd soon forget about her.

Ronan, if he ever thought about her at all, would remember her as someone who eased him back into a healthy sex life, a bridge between his old life and his new.

What she wouldn't do was give him a hint of the pain that was threatening to consume her, or confess her desperate wish to be his lover, to help him raise his amazing boys.

To share his bed, his life.

Those were impossible dreams, and Joa was, if nothing else, a realist.

Twelve

Across town, Ronan sat behind his desk, trying to concentrate on Eli's conversation. But honestly, he was only hearing every fifth word and nothing Eli said made any sense.

"Are you even listening to me?" Eli demanded.

"Not really," Ronan admitted.

Because thoughts of Joa, and the spectacular night they'd shared, kept invading his brain. Images kept appearing on the big screen of his mind: Joa's wet hair streaming down her back as he kissed his way down her spine, the tiny dimple in her butt, the fact that his hands could almost span her waist. The noises she made when she was about to come, the tenderness in her eyes.

Ronan was glad he was sitting down, that his pants were hidden by his desk. Damn, he needed a cold shower. And a brain transplant.

Joa was his temporary nanny, a friend's sister, barely more than an acquaintance. He shouldn't be this consumed by her, thinking about her so much. He had work to do, kids to raise, an assistant to listen to. He couldn't afford the time to indulge in fantasies and memories...

No matter how amazing a night it was. No matter that he wanted many more of those nights...

"Beah should be here any minute," Eli said, standing up.

Ronan's mouth curved up into a smile. He'd never really liked Carrick's ex-wife but he adored Finn's ex, Beah, and Ronan had been sad when they called their marriage over.

Ronan had no idea why they never worked out but suspected it had something to do with the fact that Finn was as chatty as a rock and didn't wear his heart on his sleeve, or anywhere else.

Ronan looked past Eli and stood up as the tall, willowy redhead walked into the room. With copper-colored eyes and pale skin, she wasn't traditionally beautiful but there was something incredibly attractive about her. With her warm personality and stunning smile, she pulled people in and men routinely fell at her feet. Most of her clients were a little in love with her, but Beah stayed professional and they kept sending business her way.

Ronan stood up, kissed Beah on each cheek and gestured for her to sit. "I was surprised to hear you were in town."

Beah crossed her long, long legs that ended in two-inch stilettos. "I need to talk to F...someone about a wedding, not a conversation I really want to have."

Ronan frowned. "Yours?"

Beah snorted. "God, no."

Ronan updated Beah on the news, both business and family, and then they turned back to business.

"I thought that, while I was here, I'd get an update on the Mounton sale and brief you on which pieces are generating the most interest with my clients," Beah suggested.

"Excellent," Ronan replied. Talking to Beah about her clients and art would force him to concentrate on work, would push his mind off Joa and last night. He was dealing in valuable artworks and he had to concentrate because making a mistake could cost Murphy's tens of millions or more.

He and Beah were nearly done when their meeting was interrupted by a knock on his office door. Annoyed by the disruption, he was surprised to see Finn stepping into his space.

Especially since Finn always seemed to know when Beah was in the building and did his best to avoid her.

Electricity crackled between them and Ronan eventually broke the sexually charged silence by loudly clearing his throat. Both Beah and Finn jumped and Finn jammed his hands into the back pockets of his jeans.

"Beah."

"Finn," Beah replied, equally formal. "I hope you are well."

"Fine. You?"

Dear God. Ronan wanted to bang his forehead on the desk at their stubbornness. Just find a room and get it done, was what he wanted to tell them but couldn't.

He'd told his brothers to stay out of his sex life, and what was good for the goose and all that.

Ronan pushed to his feet. "What do you need, Finn?"

"Not me," Finn said, looking miserable. "It's Carrick. He's holed up in his office, not taking calls or meetings."

"Is he sick?" Ronan asked, immediately concerned.

Finn shook his head and ran his hand through his shaggy hair. "I told him something yesterday, something about Sadie, and he's, well, pissed. Not at me, I don't think, but at the situation. I think he ended things with her."

Aw, crap. Carrick and Sadie were perfect for each other, any fool could see it. And if Carrick couldn't, then Ronan was the one to set him straight.

Ronan walked toward his younger brother and as he passed him, briefly placed a hand on Finn's shoulder. "I'll talk to him and see what's up. Hopefully, I'll be able to sort him out."

Though, like him, Carrick was stubborn. It might not be so easy.

Being stubborn was something all three Murphy brothers excelled at.

Ronan rapped on the closed door to Carrick's office but didn't bother to wait for an invitation to enter. Carrick, his forearms on his thighs, looked like shit. Judging by his bloodshot eyes and pale face, it was obvious he had a hangover from hell. But underneath, Ronan saw heartbreak, an emotion that had been his own faithful companion these past few years.

Carrick sat up and glared at him. "What's up?" he asked his brother, his tone curt.

"Marsha's canceled your meetings and is holding your calls. She's worried because the last time you cut yourself off so completely, Tanna had her accident."

Carrick frowned at him. "And you didn't think that maybe I needed some time alone?"

His brothers hadn't left him alone when Thandi died, no matter how much he begged them. In hindsight they'd been right—he'd needed them to be his buoy in a very wild sea. Well, it was time to repay Carrick. He'd never be able to fully reimburse him for all the long nights his older brother spent with him after Thandi died, but he could try.

"Want to tell me what's the problem?"

"No."

Ronan winced at Carrick's one-word answer.

"I want to be alone," Carrick stated, looking pointedly at the door.

"But what you want and what you need are two totally separate things." As he knew.

"I know what I need, Ronan."

"No, Carrick, you *think* you know. You think you want to be alone, to protect yourself from hurt, from having another woman leaving you. I hate to tell you this, but you can't control anyone's actions. People leave, people die and people mess up."

Jesus, where did that come from? And was he talking about Carrick, or himself? No, he had to be talking about Carrick because if he wasn't...

No, he wasn't ready to go there. He wasn't ready to let Thandi go.

She left you three years ago... She died, remember?

Shut up, inner voice.

Carrick tipped his head to the side and rolled his finger, gesturing for Ronan to keep speaking. Which, come to think about it, was strange. Like them all, Carrick didn't open up easily, and while they all argued about business all the time, they didn't talk much about their personal lives.

"You and Sadie called it, didn't you? Or, to be more precise, you did." He wanted to tell Carrick that he was a complete moron for letting Sadie slip away but he knew that Carrick would either kick him out or punch him and Carrick would stew in his stubbornness.

Carrick needed Sadie, dammit. He deserved a second chance at marriage, to be happy.

Didn't they all?

Carrick shrugged and Ronan felt a surge of frustration. "She was your one, Carrick, the person meant for you. How can you not see that?"

"How do you know?"

Was Carrick really going to make him explain? Well, if talking sliced through his brother's stubbornness, he'd give it a shot. "Because I know true love when I see it, Carrick! I lived it, I had it and I recognize it. She is your other half, the person you are supposed to be with."

"I thought the same with Tamlyn."

Ronan didn't know how Carrick could compare the bright, funny, lovely Sadie with his ex-witch. Annoyed, the words tumbled out of him. "You don't only get one person to love and you love people differently, at different times of your life. You loved Tamlyn, but you're a different person now to the person who loved her. You don't only get one shot at marriage and love, Carrick."

Ronan heard his words, knowing he was walking straight into a trap, a trap his brother wasn't going to let him wiggle out of. "I hear you, Ronan, I do."

Okay, maybe Carrick was too deep in his own misery to toss Ronan's words back in his face.

"So, you are going to sort out this mess with Sadie?"

"I am. But before I do, can I ask you one question?"

Ronan nodded, then shrugged. "Sure."

"Why is there one set of rules for me and a different set for you? If I get to take another shot at a relationship, why can't you?"

"Why is there one set of rules for me and a different set for you? If I get to take another shot at a relationship, why can't you?"

After leaving Carrick's office, the tough question burning in his brain, Ronan walked straight to his car and headed home, needing to be where Thandi was. Because Thandi wasn't in a grave; she lived within his sons, in the memories they shared in their West Roxbury house, in the rooms she'd walked and lived and loved in.

Before entering, he'd checked his security cameras and knew that Joa wasn't home. She'd left somewhere around eleven and, hopefully, she wouldn't be back anytime soon. He needed time alone, time to think.

With Carrick's question floating around in his brain demanding an answer, Ronan entered his house, thinking that he was seldom here when the kids weren't. Ronan didn't bother to shed his coat; he just stood in front of Thandi's portrait, the first thing anyone saw as they walked into his house. His beautiful wife, the beat of his heart.

Was she, still? Was he still in love with her? Oh, he still loved her but was he still *in love* with Thandi?

If I get to take another shot at a relationship, why can't you?

He'd gone into Carrick's office to straighten him out but he'd been the one who'd come out of that encounter feeling scathed and shot, his entire world upended. He'd been so damn arrogant, telling Carrick he had a right to another relationship, that he was throwing away the chance of happiness because he'd had a bad marriage with a bad woman.

You don't only get one person to love and you love people differently, at different times of your life.

Did that mean he was allowed to fall in love again? Could he? Was Joa the one he could take that chance on?

Ronan turned his gaze onto the photograph on the hallway table, the photograph of he and Thandi on their wedding day. They'd been so happy. Could he even be half as happy with someone else?

Yet he had been, these past weeks, with Joa. A different type of happy. Not better or stronger, just different. Ronan looked into the great room, saw the many photographs of Thandi on the mantelpiece, the massive silver frame on top of the piano. There were photos of her on the fridge. In fact, there were photos of her everywhere.

Ronan mentally moved up the stairs, picturing the photos of her on the walls, photos of her on the table on the landing, photos of her scattered around his bedroom. What did people think when entering his house? How did they feel about being surrounded by images of his dead wife? His entire house was a shrine to Thandi, and maybe it was time to let her go.

Time to embrace something, *someone* different.

Maybe it really was time for him to start living again…

Ronan turned at the sound of the front door opening and his heart rate accelerated as Joa stepped into the hallway, black hair glinting in the sunlight streaming in from the glass insert above the door. She looked surprised to see him, then her face settled into a bland expression, the expression she used to put distance between them.

Joa was acting like his employee, like his reticent nanny. He wanted the warm, exciting, hot-blooded woman who'd shared his bed last night, not this cool beauty with flat eyes and a taut mouth.

"What are you doing home?" Joa asked, placing her bag on the hall table. She never hung anything up. It should annoy him, but it didn't. He was just happy she was there, sharing and messing up his space.

How could he explain? How would she react if he told her that she brightened his life, that he wanted to see whether they could, maybe, make this work? That he thought he might be falling in love with her…

"Uh…"

Joa jammed her hands into the pockets of her coat and rocked on her heels. She stared at a spot past his shoulder and later, when he remembered this conversation, he'd pinpoint this moment as the start of their downward slide. Before he could form any words, she spoke. "I think I've found you a nanny."

Ronan felt like she'd punched him in the gut. He'd totally forgotten her search for a nanny. "I thought you liked my kids, that you enjoyed looking after them."

"Ronan, I told you this was temporary. That I didn't want to be an au pair anymore."

Well, yeah, she had said that...

"She's really rather wonderful. She's a grade school teacher, and the boys really like her. She lives close by..."

He didn't want another nanny, he wanted *her*. "I don't care. I want you to stay."

Ronan knew, from a place far away, that he was botching this, that he needed to explain, but his feelings were too new, too fragile. He hadn't had any time to work through his thoughts, to come to terms with the idea that he could be happy again, with someone else, that he could put aside his guilt and start to live again. He needed to do that, he needed time, but he also didn't want to lose Joa. Because, God, if she left him, left this house, she might get on a plane to Bora-Bora or Brisbane, Taiwan or Tennessee. If she left, he wouldn't be able to get her back.

"Best thing is, she can start straight away," Joa said, ignoring his previous comment. "I've arranged for her to pop around tonight. You can meet her then."

"I don't want her, I want you!" Ronan roared.

His bellow didn't scare Joa; she just planted her feet and kept her gaze on the wall behind him.

"Will you damn well look at me?" he shouted. He gestured to Thandi's portrait. "I'm here, she's not!"

Joa finally wrenched her eyes off Thandi's portrait. "Of course she is, Ronan. She's everywhere. In your head, in your house, in everything you do, every decision you make."

Joa held up her hand and tossed her head, blinking back tears. "It's okay, Ronan. It really is. I get it. She was the love of your life, the mother of your kids. I can't compete with that. I don't want to compete with her."

Ronan wanted to tell her that he loved them differently—he *loved* Joa? Jesus, did he? Maybe...

Man, this was all too much, too soon. He felt like he was being emotionally sideswiped from all angles.

"Let's not make this more difficult and emotional than it needs to be, Ro. Let's keep this simple, okay?"

Simple sounded good. It really did. Simple was him living his life as a widower, alone. Raising his boys, working, his life uncomplicated by a silver-eyed goddess who made his blood sing. He liked simple. Simple made sense.

But simple was also boring, unimaginative, lonely...

"I know that Tanna is taking the boys to spend the weekend at the Lockwood estate. They've been invited to Darby's stepdaughter's birthday party."

Ronan rubbed his forehead with the tips of his fingers, trying to think. Yeah, that sounded right. God, he was so tired. He felt like he could sleep for a week...

He'd forgotten how exhausting emotions could be.

Joa pushed her hands into the pockets of her coat. "I've booked a flight to go to Miami, to spend the weekend with Keely. There's so much we need to discuss with regard to the foundation, including a very impressive résumé we received today. The applicant might be perfect for the CEO job."

No, that job was Joa's. Nobody was better suited to running Isabel's foundation than the resilient, amazing girl-turned-woman whom Isabel had rescued all those years ago. Ronan wanted to tell her that, insist that she fight for the job, but he couldn't form the words because there were so many others on his tongue.

Don't go.
Don't leave.

I think I'm falling in love with you...

Joa sucked in a breath, emotions he couldn't identify tumbling through her eyes and across her face. "Interview Abigail tonight and if you like her, why don't we all go out to dinner on Sunday night? You, the kids, Abigail and me. We can tell them that Abigail will be their new nanny. And I can say goodbye."

The thought of her leaving them—*him*—forced his brain to kick into gear and form some words. "You're leaving? Where are you going?"

Joa shrugged. "I don't know yet. I'll see. But I think it's best if I leave Boston, put some distance between me and my memories of Iz."

Put some distance between you and me. Ronan heard the words as clearly as if she'd spoken them.

"Are you really leaving me?" Ronan asked, feeling like she'd reached into his heart and yanked it out of his chest.

Joa swallowed, closed her eyes and nodded. Her "yeah" was small but still audible.

"Did you hear me when I said that I want you?" Ronan asked, his voice cracking.

Joa placed her hand on his heart, a touch that briefly cut through the cold fog enveloping him. "I know you want me, Ro. That was never the problem. But what I want the most belongs to someone else and I'm not going to fight her for it."

Joa turned away and Ronan watched her walk up the stairs, feeling overwhelmed, a little pissed and totally at sea. He started to go after her, suddenly terrified by the thought of her not returning. What would he do? How would he cope? Oh, this had nothing to do with her looking after the boys, and everything to do with where he wanted her in his life...

No!

Not yet, think it through.

Ronan knew he couldn't be impulsive. He couldn't go on his gut. He had to think, pick this situation apart. He couldn't throw himself at her feet, because she was vulnerable, too, and might agree to stay, to move into his life, his world, as his partner and lover, not just as a nanny. And, when the novelty of fantastic sex faded, would one or both of them realize that they'd made a huge mistake?

He couldn't just think about himself. He had the boys to consider.

He needed to think, dammit. Ronan scrubbed his hands over his face and was surprised to feel the hint of tears on his cheeks. Tears? Really? He had never thought he'd cry again, and especially not over a woman.

Ronan dropped his hands and his gaze landed on the silver photo frame, the picture of him, Thandi and Sam, back when he was completely happy, so damn sure of himself and his place in the world.

Ronan placed his fingertip on Thandi's cheek, ran it over her jawline and then slowly and deliberately lay the photograph facedown.

Thandi was dead, and life, so it was said, was for the living.

So that begged the question, how was he going to live his?

Thirteen

Joa stared past Keely's shoulder to the placid Atlantic Ocean behind her.

It was Saturday afternoon or, as Joa liked to call it, day two of her crappy, Ronan-free life.

She'd have maybe an hour or two more with Ronan and the boys when they had dinner tomorrow night and then she'd leave their lives forever.

Forever.

God, that was a long, long time.

She didn't know if she could bear it. She'd been so stupid, falling in love with a man who was unavailable. When was she ever going to learn?

Keely looked up from reading the résumé of the latest applicant for the foundation's CEO position and rolled her eyes. "Are you going to spend the entire weekend sighing?"

"Probably," Joa admitted, lifting her glass of iced tea to her lips. She gestured to the résumé lying across Keely's thighs. "She sounds great, doesn't she?"

Keely tapped the paper with her index finger and shrugged. "You seem to think so."

"She's smart, has the right qualifications and has a solid track record of working in the sector," Joa countered. "She's perfect for the job."

"Or you *want* her to be perfect for the job," Keely said, tossing the résumé onto the wooden table between them. They were seated on the deck of Keely's luxurious rented house and it was so nice to be in shorts and flip-flops again.

Well, her body was warm; her heart still felt like it was encased in ice. *Might as well get used to the sensation, Jones.*

"What are you trying to say, Keely?"

"Her being so great gives you the out you're looking for."

Joa tried to make sense of her words but came up blank. "I'm sorry?"

"You want her to be wonderful so you can leave Boston, the foundation, me," Keely stated, her voice holding an edge that Joa had seldom heard before.

"You left out Ronan and his boys and Mounton House and Boston and Isabel's memory," Joa quipped. When Keely's eyes turned stormy, Joa realized Keely didn't appreciate her flippancy. But Joa had to pretend everything was fine, because if she didn't, she'd curl up in a ball and sob.

"Oh, we'll get to Ronan in a minute," Keely crisply told her. She leaned forward and nailed Joa with a sit-there-and-listen stare. "When are you going to stop running, Joa?"

Wow. That was unfair. "I am not running. And how did we get onto this subject? We were talking about the CEO position."

"A position that you want, that you would be so good at!" Keely's voice rose.

"I'm not qualified, Keely."

Keely threw up her hands in frustration. "Oh, sure, you

couldn't possibly acquire some new skills. You don't have a brain in your head, and you *only* have a master's degree in psychology. Yeah, you couldn't *possibly* learn anything new. And we couldn't possibly afford to pay for any advice we might need."

Wow, while she was gone Keely had become very proficient in sarcasm.

"Uh…you'd support me running the foundation?"

Keely overexaggerated her eye roll. "Argh! Yes! You have passion and empathy and you get what Isabel was trying to do. I kept an eye on the foundation while you were away because someone had to, but it's not what I want to do. You, however, just jumped in feetfirst."

She had. And it *was* her dream job, her connection to Iz, to her past. But if she chose to take the job, and it seemed like it was hers if she wanted it, she'd have to stay in Boston.

Staying in Boston would mean she would, occasionally, run into Ronan, as she explained to Keely. That meant being around someone, three someones, she couldn't have.

"And why can't you have a relationship with him and the boys?" Keely asked. "Any fool can see you two have a connection."

"He's still in love with his wife," Joa muttered.

Keely held up her index finger and pointed it at Joa. "Oh no, you can't blame all of this on him. You have your issues, too."

"Which are?"

"You're terrified to be all in with someone."

"Can you blame me since I was hurt every time I left a family?"

"It couldn't have hurt that much," Keely retorted, "or else you would've stopped au pairing a long time ago. But you didn't leave until you were asked to leave because you felt safe there. You could love your boss from afar, pretend you were part of his family, act out your happy-family fantasies because there was no chance of anything happening, no risk to you. Because a real family comes with the *potential* of heartache, with the potential of someone leaving you, someone not loving you. Pretending is so much easier, so much safer than actually living."

Joa stared at Keely, her mouth opening and closing, feeling hot, then cold. She wanted to argue, to tell Keely she was talking nonsense, but Joa couldn't. She'd never considered *why* she fell for unavailable men.

Her sister was right. Joa had been trying to protect herself, to put a barrier between her and any potential loss.

Ronan had started to say something about wanting her to stay, but because she was scared, because that conversation felt too real, too scary, she'd tossed Thandi in his face and made his dead wife the barrier between them.

Maybe Ronan did still love Thandi, maybe he wasn't ready to move on with Joa or anyone else, but she didn't know for sure because she hadn't given him a chance to explain.

She had just run out of there because what she felt for him was so damn tangible. Tangible meant scary. And she hated feeling scared, vulnerable, like she was fourteen again, and alone.

Joa didn't realize that tears were running down her face until Keely touched them with her fingertips, wiping them away. "I'm not telling you that he loves you, Ju. I don't know if he does or doesn't. But he hasn't looked at anyone else in three years the way he looks at you. I haven't seen him this happy for the longest time. I haven't seen you glow like this for years and years. There's something there and you owe it to yourselves to explore it, to see where it goes."

Joa placed her elbows on her thighs and her hands on her head. "I hear you, Keely, I do. And I know that I run away to keep myself safe. But she's still such a big part of his life…"

"She's the mother of his kids, babe. She'll always have a special place in his heart." Keely pulled a face. "And maybe he'll never be able to love you the way you need him to, but you can't run without giving him the chance, or at the very least, without talking to him about the way you feel."

Joa's heart bounced off her chest. "Are you saying I should tell him that I love him?"

"If that's how you feel," Keely replied. "He might, or might not, love you back. But that's his choice. Your choice is to tell him how you feel. It's also your choice to take the job you love and not let him, or the way you feel about him, influence your career."

"Ooh, ouch. The punches keep coming."

Keely squeezed her knee. "The truth is an ugly thing, baby girl." Keely rested her forehead on Joa's knee before sending her a sympathetic smile. "You need to be brave, Ju. You need to take a chance on *something*. And you need to start living in the real world, not a pretend one."

The truth was undeniable, but it wasn't fun. Or fair. Or easy or nice. But it was the truth. And if she wanted to look at herself in the mirror with any sense of self-respect, she had to face it and deal with it.

A few months shy of her thirtieth birthday and she finally, emotionally, felt like an adult.

Ronan taped down the bubble wrap on Thandi's portrait and looked at the bare spot on the wall. He'd expected to feel sad, but really he just felt…content. Like it was time to let his wife go.

Thandi wasn't in a picture on the wall, she was in Sam's smile and Aron's eyes and in the million memories Ronan had of her.

He felt Carrick's hand on his shoulder and Finn moved to stand on his other side, and he was grateful for his brothers' presence. He'd unhooked pictures off walls and taken them off sideboards and tables and corkboards—leaving the silver frame containing the picture of Thandi and Sam—Aron in her huge tummy so he was there—on the table between his boys' beds. Ronan had removed all the photos from his own bedroom and put Thandi's notes from the fridge in a shoebox, along with the other unframed photographs he found along the way. The framed photographs were packed into the cardboard boxes at his feet.

But he'd needed help to take Thandi's massive portrait off the wall and there were only two guys he could ask to help him with that.

Carrick looked at the bare spot and grimaced. "You definitely need a painting to cover that spot."

"Can't think where we might be able to source one," Finn replied, his tongue in his cheek. The attic at their family home, the house Carrick inherited and lived in, was crammed with art.

Correction, the house Carrick and Sadie now lived in. And Carrick was so besotted with his new fiancée that Ronan knew he could ask for anything and Carrick would hand it over…

"I've always been partial to the landscape on your bedroom wall." Ronan teased, knowing it was one of Carrick's favorite paintings.

"Let me think about that…" Carrick held up his index finger, "mmm…no."

Oh, well, it was worth a try.

Ronan shrugged. "I'll find something." He looked at the empty space on the wall, hauled in a deep breath and folded his arms. "What do I tell the boys when they ask where their mom has gone?"

"If they even notice, you tell them the truth. That there's a photo of her in their bedroom if they need to look at her," Carrick replied. He nodded to the big boxes containing the rest of the frames and photographs. "Do you have space to store these boxes or do you want them to go into the vault or up into the attic at the house?"

Ronan was grateful that neither of his brothers suggested getting rid of the photographs. They understood that Sam or Aron might want them someday. Hell, he might want to look at them again, although he had copies of all of them in his cloud account.

"I'm not sure yet," Ronan replied, rubbing the back of his neck. "Can I let you know?"

"Sure." Carrick walked into the great room and headed straight for the cupboard in the kitchen where Ronan kept a bottle of Jack. After grabbing three tumblers, he poured them each a shot. Passing the glasses out, he raised his. "To Thandi. May she rest in peace."

Ronan nodded, touched. "Yeah."

Finn tossed his drink back and rested his forearms on the granite counter of the island. "Are you going to tell us what prompted this, Ro?"

Ronan pushed his hand through his hair. "A combination of things. I thought it was time to say goodbye, to let her go. Partly because of Joa…"

"How's that?" Carrick asked.

"Well, it can't be fun walking into your lover's house and seeing his dead wife on the wall. On *every* wall."

"Fair point." Finn agreed. "So, does that mean you are going to try and work it out with her?"

Ronan shrugged. He'd missed her terribly these past two days and couldn't wait to see her later. But he wasn't sure if he was rushing into things. Maybe he just thought he was in love with her because she was the one who'd broken through his icy walls. He explained his dilemma to his brothers, both of whom took a minute to give him their considered and thoughtful opinion.

"Bullshit."

"Horse crap."

Well, okay, then. Carrick poured another shot, but Ronan shook his head. It had been a hell of a day already and his boys would be arriving any minute from their weekend away with Tanna at the Lockwood estate. And later, they'd all be going out to eat. He most definitely needed his wits about him.

"You're looking at this wrong, Ro. Maybe she was the one who broke through because she was the only one who could. Despite being our resident charmer, you've never been a player. You've always taken love and relationships very seriously." Carrick held up his hand. "That's not a criticism, just a statement of fact. You take a while to fall in love but when you do, nothing much budges you off it."

"Yeah, Joa has to be special for you to do all this. To move on," Finn agreed. "If she wasn't, you wouldn't be doing this. And I think Thandi would approve. I think that, had she met Ju, they'd be friends."

They were completely different people, but he agreed. They would've been friends. Ronan pulled in a deep breath, trying to ignore the prickle of heat in his eyes, the slight burn. "Thanks. For being here... For doing this. For—" Jesus, his voice was cracking "—you know, everything."

"You should be grateful since I left my brand-new fiancée to be here." Carrick's fist smacked his arm. Ronan audibly cursed Carrick but silently thanked him. Had he not punched him they might all be in tears by now. They all preferred pain to pathos.

Finn snickered. "You should be grateful to Ronan for

giving you a damn fine excuse to take a break from Sadie. You're not as young as you used to be, Carrick."

Carrick nailed Finn with a hard look. "Bastard."

Finn's phone beeped and he pulled it out. He swiped the screen, read the message and cursed. Happy for the change of subject, Ronan asked him what the problem was.

"Obviously you remember Ben? He spent a lot of time at our house when I was a teenager?"

Ronan nodded.

Finn continued. "Well, he and his girlfriend from way back then have recently reconnected. They both ended up working for the same company in Hong Kong and are getting married. But because they are there and not here, they want me to organize their wedding."

Ronan exchanged a glance with Carrick, thinking that there was more to the story. But he couldn't help laughing at Finn's uncomfortable expression. "Really? You?"

Finn looked miserable. "No, Not only me. Beah's going to help me since Ben and Piper attended our wedding ceremony in Vegas."

Carrick frowned. "About that…"

Finn rolled his eyes. "It happened nearly ten years ago and we got divorced. You can't still be pissed that we didn't invite you to the wedding."

"You didn't even tell us you were getting married," Carrick retorted.

Ronan listened to the oft repeated argument and tuned them out. He turned his head at the sound of his front door opening and noticed a shadow crossing his hallway. His boys were home and he hurried into the hall to see them standing statue still, looking up at the empty wall. Ronan uttered a quiet curse and skidded to a halt when he saw Joa standing in the open doorway, snow dusting her dark hair. The icy wind blew snow inside and Ronan shivered. He walked over to her, tugged her forward and pushed the door closed, looking from her to the boys. "Where's Tanna?"

Joa's big eyes flicked off the bare spot on the wall to his face and immediately went back again. "Um, she pulled up as I did. She was in a hurry to get back, so I brought the boys in."

Ronan nodded and went over to his boys, dropping to kiss each on his small head. "Hey, guys, did you have fun?"

Aron nodded enthusiastically and held up his arms to be picked up. Ronan hauled him up and settled him on his hip. "There was lots of ice cream and a horse and a clown—"

"Where's my mom gone?" Sam demanded.

Ronan tightened his grip on Aron as he dropped to his haunches to look Sam in the eye. "Your mom hasn't gone anywhere, Sam. I've just taken her painting off the wall, that's all."

"Why?"

Explanation time. *Hell.* "Because she's not here anymore and I think it's time we start to remember her in our hearts and minds and not because there's a huge picture on the wall."

"But what if I start to forget what she looks like?" Sam asked, panic in his voice.

"There's a photo of her next to your bed. You won't forget, Sam." Ronan darted a look at Joa. "We won't forget her, Sam, I promise."

Joa dropped her head to stare at the floor as Ronan pulled his older son in for a hug. "It's time, Sam."

Ronan felt Carrick remove Aron from his arms and he looked up to see Finn place his hand on Sam's shoulder. His younger brother waited for Sam to look up at him. "Hey, bud. Want to come home with me? We can have a movie and video game night."

They were supposed to be going out for supper with

their new nanny but Ronan couldn't face it. Besides, he had something important to do, much to say.

Ronan stood up, pulled his phone from the back pocket of his jeans and quickly sent Abigail a text message, asking to postpone their arrangements for the evening. He saw that she'd read the message and then a thumbs-up emoji appeared on his screen.

Right, one very small mission accomplished.

Ronan returned his attention to the conversation between Sam and Finn, who were discussing what movie to watch.

"Popcorn?" Sam asked. His boys were such boys, Ronan thought. Easily distracted with the thought of junk food and some age-appropriate violence.

He sent Finn a grateful smile and looked at Aron. "Want to go and hang out with Finn, A?"

Aron shook his head and wound his arms around Carrick's neck. "Want to go with 'Rick."

Ronan arched his eyebrow at Carrick. His brother was in love and surely wanted to spend some alone time with Sadie. He expected Carrick to make an excuse. But Carrick just looked from Ronan to Joa and quickly nodded. "Sure, bud. We'll hang out."

It took a village—or, in his case, his brothers—to raise a child. God, he was lucky to have them. "Thanks, guys."

Ronan gave his boys another quick hug, sad to see them go after not seeing them for two days. But he and Joa had things to talk about, and they didn't need the distraction. They were only trying to sort out the rest of their lives…

After Carrick and Finn scooped up the boys and the bags they'd walked in with and left, each with a child in tow, Ronan took Joa's coat and hung it up on the coatrack.

Joa unwound her scarf, not sure what was happening. The boys had left, she didn't know if they were still going to dinner with Abigail and there was a damn big empty patch on the wall. Joa looked at the plastic-covered portrait and wondered whether she was hallucinating.

But no, there were two other boxes filled with—she lifted the open lid—more photographs. The wall going up the stairs was bare of photos and Thandi's scarf and hat weren't on the coatrack to the left of the door.

Joa looked at Ronan, so handsome, so serious.

"It was time."

Joa looked at him. "Really?"

Ronan nodded. Placing a hand on her arm, he tugged her over to the staircase and sat down on the third step up. He patted the spot next to him and Joa bit her lip, not sure what to do. She felt totally spacy, like she'd been tossed into an alternate reality where nothing made sense. She debated whether to sit or bolt. But Ronan's gaze was steady on her face and his beautiful, serious eyes begged her to trust him or, at the very least, to hear him out.

So she sat down, keeping a solid ten inches between them.

It took a few excruciating minutes for him to speak. "Thandi is a part of me, Ju. Death has marked me. I'd be lying if I told you it hasn't. Losing her ripped me apart, it really did."

"I know, Ronan. I mean, I don't *know* know but—" Joa's words tumbled out, desperate to reassure him. How lucky he was to know love like that, how lucky Thandi was to be loved so fully by this amazing man. How brave they'd both been.

Ronan's hand gripped hers and squeezed. "Just listen, please."

Joa expected him to remove his hand, but instead he just slid his fingers between hers, his palm warm against her skin.

"Thandi was amazing and I loved her very much and I want to remember her. She *deserves* to be remembered."

Joa tried to remain impassive, but Ronan must've seen the distress on her face because he squeezed her fingers gently. "I'm not trying to hurt you, sweetheart, but I need you to understand. Because if you don't, there's no hope for us. So will you try?"

God, didn't he know that she'd do anything for him? Not able to speak, Joa just nodded.

"It's taken me a long time to realize, to accept, that it's not all or nothing. We can't shove emotions into boxes and pull them out when we want. Death is far more complex than that and I need you to accept that I can still love and miss her and be totally, wildly, crazy in love with you."

Joa thought she heard that he loved her but that couldn't be right, could it? "I've been happier with you these last few weeks than I have been for years and I'd like to keep being that happy. But the thing is, I know I'll still think of her occasionally and I don't want you to feel threatened by that. I love her, but I'm not *in love* with her anymore.

"I'm so in love with you, though."

Joa stared, trying to make sense of what he'd said. Could she love this man, knowing a part of him would always love his wife?

"Do you compare us?"

Ronan released a small snort. "Hell, no. You two are as different as night and day."

Well, that was a relief. Joa, needing to move, stood up and paced the area of the hallway in front of him, her thumbnail between her teeth. Could she do this, could she take a chance on him?

Ronan started to speak, but Joa shook her head, holding her hand in a silent plea to let her think.

She could walk away right now and resume her solitary

life, hiding out behind her walls and not letting anyone get close. Or she could let Ronan in and give love a chance.

He was a good man, a *sexy* man and she loved him, she did. But could she play second fiddle? She needed to know…

"Do you think you can ever love me as much as you love her?" she whispered.

Ronan released a curse as he jumped to his feet, his expression revealing his distress. And at that moment, Joa understood. His expression told her that it wasn't a more or less kind of thing. It was equal but different and maybe she had the edge because she was, obviously, *here.*

Ronan cupped her face in his big hands. "Oh, Ju, not for one minute did I mean for you to think that it was a matter of levels. I just need you to understand that although I've put her away, although I've moved on because you stepped into my life, I am, occasionally, going to think about her. But I promise this won't be a three-person relationship. This is you and me."

"And the boys," Joa added, covering his hands with hers.

"Yeah, them," Ronan teased. "Do you understand? You will be my priority. I won't live in the past when I have you in my present."

"Ro…" Joa lifted her face, leaning on her toes for a kiss. Ronan's lips covered hers and Joa finally, finally felt like she was home, that she was part of something bigger and better than herself.

Then Ronan stepped back and his hands left her face to rest on her shoulders. His intense eyes bored into hers and Joa knew their conversation wasn't over, that it was her turn. Her man—so self-assured and confident—needed to know where he stood, whether he was as important to her as she was to him.

Joa held on to his wrists and briefly closed her eyes.

Pulling in all her courage, she gave him the words he needed. No, the words she needed to say.

"I've been on my own for so long and I knew I wanted a family but I kept falling in love with unavailable men. Because I was scared of the one thing I wanted most. Scared of being happy, of being loved, scared of losing that love. It's easier to be on your own, you know?"

Ronan squeezed her shoulders. "I do. Falling in love is terrifying."

"But I'd rather be scared with you than lonely on my own," Joa confessed. "I love you. I'd love you even if you didn't have those two monsters."

"Good to know," Ronan said, smiling. "Make you a deal?"

Joa tipped her head. "I'm listening."

"When you're feeling scared and overwhelmed, tell me and I'll remind you how much I love you. Look, Ju, I'm old enough to know that it's not going to be all roses and dancing on clouds. We both have a lot of baggage. But that's life. We're two strong people and I like us that way. But if we try to communicate, if we're brave enough to tell each other how we are feeling, *what* we are feeling, we can love each other through anything."

Joa felt the burn of tears, the warmth of happiness. She wound her arms around Ronan's neck and buried her nose in his neck. "I love you so much."

Ronan pulled her into him, one hand on her butt, another on her back. She felt safe and secure in his arms, like no one could touch her, like she'd never have to be alone again.

She had Ronan, Sam and Aron, and hopefully in a year or two, a child of her own. She jerked back, thinking she might as well start practicing her rusty communication skills as soon as possible. "I want a child," she said, her words rushing out. "Not today, or tomorrow, but sometime in the future."

Ronan didn't blink. He just pushed her hair behind her ears and nodded. "Sure."

Wow, okay. That was easy. While she was on a roll, she thought she'd raise another subject. "And I'm going to head up the foundation. I mean, I intend to help you raise Aron and Sam, but I want to work, Ro. It's important."

Ronan nodded. "I assumed so. That's why I hired Abigail. She starts on Monday."

Joa grinned at him. "So, no dinner tonight?"

Ronan's grin turned seductive and Joa felt the special place between her legs heat up. "Oh, there will be dinner. And you're on the menu."

"Really? That sounds interesting."

Ronan's lips curved as his mouth descended toward hers. "Mmm, I need to practice making babies."

Joa laughed, happiness a new, foreign and completely wonderful feeling "Yeah, I think you've proved you can do that, Murphy."

"Boy babies, maybe. Girl babies take a little more practice."

Ronan led her up the stairs and then up another flight of stairs. He paused outside his bedroom door, his eyes green and gold and blue. He cupped the back of her neck with his big hand and rested his forehead against hers. "I want you in my bed, Ju. Just you and me, a blank page, the start of a new chapter. Will you come inside with me?"

Of course she would. She would go anywhere with him. Because, as she knew, as he'd just proved, fairy tales could come true.

Epilogue

Murphy International often held a presale cocktail party the evening before an important auction and the world's foremost collectors of Fabergé were present, peering through glass cases to look at the items going on the block the next day.

Joa, like everybody else, had done her fair share of drooling over the objects she'd first laid eyes on in the vault somewhere way below her feet in the bowels of the building. But she kept coming back to the miniature egg, dotted with diamonds and rubies, edged with gold. She'd asked Keely if she could pull Isabel's miniature egg pendant from the Mounton sale and Keely had agreed. Joa touched the silver egg that hung in the deep, plunging V of her black cocktail dress and wondered if she could justify owning two miniature eggs by Fabergé.

She was rich, but she wasn't—she hoped—spoiled.

But damn, it was beautiful.

Joa felt Ronan's possessive touch on her back and smiled when he dropped a hot kiss on her bare shoulder. Tipping her head to rest it against his, she sent up a quick prayer of intense gratitude...

For this man, for his boys, for her completely extraordinary life.

"Careful, darling, you're drooling," Ronan said, wrapping his arm around her waist.

Joa leaned into him. "I know, but it's utterly fantastic." She bit her lip and shrugged. "I'm thinking of buying it at the auction tomorrow."

Ronan lifted one eyebrow. "It's your money, darling. You can do anything you damn well like." Then he winced, as if remembering something. "But maybe I should tell you that I've just heard that this pendant has been withdrawn from the sale by the owner."

Joa's shoulders slumped in disappointment. "Aw, no. Seriously?"

Joa saw Finn and Keely approaching them but, as per normal, quickly returned her attention to Ronan, looking utterly debonair in his classic black tuxedo. The shadows from his eyes were gone and his sensuous mouth was quick to smile. She'd done that, she thought, proud.

She'd made him happy and she intended to keep doing that—she glanced down at her simple engagement ring with its huge diamond—for the rest of her life. Not being able to buy this pendant was the first blip on her completely perfect life.

Maybe she *was* becoming spoiled...

"Has it been sold to someone else?" Joa demanded. "Can I make a counteroffer?"

Ronan shook his head. "Sorry. The new buyer has no intention of selling it. It's a gift to someone he loves with all his heart and soul."

"What are you two discussing so intently?" Keely demanded, stopping next to Joa. Then she wrinkled her nose. "But if it's anything mushy, you can skip the explanation."

"Yeah," Finn agreed, "between you two and Carrick and Sadie, and Tanna and Levi, you're making the rest of us feel nauseous."

"I agree! What's with the constant PDA? Can't you keep your hands off each other for more than a millisecond?" Keely demanded.

"Shut up," Ronan genially told them, not taking his eyes off Joa, whose heart was bouncing around her rib cage. Ronan was teasing her about something, she was sure of it…

What was he up to?

Finn bent down to look at the pendant before standing up and looking at Ronan. "Is this the pendant you bought off the Fabergé collector?"

Ronan released a loud groan. "Jesus, Finn! It was supposed to be a surprise!"

Finn pulled a face at Joa. "Oh. Sorry."

"Go away," Ronan told him through gritted teeth.

Joa watched his brother and her best friend walk away, idly noticing that they both darted glances across the room. Finn was looking for Beah and Keely was glaring at Dare…

Situation normal, Joa thought.

Bringing her attention back to her fiancé, she lifted her eyebrows. "Did you really buy this pendant for someone you love with all your heart and soul?"

Ronan cupped the side of her face with his big hand and Joa turned to kiss the palm of his hand. "Yeah, I plan on giving her one as often as I can…"

"That could be quite expensive," Joa murmured as Ronan's mouth moved toward hers.

"Trust me, she's worth every damn cent. She's, quite simply, my life."

As he was hers.

"Thank you, Ro."

And they both knew she wasn't just thanking him for the pendant but also for giving her a place to belong, for giving her a forever family.

* * * * *

HER ONE NIGHT
PROPOSAL

KATHERINE GARBERA

For Rob, love of my life and my partner in crime.
I'm so glad to be sharing this journey with you.

I don't know that I would have finished this book on
time without my afternoon sprints with Renee Ryan,
Cindy Kirk and Nancy Robards Thompson.

Thank you for inspiring me to stay on track and get my
word count every day.

Also, a special thank-you to my editor,
Charles Griemsman, for his insight and judicious
editing that makes my books shine!

One

Lunch with her family was always one of the highlights of Iris Collins's week. It was a Wednesday afternoon tradition that had started when she and her twin sister, Thea, were home from boarding school and had followed them into adulthood. They always dined at the club in her father's high-rise office building in the financial district of Boston. Hal Collins was the sole owner and proprietor of Collins Combined, a firm that focused on long-term investments in publicly traded companies.

Iris's phone pinged just as she entered the lobby of the building. She pulled it out of the pocket of her sheath dress and glanced down at the screen to see it was from her so-called boyfriend. She put the phone back in her pocket as her sister came over to hug her.

"I knew you'd be early. I figured I'd get here first so we could chat before Mom and Dad get here," Thea said. "We haven't talked since your trip with Graham. How'd it go?"

"Okay," Iris said.

"Just okay?"

Actually, less than okay if she were honest. During their Bermuda vacation, Graham had pushed her to be more adventurous in bed and that had ended badly. He'd gone down to the bar to drink all night while Iris had sat on the balcony alone listening to the waves. She was trying to keep things going with him until her college roommate's wedding in ten days' time. Graham was her plus one at all the events and she was a bridesmaid so it could get awkward if they broke up. She knew the bride, Adler Osborn, had planned for them to attend as a couple and the last thing that Iris wanted to do was add any extra stress for her friend.

Her phone pinged again, and her smart watch vibrated on her arm. She glanced down to see it was another message from Graham.

"Speak of the devil," she said, pulling her phone out to read the text while Thea looked over her shoulder.

Listen, things aren't working out between us, so I'm done with dating you. I hope you understand.

"Are you kidding me?" Thea said. "He's breaking up with you over a text."

Iris wished she could be surprised but was relieved instead. She quickly typed, Sure, I understand.

Great. Figured you'd get it.

"Get what?"

"Nothing," Iris said to her sister. The last thing she wanted to do was talk about sex in the lobby of their father's building. She was starting to wonder if she was the prude that Graham had labeled her…and did that matter to her?

Thea took her phone from her before she could stop her, typing in a quick message.

That's okay I want more from life than you can offer.

"Thea. Give me back my phone."

She saw the dancing dots that meant Graham was responding and her stomach felt tight. There was no way he was going to take that kind of insult without replying. That was just the kind of person he was.

That's okay I want someone who's not beige, boring and basic. Bye, bitch.

Thea reached for her phone, but Iris just held it away from her and texted back the thumbs-up emoji.

"Why did you do that?" Iris said to her sister. "He was my plus one. I'm going to have to deal with him not being there."

"Who do you have to deal with?" their mother asked as she came up behind them and hugged them both. Always larger than life, Corinne Collins, known as Coco to her close friends and bridge group, was wearing Ralph Lauren.

"Graham. That guy I was dating."

"He just broke up with her over text," Thea added. "How rude."

"Very rude. But not everyone pays attention to etiquette these days."

"They don't," Iris said. "Where's Dad?"

"He's running late," Mom said. "I warned him not to be too late or I'm taking you two on a shopping spree."

They all laughed as it was a family joke between their

parents from back in their early days when her father said time was money and her mom had said she agreed and liked to use her time to spend it.

As Iris followed her mom and her sister to the hostess stand at the entrance to the restaurant on the second floor, she was seething. How dare he say something so rude to her? Of course, she knew he thought she was boring…but basic? She was *so* not basic. She was Iris Collins, television lifestyle guru. Known for her trendsetting style and Instagram-worthy jet-setting.

She'd known he was douche bag when he'd suggested a three-way, but this was beyond.

Her mom saw a friend from her bridge club at the bar and went to chat with her, which meant that Thea and she were alone again.

"You need to bring someone so hot to the wedding. Show him who's basic. I can't believe he had the nerve to say that," Thea said.

"Agree. But who? I don't know anyone. I really don't have time to cultivate a relationship in only ten days."

"Let me think," Thea said.

"It can't be anyone I know," Iris added. Graham knew most of the people she worked with.

"True. You should hire someone. Just be straightforward about it. Like a Julia Roberts movie. You can do that."

"No," Iris said.

"Why not?"

"Because it's embarrassing, that's why."

"It's not embarrassing. You could have a hot guy on your arm, and if you're footing the bill, he has to behave the way you want him to," Thea said. "I know some hot guys who might be interested."

"Like who? You work at home with two cats," Iris pointed out. Her sister ran a very successful blog about etiquette and deportment. There was a high demand for people who wanted to actually live the life in those swank Instagram photos they saw online, and Thea was in demand when it came to social events.

"I have friends," Thea added.

"Thanks, Thea," she said. "But I'll sort this out. We don't need to waste any more time on Graham."

Their father arrived and they had a nice lunch. Iris had that feeling deep inside as she watched her parents holding hands under the table during coffee and dessert. That longing that she always felt. Was it too much to ask that she could find a partner? She wanted what they had but she seemed to attract men like Graham.

But for now, maybe Thea was right. She could find a hot guy to hire as her date for the wedding. It was only four days and three nights…

Zac Bisset hated being in Boston but there were times when real life intruded on his training schedule and he was forced to leave his yacht and deal with it. It didn't matter that it was a perfectly nice June day. He was wearing a suit and loafers instead of a pair of swim trunks and bare feet. Being born into a family that had wealth, privilege and way too many constrictions had never suited Zac well. He'd found his escape on the sea, sailing. It was a passion he'd pursued through his college years. Then he'd joined an America's Cup team from the UK and done that for the last few years, but he'd recently left the team to start his own bid.

Putting together an America's Cup team was expensive. He could easily ask for and receive the money from his family's company, Bisset Industries. But that money would come with too many strings. His father had been dying to get him to be more active on the board and the last thing Zac wanted was to answer to August Bisset. Or worse, his older brother Logan. He liked having the freedom to do his own thing.

But his options were limited. After the US-sponsored Oracle team won, Zac had craved creating his own team and putting together his own bid to win. He needed a big company to sponsor him or his own inheritance to make a successful run. Time was running out since they needed to already be training.

He left the meeting at the corporate offices of the large telecom company where he'd been discussing a sponsorship. When he got to the bar in the lobby and ordered a club soda, his phone pinged and then started buzzing as a slew of messages came in. The first was from his eldest brother, Darien, who was a politician and not in the family business; he wanted to meet up for drinks before their cousin's wedding festivities kicked off. Then there was a message from the group chat he had with his teammates who were waiting for an update. The last was from his mom, saying she was on Nantucket at Gran's place and urging him to come by early so they could have some mom-and-son time.

He rubbed the back of his neck, not interested in responding to any of them at the moment. Of course, his two favorite people in the family had reached out, which he appreciated. Logan and his dad wanted to boycott Adler's wedding because she was marrying into the Williams family. They were the chief competitors of Bisset Industries; their business had been started by a man his father hated. So there was that.

Zac had no beef with the groom, so he'd volunteered to go to all the events. He liked a wedding party. With booze, pretty girls and lots of dancing, it was his kind of shindig. It was a destination wedding, so everyone was being put up at a luxury resort on Nantucket, the flagship of Williams Inc.'s newest venture. The groom and his family were slowly encroaching on every line of business the Bissets were in. But Zac's youngest sibling and only sister, Mari, had been to a press party there a month ago and couldn't stop singing the resort's praises.

Which had done nothing to make Logan and his father happier about going. Family was trying at times and one of the reasons he preferred to stick to training for the America's Cup.

He texted his teammates first. They had a group chat nicknamed the Windjammers. The team was pretty small at the moment, just Zac, Yancy McNeil and Dev Kellman. The three of them were in New England searching for sponsors and working on a new design for their yacht. The competition was won as much with skill on the seas as it was with the aerodynamic design of the craft.

No-go on the money. Got one more meeting before we are going to have to brainstorm more options.

Yancy was the first to respond.

Damn. I have some feelers out. Heard from a friend that she has someone who is looking for a long-term investment. I'll text you the deets.

Dev quickly chimed in.

I don't have any leads but I do have some margaritas ready to go once you both get back to the Blind Faith.

Zac wrapped up the chat with, Thanks. I'll check out your lead, Yancy.

Yancy texted over the information as Zac signaled the

waiter for a refill of his soda water. He glanced up, his breath catching in his throat as he saw the blond woman walking into the bar. She wore a formfitting dress with tiny sleeves that left her long arms bare. She was tan and fit, and she moved with confidence and purpose. Their eyes met and she stopped, her lips parting in a slight smile. Her eyes were blue like the seas around the southern island of New Zealand. Her mouth was…damn, all he could stare at now. Her upper lip was fuller than her bottom one and it seemed to him that she was very kissable. All he could think about was how her mouth would feel under his.

He stretched his legs under the table and looked away. Yeah, he'd been at sea for too long if his first thought when seeing a woman was kissing her. He needed to get himself under control before he was surrounded by family for a week.

He heard footsteps and looked up, expecting to see the waiter, but it was the woman. She smelled good up close like the summer blossoms in his mother's garden at the house in the Hamptons. She had a direct kind of gaze that he liked. He wasn't a timid man and he didn't always know how to deal with people who were. Up close he could see that her hair wasn't truly blond but darker shades of caramel were shot through it. It curled around her shoulders and he noticed how slim her neck was and the tiny necklace with a flower charm on it.

Iris was still thinking about her sister's outrageous advice as she went to the bar across town after lunch. She glanced around the room; it was midafternoon, and she was meeting her "glam squad" to go over her prep for the wedding in Nantucket. The fact that Adler's wedding was going to be televised and there would be lots of vloggers and online society gossip websites meant that she was going to have to be camera-ready at all times.

She'd built her own platform over the last five years, working her way up from an assistant to Leta Veerland to her having her own style television show. Leta had taken reality television by storm in the late 1990s and early 2000s, starting out by showcasing her sister Jaqs' bridal designs. She had set a standard that many young video channel content creators tried to emulate, with her style and advice on creating the perfect personal habitat. Iris had learned from Leta that she had to always look the part when she walked out her door, even if she was only going to the grocery store. If one of her viewers saw her acting or looking in a way that contradicted her brand image, then she'd lose her believability.

Thea texted to say she'd found a guy who would be her date for the entire weekend for a thousand dollars. She tucked her phone away, not at all interested in some guy her sister found for her.

She glanced around and didn't see her makeup artist, KT, and her stylist and personal assistant, Stephan, so she headed toward one of the tall tables in the back. She almost stumbled when she saw the hunky blond sitting in one of the large leather club chairs near the entrance. He had a clean-shaven, chiseled jaw. His hair was long and brushed the tops of his shoulders, but it was clean and lustrous and reminded her of a Viking…not the pillaging kind but the hot, yummy kind.

Make him an offer he can't refuse.

Thea's voice whispered through her head and she shook it to dispel her sister's ridiculous idea. It absolutely wasn't happening.

But now that Thea had planted the seed, Iris did sort of wonder if she could do it. She ran a multimillion-dollar business. She remembered something her mom had said when she had started to make real money as a social media influencer: *don't be afraid to pay people to do the things you need done.*

Technically there was nothing wrong with showing up at a destination wedding without a date. But the wedding was going to be televised. She was getting ready to launch a domestic goddess–themed range of products and a book. Everyone from her management team to her own staff were looking at the numbers that said she was stagnating while her competition made advances. People like Scarlet O'Malley, the heiress and social media influencer, who was now married and expecting her first child. Iris's peers—her competition—were moving on from single-girl-in-the-city to new-wife-and-mama and she was still stuck in…boring-and-basic land.

Ugh!

If she showed up with someone like the Viking on her arm, it would be a boost to her social image, and it would give her a man to pose with. She could even frame it as a business deal…

He glanced up and caught her staring and she smiled at him. He winked and smiled back. She walked over to him. She wished she'd paid more attention to that movie her mom had made them watch on girls' night… *Indecent Proposal.* She needed to channel her best Robert Redford…or she could *Pretty Woman* him and be Richard Gere.

Confidence was key. She could be confident. Hadn't she convinced her parents to let her start her own YouTube channel when she was fourteen?

"Hello," she said. She'd charm the socks off him, she thought. Glancing down at his feet she saw he hadn't worn socks with his loafers. Fate was giving her a sign that she wouldn't mess this up.

"Hi. Want to join me?" he asked.

She glanced at her watch. She had about fifteen minutes until she'd have to call her team. And Thea's idea was there, nagging at her…though really, if she was going to do this, she had to stop thinking of it as Thea's idea.

"Sure, but only if you'll allow me to buy you a drink," she said.

"I'm never one to turn down a pretty lady," he said, standing and holding out a chair for her to join him.

"You aren't?" she asked.

"Not at all."

"Have you ever regretted that?" she asked. This man seemed daring, just like the Viking she'd compared him too, but she knew that she might be seeing what she wanted to see and not the real man.

"Never. Sometimes it has turned out differently than I anticipated but that's life, isn't it?"

"Your life maybe. I'm pretty much always following a plan," she said. She watched him, carefully trying to gauge his reaction. Was she seriously thinking about Thea's outrageous suggestion?

Yes. She was.

"I've never been one to follow a plan," he said.

"How does that work?"

"I go where the wind takes me," he said.

"The wind?"

"I'm a sailor and compete in yacht races," he said.

Hah, she thought. She'd known he was a Viking and instead of pillaging he was out there conquering the sea.

"Like the America's Cup?" she asked. She really didn't know that much about yachting.

"Exactly like that. I'm currently putting together a team and looking for investors for my bid in four years," he said.

He needed investors…

"Why are you asking?" he asked.

She took a deep breath. If she was going to do this then she wasn't going to find a better man than this guy. He looked good, he needed investors and she liked him. "I need a favor," she said.

"And only a stranger will do?" he asked.

She noticed he had a pile of papers on the table in front of him and as she glanced down, she recognized it as a prospectus—the kind of document someone looking for investors would use to showcase their product. She quickly looked away as he sat back down and straightened the papers, turning them facedown on the table.

"Sorry, didn't mean to read your stuff," she said.

"No problem. But you mentioned you need a favor. I'm already intrigued. Please sit down and then you can tell me all about it," he said.

She sat down, crossing her feet at her ankles and keeping her back straight. Her father had once said that posture was the first step to giving off the air of confidence. She swallowed and then took a deep breath. She had to be careful: sexual harassment went both ways and she didn't want to come across like she was propositioning him.

"I'm going to make you an offer that you can't refuse," she said. Wasn't that what Robert Redford had said? Was that right? Wasn't that the line?

"What are you, the Godfather?"

"No, I'm trying to say I need a man for the weekend, and if that prospectus is any indication you're looking for investors, you need some money, so… I'm making a mess of this."

"Is this an indecent proposal?"

Two

She blushed and blinked at him and then sat up even straighter and tipped her head to the side. "It's more of a business proposal that is personal in nature."

He'd been propositioned before but usually by women who wanted entrée into his jet-set world.

"I'm intrigued," he said. And he wasn't lying. This woman was beautiful. And though the fact that she was offering him money out of the blue was crazy, it was a nice fantasy to think of someone like her sponsoring his America's Cup bid, not a bloodless corporation or his controlling father.

"I'm going to a destination wedding and I need a date. It's four days, three nights, and I'm willing to invest in your project there in return for you accompanying me. It would be strictly for show. I'm not expecting you to do anything indecent."

"Too bad. I sort of liked the idea," he said. Funny, he

was about to attend a wedding that was scheduled to run for the same amount of time. Was she attending Adler's wedding, too?

Her shoulders stiffened and she sat up even straighter if that were possible. He liked her, he realized. She was different from the sporty women he usually hung out with, and though she was polished and clearly moved in the same social circles he'd grown up in, she felt different.

"Well, that's not on the table," she said.

"Why are you hiring a guy?" he asked. Frankly she didn't seem like the type of woman who had to pay someone to be with her, and if she was, what was he missing?

"It's a long story," she said. "And I really don't want to get into all the details. Suffice it to say, I was dating someone, and he broke up with me and I don't want to go stag to this event. It's televised and I'm filming while I'm there so…"

"It's about image?" he asked, a bit disappointed because she'd seemed to be more real than that. But he'd been fooled before so he shouldn't be too surprised.

She shook her head. "Yes, but it's not what you think. It's my business. I'm a lifestyle guru… I have a show and line of products and my mentor's sister designed the wedding dress so I'm doing an entire behind-the-scenes thing. If it was just me and not all the other brand stuff, I wouldn't care."

"Who are you?" he asked. "I hope you don't mind me asking but I've been out of the country and spend most of my time on the water."

"I'm Iris Collins."

He had heard of her, mainly from his sister, Mari, who had mentioned her as someone she wanted to grow her brand to be like. Which Zac had freely admitted he had no clue about. "I'm Zac."

"Am I right in assuming you need investors for your America's Cup bid?"

"Yes, I'm trying to find investors to fund my run. I have some new people and ideas I want to try," Zac explained.

"I think I can help you with that," she said.

"Lifestyle guru-ing pays that well?"

"Very well," she said with a laugh. "Which is another reason why I really need to present the right image. It would mainly involve you dressing up and holding my hand. Maybe there'd be a kiss or two but I just need someone to be my partner at all the events."

He was 100 percent sure that his answer had to be no. He didn't need Carlton Mansford—his father's PR-spin doctor—to explain that hiring himself out as a date for the weekend wasn't going to play well if it ever got out. And he'd been a Bisset long enough to know that this kind of thing wouldn't stay a secret.

He had to come clean with her. Let her know he wasn't desperate for money.

"I…"

He trailed off. He wanted to let her know it was a no-go but didn't want to embarrass her. Under different circumstances he'd have asked her out to dinner, but this wasn't that time. He had a problematic wedding of his own to attend, and he needed to really focus on getting serious investors for his team, not a nice lady who had some money to pay him for a weekend together.

She gave him a wry smile. "Don't say anything else. I knew it was a long shot. My sister said I should be Richard Gere and find myself someone pretty to have on my arm."

"She's right. But I'm not that guy," he said.

She nodded. "Thank you for your time. And the drink is of course on me."

She got up and walked away with way more class and

elegance than he knew he could ever muster. She held her head high and back straight as she went over to the bar area.

Then there was a commotion near the entrance, and he noticed a TV cameraman and several photographers entering as the seating hostess tried to stop them.

They made a beeline for Iris and Zac turned to watch them.

"Ms. Collins, rumor has it that you were dumped by Graham Winstead III?" one of the paparazzi shouted out. "Will this affect the launch of your new Domestic Goddess line? How can you claim to know anything about domestic bliss when you're—"

"Boys, please. Rumors are just that. Rumors. I'm not going to deign to answer them. As my father always says, keeping your ear close to the ground and listening is good business, repeating what you heard is asking for trouble."

Iris Collins smiled winningly at the cameras and then glanced at her watch. "I have to run. I'm meeting someone important."

She turned and started to walk past the paparazzi, but bumped into a table and lost her balance. Zac was on his feet before he had a chance to remind himself he'd already decided this was a bad idea.

But somehow watching her maintain her poise and dignity as she dealt with the gossip had made him forget that. He wanted to know more about this woman. He caught her and pulled her into his arms, looking down into her startled face.

"Angel face, I've got you," he said, making sure he only looked at her.

Angel face?
She clung to his big shoulders and automatically smiled but she was pretty sure she looked like Jared Leto's version

of the Joker from *Suicide Squad*. Being ambushed in person wasn't something she'd ever get used to. She preferred to deal with this kind of gossip online when she could rant to her assistant, then just smile and type out a response. Even more embarrassing had been the fact that she knew that Zac had overheard it all.

She'd pretty much used up all of her stores of bravado talking to the paparazzi and the last thing she wanted now was to make things worse. There was a knot in the pit of her stomach, and she was angry. And she couldn't help it; ever since she was a young girl, when she got mad, she cried. She blinked a number of times, refusing to let anyone see tears in her eyes.

Including Zac, but he seemed to get that she needed someone at her side. And here he was, holding her and calling her *angel face*. She had been doing photo-calls for her blog and TV show for the last five years so she was polished and professional or at least she hoped she was on the outside. Inside she wanted to hammer out the details. Did this mean he would come with her to the wedding?

"Thanks," she said, straightening back up. But he continued to hold her close to him.

"Go with it," he said.

"Did you change your mind?" she asked, staring into his blue eyes and hoping that he had. Though a part of her wanted him just for her own, this was easier. No messy feelings, no falling for someone who thought she was basic. Just a simple exchange of favors.

"Yes," he said under his breath.

She wrapped her arms around his neck and planted the biggest, juiciest, showiest kiss on his lips that she could. She knew it had to look good for the paparazzi and she put everything she had into it. She thought he was surprised at first, but then he dipped her low, his tongue sliding over hers, and she forgot about the cameras and the game. Forgot everything but the fact that this man was holding her in his arms, and he made her feel alive.

He straightened them both up and she still felt dazed. She had no problem ignoring the paparazzi, who were calling out questions to them as they walked out of the bar. He just sort of directed her and she followed. As soon as they were on the street, a large Bentley pulled up and a driver got out and opened the door.

"Sir."

"Malcolm," Zac said as he held the door open and she slid in the backseat.

As soon as the door closed behind them and they were on their way, she grabbed her phone and texted someone. Then she turned to him.

"Sorry, I was supposed to meet my hair and makeup people back there. I just texted them to cancel. Now what's going on? Who are you? Did you really agree to be my date for four days? I'm pretty sure you don't need the money... unless you're a professional gigolo—you're not, right?"

He rubbed his finger over his lips and just stared at her as if he couldn't stop thinking about their kiss. If she were 100 percent honest, she couldn't either, but she wanted to pretend nothing had happened. She was beige, right? She didn't kiss a stranger and feel instant passion like this. It was probably a fluke, she thought. Yeah, a total fluke.

"You asked me to help you out in exchange for investing in my project," he said. "I wasn't going to do it, but when I saw what you were up against, I couldn't resist."

"Are you doing this out of pity?" she asked. If so, she was turning into a total loser. She really should never have started this whole indecent-proposal thing.

"No, I'm doing it for money," he said, winking at her. Damn, he was so handsome for a minute she just smiled back at him and then his words sunk in. "But do you need money? You're not a gigolo, are you?"

"I don't know anyone younger than my grandmother who uses that word."

"I don't like the term man-whore," she quipped. "Listen, just answer me. Do you take money from women to hang out with them?"

"Just you," he said.

He was being cute, and she couldn't blame him, but this situation had just gone from a jokey idea to reality and she was committed because those photos of the two of them were going to go viral. Having him by her side would seriously save her bacon, but at the same time it created a bunch of issues she and her team were going to have to deal with.

"Glad to know I'm special. Where are we going?" she asked as she realized the driver seemed to be making a big circle around downtown.

"Wherever you want to discuss this," he said. "Malcolm will keep driving until we give him a location, right?"

"Yes, sir. Ma'am, where should I take you?" the driver asked her, without taking his eyes from the road.

"Take us to Collins Commons," she said, naming her father's compound in the financial district. They could discuss the details in one of the conference rooms there. Her phone started blowing up with texts and she glanced at them. Her team wanting to know where she was and who that hottie was with her.

"What's at Collins Commons?" he asked.

"My father's office. We can discuss your project, my investment in it and what I will need from you this weekend," she said. "I think it's best to get that all in writing so that we don't have any confusion."

"This weekend?"

"Yes. The wedding is the Osborn-Williams one on Nantucket."

Zac stared at her for a long moment and seemed to be pondering something but he finally just took a deep breath and nodded more to himself than to her.

"Your dad does this kind of thing?" Zac asked.

"Investments and contracts, yes. Hiring a man for the weekend, no. I think I'm the first one in our family to do this."

Zac had to give her props for recovering quickly; he realized there was much more to Iris Collins than met the eye. She had handled the online-gossip-site stringers with more aplomb that he ever had. He had seen her mask slip only once and that was when he kissed her.

She was attending his cousin's wedding. He should tell her who he was, but then she might not believe he really wanted outside investors. They were still essentially strangers and telling people he was a Bisset, had complicated his life in the past.

He knew the embrace was meant to be all show for the photographers, but he'd never been good at hiding the truth of who he was. He was ambitious and some would say militant when it came to what he wanted. But then he was a Bisset, and even though he hadn't gone into the family business, he'd brought the cutthroat Bisset drive with him to the world of competitive sailing.

But this was an entirely new situation and he was trying to be chill until he got the lay of the land. The conference room they were led to in the Collins Commons building was well appointed. Not unlike the massively impressive boardroom in the Bisset Industries headquarters in New York.

He knew that at some point he needed to clear up who

he was, but not yet. He was enjoying this. She'd wrested control back from him, and though it was counter to his nature, there was something about her that fascinated him.

Maybe it was that for the first time since he'd left Team GB and came back to New England to start his own team, he wasn't facing a choice that he didn't want to make. He had always been the kind of man who forged his own path. He'd known from watching Larry Ellison's attempts to win the America's Cup with his Oracle backing that it wouldn't be easy. But he hadn't realized how hard it would be to convince investors to take a chance on him without Bisset Industries' money also backing him.

He had always been able to make things happen without his father's assistance. It had been a point of pride for him and now... Well, unless he missed his guess, Iris had the connections to the kind of investors he needed. All he had to do was be her date for a long weekend. Simple enough.

Except his family would be at this wedding and, though he kept his private life private, the kind of splashy relationship she wanted from him...might raise questions. He had to make some decisions quickly.

"Are you freaked out now?" she asked.

"Aren't you?" he countered.

"Yes. I am. Listen, you were so sweet to come to my rescue when I tripped, but I'm not sure you know what you've gotten into," she said.

He leaned back in the large leather chair and steepled his fingers across his chest in a move he'd seen his father make many times when facing an opponent in the boardroom. The fact that the opponent was usually his aunt or his mom had always made Zac smile, but right now he was glad to have that model to draw on.

"Tell me about it," he said.

She nodded and stood up, moving to the other side of the

large boardroom table and pacing in front of the windows that looked down on Collins Commons. The summer sun was filtered through the tinted windows but still provided enough light for him to admire her slim silhouette.

"As I mentioned, I'm a lifestyle television personality. My career started with a blog, and I was a personal assistant to Leta Veerland. I'm not sure if you've heard of her," Iris said.

"I know her," he said.

Leta Veerland was on par with Martha Stewart. She'd built her career in the 1980s and '90s with her lifestyle books, monthly magazine and television show. Yeah, he'd heard of her. His mom had considered her the gold standard for entertaining and had emulated Leta Veerland at all her Hamptons summer parties and events.

"I figured. She's a household name. Anyway, she wanted to cut back on the show and I transitioned into it and brought a younger, fresh perspective—her words—to it. And people seemed to respond. So, I've been doing this for about seven years now. My market has been growing from single-girl-in-the-city to coupledom-and-settling-down—"

"But you're not in a couple?" he asked.

"Well, yes. I mean I was dating someone but that didn't work out. And I'd been teasing that I'd reveal my new guy at this wedding that I'm a bridesmaid in. I'm also promoting a new product launch for brides-to-be and new wives so…"

"It would look really bad if you showed up stag," he said. "Okay, that makes sense. So what exactly do you need from me if I do this?"

She turned around, and he noticed when she talked business there was none of that sweetness to her. She had a very serious go-getter expression that reminded him a lot of his father and his brother Logan when they were going in to close a deal.

"If? The paparazzi just caught us embracing. I'm afraid it's you or no one else," she said. "We just need to work out a price."

He stood up and walked around the long conference table, taking his time. He had somehow gotten the upper hand and while he knew funding and financing an America's Cup bid was way too high a price to ask her to pay for four days as her "boyfriend," they were both in a position where there wasn't an out.

She didn't back up when he moved closer, not stopping until only an inch of space separated them. "I'm afraid what I need is very pricey."

Three

Coming home to Nantucket was always bittersweet for Juliette Bisset. She and her mother, Vivian, had continually had a difficult relationship when they were in the city but on Nantucket they'd always been strangely close. Maybe it was the beach-hair-don't-care attitude that seemed to infuse the island. Juliette had never really thought too much about it, had simply vowed she'd be less harsh if she had a daughter of her own, something she'd failed at.

Her younger sister, Musette, had loved it here as well when she was alive. She'd been gone almost twenty-five years now. Juliette still missed her even though during the last few years of Musette's life, it had been difficult to love her and not live with the constant fear that she was going to kill herself with her reckless lifestyle.

"I figured I'd find you out here."

Juliette turned around to see her niece, Adler, standing there. Musette's daughter. She was the reason the entire family was descending on the island.

Adler's was going to be a no-holds-barred, celebrity-studded, televised ceremony. And as if that wasn't enough to cause stress, she was also marrying into the family of Juliette's husband's business rival. It was completely insane and yet seemed perfectly normal considering she was Musette's daughter. A part of Juliette imagined her sister, who'd never like August Bisset, chuckling in glee at the fact that her daughter was marrying into his rival's family.

"I can't help thinking about your mom this week as we are all here for your wedding."

"Me too. I miss her," Adler said.

Juliette put her arm around Adler and hugged her close. "Me too. I feel like she's here with us."

"I hope so," Adler said. "That's one of the reasons why I picked Nantucket for the wedding. This is where we were always happiest when she was still alive."

"I'm hoping the gardenias bloom in time for my wedding bouquet," Adler said.

Juliette knew that Musette used to leave the blossoms in Adler's nursery when she was a little girl. "I'm sure they will."

Adler turned away to the other headstones in the private family cemetery. This land had been in the Wallis family for six generations and most of their ancestors were buried here.

"Why is this gravestone blank?" Adler asked.

Juliette's stomach felt like lead and her throat tightened. That tiny gravestone held her deepest, darkest secret. "It's for a baby who was stillborn."

"Oh. That's sad. Was it Gran's?" Adler asked.

"No, it wasn't," Juliette said. "Let's get back up to the house before that storm blows in."

Adler slipped her arm through Juliette's as they walked back up the cobblestone path toward the house. Adler was talking about her wedding and the last-minute things she needed to do in the three days before all of her guests arrived. But Juliette's mind was elsewhere—back there with that tiny unmarked gravestone. There were times when she'd wished she'd never hidden that baby.

But there were other actions she'd taken...things that couldn't be undone, so her little stillborn baby boy would always be hidden there.

They went through the house's beachside entrance, switching their sandy shoes for slippers that the butler, Michael, thoughtfully left for them. As soon as they entered the hallway, Dylan, Vivian's corgi, ran toward them. Adler dropped down to her knees, petting Dylan and getting several sloppy kisses.

Juliette petted Dylan, as well.

"Nice walk, Juliette?" her mother asked as she entered the hallway. Vivian was in her seventies but looked younger. She wore a pair of slim-fitting white jeans and a chambray shirt that she had loosely tucked in on one side. While on Nantucket and in beach mode, she let her naturally curly blond hair actually stay curly instead of having it straightened by her lady's maid, Celeste, each morning. She held a martini glass in one hand, and as she came closer to Juliette, she reached over and gave her a loose hug.

Then her mom did the same with Adler but added an air kiss. Juliette had compared herself to others for so many years, and for a moment she started to let the old feelings of jealousy well up before she shoved them aside. She had a daughter of her own that she was finally getting close to. Something she'd never expected to happen at the ripe old age of sixty-one.

"Martini, girls?"

"Yes, ma'am," Adler said.

"Definitely," Juliette said. This weekend was going to be

hard for her in more ways than one, but she was going to do her best to face it with charm and a smile firmly in place.

"When is August coming?" her mom asked when they were all seated in the sunroom.

"I'm not entirely sure. He and Logan have a meeting with a client this week and they will be coming together," Juliette said.

She and her husband were enjoying a new closeness since he'd stepped down and handed the reins of Bisset Industries over to their son, Logan.

"I hope Logan and Uncle August are nice," Adler said. "Zac promised he'd help me ride herd on his older brother, but you know how Logan can be."

"I do. He's so much like your uncle," Juliette said, trying not to let her mind linger too long on that thought.

"How pricey will it be for you to join me?" Iris asked Zac as they continued their negotiation. She was trying to stay focused on business but he smelled good and that kiss earlier... How she'd felt when he'd kissed her kept distracting her. Was it a fluke? That was the one thought that was going through her head.

His mouth continued to be a distraction. It was firm looking, but his lips had been so soft when he kissed her. Had she just imagined it? She wasn't sure that hiring a man to be her date at the wedding was a good idea. She'd barely kissed Zac and she was already losing her focus on the big prize. She had to hustle to stay ahead of the competition. And instead of worrying about that she was wondering about his kiss.

Focus, girl.

"I'm actually putting together my own team for the America's Cup."

She blinked. That wasn't what she'd been expecting to

hear. She knew very little about the America's Cup except that the CEO of Oracle had won for the United States a few years ago and that it had taken him a lot of money and time. "Is that what you do for a living? Sailing? Or is this a new hobby?"

"Yes, it's my job. I have some other interests as well, but the bulk of my time is spent training and participating in yachting competitions around the world. I've been in Australia for the last few years and I had hoped to captain the team I'd been training with, but they went in a different direction and I'm not really that great at taking orders so I'm doing my own thing. I need investors to help sponsor us."

"Okay. I think I can help," she said. "Actually, my dad manages all of my investments and I think this might be something that he would be interested in. He's always trying to diversify but this is niche."

"It is," he said. "You want your dad to know you hired me?"

"No. What I'm now thinking is that you and I would be together the four days at the wedding and then, since this is going to be a big investment, could we possibly extend the arrangement for, say, three months to get through my new product launch? Then you could go off to do your yachting and we could drift apart but it won't look like it was just for the wedding," she said. Now that she knew what he wanted, it was easier to get her head where it needed to be. She turned away from him and moved to the sideboard where she knew pens and paper were kept.

She took two legal pads out and pens and then hit the intercom button on the phone and rang her father's assistant.

"Hello, Bran. It's Iris. Could we send some refreshments into the small conference room and I'll need some time on my dad's schedule in an hour or so," she said.

"Certainly, Iris. I'll get some fresh fruit and those cookies you like sent up. Shall I also bring in cold beverages and some coffee?" he asked.

She looked over at Zac. "Do you want coffee?"

"That'd be great," he said.

"Yes, please. Coffee for two."

"Certainly, Iris," Bran said, hanging up.

She walked back to the table and pushed one of the pads of paper and a pen across to Zac, and then pulled out a chair for herself. He took the paper and pen, then came around and sat down next to her.

Dang, but he was impossible not to watch as he moved. He had a lithe, masculine grace. She was still staring when he sat down next to her.

"What are we doing?"

She shook her head. She had to get over this ridiculous attraction to him. He would be an employee like KT or Stephan. She had to treat him as such.

"I thought we could each write down the things we need. I know you already have a prospectus. Do you have a profit-and-loss sheet?"

"I do," he said.

"Good. How do you feel about the three months?"

"I'm not even sure what it is you want from me," he said.

"I need you to be my boyfriend in public. Take photos with me, of course. You'd have to give me permission to use them on all social platforms. There are four days of events at the wedding, so I'd want you there at all times by my side. Once the wedding is over, I'm thinking we'll need one or two dates a week, as well as some cute social media exchanges and maybe a couple of live videos so I can keep us relevant. My product launch is in six weeks and once it does, I'll be traveling and doing events. We won't be together so maybe we can do some exchanges on social media again and possibly, if it works for your schedule, you could fly out and meet me at one of my appearances. I will give you the full schedule so we can see if that works."

"Uh, I don't know about that. Being your boo for the weekend is one thing, but all that other stuff is a big commitment. I'll have to start hiring my team and get to work on having the yacht I've designed manufactured. My time is going to be pretty well spoken for. I can do the wedding but beyond that you are on your own."

"Forget it then. I need someone… Actually now that you were photographed with me, I need you, Mister… I don't know your last name," she said.

"It's Bisset. My dad is—"

"Mr. Bisset, I don't think we need to go into families right now. All I'm interested in is the details. I'm going to be giving you a large amount of money, you are going to have to work for it."

"You are investing in my racing team, Iris," he countered. "You will see a profit from it when I win. I'm doing this as a favor because I like you, angel face."

He leaned in closer and she felt the brush of his minty breath across her cheek. "I think you like me too or you wouldn't have suggested this in the first place."

Her skin was as soft as it looked and the more time he spent with Iris, the happier he was with his gut decision to help her out. He hadn't liked watching the paparazzi question her, but he knew that was in no small part due to the way that they had treated his own little sister, Mari. Mari had had an affair with a married man when she was younger, and the press had sniffed that story out and made her life a living hell for a while.

As much as he knew that everyone seemed to live for the latest tea, he didn't like it. His sister said that being in the spotlight meant taking the good with the bad, but he wasn't sure about that. And because he wasn't going to lie to himself, that kiss between him and Iris had been hot. Hell, hotter than he'd expected. He didn't want to just walk away. But hanging out with her at the wedding was one thing. Three months of fake dates and appearances would be hard to maintain.

He wasn't at the point in his life where he wanted to focus on anything but winning the America's Cup and that meant his next few years were taken. But she wasn't going to back down; he could easily read the determination in her eyes. And as she'd said, now that they'd been photographed together, it was either him or no one. And he didn't want to leave her in the lurch.

"I do like you," she said, at last, touching her finger to his lip and then drawing her hand back.

A tingle went through him at her touch.

"So then. Let's make this work," he said, shifting back because he couldn't allow this to be anything more than a business deal. He needed investors and unless she was lying—and Iris didn't strike him as a woman who would make things up—she could provide solid backing. This place belonged to her father; she had real money on the table. He would make the three-month arrangement work.

"Yes, let's," she said. "I'm going to make a list of every event I need you at for the next three months. You jot down your schedule, as well."

"Before we do that, shouldn't we make sure that your investors are on board?" he asked. "Or did you anticipate that it would just be yourself?"

"Um, yes, of course," she said. "Let me see what you have. I think an investment group would be better, but I'll ask my dad."

He handed her his prospectus and she started going over

it, making notes off to one side of her notepad. He watched as she flipped through the prospectus and the profit-and-loss sheet. Finally she sat back. "Okay I think you've got a solid plan here. I'm not sure why you weren't able to secure investment on your own."

"Me neither," he said.

"I wanted to sort our part of the arrangement out first, but I think my dad is going to need some time to look into this. So let's get him in here and we can discuss that. Regardless of his opinion, I will be investing in your run."

"Why?"

"Because you are going to help me out," she said. "I like a man who honors his word, and from what I've read in this document, you are qualified and know what you're doing."

"I'm not looking for handouts."

"You're not getting it. I'm not a passive investor. I'll be looking for updates quarterly."

"You will?"

"Yup, but don't worry, you'll be hanging out with me a lot so I can keep up to date," she said, with a wink. She pushed her chair back and stood up, but he stopped her with his hand on her wrist.

That electric tingle went up his arm again and his touch drew her off balance. She started to fall and he caught her and steadied her as he stood up. "I don't want you to think you're the boss."

"Why not? I clearly am. I'm going to work up an employment contract for the next three months for our personal arrangement," she said. "And we will have the investment contract separately, okay? You were right. I don't want my dad to know about this. It would be better for everyone if it seemed like you were into me."

"I am," he said.

"Perfect, keep that up," she said. "I'll go get my dad."

"Not yet," he said.

"What? Why not?"

"Because you're giving me credit for being a much better actor than I really am," he said, putting his hand on her waist and waiting to see if she pulled away.

She didn't. Instead she tipped her head to the side, watching him with those wide brown eyes of hers. She nibbled on her lower lip as she waited, and he was struck again that she was two very different women. Strong and confident in business, a little shy and reserved personally. Which of course made a certain kind of sense when he thought about her asking to hire him for the weekend.

"I'm not sure this is a good idea," she said, putting her hand on his chest. But she didn't push him away.

"Why not?"

"We're *pretending* to be a couple," she said. "I don't want to blur the lines."

"We have to make it look real," he said. "If you push me away when I touch you, no one will buy the act."

She nibbled her lower lip again and he bit back a moan. She turned him on like no one he'd been with in a long time. But he was here for business. Which was part of the point he'd been trying to make to her. They had to appear to be lovers even though they were strangers.

He'd also been determined to make his own path and that had sometimes led him astray, but he had to be honest, this detour was the most interesting one he'd found himself on. Pretend boyfriend/lover to a lifestyle guru…who knew?

Four

"So, my daughter tells me you're putting together a group of investors for an America's Cup bid. I read Ellison's book. That's a risky venture," Hal Collins said. He wasn't a tall man, but he carried himself as if he were. There was a sharp intelligence in his gray-blue eyes and a hint of the warmth that Zac had glimpsed in Iris's. He also recognized where Iris got her confidence and backbone.

"Yes, sir," Zac said. "I've been on two teams since I graduated from college and have a lot of experience and knowledge."

He'd been in the boardroom with Iris for what felt like hours and now her father was here to determine if investing in Zac's America's Cup bid was viable.

"Good to hear," Hal said. "Why are you striking out on your own?"

"The honest answer?"

"Always," Hal said.

"I don't take orders well. I know how to win but when you're cashing a paycheck and not the man footing the bill, not everyone will listen. I'm tired of coming in second," Zac said. Hal reminded him a bit of his brother Logan, who would have asked the same sort of questions. Zac knew he had to prove himself to Hal and he was willing to do that.

"Understandable," Hal said. "I don't take orders well either. So how do you know Iris?"

He glanced over at her where she sat a couple of seats away from him and her father. Her eyes widened. They hadn't finished working out the details of the "favor" she wanted from him. "We're dating, sir. I think you should know that I started dating Iris before I knew she was your daughter, so in no way did that influence me."

Hal glanced at her. "I thought you were seeing someone else."

"I was, Dad, but that ended. Zac and I just met and hit it off," she said. "This isn't about my personal life. It's about a pretty solid investment. You are always urging me to diversify."

Hal looked like he didn't want to let the relationship questions go but he just nodded. "This is a risky investment, but from what I've read, I think you might be worth the risk. I need to do some more research, and I'm not sure when you need an answer?"

"The sooner the better. I have already started the design process and I have two team members, but I'll need to recruit more. To be successful in an America's Cup bid, the longer we have to train and prepare the better we will be."

"Fair enough," Hal said. "I should be able to have an answer for you tomorrow. Iris, will you still need the conference room?"

"If you don't, then yes. We're discussing a few details about our schedules," Iris said.

Hal seemed surprised that she'd choose a business setting for a personal matter and Zac knew they were going to end up answering more questions, so he just stood up. "Sorry, that's my fault, sir. I don't live in Boston and didn't want to suggest she go back to my hotel room to talk or to her house. As Iris mentioned, we've just started dating."

"I like that. The other guy was too pushy," Hal said, standing. Iris stood too and smiled at her father as he left the room, carrying all of Zac's financial information with him.

Zac realized he should have mentioned his father and his own fortune and made a quick decision. "I need a private word, Mr. Collins."

Iris seemed surprised and he wondered if she thought he was going to tell her dad about the offer she'd made him. But he just smiled as reassuringly as he could at Iris.

"I need to return some calls. I'll wait in the reception area, Dad."

Iris left the room as Hal sat back down.

"Are you August Bisset's son?" Hal asked.

"Yes."

"Why haven't you mentioned this to Iris?" Hal asked. "I'm not sure keeping this kind of secret is a good idea."

"It didn't come up, but I'm planning to tell her. As you know my family owns Bisset Industries and I have a large investment portfolio of my own. I'll be putting up some of my own money but I need outside investment."

"Why don't you just go to your brother and ask him to invest?" Hal said.

Zac wasn't surprised that Hal knew his brother, Logan, was the CEO of Bisset Industries. "I don't like the strings that come with that. I need to be free to do this on my own. I'm not saying I won't answer to investors, but when it comes to doing business with family…it's difficult."

"I've heard it can be," Hal said. "Thank you for telling me. I think you'd be safe telling Iris, but my wife has warned me not to interfere in either of my daughters' relationships."

"That's probably good advice. I will tell her but thought you might find it odd when you start doing your research and realize I didn't mention it," he said.

"Makes sense. I have a few investors who like long shots and can take the hit if we lose money. I was thinking of a five to six person investor group. We'd form it as an LLC and you would work for us. I know Iris wants to invest in you and you could put your money in through the LLC too," Hal said.

"That sounds like the right approach. And I've been working on a new cutting-edge design for the fin that I think we might be able to monetize after the race," he said.

"Good to know. I think we can at least get the ball rolling this week once I've done a bit more research," Hal said. This time when he stood, he held his hand out to Zac.

He shook the older man's hand, realizing that Iris had given him exactly what he'd been looking for. So he was going to have to give her what she'd asked for from him.

"I'll let Iris know we're done," Hal said. "I look forward to seeing more of you, Zac."

Hal left the room and Zac walked over to the window, staring out at the city. He felt just as hemmed in as he always did when he was on the land, but this trip had been full of the unexpected. And he definitely couldn't complain.

When Iris left the conference room, she rescheduled KT and Stephan for the next morning at seven o'clock, then went down the hall to the patio area. It was surrounded on three sides by glass walls. She looked out at the city, pretending that this was a normal day. But it wasn't. She had been on a roller coaster since she'd gotten that text from Graham.

Her phone pinged and she saw that it was a text from Adler. Her best friend, the bride-to-be. It was a photo of two martini glasses, captioned, Saving one for you.

She texted back that she needed a drink or two.

Adler's response was immediate. You okay?

Yeah. I'll tell you all about it when I'm on the island. Won't be with Graham at the wedding… I'm too basic for him. Whatever, right?

He's a dick. Are you sure you're okay? Want to chat?

Can't at the moment.

She hesitated.

Believe it or not, I met a guy.

Good. Tell me more.

He's cute, really bright blue eyes, and he has a bit of stubble. You know, normally I'm opposed but it suits him. Also he kissed me, and it was way hotter than anything I've experienced before.

Sounds perfect. Are you bringing him to the wedding?

Yes. Is that okay?

It's fine. Can't wait to meet him. Text me after drinks and let me know how it went.

Will do.

Bran cleared his throat and she looked up.

"Your father said he's done speaking with Mr. Bisset and you can rejoin him," Bran said.

"Thank you. We shouldn't be much longer."

"Your father pays really good overtime so it's not a problem if you are," he joked.

She followed him back into the office area and then went down toward the conference room. On the walls of the hallway were photos from the different companies her father had invested in over the years. Some of them included her father as a younger man and in many of them her mom was by his side.

She felt a pang deep inside of her.

It wasn't that she needed a man to complete her or that she was less than without a guy at her elbow. It was that she wanted a partner. For some of the companies in the photos, she clearly remembered her father struggling to decide to invest in the firm and how her mom had been his sounding board. She knew the stakes because they were in it together.

Iris wanted that. She'd thought that Graham would be that kind of guy. He hadn't shied away from the social media aspect of her career, he liked that she made more money than he did and he'd been nice to have at events and functions. Despite being douchey at times, Graham was very good at a cocktail party. But he hadn't been right for her. She'd sort of sensed it from the first but then she'd put her misgivings aside, preferring to ignore the bad stuff and focus on the good.

But she'd deceived herself.

She wouldn't do that with Zac. He was really going to be just for show, and as much as her heart ached at the thought of that, her mind and her bruised spirit applauded it. How many hits could her soul take before she just turned into... Leta. As much as Iris loved her mentor, she'd had six failed marriages and was very cynical toward the opposite sex.

"Iris?"

She turned toward the conference room where Zac stood in the doorway. She smiled at him. "Just taking a stroll down memory lane. So much of my family is built into Collins Combined that it's hard not to sometimes feel nostalgic."

And envious, she admitted to herself. But then she straightened her shoulders. She wasn't big into feeling sorry for herself. She tucked her phone into the pocket of her dress and turned toward him. "Let's get down to business on this, shall we?"

"There's nothing more to discuss," he said. "I'll do what you've asked. I think it's fair. Your father is offering more than I'd expected from you when you suggested this exchange."

As much as she wanted to hear that news, she had to be sure he understood what she wanted. "Let's go in the conference room and make sure we both have the details the same."

He stopped her as he walked by him. With his hand on her upper arm, she looked up into his eyes and felt that heat running through her at his touch. She had to get this under control. Hadn't she just realized that by lying to herself she'd end up broken? She had to stuff the attraction way down. She'd put her own personal needs and desires aside when she'd started on this path and it needed to stay that way.

She'd built her empire from showing people what they wanted to see and not by being herself. It was too late to change now. She didn't want to lose what she'd built and she had a feeling not keeping strict boundaries with Zac could spell trouble.

"I think we should only be touching when we're in public," she said. "Let's go inside and address this."

"Address what? You want me to be your—"

She put her hand over his mouth to stop him from saying anything else as she noticed her father's assistant coming out of his office.

Zac arched his eyebrows at her as she flushed and drew him into the conference room, closing the door firmly behind them and leaning back against it. She let her tingling hand drop from his mouth. She wasn't normally such a touchy person.

"Well, angel face, that was definitely touching."

Zac could see the conflict in her. There was something about her that was deeply sensual, yet she seemed to prefer to keep it hidden. It was there in her appearance. Her hair was pulled back low on her neck, her clothing was sensibly feminine and conservative, which only made her sensual mouth and her figure stand out more because there was a natural grace and femininity in every move she made.

"What did Dad say?" she asked.

"He's interested in putting together an LLC of five or six investors. You'd be one."

"Good. That works for me. Please, sit down, Mr. Bisset," she said.

"Is this the part where you explain that you're the boss?" he asked as he moved to one of the chairs. He wanted to tease her and see if he could find his way past the bow tied at her neck and maybe loosen up that hairstyle, but he needed to finalize their agreement more. He wanted to know the boundaries and parameters because he was ready to get back to his team and start the wheels in motion. He

had no doubt that once Hal started researching both himself
and his yacht-captaining career, he would get behind him.
And even if he didn't, Zac had decided he'd fund the run
himself. That was what Larry Ellison had done. But part of
the reason Zac had hesitated to do that was ego. He wanted
to know that others believed in him. So that his run was
more about proving something to himself than to the world.

"It is," she said. "So here's the schedule for the wedding.
I think those four days will be the most intense part of this.
Then I just need a few dates after. As I suggested earlier,
at first we'll do a couple a week, and then I have my book
and product launches and you'll be doing your boat stuff,
so we stay long distance—a long-distance couple."

He almost smiled at the way she cut herself off from saying lovers. It amused him that she was...well, the way she
was. He should mention he knew Adler but she was on a roll
with her requirements so he decided to let it ride for now.

"Okay. For the wedding, I'll be your guy at all of the
events. We can hold hands, kiss and do whatever else you
think we should."

"Thank you for that. But maybe we should set a limit
on the kissing—once a day," she said.

"No. We should both be acting the way we would in a
real relationship if we're going to sell it. Your dad is way
too savvy not to notice if we just kiss once a day. We need
to be ourselves."

"Believe it or not, that is me," she said.

"Well it's not me," he countered. "This has to seem like
we're both real people. I can't be someone you made up."

"And yet you are," she said testily.

"Having second thoughts?" he asked her.

"Yes. And third and fourth. And it all comes back to
you."

He scooted around so that his chair faced hers and pulled

her closer to him. "The only way this is going to work is if we are a team. We have to have each other's backs. If we're both playing our own game, it will show to everyone who we meet."

"A team?" she asked.

There was something more going on here than the conversation. He could see it in her eyes. "Yes. We have to be partners. We'll look at the events and make a plan that shows you and me in our best light."

"I… I really like that."

"Good. I know that we have an arrangement, but I think we should try to be friends. That will be fun too. We can learn about each other and that will lend a realness to the relationship."

"It will," she said.

He saw her taking notes and wondered how many relationships she'd been in. Because the way she was acting, it didn't seem like she had a lot of experience. "Isn't that what you normally do when you start dating someone?"

She put her pen down and tucked a tendril of hair that had escaped her updo back behind her ear. "I don't know. Normally I date people I meet at an event. If they are an influencer, then we try to stage photos and go places where our viewers want to see us—"

"That's not what I'm talking about. The last guy you dated—didn't you get to know him?"

"Yes. But he wasn't who I thought he was," she said. "It's so crazy because on the surface we seemed like we were made for each other but behind closed doors… Well, I'm glad that we won't have to worry about any of that."

"What are you talking about?" Zac asked. He wasn't sure what had happened, but it didn't sound like it was pleasant.

"Nothing. I like this," she said, flipping to a blank

sheet of paper on her notepad and writing with clean and neat strokes. When she was done, she turned the pad to him and handed it over. "Read this and let me know your thoughts."

He glanced down at the contract she'd written on the legal pad. It stated a start date for their association, as she'd called it, and it stated an end date of three months from today. She listed out what she wanted from him and then left a blank for the dollar amount of her investment.

"Should we make sure we have chemistry before we try this?" he asked.

She nodded a few times. "Yes, you're right. We need to make sure we're believable as a couple."

He stood up. She did so as well and then held out her hand. He reached out to take it, then tugged her toward him and lowered his head for a kiss.

Five

She clung to his shoulders as every nerve ending in her body went on high alert. His lips were close but he wasn't kissing her but she was so close to those lips of his. And she needed to prove to herself that earlier had been a fluke. That she was the highly business-focused and driven woman with a low sex drive she'd always been.

So she shifted slightly, leaning up until her lips brushed his. That tingle started again in her lips and she saw his eyes widen slightly before he took control of the kiss. Oh, dear Lord, the man tasted so good. Better than anything she'd tasted before. She held on to his shoulders; they were strong and muscly, probably from all that time spent captaining a yacht.

She felt one of his hands on the small of her back and the other at her waist. His fingers moved against her skin, caressing her as someone cleared his throat behind her.

Zac broke the kiss and straightened, turning them both so that the boardroom table was at their backs.

"Dad," Iris said. "Sorry about that. We were just wrapping up in here… I mean it's not what it—"

"Stop explaining, Iris. The last thing either of us wants is to discuss you kissing Zac," her father said.

Iris smiled because her father was right and it seemed like that kiss had lent authenticity to their story that they were dating. "Did you need one of us?"

"Actually, both of you," her father said.

"Both of us?"

"Yes. I spoke with your mom and mentioned I'd met Zac and she wants to meet him too. You know she hates when I know something she doesn't," her father said with a wink.

All the enjoyment Iris had had from the kiss and feeling like she'd fooled her dad went out the window and instead panic started to fill her stomach, making her queasy. Fooling Dad was one thing, but her mom? That was going to be very difficult.

"Oh, I wish we could, Dad, but I promised Adler we'd be on Nantucket in the morning, so Zac and I were going to have a quiet night in."

"That's perfect, sweetie," her father said. "Your mom invited you both to dinner. I think Thea will be there too."

Of course, she would be.

"Zac, will that be okay? I know you said you had a call you needed to make tonight," she said, hoping he'd pick up on her subtle hint and make an excuse so they could skip dinner.

"That's fine. My call can wait," he said, wrapping his arm around her waist and squeezing her close to his side. "I look forward to getting to know your family better."

"Great. That's settled then. I'll text your mom. Be at ours at six-thirty," Iris's father said.

He turned and walked out of the boardroom, closing the door behind him. Iris took a deep breath before turning to face Zac. Before she could say anything, he ripped the page off the legal pad. "We should have two of these so we each have one."

"What?" she asked, not even thinking about the contract. "Yes, of course. Why did you say yes to dinner?"

"If we can't fool your family at dinner, how are we going to make a lot of people buy us as a couple for four days?" he asked. He pulled the legal pad to him and started copying what she'd written word-for-word.

"It will be harder with my mom and Thea. Dad's easy because he only sees what he wants to. But Mom is shrewd, and you should know that Thea suggested I hire a guy for the weekend so she might try to trip you up."

"Thanks for the heads-up. See, this will be a good test run."

"Yeah, probably," Iris said. "I mean, yes."

She felt a little light-headed. Maybe it was that kiss he'd laid on her...or she'd laid on him.

"I'm sorry about that kiss," she said. "I know you meant for it to seem as if we had been kissing if my father came in. It won't happen again."

"I didn't mind at all. I was going to do more than just hold you. I wanted whoever entered to pay attention to us and not this," he said, gesturing to the legal pad. She saw he'd signed his name on both copies. "You sign now and we'll both have a copy."

She went over and signed the second one and then took it and folded it neatly into thirds so it would fit into her purse.

Then it occurred to her that there was no termination clause. "We didn't give ourselves an out."

"You said there was no other option than to see things through for the three months. I'm a man of my word," he said. "And I can tell that you are a smart lady. You won't back out."

She nodded. "Do you have a hotel in town?"

"Yeah, I've got a place," he said. "I have a car there too."

They exchanged phone numbers and she gave him her address. "Do you want to just meet at my parents'?"

"No. I'll pick you up. I think your dad is an old-fashioned kind of guy," Zac said.

"You're not wrong, but he gets that we live in a modern world," she said. "I'll take my car and meet you there."

"You know your family best so that sounds good," he said.

"Okay, so see you tonight," she said, then led the way out of the conference room. As they walked down the hall, she realized she'd said goodbye too soon and now she had to either figure out something to say to him or just walk awkwardly in silence next to him.

In the elevator, he hit the ground-floor button.

"Zac, thank you," she said.

"You're very welcome," he said.

"So how did you get the money for this?" Dev Kellman asked when Zac arrived back at his family's Boston home where he and his friends were staying while they tried to drum up financing. Yancy McNeil was there as well, standing by the bar when he entered.

"Through Iris," Zac said. His friends had never heard him mention a girlfriend, so he figured he'd better start talking about her soon. From watching his sister—whose channel and media following were a lot smaller than Iris's—get dragged when she started dating Inigo, he knew that the attention he and Iris would receive was going to be a lot more intense.

"Who's Iris?" Dev asked as he pulled three longneck

bottles of beer from the fridge behind the mini bar, gave one to Yancy and held one up toward Zac. Zac nodded.

Who was Iris? His objective had been to get financing, and of course he was on the verge of securing it in the most bizarre way possible. Dev and he had been good friends for the last ten years, having met at boarding school. He knew that Iris only wanted the two of them to know about their arrangement and he was going to honor that, but he hadn't really thought through the logistics of being her for-hire man. He was going to have lie to his friends and family or just shut them down with a few terse words. "The lady I'm dating," Zac said.

"Since when?" Dev asked. "We landed two days ago, and you broke up with Zara before we left Sydney so I don't think you had time to get—"

"Since none-of-your-business," he said. He wasn't about to start making up stories about the two of them and Dev and Yancy didn't really need the details.

"Okay, okay, don't get cranky. I was just asking. It's not like you to hook up with a woman this quickly."

"She's different," Zac said at last. "You know I'm not all touchy-feely and *let's talk about our emotions*."

"Me neither. Just when you tie our business to a woman, I want to make sure it's a good decision."

Dev and he both. It was risky. Which was why he'd almost come clean with Hal. He wanted to make sure that the deal with Hal went through regardless of this thing with Iris.

"I'm being careful. The money isn't tied to me dating her."

"Fair enough, but you've got tons of money. Why not just use yours?" Yancy asked.

"I am. Her dad is an investment guy. He puts together groups of investors who go after different ventures. When I mentioned to Iris that I was in Boston trying to raise funds, she mentioned her father might be interested. She said that he was always looking for new things. I don't think this is quite what he had in mind when he said that, but he was game. He's doing some research and is putting together an investment team. I'll be one of the shareholders as will Iris," Zac said.

"Cool. How will it be structured?" Yancy asked.

"I'm not sure yet, but he mentioned an LLC. I want you and me as COOs so that we can be in charge of getting who we need in place. We should know in the next few days about the funding, but I think it's safe to start shopping for a design company that can manufacture our yacht," Zac said. "I mentioned that we are planning to sell our design after the next Cup run."

"The patent is in our names," Dev reminded him.

"They know that. They'd get a share of the profit but no intellectual property claim."

"Great. I'll get the ball rolling. I'm having dinner with some guys who might be interested in joining our team tonight and then we can meet tomorrow to talk more," Dev said.

"Let's meet next week on Nantucket. I've got to be there for Adler's wedding and Iris is a bridesmaid," Zac said. He really needed to tell her about his connection to Adler.

"Ah, so that's how you two met. Cool. Can't wait to meet her. Thanks for putting this together. I was really getting sick of having our ideas overlooked."

"You don't have to thank me. We're a team," Dev said. "I've got to go. Talk tomorrow."

He did the one-armed bro hug with Dev and Yancy that had become their habit, then his friends left and Zac was alone in the town house. He went up to his room and stood in front of his closet. It had been a while since he'd had to socialize with upper-class people so he wanted to look the part.

He had a closet of clothing that the staff kept clean at all times. He didn't know how casual or formal dinner at the Collinses' house would be. He opted for some dark trousers and a button-down shirt and paired it with some dress shoes.

He rubbed his hand over his beard. He kept it neatly trimmed but it was summer and hotter here than it had been in Australia, so should he shave? He'd leave it for tonight.

He showered and dressed, then headed to the address that Iris had given him. When he pulled into the large circle drive, there were two cars already parked there: a green VW Beetle and a sleek beige BMW. He parked behind them, got out of the car and walked up the drive. He had a bouquet of flowers he'd picked up on his way over and a bottle of wine he'd nicked from his parents' wine cellar.

Did he look like he was trying too hard to impress her?

He texted Iris that he was in front of the house, then rang the doorbell. He heard a dog barking, and then the door opened and Iris stood there. She wore a pair of white trousers and a halter-neck top that showed off her shoulders and collarbone. Her hair was down around her shoulders and her brown eyes were warm as she smiled at him.

He wasn't sure why it mattered but he really hoped he impressed her.

"So, when did you meet this guy?" Thea asked as they sat at the counter in her mother's kitchen. She'd arrived twenty minutes earlier and she was just full of questions tonight.

"A few days ago," Iris said, keeping it vague because she'd been so busy making sure they had a legal document that she'd forgotten the details of their cover story. "I didn't want to say anything earlier because I hadn't broken things off with Graham."

"It's kind of quick," her mom said. "But your father was impressed by him."

"He's that kind of guy," Iris said. There was something solid and formidable about Zac. He wasn't like Graham, who, though charming, had at times seemed like he was trying too hard.

"I'm not sure I believe that," Thea said. "Remember what we were talking about at lunch?"

"Thea," Iris said. "I told you that silly plan you had wasn't necessary. You just didn't trust me."

"Sorry, Iris," Thea said, her eyes growing wide. "I was trying to help you. You didn't mention him so I thought that jerk Graham was humiliating you."

"It's okay. I know you were just trying to protect me," Iris said.

"What are you two talking about?" her mom asked, mixing some Aperol spritz drinks for them.

"I suggested Iris hire a guy to act as her date for the wedding weekend. Graham kind of left her high and dry," Thea said. "But you knew that he wasn't right before that text, didn't you?"

"Yes. This weekend he was…well, not what I had hoped he'd be. So I'd already made plans to move on," Iris said.

Oh, God, this had to work, because if it ever came out that she'd hired Zac, she was going to lose a lot of followers. She'd never lied to her audience before. She might stage photos but it was always based in honesty.

Had she made a mistake?

The doorbell rang just as her phone buzzed. She glanced down to see it was a text from Zac. Thea looked at it too. Angel face, I'm here.

"I'll get it."

She left the kitchen and wiped her sweaty hands on her legs as she went down the hall. This would work. She had no choice but to make it work.

She took a deep breath and opened the door. Zac looked good. Damn good. He'd put on a dress shirt and had it neatly tucked into a pair of nice trousers that showed off his slim waist. He had put on dress shoes and socks and his hair was nicely styled. As he took off his aviator-style sunglasses, she realized the navy shirt made his blue eyes more brilliant.

"Hi."

"Hello. I need to talk to you about the wedding."

"Come in," she said. "We can do it later. Not in front of everyone."

Zac stepped into her parents' house as Riley, her mom's thirteen-year-old miniature dachshund, came running down the hall, dancing around Zac's feet and barking.

"Riley, shush," she said, bending to pet the dog.

Zac stooped down next to her and shifted the bouquet of flowers and the bottle of wine he'd brought to the same hand so he could pet the little dog.

"Hello, Riley," he said. Riley loved the attention and started licking Zac's hand. Then after a final pet, Riley trotted back down the hall to the large kitchen where Iris's mom and sister waited.

Iris and Zac stood up. "Thanks for coming tonight. Dad's still at work. Thea and Mom are anxious to meet you. I said we met two days ago."

"Good," he said. "I was in Australia before that."

"Oh, okay. I was on a weekend trip with my ex. They might ask. Maybe we should say we met at the bar today," she said.

"Sounds good."

"Yes."

"Perfect," he said. "You look nice."

"Thanks. So do you. That shirt makes your eyes seem even bluer than before," she said.

He smiled at the compliment. "Should I have shaved? My mom hates stubble, but I figured I didn't want to look like I was trying too hard. Your dad would notice."

"I like the beard," she said, lifting her hand to touch it. It was soft and abraded her fingers slightly.

"Iris, are you going to keep him in the foyer, or can we meet him?" Thea said from the end of the hall.

"We're coming." Iris turned to face her sister and led the way to where Thea was standing. "Zac Bisset, this is my sister, Thea."

"Nice to meet you," he said, holding out his hand.

"Nice to meet you too," Thea said. "Come meet Mom. She's made Aperol spritzes as an aperitif. Do you like those?"

"My brother Darien calls them Kool-Aid for grown-ups."

"He has a point. They are very easy to drink," Thea said.

"Mom, this is Zac. Zac, this is my mom, Corinne," Iris said.

"Nice to meet you, Corinne," Zac said. "These are for you."

He handed her mom the flowers and the wine, then gave her an air kiss on the cheek, which her mom returned. "Thank you, Zac."

"You're welcome. Thank you for inviting me to dinner," he said.

"I'm sure Hal told you that once he met the guy Iris was seeing, I was curious and wanted to meet you too," her mom said.

"He did," Zac admitted.

"No use pretending that we aren't very curious about you," Corinne said.

"I'm an open book," Zac said. "I'm glad to have the chance to meet Iris's family too."

Oh, great. Zac was saying all the right things. And doing everything as if she'd handed him a script. She had to remember it was an act or it would be very easy to fall for him.

Six

Iris walked Zac out after drinks and dessert were over. He had enjoyed meeting her family and it was easy to tell that, despite her online presence and social media persona, Iris lived a very normal life behind-the-scenes.

Thea had done her best to try to trip him up but one thing in their favor was the fact that they'd simply just started dating. There weren't a lot of things a two-day old couple were expected to already know about each other.

"Thea was tough," he said as he leaned back against his car. The sky was clear, and though the stars weren't as visible here as they were in the middle of the ocean, it was still a beautiful night.

"She's a pain in the butt," Iris said. "But I think this was really good practice. So I know I said we wouldn't need to be on Nantucket until Thursday but would you mind going over tomorrow? Adler wants to catch up and of course meet you before everything gets started. She's my bestie so she's curious."

"Not at all. Actually, about that—" he said. He probably should mention that Adler was his cousin at this point.

"Good," Iris interrupted. "I'm going to be bringing some staff with me so we could meet at the hotel in Nantucket or drive down together."

"Staff?" he asked. "Besides me?"

"Yes. I have a glam squad who makes sure I'm camera-ready. Also my production assistant will be there. Aside from my bridal duties, I'm going to be doing a few on-air interviews as part of the recorded show. You'll be free to do your own thing during that time."

"I didn't realize the wedding was going to be televised," Zac said. "I can't drive down with you. I have a meeting with my team tomorrow. I'll meet you at the hotel."

"Yes, it's part of a show that features destination weddings. Adler's wedding will kick it off. Because my reality TV show is pretty much *my life* and the events I attend, I'll be doing some live shoots that will be aired later. I want you in some of them but just to add flavor—that's the part we spoke about earlier."

"Of course," he said, but he really wished he'd paid better attention when they'd negotiated terms because this was sounding more like work than he'd imagined. "Do I need a glam squad?"

She laughed. "No. KT and Stephan will get you camera-ready if need them but I really want to just use shots of the two of us from the weekend in a montage. I don't want you to feel pressured especially since that isn't what you signed up for."

He was beginning to feel like he didn't know what he'd signed up for. Iris wasn't what he'd expected. She intrigued him and he wondered if he'd ever really figure her out. It had been easy to see her as the good daughter tonight but she had demonstrated a wicked sense of humor and her family did a lot of gentle teasing. It was very different from the formal meals he was used to when his father was present. Then everyone was polite and traded thinly veiled barbs. The dinner with the Collins family tonight reminded him more of the meals he had when it was just his mom and his siblings.

Hal Collins was a very different man than August Bisset. Where August was domineering and forceful, Hal was… somehow gentler but in no way less shrewd.

"Great. Will they be staying in the same suite as us?"

"No. Definitely not," she said. "I want us to be able to have some downtime when we can be ourselves."

"Angel face, I'm never not myself," he said.

"Is that true? Even when you told my dad that you were a fan of opera?" she asked.

"Well, I mean, I do like *The Magic Flute*," Zac said. "But you know how it is when you meet the parents. You don't insult things they love."

"Very true," she said. "It's a good thing you'll be in training, otherwise I think he might invite us to join them the next time they go."

"I wouldn't mind at all. My mom loves opera as does my gran. On Sundays before brunch, they both would fill the house with music. Sometimes opera, sometimes jazz, and when we got old enough, rock."

"Sounds like a wonderful tradition," she said. "I would love to meet your family someday."

Uh, yeah. "About that."

"What?"

"I didn't want you to recognize my last name at first, but I'm actually Adler's cousin. My mom is Juliette Bisset, her aunt and godmother. You'll get to meet more of my family than you probably want to," he said.

"What?" she asked. "Why didn't you say anything to-night at dinner?"

"I was trying to let your family get to know me. Plus it's pretentious to introduce myself as August Bisset's son," he said.

"I get that, but you should have said something," she said. "Why do you need my dad to find investors then? Can't you fund the run yourself?"

She looked angry and hurt and he realized he should have handled this better. "I'm sorry, Iris. I never meant to hurt you."

"You didn't. This is a business arrangement. I just like to know all the facts. Does Dad know?"

"Yes, he recognized me and I didn't deny it."

"So why play games with me?" she asked.

He tipped his head back, looking up at the evening sky.

"I'm sorry. I didn't mean to hurt you. I could do it with the help of my father and my brother, Logan, the current CEO of the family business, but the truth is they both put too many strings on the money and I don't want to answer to them. I started captaining to find my own thing and if I asked them for money…it wouldn't be mine anymore."

She folded her arms under her breasts and narrowed her eyes as she studied him. "That makes a certain kind of sense. I felt the same way when I started my own brand. I had Leta's backing but I knew I wanted to establish myself before I went to Collins Combine for an investment. It was more fulfilling knowing I'd made it on my own."

"That's what I want," he said. "I'm very successful in my field on someone else's team but I want to be the cap-tain of a winning America's Cup yacht and the only way I can do that is with your help."

"Is there anything else you are hiding?" she asked. "I don't what there to be any more surprises."

"Well, I'm not faking it when I kiss you."

"No. Don't do that. This will only work if we treat it like a temporary thing," she said. "I bought you for three months."

"Angel face, I don't work like that," he said. "I'm not good at faking it and frankly, I'm better at it than you. You were way too tense at the beginning of the meal, waiting for me to—"

"I know," she said. "It's just my business and everything is on the line. I think I made a huge mistake but there's no going back."

Her honesty undid him. He was ready to push her until she admitted that they should sleep together, that the attraction between them was hotter than the sun on a summer's day. But he saw that she was confused by the attraction and this offer she'd made him, which was out of character for her.

He noticed the blinds shifting in the front room of the house and realized that they had been out here too long. "Someone's watching us. Want to go someplace and talk? I have a town house that's not far from here or we could go to a bar."

She sighed. "Okay. Is the town house an Airbnb?"

"No," he said. "It's one my family owns. We have property all over the world and the place in Boston is one my mom uses when she comes up here to visit my gran."

"There is so much I don't know about you," she said.

"That's fine. We've only been dating for two days," he reminded her. "You okay to follow me?"

"Yes. But text me the address in case we get separated."

The blinds at the front of the house were still askew so he leaned in, putting his hand on her waist. Then he kissed her gently on the cheek. "Just to allay any suspicions."

She sighed as her hands curled around his biceps. "I like kissing you too. That's why I don't want to do it too often."

"Let's talk about it at my place," he said. "Want to leave your car here? I can bring you back to get it later."

"No," she said.

He stepped back, putting his hands up. "Okay. Whatever you want."

"Let's go."

He waited for her to get into her beige BMW and then got into his car. He pulled around her in the large circle drive and she followed him the short distance to the town house. There was ample parking for two cars in the driveway and he led her into the house.

She paused in the entrance hall, looking at the picture of the Bissets on the left wall. It included his extended family and had been taken earlier this year when Mari had announced her engagement to Inigo Velasquez.

"I know your sister," Iris said. "Not well, but I do consider her a friend. The ripples from this arrangement we have just keep growing."

Iris shook her head and then walked past him into the house. "Which way to...wherever you want to talk?"

"Second door on the left, wall switch as soon as you enter. I'll be right behind you," he said.

She moved down the hall the way she had moved in the boardroom earlier. She was getting back into businesswoman mode and he was the first to admit he preferred her in relaxed mode. But she was in charge. She had concerns and worries that he knew nothing about and frankly, he didn't need to. They had a deal.

He'd almost forgotten it while they'd been at dinner. Her family had been so warm and welcoming he wanted to be the new boyfriend—for real. He wanted to somehow believe that if he—was what? Someone completely different?

He couldn't fit into that domestic scene in any scenario that wasn't pretend. He spent most of his life on a yacht and he wasn't planning to stop anytime soon. His life was on boats.

She'd taken a seat on the leather sofa in the living room. As much as he wanted to sit next to her, he walked to the large chambray-colored armchair and sat down, putting his feet up on the hassock. "So…"

"Zac, I'm sorry that I've put you in this situation. And I'm not even sure why you agreed. I know you want investors and I sort of understand wanting to do this without your family's interference, but you didn't need to agree to my dating plan in order to make that happen," she said. "I think because we're going to be lying to everyone about our relationship, we need to be honest with each other. We need to be clear so that there are no misunderstandings. Does that sound agreeable to you?"

"Yes, it does," he said. "That's why I told you I'm hot for you."

Her eyes widened for the shortest second and then she nodded. "Me too. But that's a complication I'm not sure I'm ready to handle. To be fair, you should know that I'm not very good at sex."

He was shocked for a second. Then he shook his head. "I highly doubt you're not good. Both players share the responsibility for that."

"Uh, oh…okay," she said. Then she groaned. "Why did I even say that? Even though my reputation is for saying the right thing and hosting fab events, in my personal life… I'm not as together as all that."

"I like it. It's real. I bet your viewers would get it too," he said. "Have you thought about being yourself?"

She shook her head. "No one wants that. Sure, it would be amusing for a short while as a novelty but everyone wants you to stick to the image they have of you. Everyone."

She sounded very sure and he wondered who had been disappointed in the real Iris. But that wasn't a question he needed answered right now.

"What's next?"

Next? She had no idea. She needed to get focused and stop thinking about how strong his arms had felt under her fingers. Or how warm his breath had been on her cheek. Or how she'd wanted one more real kiss instead of that brush of his lips earlier.

"Let's get the wedding details sorted out," she said. "Then I think we can plan to meet on Nantucket tomorrow."

"Sounds good. What are the details?" he asked.

"You might already know them," she said. "Since you're family-of-the-bride. Let me pull up the schedule Adler sent." Iris took out her phone and called up her calendar. "So next Thursday is the welcome lunch at her gran's— your gran's place, then the sailing competition around the harbor. I guess we should do well at that."

"We should since I'm captaining one of the yachts. Are you a good sailor?"

"I'm okayish. I really don't swim well, but I do like being on the water," she said. No use going into details of how she liked to get below deck with a few drinks to calm her nerves.

"Great. That will be fun," he said. "We can do some romantic things on the boat."

She just vaguely nodded. *Like what?* she wanted to know, but kept that question to herself. "Then there's the clambake in the evening. That's a really full day. I think we should just be clear about being a new couple, touchy but not over the top with the PDA. I mean, we want to be cute and romantic, not X-rated."

He crossed his arms over his chest and nodded his head

a few times. "I can do that. Am I staying with you in your suite? Or do I need my own place?"

"I was thinking the suite," she said. "Unless we should just not be lovers…"

"We're not lovers," he reminded her.

"I know that. I mean, will it make me seem too prudish if I don't have you in my suite? It's got two rooms so you can stay with me, and we can let anyone who's inclined to dwell on it, think what they want."

He started laughing.

"What?"

"*Inclined to dwell on it*—are you kidding?"

"No. I mean, it was kind of fussy of me, wasn't it? If people are going to gossip, it's up to them what they think."

"I agree. So, what's on Friday?"

"The golf scramble. Adler is pairing up with her side of the wedding party so we'll be separated for that. Then we have the rehearsal and the rehearsal dinner. Saturday is the big event, so I'll be busy helping Adler get ready and then there's the sunset ceremony followed by dancing all night. Can you dance?"

"I can. Mom insisted I learn. She said women like dancing and a man who says he won't is a turnoff."

"I agree," Iris said. "All that's left is brunch on Sunday and then we head home. Where will you go?"

"I'll stay in Nantucket for a few days unless your father has the investors ready by Monday then I'll come back to Boston with you," he said. "We can see each other frequently until the money is ready and then I'll have to start putting things in motion."

"That's settled then," she said. "I'll forward you the schedule. Remember, I'll be doing some filming as I mentioned. I'll also probably do some photos for my social accounts so I'll need you for those, but I'll use the events we're at for a backdrop."

She put her phone back into her bag and looked around the living room. It was very traditional but with sort of homey touches. There was a large landscape painting of Boston Harbor on one wall and candid family photos on the table by the sofa. She couldn't help smiling at the one of a teenaged Zac standing at the helm of a yacht. "When did you start yachting?"

"When I was nine. It was either that or go with Logan and Darien to the summer internship at Bisset Industries. And…well, Dad and I butt heads a lot so Mom suggested I try sailing lessons, which I loved. She calls me her water baby… I'm a Pisces."

"I'm an Aries but everyone says I'm not typical of the sign," she said.

"Uh, whoever says that doesn't know you at all," he commented.

She stuck her tongue out at him. "I am a tad bossy."

"Yeah, that's one way of putting it," he said.

She liked him. There was a part of her, the one that still secretly longed for a partner, that wished this was real. But she knew she'd never have talked to him if it hadn't been for Thea's suggestion. And he'd never be here if she hadn't made her offer. It was the only kind of relationship she was good at. It was fun and easy because she knew what she was getting and that it would be ending.

Was that really all she was going to have with him?

It was disappointing but she was glad that she had the chance to know him. Because he was so different from the other men in her life. And he made her feel like she was different…well, not different so much as that she could be herself and that was okay.

She realized that she wasn't trying to impress him and she'd have never guessed that would be so freeing.

"I guess I'll be going. Thank you, Zac."

He stood up when she did, and she turned to walk toward the door but he stopped her.

"Angel face?"

"Yes?"

"One more thing," he said, pulling her into his arms and giving her the kiss she'd been craving all night.

Seven

She was so cute, and it had been pretty hard to resist kissing her. He'd been thinking about it all night as he'd watched her and her family interact. He'd grown up in a reasonably supportive household but what he'd seen at the Collins family dinner table was something he'd truly never experienced. There was real love in the family and though he and his siblings had a close bond, their father had always encouraged them to compete against each other. To prove themselves to him that they were the best of the Bisset children.

Darien had reacted by smoking a lot as a teenager and then just skipping the family business, to leave room for Logan who was a lion and had no trouble going in for the kill when he sensed a weakness. That had been the one reason why growing up Zac hadn't wanted to go to the office with his older brothers. As much as he'd wanted August Bisset's approval, he never wanted to have to cut down Darien or Logan to get it.

Kissing Iris made him rethink the entire agreement he'd made with her. He didn't want to be bound by a contract, and for the first time in his life, he felt like he was pretending to be something he wasn't. It didn't sit well with him. He lifted his head to stare down into her face. Her eyes were closed but as soon as he broke the kiss, they flew open.

She put her hand on her lips and then she stepped back. "Did I do something wrong? I'll tell you in all honesty I'm not that great at this. I mean, the posing and looking like I'm enjoying a romantic embrace I can handle but the real—"

He put his finger over her mouth to stem the words that she couldn't seem to control. "Angel face, you're so damned good that you're making me regret I only agreed to be your man temporarily."

She tipped her head to the side and smiled up at him. "Really?"

He nodded.

"You're way sweeter than I bet you let anyone see," she said.

"I'm not sweet," he said. "That's lust talking."

"Lust? Is it because you've been at sea for so long?" she asked.

It was odd to see the woman who had negotiated with him in the boardroom like she was preparing to win *Shark Tank* be so shy when it came to personal relationships. Then again, he knew that everyone dealt with intimacy in his or her own way. Normally he liked to make it a competition because he wasn't comfortable letting his guard down.

But he was quickly coming to realize that he couldn't make this a game. She wasn't the kind of player who would be able to handle this. And that changed everything for him.

She wasn't what he'd expected; even dinner at her family's home hadn't been what he was used to. Maybe he should change his thinking and acknowledge that she wasn't going to fit in any mold he had for her.

She wasn't just the lifestyle guru with the perfect image and confidence to boot. She was real and that enchanted him as nothing else could. Maybe she was his siren, tempting him with something so outside of his normal world that he would unknowingly crash against the rocks to get to her.

But at this moment, he didn't care. His mind might be trying to send out a warning, but his hard-on wasn't having any part of it. He pulled her back into his arms. "This has nothing to do with our deal."

"Why not?"

"Because I want you regardless of that contract," he said. Also, he realized that as a Bisset he wasn't about to let someone else be in charge. He was a bit chagrined to realize he had more traits in common with his father than he wanted to admit.

"I don't... Will you still honor the bargain no matter what the outcome tonight?" she asked.

"Yes, of course," he said. "What kind of men have you—never mind—I really don't want to know. I'm not going to back out now."

"Okay," she said. "I want to say one more time—"

"Don't. Forget about whatever you've experienced in the past, Iris. We've never been together before and I feel like we should both be ready for whatever comes our way."

"Whatever," she said, and he saw a glimpse of the control freak he'd witnessed in the boardroom cross her expression. She closed her eyes and took a deep breath.

He realized thinking wasn't going to help her relax. She wanted him; he'd felt it in her kiss. But she was afraid to move forward.

He pulled her back inside his house and lifted her off her feet, carrying her down the hall to the living room. The room was in shadow when he put her on her feet in front of the French doors that led to the patio.

She tipped her head back as he kept his arms around her waist. "Okay, Google, play 'They Can't Take That Away' by Billie Holiday."

The home assistant acknowledged his request and the music started. He pulled Iris more fully into his arms, dancing with her in front of the doors that led to the backyard. He held her loosely because she wasn't the kind of woman who responded to grasping, greedy passion, at least at this point. There might come a time later in their relationship—he stopped himself from continuing with that thought. Their relationship had an expiration date. It would end. So there was no point in holding anything back.

He could be himself and he could enjoy all of her because there wasn't any expectation that they'd have more than this time together.

He lowered his head and their eyes met. Hers were dreamy, and for the first time since he'd met her, she seemed to be relaxed. Her guard was completely lowered, and he realized that she was probably thinking the same way as he was. That this moment was all they had. There were no consequences.

He put his thumb on her chin and tipped her head back a bit more so he could kiss her again. He swayed to the music and tried to ignore the white-hot passion that was making his blood flow heavier in his veins and hardening his erection. He tried not to focus on the fact that he could tell she wasn't wearing a padded bra because he felt her hard nipples pressed against his chest when she wrapped her arms around his neck and went up on her tiptoes to kiss him.

He tried to pretend that this was like every other first

time he'd been with a woman, but his gut and his heart warned him that it wasn't. His mind wasn't engaged, had been shut down, and consequences and repercussions weren't a consideration. All he wanted was this night with Iris and to squeeze every bit of emotion from it and her that he could.

Iris had to get out of her own way, and once she was in Zac's arms as he danced her around the living room, she sort of did. Part of it was the magic of Billie Holiday—the song was so old-fashioned and such a standard that Iris felt no pressure to be overtly sexy or to bring it. But the other part was just about being with Zac. He sang under his breath as he danced them around the living room; his tone was a bit off-key, but it was endearing. Something less than perfect in the breathtakingly sexy man.

When he kissed her, she forgot everything. She stopped worrying about making sure she kept her stomach sucked in and didn't breathe too heavily. She forgot all the tips she'd read about how to turn a man on and just relaxed. Her skin was wonderfully sensitized and her heart felt like it was beating a bit too fast. When she wrapped her arms around his shoulders, going up on tiptoe to deepen the kiss, she felt the brush of his erection against her stomach. She rubbed against him and would have pulled back, but he made this groan deep in his throat and then reached down to cup her butt, lifting her higher against him so that she felt the tip of his hard-on against her feminine center.

She'd never felt anything like this with a man before. Sure, when she masturbated, she could get there but this was the first time that a kiss and a touch had completely overwhelmed her.

She suspected that Zac was slowly leading her along and she didn't care because it felt so good, so right and exactly like she'd always thought sex should be. It wasn't tongues shoved down her throat or hands that seemed to grasp and pinch her breasts just a little too hard. It was soft caresses and a kiss that she never wanted to end.

He shifted her in his arms as the music changed. It was that song "You Belong To Me." Her heartbeat increased, a warning briefly going off in her mind that he couldn't belong to her, not for long. But she shushed it. The last thing she wanted was to start thinking and lose the feelings that Zac was stirring to life inside of her. When he spun them around and lifted her into his arms again, the world tilted and shifted until she was lying on her back on the couch.

"Still happy to be here with me?" he asked.

She nodded. "Yes."

"Good. If I do anything that makes you uncomfortable, tell me," he said.

"Same."

He laughed in that big kind way of his and she couldn't help smiling back. "Honestly, there isn't anything you could ask me to do that I wouldn't."

"That sounds like a challenge," she said, but she knew she wouldn't dare let herself ask him for anything too risqué.

"I hope you take it up," he said. "But not tonight."

He undid the buttons on his shirt and shrugged out of it, putting it on the coffee table before he sat down on the couch, brushing against her hips. He reached for her sandals and removed first one and then the other.

She reached out to touch his chest. It was covered in a soft mat of blond hair that tickled her fingers when she ran them over his hot skin. His muscles underneath were hard and he bunched them as she touched him. She ran her finger around his nipple and watched it harden under her caress and felt her own nipples do the same.

She drew her finger down the center of his chest and felt the jagged, raised skin that indicated a scar. She leaned closer but in the low lighting there was no way to really see it. She wanted to know more about it, but not now. She let her finger drift lower, following the line of hair that tapered as it approached his belly button. He had the kind of washboard abs that she'd only ever seen in magazines or on TV.

He sat very still and let her explore to her heart's content, but she noticed his erection growing bigger as her touch neared his cock. Her fingers tingled with the need to touch him, but what if she did and he suddenly got impatient, bringing all of this exploring to an end?

She sighed and lowered her hand, tracing the fly of his dress slacks and feeling the hard ridge underneath. He canted his hips forward, thrusting his erection against her fingers, and she curved them around his shaft, stroking him through his pants.

She felt hot and creamy between her legs and she knew she wanted him. She also felt hollow and empty like she wanted him inside of her. It didn't matter that these magical feelings would disappear when that happened. She still craved the feel of him inside her. She shifted around on the couch, reached up under the skirt of her dress and removed her panties.

She tried to straddle him, but he stopped her.

"We aren't in a hurry," he said.

"I am," she admitted. "If we wait too long, this feeling might go away."

She moved awkwardly, because once she started talking, the self-consciousness she thought she'd banished was back. She tried to straddle his lap and lost her balance, falling backward. But he caught her in his arms and lifted her, his biceps flexing under her hands as he settled her on his lap.

"I've got you," he said.

She couldn't say for certain if there was a hint of promise in his words or if she was just imagining it, but she decided to just follow her gut and take it for what she wanted it to be. Take him for what she wanted him to be. The kind of lover she'd always dreamed of finding but never had.

She tunneled her fingers through his thick blond hair and lowered herself, taking his mouth the way she wished he'd take her.

Zac slid his hands up under Iris's skirt and cupped her naked butt as she deepened their kiss. He'd wanted to take this slow, wanted to do this at a pace that worked for her, but at this point he was past thinking about timing. He wanted her and each breath he took sharpened his desire.

He was so hot and hard that he felt like he was going to explode unless he got inside her. He drew her down against his hard-on, thrusting up against her, frustrated by the layers of fabric separating them. He reached between them, pushing her skirt up and out of his way, the backs of his fingers brushing against her warmth. She moaned and lifted her head. He touched her again, holding her with his palm, and she closed her eyes, her head falling back as she gyrated against his hand. When he touched her most intimate flesh, her hands on his shoulders tightened. She made little circular motions with her hips and he adjusted his touch until she was moving more rapidly against him. He shifted his hand lower and entered her with one finger and she threw her head back as he did and moaned much louder this time.

He let her ride his hand until she screamed his name and seemed to come against him. She collapsed against his chest and he held her for a moment before she reached between them and lowered his zipper. He stopped her with his hand on top of hers. If she touched his naked cock, he wasn't going to be able to think of anything but taking her and making her his.

"Are you on the pill?" he asked.

She hesitated and swallowed hard. "Yes. Of course."

"Okay, good. I've got condoms in the other room," he said. "Want me to use one?"

She chewed her lower lip between her teeth.

"I know it's not romantic but a minute of talking now is worth it," he reassured her.

"Yes, I would prefer you use one."

"Wrap your legs around my waist and your arms around my shoulders."

She did it and he stood up, putting his hands on her backside to keep her in place as he walked to the bedroom that was down the hall. He went to the bed and sat down so that she was still on his lap.

"They are in the nightstand."

She reached over and flicked on the lamp first and then opened the drawer. Every time she moved, she rubbed against him and it was all he could do not to twist his hips, find her opening with the tip of his erection and thrust up into her. He was reciting maritime law in his head to keep from doing it and when she finally held up the condom packet, he took it from her with more exuberance than finesse. She slipped back on his lap, closer to his knees, and he reached between them to put the condom on.

Once he had it on, she looked at his erection and then back up at him. He wasn't sure what he read in her expression, but he almost felt like she was unsure again.

Damn.

"Do you still want to do this?" he asked. His voice sounded almost guttural since he was so turned on. Stopping was going to be hard but he'd do it because he never wanted to see fear or disgust on Iris's face.

"Yes," she said, putting her hands on either side of his face and lowering her mouth to kiss him again. She shifted and the skirt of her dress brushed over him. He bunched it in his fist and lifted it all the way up and out of the way. She shifted around, then reached between them to position him between her legs. She opened her eyes and their gazes met as she drove herself down on him.

Damn.

She fit him so tightly, like the best kind of glove, and he wanted more. He had intended to let her set the pace, but he couldn't. He fell back on the bed and rolled over so she was under him. She held on to his shoulders as he brought his lips down hard on hers and thrust his tongue into her mouth. She sucked it hard as he drove up into her, taking her at a pace that was faster and harder than he'd intended. His conscience made him slow down and he started to pull back but she tightened her grip on him and whispered in his ear, "Don't stop."

He didn't stop. He just kept thrusting inside her until he heard those cries he'd heard when she'd orgasmed earlier as she came again he felt her body tightening around his. He drove himself faster and faster into her until he came in one long rush, emptying himself inside of her. He kept thrusting until he was sated and rolled to his side, pulling her into his arms and stroking her back while his heartbeat slowed.

She put her hand on his chest and then rested her head on top of it. She sighed and he lifted his head to look down at her.

"What?"

"Thanks for that. I have to be honest and tell you I wasn't expecting…"

He waited to see what else she'd say. It was clear to him that she hadn't enjoyed sex in the past, but he doubted she wanted to discuss that with him.

"What?" he asked again.

"You."

She rolled to her side and sat up after saying that. Then she got off the bed and went to the bathroom. He watched her go, very aware that she wasn't the only one who'd been caught off guard tonight.

He hadn't been expecting her either.

Eight

Arriving on Nantucket one week later made Iris feel like she was in total vacay mode. It didn't matter that her glam squad had gotten her ready early this morning at her place in Boston to make sure she was casual yet sophisticated or that she had fifteen minutes before she had to meet the photographer on the beach to do a photo shoot for the summer social media shares. As she stood on the balcony of her hotel suite, listening to the crashing of the waves on the beach and smelling the salty air, she felt like she could breathe.

Sleeping with Zac hadn't been her best idea, she knew that, but damn, for the first time in her life she'd felt more than just the urge to get it over with when she'd been having sex. Zac had made her realize that something she'd thought she could live without—an active sex life—wasn't true. She'd had no idea that the men she'd been with hadn't been good lovers. To be fair, it could have been that she wasn't a right fit for those men.

Did that mean she was a right fit for Zac?

Or was it simply because she'd hired him for the week-end that she had relaxed? She wished she could talk to Adler and tell her the truth about what was going on. But she didn't want anyone to know she'd hired herself a man for the weekend.

Her phone pinged and she glanced at it. It was a text from Adler.

Hey, girl! Are you on the island?

Just got in. I have a photo shoot in about ten minutes but want to catch up after?

Yes. Where's the photo shoot? I'll come by and watch.

Private beach two houses down from your gran's place.

See ya there. Is the new guy with you?

He had a few meetings this morning. He'll be here this afternoon.

Perfect. Want to have dinner with Nick and me tonight?

Let me double-check with him.

Iris took a deep breath. This was what she needed to hap-pen. She wanted people in her life to accept Zac as her real boyfriend. And he'd agreed to do whatever she asked for the weekend. She texted to ask if he'd be available around six for dinner. He responded with the thumbs-up. She let Adler know they'd both be there.

Should she mention to Adler that the man she was dating was her cousin? She wanted to tell her in person rather than over the phone. That kind of conversation was going to bring up all kinds of questions about Zac. She tossed her phone on the bed and fell back on the covers, staring at the pristine white ceiling as if she looked hard enough, she'd find some cosmic answer to the question.

There was a knock on her door and she hopped up to go and answer it. It was KT from her glam squad. KT always looked so boho and chic, with her long legs and straight brown hair that she'd styled in a side braid today. She wore a pair of tiny denim shorts with a flouncy top. It was a look that Iris envied but she had never been able to pull off. She was too intense for that kind of outfit. By contrast, she wore a broderie white sundress with wooden buttons and a pair of Hermès sandals.

"Parking is a bear near the beach," KT said. "We should leave now. Stephan is already there and the photographer is setting up."

"I hope the weather holds out," Iris said, grabbing her phone and purse and leading the way out of the room. "There were storms yesterday."

"It's gorg out there today. As soon as your photo shoot is over, I'm going for a run on the beach."

"Sounds like a plan. I shouldn't need you until tomorrow for the clambake. I have the outfit you styled for me and know how to do my paddleboarding makeup… I really hope I don't fall off the board. Did you see that can happen?"

Her assistant put her arm around Iris's shoulders. Everyone in her inner circle knew she struggled with a fear of water. She was slowly getting over it but there were times when it became overwhelming.

"You'll be fine. My sister says the key to paddleboarding is a strong core," KT said.

"A strong core? I'm wearing Spanx 24/7. My core isn't soft at all."

"You'll do fine," KT said. "I've never known you to fail when you put your mind to something. Just remember that your followers are watching and want you to succeed. You're living that hashtag best life."

"I am, aren't I? Also the camera crew will be shooting the paddleboarding so I have that as an added incentive to stay on."

"Perfect. Plus, you'll want to impress your new man," KT said. "You're usually all about keeping up the perfect image so I know you'll do fine."

The perfect image. Was that what she was all about? "Do you think that comes off as me trying too hard?"

"Girl, it's your brand. I think it suits you." KT followed her out of the resort to her car and they both got in.

Iris wanted to be chill about everything that KT had said but it was stirring up the thought that maybe she had been trying too hard for so long that even she didn't know how to relax and just be herself. That brought her back to sex with Zac… Had it been Zac and his fabulously fit body and sensual moves that had been the difference or the fact that she hadn't been trying to be who she thought he wanted her to be?

The answer wasn't going to just show up. Plus, did it matter? He was only with her until Sunday and then for a few more dates and photos before he was out of her life for good. She'd be back to her usual self. Which was exactly what she wanted. Truly.

Now if only she could convince herself of that.

Zac left Boston late, got stuck in traffic, and when he finally arrived on Nantucket, he was ready for a beer or two. He and Dev had spent most of the day on the phone or on Skype calls talking to people that they wanted on their team. Most were excited at the prospect of a new team, but a few were skeptical that they would be able to pull off a winning run with only two years to get the team going.

Zac wasn't interested in naysayers or nonbelievers, so even when Dev had argued to keep a few of the skeptics in the potential pool, Zac had cut them. If he'd learned one lesson from his father, it was to surround himself only with people who had the same goals. His dad had often said if a person was wishy-washy before you shook hands, they weren't going to become more committed after the deal was done.

He rubbed the back of his neck as he followed the map to the hotel where he'd be staying with Iris for the next few days, which he realized was going to be awkward for everyone if he didn't let his mom know. He thought about texting but she would only call him back so he used the hands-free voice command to dial her number.

"Hello, honey. Where are you?" his mom asked when she answered the phone.

"Just got off the ferry," he answered her.

"That's great. Shall we set a place for you at dinner?"

"Not tonight," he said. "I'm not going to stay at Gran's either."

"Why not?" she asked.

All of the sweet chattiness was now gone from her voice. She'd sent all of them an itinerary for Adler's wedding and she'd been very clear that she expected them to show up to all of the events on it.

"I met a woman in Boston, Mom. Turns out she's a friend of Adler's and I'm going to be staying with her."

"Wow, that's quick work," his mom said. "Who is she?"

"Iris Collins."

"Oh, I thought she was dating someone else. She's really nice. How did you meet her?" she asked, chatty again now that she knew he was with Iris.

Zac had never realized what a difference dating a woman who was in his social circle would make. He'd pretty much always picked someone who was in the world of competitive yachting because those were the women he knew the best, so this was a new experience. He wondered if this was how Mari felt when she'd gotten engaged to Inigo Velasquez. The Formula One driver was definitely on Juliette Bisset's approved list.

"We met in a bar," he said.

"Oh," his mom said.

"*Oh?* Don't be judgy, Mom. You and Dad met at a weekend house party," he said. "I'm sure there were drinks served there."

"Did I sound judgy? I didn't mean to be. I was just hoping that you would have a meet-cute story."

"We don't live in a rom-com," he said.

"I know. I just always hope that all of my kids will have a big romance and Iris is definitely a step up—"

"Mom, I'm a second away from driving through a make-believe tunnel and losing my signal with you," he warned her.

"Point taken. Bring her with you to lunch tomorrow. Your father wants us to host the Williamses. Did you see my text?"

"I did and I will. I love you, Mom. I'll talk to you tomorrow," he said.

"Bye, sweetie, love you too."

She disconnected the call and he continued to make his way toward the hotel. His mom was not going to be very happy with him when he and Iris broke up. But that was a problem for Future Zac to deal with. Right now his mom was pleased that he'd landed someone like Iris. He wondered if he could have done it if she hadn't been desperate for a date. He liked to think so, but he wasn't sure.

He didn't know what kind of guy she usually went for but he was pretty sure she didn't often go for athletes or, as his dad like to refer to him, sea bums.

That night together last week, though… If he'd really been dating her that would have changed things for real between them. Instead he had no clue what it had done. He wasn't thinking of when he'd be able to walk away from her. In fact he'd been remembering how she'd felt in his arms all day at odd moments. Dev had accused him of losing focus, but Zac knew that his focus was fine.

It was just on Iris and not on the race or his yacht or the team he was building. Maybe there had been more of a reason to stay away from women in his own social set before this. After all, a sailor would know the score. A fellow sailor would know that he was only interested in having fun until the wind changed, and he was back on the ocean pitting himself against all the other crafts out there. Trying to be number one and conquer the sea.

He followed the signs to the hotel, pulling into line for the valet. As he did, he remembered that little sound that Iris had made when he'd entered her and the surprise on her face when she'd come long and hard. He wanted to see that look on her face again. He couldn't wait to hold her again.

Damn.

He was screwed.

It was a good thing that they had a signed contract. Otherwise he'd be tempted into thinking that Iris was the kind of woman who could make him stay ashore.

He stepped outside into the humid summer afternoon, blaming his agitation on the heat instead of the woman who'd paid him to be her companion.

* * *

Adler Osborn stood on the widow's walk and looked out at the storms brewing on the ocean. Only three more days until she'd be Mrs. Nicholas Williams and she couldn't wait. She'd had a text from her fiancé that he was en route and would meet her at the Crab Shack in town in twenty minutes. She couldn't wait to see Nick.

Growing up, her life had been unconventional to say the least. She'd never known her mother, who'd died when she was twenty-five and her father was a famous rock star who truly lived the sex, drugs and rock 'n' roll lifestyle, but also had oddly been a devoted parent. He wanted her with him on the road but her mother's family had wanted her attending the right schools and getting the proper upbringing.

Her Aunt Juliette and Gran had been fierce negotiators with her father, and they'd worked out a deal where she'd split time between two vastly different worlds. Though she loved both halves of her family very much, she'd always longed to be part of one world. It was hard to go from boarding school and socializing with a lot of rules to life on the road and no rules.

Until college, when she'd met Iris Collins and the two had become best friends, Adler had felt torn in half by her two lives. But Iris had helped her sort herself out. One of the things that Adler had realized was that she wanted all those things she'd never had growing up. A proper home—not a boarding school or tour bus. A home that she came back to every single night. A family that was her own. She wanted a husband, kids and the whole suburban life. But she needed someone who could understand her. Really got her. Not a guy who wanted entrée into her father's debauched world. Or who wanted to attend the jet-set parties her Aunt Juliette threw.

Nick Williams had been perfect. A borderline workaholic who was rich as Jay-Z and didn't give a crap about what anyone thought. He was fun, had the prettiest blue eyes she'd ever seen and the sexiest ass. When she'd first met him, she'd been dazzled. And it was only when things got rough for her, with her father's heart attack, and she found Nick standing by her side, putting work on the back burner to be there for her, that she realized that she'd found the man she wanted for the rest of her life.

She was no longer the illegitimate daughter of a debauched rock star and the runaway heiress who died of a drug overdose, but a respectable member of society. Someone who stayed out of the headlines and lived a normal life.

Gran had said that normal was overrated but then again Gran had been normal her entire life. Adler, not so much. And Iris was another one who lived and breathed for small-town suburbia…the dream, as far as Adler was concerned.

She texted Nick that Iris and her new man were meeting them. He rang back instead of texting.

"Hey, sexy!"

"Hey, gorgeous. Who's the new guy? I thought she was dating Douchey the Third," Nick said.

"I don't have the deets but he arrived about thirty minutes ago and I invited them to join us for dinner. I want to meet him and thought it would be weird if I just showed up in her hotel suite alone."

Nick laughed. "You might seem like a one-woman interrogation squad."

"I know. So, I thought if we met them together, then you could help me make sure he's nothing like Douchey."

"Good plan. Am I picking you up?"

"Nah. Uncle Auggie has just arrived and I think I'll spare us that," she said. Her uncle didn't like her fiancé, which didn't bother Adler because she'd never been a big fan of her uncle. The fact that he'd cheated on her Aunt Juliette hadn't made him Gran's favorite either.

"Thanks for that. You can never doubt that I really love you, gorgeous, because there is no way I'd put up with August Bisset otherwise."

"I know it," she said, feeling her heart fill with joy. "See ya soon."

"See ya," he said, disconnecting the call.

Adler checked her makeup and then grabbed her clutch and headed downstairs. Michael was carrying his silver tray with two martinis and a bourbon neat to the sitting room.

"Will you be joining the others?"

"Nope. Heading out for the evening. I'll probably stay over at Nick's tonight," she said. Since Nick wasn't comfortable staying at her gran's place, he'd purchased a cottage for them that was two streets over. That way she could see the family she loved, and he didn't have to.

"Heading out, dear?" Gran called as Adler walked past the sitting room.

Her Uncle August was sitting in the large leather armchair and had his back to her. His hair was mostly gray now but at one time it had been black. He turned and smiled at her.

"Hello, Adler. Juliette was just telling me that you're all set for the wedding," he said.

"I'm getting there. Still a few last-minute things to take care of," she said, coming over to give him a hug. The thing about Uncle Auggie was that he wasn't a jerk. He was charming and fun. As her Aunt Juliette said, he was hard to stay mad at.

"If there's anything I can do, let me know," he said, then took a deep breath. "I know that there's some tension because of the business dealings Logan and I have had with your fiancé and I want to put that behind us. We'd like to have Nick and his family to dinner tomorrow night. Just so we can all get to know each other. Put everyone's mind's at ease."

Adler was surprised by the offer. "Let me speak to Nick tonight and let him know. That should work with our schedule since most people aren't arriving until Thursday."

"Great," he said, sitting back down. "I'll get Carter to make all the arrangements."

"I'll handle this, Auggie," Aunt Juliette said. "Have fun tonight, Adler. See you tomorrow?"

"Yes," she said, kissing her gran and aunt on the cheek before she turned and left the house.

Her uncle's gesture was surprising and gave her hope that her wedding and marriage could mend the old rivalry between the Bisset and Williams families. Finally she was getting the life she wanted where her name was in the press for a positive reason and not because of scandal.

Nine

Iris wasn't sure how to act when Zac arrived in the suite. She'd been dressed and ready for more than thirty minutes, in fact, since he'd texted her that he was getting close. Now she was hovering in the main living area while he was settling into the smaller room in the suite and getting dressed for dinner.

"I'm ready," he said.

She swallowed hard when she saw him. He wore a pair of shorts, deck shoes and a button-down shirt. His blond hair was tousled as if he'd run his hands through it. Her own fingers tingled as she remembered how soft and thick his hair was and how it had felt to hold his head to her breast while they'd been making love.

She shook her head. *Stop it.* She needed to stay focused. This was the second test of her and Zac as a believable couple.

"Do I look okay?" he asked. "You're kind of staring at me…"

"You look fine. I was just thinking about something else," she said. Yeah, like how good he had looked naked. "So, Adler and Nick are two of my oldest friends. They will be subtle but they're going to dig and try to find out when we started dating and everything."

"So, it's dinner with the family, part two," he said with a chuckle. "Don't worry, angel face, Adler's my family as well so I know how to handle her."

Angel face.

It was a sweet endearment. To be honest, she'd never had one in a relationship before unless *babe* counted. But she'd never felt it had.

"Crapola. I didn't want to tell her in a text and we didn't end up meeting in person this afternoon. She's going to have all kinds of questions. This is a bad idea," she said abruptly. She hadn't really given much thought to the fact that Adler was Zac's cousin. That might make things complicated down the road. As if sleeping with a guy she had hired wasn't already a bad idea. This was what happened when she let Thea get in her head. She started making decisions from a place of panic instead of a place of reason.

Zac came over and put his arms around her, hugging her close and then stepping back. "Relax. Whatever happens, we will roll with it. We're still new to the relationship... By the way, my family is going to be grilling you and probably trying to figure out what you see in me."

"Why would they do that?" she asked.

"I'm pretty much always focused on yacht designs, team dynamics and how to win the America's Cup. I'm told I can be boring AF when I get on a roll about it," he said. "So there is that. I know that we have a contract for me to be here, but I genuinely like you, Iris. I think if we just are honest about our reactions to each other, throw in a few kisses and longing glances, no one will be suspicious."

She stared up into his bright blue eyes and nodded. He made it sound so simple, but she knew that it was way more complex than that. She took his hand in hers. He had some callouses, probably owing to a lifetime spent working on boats, but she liked the way he immediately squeezed her hand.

"I like you too," she admitted.

"I already knew that," he said with a cheeky grin as he led them out of the suite.

He started down the hall, but she stayed to watch the door close and then double-checked the handle. He stopped, arching one eyebrow at her in question.

"Sorry, habit," she said.

"That's a good one," he said.

Graham had hated that she did it and said it made her look like a paranoid weirdo. But then she was coming to realize that a lot of the things Graham had said about her weren't a reflection of her but rather of him. As much as she'd been trying to find the perfect mate, he'd been trying to find a woman who fit what he wanted. A woman Iris realized she hadn't ever been nor truly wanted to be. And that was okay.

Zac came back and double-checked the door as well before taking her hand and walking toward the elevators. He had his faults; she knew he did. No one was perfect—man or woman—but there were a lot of qualities to Zac that she'd never realized mattered to her before. And she knew that it wasn't the qualities per se but Zac himself.

There was an elderly couple on the elevator holding hands when they got on and they smiled at the two of them. For a moment—just the briefest second—Iris saw herself and Zac in them, but she knew that was an illusion and warned herself not to buy into it.

He had said they were friends and could make this work

for the weekend. He hadn't said anything about beyond that. He was here for the time being and she had to remember that he was going to leave once his funding came in and this destination-wedding weekend ended they would start to "drift" apart and their relationship would end in three months' time. So these four days were really all they'd have together.

The lobby was crowded with people as they exited the elevator and walked toward the hotel entrance. There was a pianist playing Gershwin and the buzz of muted conversations filled the room. Iris heard a woman's laugh and turned to see Adler and Nick talking to Nick's mother, Cora. The threesome looked happy as they were talking. Adler glanced up and noticed Iris and waved, then did a double take at Zac.

She shook her head as she started walking over to them.

"Girl, why didn't you tell me your new man was my cousin?" Adler said, hugging her and then reaching over to hug Zac.

"I told her I wanted to surprise you. I wasn't supposed to be here until tomorrow," Zac said effortlessly.

Taking all the pressure off Iris for not saying anything. Adler hugged her close and Iris actually relaxed for a moment.

"He's way better than Graham," Adler whispered in her ear before turning back to Zac. "This is a very good surprise! Come meet Nick and his mom."

"I can't wait," Zac said.

Adler led the way toward them, and Zac kept his hand firmly in hers, bringing her along with him and making it clear they were together.

Adler hadn't seen Zac in person for five years. He had signed a three-year contract with an America's Cup team and had spent the time racing and training. She didn't know the details but her tall blond cousin had fallen out with the captain and hadn't renewed his contract. For as long as she'd known Zac, yachting was his life, so it was interesting to see him holding Iris's hand and laughing at her story of how she'd botched her family's famous lobster roll recipe on the morning show two weeks earlier.

Something seemed...too perfect, too right between Iris and Zac. Adler knew she should just smile and go along with it, but she didn't want to see her friend get hurt.

The thing was, Iris looked vulnerable sitting next to Zac. She smiled when he looked over at her but when he wasn't looking, her friend was staring at him like she was...well, like she really cared for him. Something Adler had never seen Iris do when she'd been with Graham.

Nick pinched her leg under the table and she glared at him. He leaned in to kiss her neck and whispered in her ear, "Stop staring at them. It's clear you're not buying them as a couple."

"What are you two talking about?" Iris asked. "When they kiss like that, they're giving each other the low-down."

Exactly, Adler thought. Iris would know she'd pick up on whatever was going on.

The downside to having been best friends for all of their adult lives was that Adler and Iris knew each other's little social tells.

"Nothing important. I need to powder my nose. Want to join me?" Adler said, jumping up.

"You're not wearing—" Nick said, but stopped when Adler turned to face him, raising both eyebrows. He'd probably been about to point out she wasn't wearing makeup, which her wedding skincare consultant had advised for a few days before the ceremony so she'd be picture-perfect on the big day.

"I'd love to," Iris said with a giggle. "Be right back."

Iris squeezed Zac's shoulder, started to walk away and then turned back to kiss him. It seemed like she was aiming for his cheek, but he turned into the kiss and their lips met. The kiss was the first convincing moment for Adler when she totally bought them as a couple.

Was it just new couple awkwardness?

She glanced at Nick, who smiled and shrugged at her. He seemed to be thinking the same thing. But she'd get to the bottom of it in the bathroom.

Iris's skin was flushed as she brushed past Adler and led the way to the bathroom at the back of the restaurant. Adler followed her friend, knowing that she should have insisted they talk today before the men had arrived. But with her wedding planner, Jaqs Veerland, flying in midday to go over last-minute details, she hadn't had time.

"Okay, spill," Adler said once they were in the ladies' room.

"Spill what?"

"The tea, girl. And don't pretend there isn't any. You and Zac…you almost make sense but something isn't feeling right."

Iris fumbled in her purse for her lip gloss and turned to the mirror. "I'm sure I don't know what you mean."

"I'm sure you do," Adler said, swiping the gloss from Iris and putting on some herself. "That kiss looked real but the rest of it…you were watching him like you weren't sure about him. What's going on?"

Iris shrugged and took the lip gloss back. "I wish I had your skin. You're glowing."

"Thanks. But I'm not going to let you distract me."

"There's nothing to tell. He's hot and we had this zing… I mean, I almost fell and he caught me and kissed me and the paparazzi went crazy snapping photos and it's just sort of gone on from there. We are still in the very beginning of this relationship. Remember when you wouldn't eat in front of Nick?"

Adler did remember. She'd liked him so much she hadn't wanted to do anything to put him off. A previous dude she'd dated had said her chewing was too loud, so she hadn't been able to eat in front of Nick.

"Fair point. I just worry about you, Iris," Adler said.

"I know," Iris responded, wrapping her arms around Adler's shoulders as the two of them stared at their reflection in the mirror. "I love you for that."

Adler reached up and patted Iris's hands. "Nick is never going to let me live this down. He said I was staring at you both like I wanted to do an interrogation."

"You were," Iris admitted. "Which wasn't helping my nerves. Do you like him?"

"Zac?"

"Yes."

"I do. When we were kids, he was always outside on the water. And he could always be counted on to help me disappear when I needed some breathing room by taking me sailing. He's not much of a talker, but that was when we were kids. He pretty much is always away sailing now. How is this going to work?"

"We haven't figured that part out," Iris said. "Right now, we are both here and enjoying each other's company."

"And you'd appreciate it if I let you do that, right?"

"Yes," Iris said. "Also, this is your big week. We should all be thinking about you."

"You should," Adler said with a wink. "I have my final fitting tomorrow after the family luncheon. Will you go with me?"

"Yes. I'm all yours. I'm filming a segment early in the morning. I heard your dad wrote a new song for you."

"Yeah, he did," Adler said. "He's been more…sentimental since the heart attack. He won't let me hear it before my wedding day."

They rejoined the men and Adler was satisfied her friend was going to be okay, which meant she was back to worrying about how her Uncle Auggie was going to be tomorrow when he was in the same room with his most hated rival, Tad Williams—Nick's dad.

"So, you're the America's Cup guy?" Nick asked as the ladies left the table.

Zac reached for his water glass and nodded. "You're the…titan of industry, right?"

Nick gave a shout of laughter. "I'm guessing that's what Adler said. I know for damn sure your father and brother don't call me that."

"No, they usually throw in some derogatory curse words," Zac allowed. Nick was a really nice guy and it was clear to Zac that Nick truly loved Adler. Zac saw real affection between them. Having grown up with parents who had been in and out of love with each other several times, Zac knew how rare that kind of bond was.

"I do the same when referring to them. I'm trying to make peace for Adler's sake," Nick said. "I was surprised by the invitation to your grandmother's for lunch tomorrow."

"Me too," Zac admitted. "I don't think my dad is mellowing, he just knows there will be hell to pay if he upsets Adler. She's my mom's only connection to her sister and she is pulling out all the stops to make the wedding is everything that Adler wants."

"I know. It's so crazy. I like your mom, by the way. She's sweet and funny," he said. "Makes me wonder how she raised a shark like Logan."

"Fair enough, but I think Logan was always Dad's shadow, not Mom's, so that might be one explanation. He's a great guy away from the office," Zac said. He and his siblings were very close, but he was realistic enough to know that they had both good and bad qualities. "We're all very driven."

"I've seen that. What's going on with your America's Cup team? I heard a rumor that you're looking for financing," Nick said.

"I'm not," Zac said. Using the Collins connection to finance his bid was one thing, accepting financing from his families' business rivals would put Zac in direct confrontation with his father and Logan. Something that Zac wasn't interested in doing. He wanted to do this on his own; he had never been looking to piss off his family.

"Okay, but if that changes, I'm interested," Nick said.

"Dude, you know that I can't even contemplate doing business with you," Zac said. "I might spend most of my time on a yacht but if I accepted an investment from you, I'd never be able to come home again. As sweet as my mom has been to you, she'd be royally ticked at the both of us, and let me tell you, that isn't a good thing to be on the receiving end of."

Nick put his hands up. "Gotcha. I'm just always looking for new investments."

"And if it happens to piss off the Bissets, all the better?" Zac asked.

"Sometimes, but honestly that's more my dad's thing than mine. I go after sound investments, not just things I think August Bisset wants," Nick said.

"So you didn't start dating Adler because she's related to my mom?" Zac asked.

"Not at all. She's not a Bisset, which of course is a plus in my opinion, but also I don't spend all of my time trying to undermine your family," he said, leaning back in his chair, glass in hand. "Whatever happened between our fathers happened way before I was born and to be honest it doesn't bother me."

"Glad to hear it. I'm sure Logan wouldn't agree."

"Logan's a douche," Nick said. "He's gone straight after some of my business, but I don't mind a good honest fight."

"Who's fighting?" Adler asked, sitting back down.

"No one tonight," Nick said. "And I promised to be nice tomorrow so we should be good."

Zac hoped they would be. Iris seemed different when she sat back down, not so smiley as she'd been before. Had Adler figured out what they were up to?

But when he glanced at his cousin, she just winked at him so he didn't think she'd found out about their arrangement. He reached for Iris's hand as the check arrived, but she moved away from him, taking the check from the waiter. "This one is on me. Thanks for making time for a quiet meal during your special week."

"Any time, Iris," Adler said.

Zac took the check from her. "Sorry, angel face, but I'll get this."

She glared at him. He guessed that she expected her fake boyfriend to stay quiet and let her pay, but he hadn't been raised that way. And though he knew she made damn good money, there was no way he could tamp down this impulse.

"Angel face?"

"Shut it, Addie. I'm sure Nick has a special name for you," Zac said.

"Does he?" Iris asked as Zac took his American Express from his wallet and handed it to the waiter.

"I do," Nick said. "But I've been warned to keep it behind closed doors."

"Oooh, what is it?" Iris asked. "Now I'm dying to know."

"Stop it," Adler said. "If you were really my friend, you wouldn't want to know."

"Is it embarrassing?" Iris asked. "It can't be. You're too adorable to have a nickname that's not cool."

"It's private," Adler said.

"Fair enough."

Zac smiled at his cousin, who had spent so much of her life in the spotlight. It was nice to know she had someone in her life who would keep her secrets and share things just with her.

Until that moment Zac hadn't realized that there was such a thing. His parents presented a united front for show, but he'd never seen them as a couple in love. And, honestly, that hadn't been something he'd thought he'd wanted in his life until Iris slipped her hand in his and squeezed it.

Ten

A walk on the beach. It was simple. It was romantic. It was expected. Iris told herself that as she slipped her hand into Zac's and followed him down the wooden boardwalk to the shore. In the distance she heard the sound of waves and she stopped for a moment, tipping her head back to look up at the black sky and breathe in the salty air.

Zac just stood next to her, letting her have her moment. She forgot how to breathe sometimes. Not like the normal inhale/exhale thing, but how to take these moments and press them into her mind so she wouldn't forget them.

And she wanted to remember this night with Zac. He'd been funny and charming at dinner—the perfect companion. How had she never noticed that Graham only talked about himself? Zac was the total opposite, asking questions and genuinely listening when everyone spoke.

If she'd had to invent an ideal man for herself, so far he was ticking all of the boxes. The cynical part of her mind warned that he was ticking them because she'd paid him to be by her side. It was a little too convenient.

"You okay?" he asked.

"Yeah," she said, wrapping one arm around her own waist as she dropped his hand. "Why?"

"You looked so relaxed and chill. And then I don't know what happened in that pretty head of yours but you started to look stressed."

She shook her head. "I don't know what happened either. Thea says I overthink everything. She might be right."

Zac reached for her hand and she let him take it. "When I first started sailing, I had a mentor who told me that there were a million things that needed to happen and could go wrong while I was on the water. He said just take each moment as it comes, the strong wind that fills your sails, the spray of water on your face, the storm that blows up out of nowhere. Each moment. That's all you can handle and all you can control."

She knew that. She did. But it was harder to do than Zac made it sound. "I try. Somehow the future always tugs at me, making me anxious to plan for it."

He laughed. "I can see that. I struggle with it as well but then I like finding a solution or a work-around. Want me to help you figure this out?"

She shook her head. "I don't know how to work around you."

"Me?"

"Yes, you. You're not at all what I thought you'd be," she said. "You've been surprising me every step of the way and that keeps making me think things that—"

"Stop," he said, tugging her gently into his arms. "Don't do that. I told you we'd be honest with each other. The way we started out doesn't have to define every moment."

She looked up at him. The lights from the boardwalk

were dim where they stood and his blue eyes were dark. He'd shaved before he'd come to Nantucket. He looked casual, but his jaw was strong, and she couldn't help letting her eyes fall to his lips.

Those lips that she'd kissed last night. Those lips that had charted a path down her body and left her quivering in his arms. She wanted to taste him again. To pretend that they were like Nick and Adler sneaking away to be alone and enjoy the simple romance of an evening at the beach.

She put her hand on the back of his neck as she went up on tiptoe, mesmerized by the thought of that kiss. He tipped his head to the side and she came closer. The warmth of his breath brushed over her mouth as he exhaled. She closed her eyes and his lips touched hers. A shiver went down her spine and she tightened her fingers on the back of his neck.

Swallowing hard as he lifted his head, he stared down into her face. Their eyes met, and she felt like…she wanted to believe that something magical passed between them. Something that would bind them together as a couple. But the truth was she was searching for that connection and she didn't trust her chronic bad taste when it came to men. Didn't trust her gut when it shouted to take him back to the room and make love to him all night.

She wanted to believe she could keep her wits about her, but she knew she couldn't. She was lying to her best friend, lying to her parents and her sister. The one person she couldn't lie to was herself.

She wouldn't be that girl who fell for a pair of blue eyes that promised the moon and woke up in the sand underneath a cloudy sky.

She took a deeper breath as she stepped back. "I think I've had enough of the night air. I'm going to head back to the room."

"Running away from me isn't going to change anything," he said.

She wanted to pretend not to understand what he meant but she wasn't going to play games with him either. "I know that. But I need bright lights and reality instead of this."

"This?"

"This…" She gestured to the sky and the beach and him. "I'm not living a picture-perfect moment that I'm going to share with my followers. This isn't real. Any of it. And I don't want to forget it."

She pivoted on her heel and walked away from him. It was hard, but she knew in the moment that it was what she needed to do. She had to stay focused or she was going to lose control of more than her emotions. She was going to lose control of her life and everything she'd worked for would be gone.

Zac knew he should let her go. She'd been pretty damn plain when she'd said this was an illusion. But he wasn't faking it. He liked her. He wanted her. He followed her, putting his hand on her shoulder to stop her.

"What?" she asked, her tone short and curt.

"You forgot one thing, angel face," he said. "I'm real. You're real. And neither one of us is lying about that."

She chewed her lower lip and he remembered the last time she'd done that: when they'd made love the first time. He was no closer now to figuring out what was going on inside her head than he had been that night. And true, it had only been a week earlier, but it felt like they'd spent a lifetime together since then. He hadn't wanted to believe that he'd ever feel like this about a woman…especially not one that he'd made a deal to date.

He hoped he wasn't. And this wasn't love, was it? Could it be?

It was lust. He was even comfortable labeling it affection and/or infatuation. But beyond that, the answer had to be no. They were in a business arrangement and only a fool would allow it to become too emotional. And despite what his brothers sometimes said Zac wasn't anyone's fool.

"I'm not calling you a liar," she said at last. Her tone was serious and grounded, the kind of tone she'd used when she'd been meeting with her fans earlier in the lobby.

He didn't say anything because he'd noticed that at times she would drop a leading statement and see how he responded. But he wasn't sure what to say to her now.

"I'm talking about myself," she said at last. "We have a contracted agreement and I know what I wanted from it. But here in the moonlight, holding your hand and just standing next to you, I guess I wish we didn't have that. That we were just two people…"

He had thought that, as well. "Would you have spoken to me if you hadn't needed me?"

She shrugged. But they both knew the answer was no. She wasn't at the point in her life where she really wanted a man in it. He was starting to realize that. She liked him and he liked her but it was in spite of their agreement. Neither of them was ready for a serious relationship. He was leaving to train for the America's Cup and she was launching a new line for her brand.

This pact they'd made for Adler's wedding, that was all they had and neither of them should forget it.

"No," she said at last.

"Me neither."

"Why not?"

"You're complicated, angel face," he said.

"So?"

"I like it, you know I do, but the truth is, we're here together because of some very unique circumstances."

"So talking about what-ifs isn't going to work," she said. "I just feel myself wanting to believe this is real in my heart and my mind is warning me that it isn't."

He pulled her into his arms because he hated not touching her when they were this close, and he was tired of denying himself and letting her set the pace. "This is real, Iris. It's just going to end when the weekend is over and we start drifting apart over the next three months. That doesn't mean we won't feel something for each other. I think it would be odd if we didn't. All it really means is that we might look back and wish it had lasted longer…"

He wanted to add that there was no reason it couldn't but that was more complicated than he wanted to be tonight. The wind was blowing off the water and the salt air was making him long to be back out on the deck of his yacht, challenging the elements and competing for his place in history.

But…

He also wanted Iris. He wanted to keep her in his arms and hold on to her until the winds and time forced him to leave her. That was something he knew he couldn't really have.

As much as he wanted to hold her in his moment, when the sea called, he'd answer. Winning the America's Cup with his own team had long been a dream of his. Something he needed to do to prove himself, to show his old man what he was capable of.

She reached up and touched his face. There was a hint of sadness to her smile and he knew she had come to the same realization that he had. No matter how much they both might want to believe that they should have more with each other, the contract they'd signed was all that either of them was willing to give.

He'd thought of her as a siren leading him astray, but he

realized that he didn't want to disappoint Iris. He needed to be his best self and that meant that he couldn't detour from his chosen path because she wouldn't detour from hers.

She needed him to be the man she'd met. The man who was a sailor and a competitor and whose life was on the sea. Not in Boston or wherever her career took her.

He leaned down to kiss her because he knew that these four days were really the most intimate time they would have together, and the pipe dream of more time was hard to let go. But in his heart and soul, he knew that was the only option. He'd taken her up on her indecent proposal never guessing that he would ever feel anything this strong for her or that the thought of leaving her would cut like a knife.

She wrapped her arms around his shoulders, and he knew that no matter what, he wasn't going to be able to stop himself from making love to her over the next four days. They might both know that their relationship would end but he needed to give them enough memories to keep them company over the long dark nights that lay ahead.

She wanted to pretend it was a fluke, that their one night together hadn't changed her forever but she knew it had. Sitting at the table with Adler and Nick tonight had just driven home to her how much she wanted everything about her and Zac to be real. She didn't want it to be just for the weekend and just for show. He'd been funny and charming and just so damn real that it had driven home how wrong her search for a partner had gone up until that point.

He complemented her in a way no one else ever had. A part of her knew it had to be because she wasn't trying to impress him. She knew he wasn't going to leave her alone in a hotel room the way that Graham had. She was paying him to be with her.

God. How humiliating would it be if that ever got out?

But she had no regrets. Being with Zac had shown her a side of herself she hadn't even realized she'd been burying.

It was hard to realize what was missing until she'd found it. She pulled back from the kiss but didn't want to. She liked the way he tasted and it felt as if it had been years instead of a week since they'd kissed.

He kept his hands around her waist. When he turned to shelter her from the wind, she again felt her heart melt just the tiniest bit. He held her as if she were precious to him and she realized that despite the fact that she ran a multi-million-dollar company and she could hold her own with anyone on the planet, it was nice to have someone hold her and shelter her.

She reached up to touch his face, felt the light stubble that was starting to grow on his jaw. In his eyes, she thought she saw the same heaviness that troubled her.

"I know I said no sex, but would you be upset if I changed my mind?" she asked.

He threw his head back and laughed, and she couldn't help smiling. She loved the sound of his laughter. He held nothing back when he did it.

"Uh, no, angel face, I wouldn't mind at all. In fact, I think I'd be downright ticked if you didn't."

"Good. I mean you did say there wasn't anything I could ask you to do that would make you uncomfortable."

"There's something in your tone that's making me think I shouldn't have issued a blanket challenge to you like that," he said.

"You shouldn't have," she quipped but she knew he was safe. She wanted him to herself but would never do anything that would make him feel ill at ease. He had given her a freedom she hadn't realized she'd denied herself. And it was making her regret that she'd waited so long to find it.

She'd never thought sexual confidence was something

she needed in her life. But since being with Zac that one night, she was already a different woman. She wanted to see what happened if they made love twice.

How would that change her?

She was ready for it.

"This is our last night before everyone is here," she said. "Our last night as a quasi-anonymous couple. What should we do?"

"Something daring and not in the rule book?" he asked.

She took a deep breath. She wasn't worried about his suggesting a three-way the way Graham had or that she wear a dildo and take him from behind. That wasn't the kind of man Zac was. In fact, she was excited to hear what he suggested.

"Yes."

"Hmm… Want to take my grandmother's yacht out and make love on the deck with just the sea around us and the moon and stars watching overhead?"

She inhaled sharply, already picturing him nude on the deck of a yacht. She was the tiniest bit afraid of water… But they wouldn't be in the water, and the chance to be the woman with him on the yacht—sharing his world—was too powerful to resist.

"Okay. Let's do it."

He took her hand in his and led the way back up the beach toward the marina. He talked to her as they walked, telling her about his earliest memories of sailing. "It was my gran who first took me out on the ocean and let me get behind the wheel. She taught me about the jib and the wind and how to harness it. She made it seem okay that when my father bellowed and yelled, I ran and hid."

Iris caught her breath as he talked about his childhood. She'd heard from Adler that August Bisset wasn't an easy man to live with. Adler rarely saw her uncle, but Zac had grown up underneath his roof and his upbringing was so different from Iris's. So foreign. Her parents had wanted them to achieve but nothing had been more important to them than making sure that she and her sister were loved.

Something that Iris realized she'd taken for granted.

She stopped Zac when they were on the slip about to board his grandmother's yacht, the Day Dream.

"Changed your mind?" he asked.

"Not at all," she said, hugging him and pulling him closer to her so she could whisper in his ear. "Thank you for being you."

He squeezed her close for a long minute and then let his arms fall to his sides. He didn't respond and she hadn't expected him to. She knew how hard it was to live with someone so demanding, and the fact that Zac had made the relationship with his father work by going his own way was more impressive than he knew. He hadn't chosen the easy path; he'd moved halfway around the world and started over. He thought he was a man who always looked for the horizon because he was running but she knew now that he did that because he was harnessing the bluster he'd inherited from his father and charting his own course.

She wished she could chart a course that would keep her by his side and didn't even care if that made her seem weak. She liked him and she wanted to keep him in her life but she had no idea if that was something that was even possible.

Eleven

Piloting the small yacht out of the marina at night was as familiar to him as the back of his hand. Once he'd gotten them out into Nantucket Sound, Iris stood in his arms at the helm of the boat. He steered them far away from the lights of Nantucket until it felt like they were the only two people left on earth.

And knowing that tomorrow he'd be surrounded by his family and there would be all of the activities of Adler's wedding party, he wanted to make this night last forever. As much as he prided himself on being the anti-Bisset Bisset he knew once he was with his brothers and sister that he'd fall back into the role that he always played with them and, of course, he had the added role of being Iris's boyfriend for the weekend.

But tonight they were Zac and Iris. "I almost wish we were living in a different time. I'd spirit you away on the high seas and we'd stop wherever we hit land, and no one would know who we were."

"You'd run away with me?"

"Hell, yes. Would you?"

She thought about it too long and he knew the answer was no, no matter what she said. Of course, Iris wouldn't run away. She wasn't about running away. She was about making a plan and then following it until its end. No matter what.

"I'm kidding," he said. "The sea just calls to me."

But it was too late to pull back that feeling even though he'd tried to cover it. He'd always know he'd thrown out something that was real and she'd drawn back. He reminded himself that she was a very attractive woman who had decided to hire a man for the weekend instead of finding a real boyfriend.

His thoughts were ruining the night. He needed tonight to be a happy memory for both of them, but maybe it was Nantucket or just thinking about his family that had soured him.

"I'm sorry," she said. "I want to say yes, but I'd be so freaked out about not knowing where we were going and not having a plan that I'd make you miserable. Do I want to be with you…?"

She stopped talking and turned in his arms as he hit the anchor release button and was about to turn away from her. She put her arms around his waist and rested her head on his chest right over his heart.

"More than anything," she said. Her voice was low, but he still heard her.

"Then why do you hesitate?"

"I'm afraid," she said, then let out a deep breath that sounded like a sigh. "I can only let my guard down because I know whatever I do you're not going to leave me. And if we started really dating, I'd let the pressure of that expectation overwhelm me. I know that makes me sound shallow."

"No," he said. "It doesn't. It makes you human, angel face."

She looked up at him then and he didn't care that she knew he wanted to run away with her. He could make whatever excuses he wanted to, he was going to miss the hell out of her when their arrangement was over and he started his training for the America's Cup. He'd go because that was his life, but he'd always look back to this moment and this night with her.

"Want to skinny dip?" he asked, because if he didn't do something, he was going to say all kinds of things that would scare her so much it would send her swimming back to shore.

"I'm afraid of the water."

"I'll protect you," he said. "But no pressure if you don't want to go in."

She chewed her lower lip. "How about if you skinny dip and I stand on the deck and watch?"

"Will you be naked?" he asked.

"I could be," she said. "Seems only fair if one of us is going to strip down, we both should."

"It does," he said, trying not to let himself fall a little bit more for her. There was so much daring inside her but she was afraid to let it out except in little controlled bursts. And he had to admit that made her all the more attractive.

He took her hand and led her to the deck of the yacht, then waggled his eyebrows at her as he took off his shirt and then his pants. He stood in front of her in his boxer briefs and put his hands on his hips. "One of us is a bit ahead of the other one."

"One of us is just wearing a thong under their dress," she said, untying the halter neck and letting the dress fall from her.

His breath caught in his throat as he stared at her beautiful nearly naked body. She stood there in the light of the full moon and the illumination provided by the running lights and reached up to undo the clasp that held her hair back. Her hair spilled down over her shoulders and she lifted her arms as the gentle summer breeze blew around them.

It should have cooled him off but even an Arctic breeze wouldn't have lessened the heat she stirred in him. He was hot and hard and at the same time he wanted to cuddle her in his arms and just keep her safe. He wished the world could see this Iris. The one with her arms in the air, bare breasts uplifted and a huge-ass smile on her face. Gone were her barriers and the proper behavior she used to keep the world at arm's length.

"God, you're gorgeous," he said. His words were low and rumbling but that was all he could manage.

She tipped her head to the side and smiled at him. "I want to point out all the places I'm not, but I can see you think I am, so I'll keep it to myself."

"I'm glad because I wasn't just talking about your body. There's something about you, Iris, that I can't resist."

Zac made her feel different and she wasn't sure she wanted to resist it. She let her arms fall to her sides and stood more fully facing him. He was turned on by her—that was easy to see—but there was a lot more than sexy times between them.

He'd asked her to run away with him and she'd panicked. Not because she didn't want to but because, for a split second, she wished she was the kind of woman who would. But she knew that the contract had freed something inside of her. It was novel and new, and she was enjoying it because it was shocking her to her staid core. But if that was her norm, she didn't think she'd enjoy it as much.

And she knew he would. She didn't want to hurt Zac.

Heck, she'd been hurt too many times by relationships to want to risk another one—hence, the contract.

"Are you still feeling like a swim?" she asked, coming closer to him. She loved his body and honestly it would be perfectly okay with her if he were naked 24/7 when they were alone together. He had been sweet to compliment her but he had the kind of body that would make anyone stop and stare.

"Well, not exactly," he said, reaching out to cup one of her breasts in his hand. He rubbed his thumb over her nipple, and it beaded under his touch.

Remembering the scar she'd felt the first time they'd made love, she reached out and touched it again. She leaned in closer and saw it was jagged and still had some redness around it. "What is this from?"

"Stupidity," he said.

"I've done a lot of stupid things but don't have a scar like this," she said, tracing the edges of it with a gentle finger, wishing she could have soothed the hurt it must have caused him.

"Well, when you combine alcohol with ego and a competitive nature, this is the result. I did a kite-surfing challenge with a teammate, won, celebrated too vigorously and ended up crashing into an outcropping of rocks I hadn't noticed."

"That does sound…"

"Dumb. You can say it. My mom and sister both said it was what I deserved. Apparently, my victory dances are a little OTT."

She had to laugh at the way he said it, but her laughter turned to sensual awareness as his hand moved from her breast to her waist and he drew her closer to him. Her naked breasts were cushioned against his upper body. His chest hair was soft against her skin and his heat was a contrast to the breeze blowing around them. He smelled of his aftershave—a clean, crisp scent—and the sea breeze. She closed her eyes and willed her mind to stop thinking. To just relax and enjoy this. But she wanted to record every second.

Her life had been played out on TV and on social media since she'd entered college. By her own design, of course, but so many of her ups and downs had been recorded and scrutinized on the gossip websites that she almost didn't believe her own reality until she saw it played back. Until she flipped past her profile and saw that smiling face.

She knew she was here with him. She wanted to just enjoy him but—

"Stop thinking," he said. "It's disconcerting to watch you go from enjoying my touch to suddenly seeming to analyze everything."

Busted.

"Damn. I'm sorry. I'm such a freak about things like that. I don't know what my deal—"

He stopped the stream of words with a kiss. She stopped thinking, stopped worrying and calculating her responses. She just clung to his shoulders as his tongue rubbed over hers and his hands splayed warm and wide on her back. She arched into the curve of his body and felt his erection pushing against her. She flexed her fingers against his skin and couldn't help the groan that started deep inside her as her entire body seemed to start pulsing in time with her heartbeat. She wanted this.

She wanted him.

And she wasn't going to allow her own self-consciousness to stop her from enjoying this.

She ran her hand down his arm, felt the flex of his biceps and squeezed them. She loved his strength. Loved how easily he held her and yet how gently he did it. He was aware of his strength and never used it to overwhelm her even though he easily could. He broke their kiss, his mouth moving down the column of her neck, biting gently at the junction where it sloped into her collarbone.

She caressed his chest, flexing her fingers and letting her nails scrape over his skin. He shuddered at her touch and she continued to move her hand down his body. But he stopped her, turning her in his arms and pulling her close against his chest. His erection nestled between her buttocks and he put one hand on her stomach and the other between her legs.

She rocked her hips back against him and he brought his hand up to her chin, tipping her head back and to the side to kiss her again. His mouth was warm and wet, drawing her deeper into the sensual web he was weaving around them. She felt his finger move under the fabric of her underwear to the juncture of her thighs. She reached back between their bodies, fondling him through his boxer briefs, realizing that the only thought she had was how to get him inside of her.

Iris felt so good in his arms that he wanted the moment to never end but he also needed to be inside of her. To take her and pretend that this night could last forever. He pushed her thong down her legs, and she kicked them aside as she turned in his arms and he shoved his underwear off so that her hand was on his naked shaft. He continued kissing her as he walked her backward to the soft cushions on the deck near the railing. He lifted his head for a moment, trying to gauge how quickly he could get to the cushions and get inside of her but she pushed him back on the padded bench and straddled him as she had for a few moments the first time they'd made love.

"I want to be on top the entire time," she said. "I feel

like I let you take control from the very first moment and this time it's all me."

"Yes, ma'am," he said. "I've got a condom in my pants pocket."

"Stay right there," she said.

He did as she ordered, watching her walk across the deck to where he'd dropped his trousers. She bent over and as she did, glanced back at him and realized he was watching her. She stopped just like that, her beautiful backside pointed at him, her hair hanging down as she smiled back at him. She took the condom from his pocket and then slowly stood back up, turning to face him.

He was stroking his cock as he watched her, and this time when she walked toward him, her gait was deliberate and her intent was to turn him on. Her full breasts bounced with her steps and her hips swayed. She was taking control of not just their lovemaking but of the night.

He felt like he was going burst as she stopped in front of him and dropped to her knees. Leaning forward, she stroked her tongue along the side of his shaft before taking him into her mouth. His hips jerked forward and he put his hand on the back of her head, touching her briefly before moving his hand away. She reached between them, stroking his shaft while she continued to suck on the tip. He felt like he was going to come in her mouth and that was the last thing he wanted for this night. He shifted his hips and went down on his knees next to her on the deck, taking the condom from her hand and quickly sheathing himself with it. He turned her around so she was facing the ocean, then took one of her hands and put it on the bench underneath his.

He put his other hand on her stomach, pushed her hips back toward him and entered her from behind. She moaned and turned her hand over underneath his, twining their fingers together, her hips rocking back against him as he entered her deeper. He palmed her breast with his free hand and kissed the side of her neck. She threw her head back as he started to pump his hips and drove himself into her again and again.

She turned her head and he found her mouth with his. He was totally in tune with her as they both ground harder and harder against each other until he felt himself about to come. But he wasn't sure she was with him. He reached between her legs, flicking her clit with his finger, rubbing it the way she'd liked it the other night. She ripped her mouth from his, threw back her head and screamed his name.

He held her hips with both hands, thrusting into her one more time, harder and deeper than before. But it wasn't enough. He drew back and drove himself into her again and again until his release washed over him and he collapsed forward, putting his hand on the bench to make sure he didn't crush her. She wrapped her hand around his wrist, her breath sawing in and out of her body.

He lifted himself from her, pulled her to her feet and then sat down on the bench and cuddled her in his lap. She looked as dazed as he felt. He was totally sated from their lovemaking. She'd done something to him. Snapped that control he'd always relied on to keep his wits about him and make sure he didn't dive in to deep.

But he knew he had. As she curled up on his lap, putting her head on his shoulder and wrapping her arms around him, all he could do was stroke her back and remind himself that he was a man who loved the next horizon more than anything on shore, even though at this moment, with the moon shining down on them, it felt like a lie.

He knew he should say something or get up and start steering them back to Nantucket. But he didn't want this moment to end. She didn't say anything either, just held on to him. He felt like they both knew that something had changed between them.

He thought he might be overthinking it, but he couldn't deny the truth that he felt deep in his soul. Iris Collins was changing him, and he was half addicted to it, half resentful of it. His life had worked for so long because he'd found his place and his way of coping with it. He wasn't sure he was ready to change for her or for anyone else.

And he damned sure knew he didn't want to go into this weekend feeling like this. He needed to be his strongest self, not whatever this was that making love to Iris had made him.

Twelve

Iris had woken up in Zac's arms at 4:00 a.m. in a total panic. She didn't want to dwell on the night before. The moonlight, the ocean, the man.

She was losing control of herself and of the situation with Zac. Last night had changed something inside of her and she didn't like it. She wasn't about to give up on everything she'd worked for because she had a lover who knew how to please her for the first time in her life. And she was ashamed of boiling Zac's good qualities down to the fact that he knew how to make her orgasm, but that was how she was going to cope with him.

She had gotten out of bed at seven o'clock and snuck into the bathroom to change into her exercise clothes. She'd only packed them for lounging in her room, but she needed to get out of the hotel and away from Zac. She needed to think and put everything in perspective.

She had wedding fever, she thought as she started out

on a slow jog down the path toward the beach. But she hated running and as soon as she was out of sight of the hotel, slowed to a walk. She wished her walk would bring her a solution to what she should do. But she'd really made a mess of things this time. It would have been easier if she'd just had Zac show up on the day of the event and look pretty on her arm. But no, she'd found a guy who knew the bride and who was…well, more than Iris had expected him to be.

He was complicating her well-ordered life and she wasn't too sure she liked it.

"Iris?"

She glanced over her shoulder to see Juliette Bisset. "Hi, Mrs. B. What are you doing out here so early?"

"Same as you, I imagine," Juliette said.

God, Iris really hoped not. "I guess hosting your husband's rivals at your mom's house would be a little bit stressful."

Juliette smiled and shook her head. "You have no idea. I've never met Nick's family because…well, Tad and Cora didn't want to meet me. But I'm glad that August is making the effort for Adler. The last thing a new bride needs is tension in her marriage."

It sounded like Mrs. B was speaking from experience. Iris wanted to know more—she couldn't help it—but manners and breeding kept her from asking. "That's true of any relationship."

"I heard you're dating my son," Juliette said.

"I am," Iris said, not sure what Zac had told his mom about them. "It happened kind of quick."

"That's what Zac said," Juliette said. "I'm not going to pry or anything. Just wanted to say I like the idea of you and Zac together."

"I do too," she said. Not just because she thought that's

what she should say but it was the truth. And as Zac had pointed out when they'd signed their pact, if they stuck to the truth as they went along, it would be easier.

"Good," Juliette said. "I should be getting back but I'm not ready for everyone to be here. I hope that Adler is enjoying this quiet before the wedding events take over our lives."

"I'm sure she is. Last night she and Nick seemed to be taking a few moments to themselves. My mom said that she wished she'd done more of that."

"Your mom has always been so wise about relationships," Juliette said.

"You have too. I mean you and Mr. B are a really strong couple," Iris said. She'd heard the gossip about August Bisset's affair that had led to a reconciliation and the subsequent birth of Zac's youngest sibling and only sister, Mari. But since then it seemed that Juliette and August had been solid.

"Thank you for saying that. It hasn't been easy but we are stronger today because of it."

Iris couldn't help but sigh at the way she'd said that. "I want that someday."

"I hope you don't have the rocky road to it that I did," Juliette said.

"If I do, I hope I weather it as gracefully as you did," she said. "I don't feel like exercising. Care to join me for a mimosa before you head back home?"

"I'd love to. I think it's just what I need this morning. I keep thinking about Musette. She'd be completely trying to take over Adler's wedding and I know she'd love every minute of it," Juliette said, referring to Adler's deceased mom.

"It must be hard for you, but I know that Adler thinks of you as her second mom," Iris said.

"And she's my first daughter. I know that sounds bad but I had Adler before Mari and I've always thought of her as mine."

"You two have such a close relationship," Iris said. "I know it means a lot to Adler."

They walked back up toward the resort and went to the restaurant in the lobby for a light breakfast and mimosas. As they were finishing up, Iris's phone pinged. She glanced down to see it was a text from Zac.

Are you okay?

"Excuse me, I have to answer this," Iris said to Juliette.

"Go ahead. I'm going to finish this drink and then head back to the big house. I'm glad we ran into each other this morning."

"Me too." Iris said goodbye, then typed out a response to Zac after Mrs. B left.

I'm in the lobby restaurant with your mom. I'll be back in the room in a few minutes.

My mom?!

Worried? ;)

No… Should I be?

No!

She settled the bill and sat there, taking her time with the final sip of her mimosa. Talking to the older woman this morning had relieved some of the tension she'd been carrying. It was clear that no matter how together a woman appeared on the outside, men and relationships could be a struggle. And in a weird way, that reassured her.

Waking up alone was nothing new to Zac, but when he rolled over and realized that Iris was gone, he wondered if he'd pushed too hard last night. He had a shower, thinking she must have gone for coffee. Then he shaved because he was going to be seeing his father for lunch. And there was no use going into that encounter with one hair out of place.

August Bisset could be charming, and there were a lot of times when Zac actually enjoyed being with his father. But not in social situations where he had to rule the room and the conversation. In such circumstances, his father wasn't afraid to point out the flaws in any of his children. It had been drilled into them to be the best from…well, for as long as Zac could remember.

After he'd shaven and gotten dressed for lunch, he started to worry about Iris. Where was she?

Was she okay?

He fished his cell phone out of his pocket and texted her. He wished he'd thought to tell her to turn on Find My Friends so he'd know exactly where she was, but he hadn't. He was stuck waiting for her to respond.

He saw the dancing dots on his screen and felt a sense of relief until she texted back that she was with his mom.

Dear God. That had *bad idea* written all over it. What were they talking about? He didn't even want to know.

She was cute and funny in her reply, which eased his mind about the night before. He'd be cool today. He was her hired date, and he'd give her what she'd paid for and a little bit more. If he focused on Iris, then he'd be able to deal with his dad without issue.

Or at least that was his hope.

He heard the door open and glanced over to see Iris

entering the living area of their suite. She had on a pair of flower-print leggings and a tank top that hugged her curves. After the night they'd spent together, he shouldn't want her again, but he did. She smiled at him and raised her eyebrows as she took in his navy pants, button-down oxford shirt and loafers.

"You're ready really early," she said.

"Usually we have a family meeting before events like this, so I'm anticipating a text from Carlton," he said.

"Good to know. Who's Carlton? Is that your dad's PR guy?" she asked.

"Yeah, he is. He kind of goes over the family image and the dos and don'ts for the event. Normally I'm not in town so I get to miss them, but I'm pretty sure I can't skip this one."

"Probably not. I'm going to shower and get dressed for the day. Should I plan to meet you later or come with you?"

He rubbed the back of his neck. "I'd like you to come with me. I mean, you don't have to, but if you are there, you're going to up my image rating."

She shook her head. "Your image rating is already pretty high."

"With you maybe," he said. "But I'm not as polished as Dad and Carlton would like. And I seem okay now, but when you see me next to Dare, Logan and Leo, I do seem like the scruffy one."

"Good thing I like scruffy."

"Good thing," he said.

She gave him a little wave as she walked toward the bedroom. "I better get moving."

He leaned back against the sofa and turned on ESPN as he waited for her. She'd been so peppy this morning. He'd thought she'd be dwelling on what had happened last night.

Well, hell.

She was ignoring it, wasn't she?

Was she going to pretend that nothing had happened? Should he?

He knew that he couldn't do that. He wasn't built that way. But she was in full-on wedding-pact mode and that meant they were the picture-perfect couple. He had planned to use their arrangement to sooth his father and keep the criticism at bay, but now that he knew Iris was back to just playing a role, it bothered him. He wanted her to talk about last night or at least be thinking about it so that he'd know she was as affected as he was.

Didn't it mean anything to her?

He got up and went into the bedroom. He stood there, staring at the closed bathroom door until he heard the shower shut off. Then he ran for the bed and lay down on it, trying to look casual as the door opened and a cloud of steam preceded Iris into the room.

"What are you doing in here?"

"Waiting for you? We're lovers now, angel face," he said.

"I know but that was last night. The wedding stuff starts today. This is the contracted thing—"

"I'm not going to embarrass you but I'm also not going to pretend that last night and the other night didn't happen. There is more between us now than a contract."

She put her hand on her chest and toyed with her diamond necklace. "You know it still has to end, right?"

"Yes, of course, I'm not sticking around, hoping you'll put a ring on my finger," he said. "I have other commitments, as well."

"Good. Then I see no reason for you not to be in here."

But she didn't smile or talk to him while she got ready and he knew that something had changed between them again. They weren't closer now; there was a new barrier between them and he had the feeling it came from both of them ignoring the truth of what they felt and wanted to say.

Iris didn't want him as her lover while she was doing the wedding stuff this weekend. And he wanted her to be that. He wanted more from her than he'd contractually asked for and it was too late. He'd signed the agreement and he had to live up to it.

And he would. Come hell or August Bisset.

Iris didn't like the fact that Zac was on the bed, but she wasn't about to let him see he had shaken her. And he did have her in a state. Enough of one that she'd had to leave the room to clear her head and get it on straight. Which was when she'd run into his mom.

Ever since Thea had grabbed her phone and responded to Graham's text, nothing had been in her control. Her sister had goaded her without even realizing what she was doing. It wasn't Thea's fault that Iris always had to appear to be in control. And as much as she hated to admit it, it wasn't Zac's fault she'd blurred the lines between them.

She could admit that the first time she'd fallen into bed with him had been sheer lust. She hadn't had that kind of experience with a guy before. But she'd been hot for him. The second time… Hell, she had no excuse. Last night had been a slip in judgment and from where she stood in the slightly steamy bathroom, pretending she was still putting on her makeup, it seemed downright stupid.

He was hot and sweet and unexpected. And not for her. She wasn't trying to talk herself out of a good thing; she was reminding herself of her reality. She couldn't let the romance of Adler finding a great guy influence her. It didn't matter that she'd wanted a man to grow her brand into "coupledom." Zac wasn't that guy—he was only acting the part.

No amount of sex was going to change that.

But would it hurt her to keep having sex with him?

That was the million-dollar question.

She wanted to be a modern woman and say no. She could have sex with a guy and not fall in love with him. After all, look what had happened with Graham. But that had been bad sex. Not the melt-her-panties-off sex she had with Zac. That kind of sex made a girl dream of something more. Something forbidden and as hard to find as a unicorn in Times Square. And as much as she was all about her preppy, practical lifestyle, she was still a dreamer at heart. Underneath her Lilly Pulitzer navy dress with the white embroidery, she was dreaming of a man who'd stand by her side.

The knock on the door startled her and she put her hand to the diamond charm on the necklace before opening the door.

"You okay?" Zac asked.

He looked so sincere and sexy, dressed up to impress his parents. She wanted to tease him about it but frankly she got it. It didn't matter how grown-up or successful she became, she still wanted her parents' approval and it made her fall a little bit more for him that he wanted his.

"Yeah," she said. Her heart wasn't in putting up her normal shield this morning. Or at least not with him.

"We said no lies between us."

She sighed and brushed past him, trying not to let the scent of his aftershave send sensual tingles of awareness through her body, but she couldn't help remembering how strong that scent had been on his naked chest last night.

"I know," she said, going to the wardrobe where she'd stored her shoes and pulling out a pair of strappy white sandals that would give her a few extra inches of height. "But you're throwing me off my game, Zac."

"What? How am I doing that?" he asked.

She wished she could be Thea and just bluntly tell him that sex was making her addle-brained, but she wasn't her twin. She was Iris, and there was no way she was going to bring up sex now. They were on their way to lunch with his entire family, and she had to keep the new girlfriend act going.

"Nothing. I think I'm just tired this morning and nervous about meeting your family."

He nodded, then walked over to her and put his hand on her shoulder. "They're going to be so impressed that you're with me, you're not going to have to worry about anything. I'm the black sheep of the family."

Only the Bissets would consider an America's Cup team member the black sheep. She smiled and realized he'd done it again: eased her nerves by being himself. She had to find a way to make her feelings more casual. But everything about him made her want to cling.

She wasn't a clinger.

She didn't want to be the woman Graham had accused her of being.

Heck, was she reacting this way because she was trying to prove something to Graham?

She hoped not. She wouldn't be that petty and spiteful. But she always knew a part of her would love to rub in his face that she'd had a fabulous night of orgasms in Zac's arms.

She groaned.

"Iris?"

"Sorry. I just had the worst thought."

"Want to share it?"

"No, you'll think I'm a lunatic."

"Now I have to know what it was," he said, with that crooked smile of his.

"You know that guy who broke up with me, forcing me

to hire you?" she asked. "Well he called me a cold fish because I couldn't climax with him and said lots of other mean things about me in the sack. And I was just thinking I wish I could tell him about last night. I think the issue was him, not me."

Zac smiled at her, pulled her into his arms and kissed her with passion. When he lifted his head, he said, "Angel face, it definitely wasn't you."

She put her arms around his shoulders and kissed him back, pouring all her fears and hopes into the embrace. When she stepped back, she told herself that was the last behind-closed-doors kiss they'd share. From now on, everything between them would be for show.

Really.

Thirteen

Juliette stood in the corner of the large conservatory that her mother always used for welcoming guests when the weather allowed. The July sky was gorgeous. Juliette almost wished she were the kind of woman to allow herself to believe in things like signs from heaven because she could have sworn that it was her sister looking down on them and giving Adler a perfect day.

But she didn't.

Her husband had changed his jacket three times, wanting to appear casual as he welcomed his one-time friend—and now enemy for more than thirty-five years—to lunch. Over the years Juliette had seen newspaper articles and some photos occasionally of Tad and his wife, Cora, but August always left events if they showed up so she'd never met them. Watching him try had always been the one thing that she hadn't been able to resist about him. August was a big man with big appetites, big ambition and a very big temper, but she'd glimpsed the vulnerability in him that he hid from the world.

They'd been married almost forty years so she knew that was to be expected.

"There you are, Jules," her mother said as she entered the room. "I have Michael and his staff ready with the welcoming drinks. I assume most of our guests will drink but he told me you asked him to include a nonalcoholic one, as well."

"I did, Mother. I hope you don't mind," she said. "I'm not sure what to expect from the Williams family, but I wanted to give everyone a choice."

"Good thinking."

Her mom had a way of making her feel like her party-hosting skills had stopped developing when she'd been throwing tea parties for her dolls even though she had a reputation for throwing the best parties in the Hamptons.

"Thanks."

"Do you really think she might make you a grand-mother?" her mom asked.

"I don't know. And we shouldn't be discussing this now. Though I am ready," Juliette admitted.

"I am too. And what's with your boys? I thought they'd be more like Auggie and marry young, but they seem to be waiting," her mother said.

"They are like Auggie but on the business side, not in terms of starting a family," Juliette said. All of her children were determined to make their mark on the world, and she didn't blame them. She'd often wondered if she'd had a career whether her marriage would have been different. Her life certainly would have. She might not even still be married to Auggie.

They heard the door open and Juliette was glad that the

guests had started arriving. She liked socializing because it distracted her from her own thoughts and her own life.

"Gran," Zac said, coming into the conservatory with Iris Collins on his arm.

Iris was too sophisticated for her son, and if Juliette were being honest, she thought the younger woman was a little too prim. Zac liked his women more...well, sporty for one thing. And loose but not in a negative way.

"Zac, so good to see you. Your mother and I are both delighted you're back from Australia," her mom said as she went to hug him.

Juliette hugged Iris and then stepped back to hug Zac. Her boys were all taller than her now and his hug engulfed her. She held him longer than she knew she should, but she'd missed this tall blond boy of hers. He always made sailing seem like it was a gentleman's sport but she knew it was dangerous and she worried about him.

"Mom," he said, kissing her on the forehead.

"Sweetie," she answered. "Tell me why you were in Boston and how you met Iris. I know that's where it happened but the details are murky."

Zac put his arm out, drawing Iris in to the curve of his body. "Nothing murky about it, Mom. I quit my old America's Cup team and was in Boston looking for sponsors for my run in the next one. If I asked Dad, there'd be strings attached. Iris's father runs an investment group and we met when I was waiting to speak to him."

"I stumbled and he caught me," Iris said.

Zac looked down at Iris and winked and suddenly Juliette loved seeing her son with this woman. There was something about them that made her want to smile.

"Your dad won't be happy about the investment but I think everything else will be fine," Juliette said.

"I know but once I caught Iris I told myself not to let her go. It's not every day I meet a woman like Iris."

"So true," Nick Williams said, coming up behind Zac and clapping him on the shoulder.

Juliette smiled at Adler's fiancé. She'd met him a few times before and found him to be a very likeable man. But, of course, he was a thorn in Logan's side, always foiling his business deals and trying to beat him to market. So she understood that not everyone in her family was happy to see him, not to mention that he was marrying Adler.

"Hey, man," Zac said, turning to shake Nick's hand as Adler came in with an older woman.

There was something familiar about the tall brunette, Juliette thought as she came closer. Then their eyes met and both women froze. *Dear God.*

It was the other woman who'd been in labor the night Juliette had given birth to her unnamed stillborn baby. Except she was a brunette now, not a blonde, and she wore the trappings of wealth as easily as if she'd been born to it.

Was this Cora Williams? The girl—Bonnie, she'd said her name was. Bonnie Smith. They'd both been in that post-delivery room crying. Juliette because she'd lost her baby that she'd hoped would save her marriage and Bonnie because she'd been cut off from her family, had no job and no way to support twins.

She remembered that moment when they'd realized there was a solution that would serve them both. If Juliette raised one of the fraternal twins as her own son, it would solve their problems.

Juliette had made a deal that only she, Bonnie and the nurse Jennifer had known about. They'd switched her still-born child for one of the healthy boys. Juliette had given Bonnie a large sum of money from her private trust fund so she could go back to school and raise her son. Jennifer had taken a small sum to falsify the documents.

There wasn't a day that went by that she didn't think about the deal she'd made. How her Logan wasn't really hers. But until this moment she'd expected to keep the secret until her grave.

She'd never met Nick's parents…that meant that Nick was probably the other twin. She saw stars and thought she was going to pass out.

Crap.

This wasn't good.

The woman… Cora. Heck, she remembered everything about that night but at the time she'd called herself Bonnie Smith.

"Auntie Jules, this is Nick's mom, Cora," Adler said, bringing them both face-to-face. Cora seemed as shocked as Juliette felt.

But manners guided her and Juliette put out her hand. "So nice to meet you."

"You, as well," Cora said, but her hands were clammy. "I feel like I know you from all of Adler's stories."

"Me too," Juliette said. She knew they needed to talk but not now. Not today.

"Adler, is this your fiancé? I'm so eager to meet him and get to know his family," Auggie said as he came in.

Cora turned and Juliette saw the look on her husband's face as he saw her. She knew that look. Cora and Auggie had been lovers.

"Cora?"

"August," Cora said, then turned to Juliette. "You never said your husband was August Bisset."

"I didn't know you knew him."

"We need to talk," Cora said.

"I think we do," Juliette said.

* * *

Zac saw the color leave his mother's face and the shock on his dad's when he saw Nick's mom. Nick looked at him and they both seemed to be of the same mindset. Carlton had entered the room and looked at Cora and then blanched.

"Why is Bonnie Smith here?" Carlton asked as he came into the room. The older man had been his father's PR man and spin doctor since the beginning of his career. In fact, Zac had never been at a family meeting that wasn't chaired by Carlton. He was the one who cleaned up messes for the family. There were times when Zac liked the older man; he was nicer than his father. But there were other times when Carlton could be tough as nails. This was one of those times.

"Bonnie? This is my mother. Cora Williams," Nick said, stepping to Cora's side and putting his arm around her shoulders. "Is there a problem?"

"Don't worry about it, Nicky. I need to speak to August and Juliette alone. Will you keep an eye out for your dad?" Cora said.

Nick pulled his mom aside, away from everyone else, and Adler was looking at Zac's mom like she wanted to ask a million questions, but she wasn't saying a word. His father just walked out of the room with Carlton, turning around briefly. "Vivian, may we use your study?"

"Of course, Auggie."

"Ladies, will you please join me in there?" August asked.

Zac watched as his mom nodded but Nick stepped in front of Cora. "I don't think so. She's not going anywhere with you. I want to know what's going on. Why are they calling you Bonnie?"

"I agree with Nick," Adler said, going over to her fiancé and taking his hand. "What's going on?"

Juliette stood up and looked at Iris and Gran, and both

of the women walked out of the room. But Zac stayed. This was his family and he wanted to know what was happening.

The butler closed the door to the conservatory. The groups in the room formed an odd triangle. Zac and his mom were on one side, his father and Carlton on another and Nick, his mom and Adler finished the formation. His father looked like he was going to lose his temper, his mom looked scared and Cora looked defensive.

He glanced over at Adler. She looked pale and afraid.

"Dad, how do you know Nick's mom?" Zac asked.

"I don't think you should be—"

"Just answer him, August. Tell our son how you know Nick's mom," his mom said.

From the tone of his mom's voice, Zac had the sinking feeling that Cora had been one of his father's other women. God, this was a mess. Had his father become her lover to get back at his rival Tad Williams?

"They were friends," Carlton said. "A long time ago. She was an intern who worked at the company just after Darien was born."

"Friends?" Nick asked, looking down at his mom. "With August Bisset?"

"Yes, dear," Cora said. "It was before I knew your father. We were friends."

"How do you know Juliette?" Nick asked. "Were you all friends?"

His mom's shoulders straightened and she shook her head. "No. That's not how we know each other. I met your mom the night I gave birth to Logan."

"We were in the hospital together. Both of us. In that rural hospital in the middle of a storm."

August looked at Cora and then shook his head. "You gave birth the same night as Jules?"

"I did," she said. "Unfortunately, I was a single mom and Juliette was kind to me."

"I know how hard it can be," Zac's mom said.

There was more to it. He could feel it in the room. A single woman giving birth at the same hospital as... Zac looked at his dad as he came to a conclusion that he hoped was wrong. Had his dad been Cora's lover? Was he Nick's father? *Hell.* He hoped not because then this entire wedding weekend was going to be a lot tougher than he'd thought it would be.

"Dad?"

"Zac."

"Is Nick your—"

"Niece's fiancé?" Carlton asked. "Because that's really the only question that makes sense, Zachary."

"Carlton, enough. It's just us. I want the truth," Zac said. "Adler deserves that. Hell, I think we all do."

He turned to look at Nick, who was staring down at his mother, and he saw the truth on the older brunette's face. She started to cry and before anyone could say anything else, the door burst open and Tad Williams walked in. He went straight to his wife's side. "What did that bastard say to you?"

But Cora couldn't answer. She just shook her head and Tad pulled her into his arms. Nick was looking at his mother and then back at August and then he just walked out of the room. Adler ran after him and Zac wondered if he should leave, but when he started to go, his mom held on to his wrist, keeping him by her side. He looked over at her.

"Please."

He nodded and put his arm back around her shoulder. Zac knew he shouldn't be surprised because his father had never been a one-woman man. But in recent years he'd started to mellow and settle down. He'd been a good husband to his mom since Mari's birth. But this was a secret from the past and it was coming back to bite them. The kind of secret that could hurt them all. Not like the secret he and Iris had. That one was just between the two of them.

He'd made damned sure of that. "Dad, is Nick your son?"

"What?" Tad asked. "What is he talking about?"

Juliette had never felt like this before. She knew that Nick was August's child, which meant that Logan, the twin she'd raised, was August's child too. She'd always felt bad about deceiving her husband but now she felt sick. This complicated game that she and August had been playing with each other for forty years was now going to ensnare too many other people. And their sons would be hurt. Mari had been the product of their reconciliation after August's blatant affair in the early '90s but this was from almost a decade earlier. At the time, Juliette had never suspected her husband was having an affair.

She'd had some postpartum depression after Darien's birth and it had taken her a long time to get pregnant with her second child. The pregnancy had made things start to feel better between them. She had the feeling now that she'd been fooling herself. Because Cora had been pregnant at the same time with who she now truly believed were August's twins.

"I asked a question," Tad said.

"Tad, honey, August and I—"

"She worked for me, Tad. After you left the company, we had those interns come in and Bonnie—I mean Cora—was one of them."

Zac knew there was bad blood between Tad Williams and his father but not being a part of the day-to-day operation at Bisset Industries, he didn't know the details.

"Did he work for you?" Zac asked.

"I was an intern at the company for a short while until your father had me fired," Tad explained.

"You weren't performing up to expectations," August said.

"Whatever. How could you have an affair? You had a new wife and baby at home," Tad said.

"You're right, I did," his dad said. "I can make no excuses, only apologies. I wasn't the man I am today. When I saw something I wanted, I went after it. I didn't care who I hurt. And, Jules, my love, you know I regret that. I don't regret it if Nick is my son. Cora was my lover at about that time. But I assumed he was your son."

"No, Cora and I started dating when Nick was three months old," Tad said. "Cora?"

"August is the father. I never told him I was pregnant. I ended things as soon as I realized that he had a wife and baby at home."

Zac wasn't sure what to say. This wasn't at all what he'd been expecting when he'd come to his gran's house for lunch with Adler's fiancé's family.

The conservatory doors opened again, and this time Logan and Leo walked in. Both of his brothers came straight toward him and his mom.

Logan put his hands on his hips, "What's going on? Adler is in tears. I really couldn't understand a word she said but she mentioned Dad…"

"Oh, God," Zac said. "Dude, there's no easy way to say this but it seems like your archenemy in business might be related to us."

"What the f—!" Logan didn't handle the news well. He turned on their father, who held his hands up.

"I just learned about it a second ago," their dad said.

Their mom put her hand to her throat and walked out of the conservatory and August followed.

"No one talks to the press. We need a meeting to figure out how to do this properly," Carlton said. "Mr. and Mrs. Williams, do you have a PR person, or would you like me to run point on this."

"We don't have a PR person," Cora said. "Nothing like this happens to us."

"I'll handle it for you," Carlton said, patting Cora on the arm. "Don't worry. This isn't going to be a big deal."

"I guess when you're used to cleaning up after August Bisset, it seems that way to you," Tad said. "But we are straight shooters. The Williams family doesn't cover up the truth."

Carlton nodded. "I know you and August have had issues in the past, but there is no way that you and your wife look good in this scenario if you go public with just the truth. August has a child he knew nothing about. You can see how that will play in the press."

Cora started crying and Tad put his arm around his wife. Zac walked over to them. He wasn't involved in the Bisset business. He felt that of all his brothers, he was the one who could liaise most easily with the Williams family.

"Carlton will make this right for all of us," Zac said. "He's not going to do anything that will put you in a bad light, Mrs. Williams. Isn't that right?"

"Of course. I'm sorry if it seemed I might," Carlton said. "We just have to cover all of the bases."

"I can't do this right now," Cora said.

"You don't have to," Carlton said. "I'm sorry I came on strong. Would you both come with me and we can figure out how you want to handle this announcement? I can tell you from past experience that we want to be the ones controlling the narrative."

Carlton led the Williamses out of the room and Zac turned back to his brothers. He hadn't seen them in person in over six months. "This isn't how I envisioned our reunion."

"Damn," Leo said, coming over to hug him. "It's good to see you, but what the hell happened?"

"Let's go get some cold ones and I'll tell you," Zac said.

"I can't," Logan said. "Is Nick really related to us? I mean, I hate that guy. I know Adler's marrying him and I was willing to be cordial but he can't be our half brother. I mean, he's the worst."

Zac clapped his older brother on the shoulder and squeezed. "I think he is. We'll figure out how to deal with him. Maybe he's not as bad as you imagine."

"Who's not?" Dare asked, coming into the room. He had his phone in one hand and a whiskey glass in the other. "Carlton told me you'd catch me up."

"We're all going to need something to drink," Leo said, leading them out of the conservatory to the lounge down the hall with the built-in bar. Iris and Gran were already sitting there and the women glanced up as they came in. Zac heard his brothers talking to his grandmother but he ignored them as Iris smiled at him. Who knew their charade would be the least exciting secret this weekend?

Fourteen

Iris didn't know how to help the actual situation they were in, but she did know how to be a good friend. When Adler came to the doorway and Iris saw the tears on her friend's face, she didn't even hesitate. She grabbed her friend's hand and took her upstairs to the bedroom that she knew Adler used when she was at her grandmother's house.

"What's going on?" she asked. "How's Nick?"

"Nick's mad. He's mad at his mom, his dad and August. It's just too much. You know I never thought that he'd have anything like this happen in his life. Oh, my God, this is something I'd expect from my dad. He's going to be completely crazy about this. He told me that I couldn't escape the chaos of life," Adler said.

Her friend was rambling and pacing around the bedroom. Iris saw that her hands were shaking.

"It's okay. Chaos is your friend," Iris said. "Your dad is going to be protective. Is he on Nantucket yet?"

"I don't know. I was supposed to text him when everyone was here. He was planning to come over and diffuse the tension between the Bissets and the Williamses," Adler said. "Given these new developments, I don't think even Dad can do that."

Adler stopped in front of the big bay window looking out at the ocean and Iris went over and hugged her. "What do you want me to do?"

"Make this all go away," Adler said.

"I can do that. We can leave Nantucket and go off grid until this passes."

Adler started crying and Iris hugged her friend harder. She didn't know how to fix this. She didn't know what impact Nick's paternity was going to have on Adler. Clearly she and Nick weren't related, as Nick was Cora and August's son; Adler wasn't a blood relation to August. But still, this was the kind of thing that Adler hated. She didn't like the jet-set party scene, or the bohemian live-for-the-moment mind-set. She wanted normal.

"Nick was supposed to be my Cory."

"I know," Iris said. Adler was referring to Cory from *Boy Meets World*. Growing up, the show had been their favorite to escape into. They'd loved that family dynamic and Adler had craved it for herself.

Adler's phone started ringing but she didn't make a move to see who it was.

"Want me to handle that?"

"Who is it?"

Iris glanced down at the screen. "It's your dad."

"Let me talk to him," Adler said. She took the phone and Iris stepped away to give her some semblance of privacy.

Iris was worried about Nick and Adler. This wasn't the news they needed two days before their wedding. She pulled out her own phone and texted Nick to ask if he was okay.

She got back a thumbs-up emoji.

She couldn't leave Adler and she knew that Nick needed someone. She didn't have any of his siblings' phone numbers and she wasn't sure if it was the right solution or not but she texted Zac.

Would you go and check on Nick? I think he's alone and he might need someone to listen.

She got an almost instant response. Where is he?

Iris used the location service on her messaging app. Nick was at the yacht club. Probably in the bar. At least he wasn't driving.

She sent the information to Zac.

On my way to see him. I'll tell him you sent me. He might not want to talk to me.

At least he won't be alone. Thanks.

No problem. This wasn't how I saw the day going.

Me either.

I'm glad you're here with me.

Me too.

She didn't have to think too hard about it. Seeing the people she loved, a family she thought she knew, thrown into a maelstrom was hard to witness. Knowing that they were going to have to put on a good public face when all of the guests started arriving made her glad she was here. She could help with that. And being with Zac was giving her a safe base to do it from. She wasn't just Adler's friend; she was posing as Zac's girlfriend and this family drama included her.

Adler collapsed back on the bed as she ended her call with her dad. "What am I going to do?"

Iris went over and lay down next to her on the bed. "About what?"

"Nick. The wedding. Everything. This isn't what I signed up for."

"Do you love him?"

"I thought I did."

"Do you still want to marry him?"

Adler leaned up on her elbow. "I don't want the media circus that this could become but I do want to marry him. But Nick isn't the same guy now."

"I wish it were simple. I've never seen two people as in love as you guys were," Iris said. "Are you strong enough to handle this?"

"I don't know," Adler said. "Our love has been easy. We've never been tested like this."

"You've handled way worse," Iris said.

"But that was easy because I was sort of removed when dad was having his issues with the media," Adler said. "It's simpler when I'm not in the direct spotlight."

"I know. But you won't be for long. If I know your dad, he'll do something outrageous to keep the attention off you. He loves you more than any other person on the planet."

Adler nodded. "That wouldn't be good either because he's just started to settle down. He can't go back to being outrageous again and living that rock'n'roll lifestyle. I mean he's barely recovered—"

"He won't," Iris interrupted. It was hard enough for

Adler to worry about Nick, let alone having to worry about her dad.

"Oh, my God. I shouldn't have let Nick leave alone. I freaked out about my perfect wedding," Adler said. "He's just found out a man he hates is his father."

"I know. I sent Zac to find him," Iris said.

"I think I need to go to him. We have to talk about what this means for us."

Iris agreed. Her friend was too emotional to drive so she went with her. They snuck out of the house because Adler didn't want to risk running into any of her cousins or her uncle on the way.

Zac picked up two Maker's Marks, straight, before approaching Nick. The other man looked like Zac had felt when he'd walked away from the UK team he'd been part of and decided to strike out on his own. He'd had no idea if any of his friends would come with him and it had been a lonely, lonely feeling.

"Nick, would you like some company?"

Nick glanced up at him and for the first time since Zac had known him—which, granted, wasn't long—the man didn't look at ease. His eyes were bloodshot and Zac noticed that his knuckles were scraped as if he'd punched a wall.

"I brought a double, figured you could use it," Zac said.

Nick took the drink and pushed the chair opposite him out with his foot. Zac sat down and took a swallow once Nick drank some of his.

"Iris sent me. I would have come on my own but had no way of getting in touch with you."

"Thanks, man. I'm not sure what the hell is going on and I know I'm not the best company right now."

"That's cool. I spend most of my time on the ocean fighting against the wind and waves and trying to prove I'm nothing like the rest of my family," Zac said.

"Your family…"

"It's yours too, right? I mean we don't have to talk about it but I want you to know that we're not as bad as you might think."

Nick downed the rest of his whiskey. "I can't do this right now. I was already a little nervous thinking of marrying Adler and starting my own family and then to learn that everything I knew about myself was a lie…"

"It wasn't a lie," Zac said. "I don't know much about your family but your dad is Tad Williams. No matter what biological matter my dad contributed, Tad raised you and the man I saw today is a good man. He defended your mother and mine."

"He is a good man. I've always wanted to be just like him," Nick said.

Zac realized that Nick might not know it but he had a better relationship with Tad Williams than he ever would have had with August Bisset. August was mellowing but he was still a difficult man to have as a father.

"That's good," Zac said. "Nothing's changed. Did you know he wasn't your biological father?"

"I did."

"Did your mom ever say anything about my dad?" Zac asked.

"She said she'd fallen for a man who was charming and funny, and when she'd realized he belonged to someone else, she left. She said he wasn't in the picture and that Tad was the only father I'd know."

Zac wished that had been the case. "I'm sorry."

"Thanks," Nick said, pushing the glass back and forth between his hands.

"Want another?"

"Yes. But I have to fix things with Adler. She tried to say things would be okay and I yelled at her."

"I think I'd do the same thing in your situation," Zac said. "That kind of news is hard to hear."

"It is, but Adler didn't deserve that. She was freaking out too, I know it, even though she didn't say anything."

"But she loves you," Zac said. "I've never seen her this happy before."

"That's the worst part about finding this out now. It's going to be a cloud over the wedding. Hell, I don't even know if she'll still marry me after I yelled at her the way I did."

The door to the bar opened. Zac caught sight of Iris and Adler. Leave it to Iris to get the couple back together and salvage the weekend. That was one of the things he admired about her. She didn't hesitate to do whatever she needed to in order to make things run smoothly.

Look at how she'd contracted him to be her man when she'd been dumped.

Where had that thought come from?

There was a hint of resentment inside him as he realized he might be just another quick fix that she was so good at administering.

"There's only one way to find out," Zac said to Nick. "Adler just walked in."

Nick pushed his glass to one side and sat up straighter. His shoulders went back and all the doubt and anger that had been dominating his expression and posture were subdued. It was as if he were putting on a show for Adler.

Instead, he was the confident man that Zac had seen the night before at dinner. He ran his hands over his hair and then noticed the scraped knuckles. Zac pulled his pocket square out and handed it to the other man. "Use this."

"Thanks."

Nick cleaned his knuckles, passing the square of fabric back just as the ladies arrived at their table.

Nick and Zac stood and when Nick turned to Adler, Zac looked away. They were hugging each other, and it was so intimate that really no one should be watching them.

He glanced at Iris and saw the longing on her face. She wanted what Adler and Nick had but she'd settled for a contracted boyfriend.

He wondered why. Was it convenience? Or was there something deeper that kept her from really committing to a man?

"Let's give them some privacy," he said.

She nodded and slipped her hand into his as they turned away. He looked down at their joined hands. After the morning they'd had, filled with lies and betrayals and secrets that should have stayed that way, he wondered what he was going to do about his woman he'd agreed to pretend to care for, since he had already realized that he had never been pretending with her.

She had gotten to him from the first moment they'd met and he should have done the smart thing and walked away. But she had him ensnared, and he had to admit he didn't mind it as long as she felt something for him.

Which he couldn't be sure of.

Iris walked with Zac to the other side of the yacht club bar, which wasn't very busy at this hour. She was worried about Zac. She knew he and his father had a contentious relationship and finding out that his dad had cheated on his mom…that had to be a blow.

"Are you okay?"

He held out a chair for her and nodded. "Do you want a drink?"

"I'm okay, but you can get one if you want to."

"I don't like to drink alone," he said.

"I'll have a Perrier with a lime," Iris said, realizing he needed something to do. She would bet that everyone in his family was doing their best to keep busy and not think about what had happened.

He walked to the bar and Iris realized she should probably cancel all of the filming she'd planned to do around the events for the day. She sent a text to her staff, letting them know that the family had decided to have a quiet day together and told them to enjoy the bonus day off. She also texted her friend Quinn, who was producing the televised wedding ceremony, and told her that Adler wasn't going to be available today.

Quinn called back instead of texting. Considering that Iris, Quinn and Adler had been good friends since their freshman year of college when they'd met at the sorority house, she wasn't surprised.

"Is Adler okay?"

"Yes. There was some unexpected drama with the Bissets and the Williamses and I don't know that she's in the right state to film. Just wanted to give you a heads-up."

"Thanks for that. Is she okay? I'm going to text her. Just send her some virtual hugs. I'm on the damn ferry right now. This thing seems to go slower and slower every time I get on it."

Quinn was a big city gal used to moving at a fast pace. Iris had once seen her friend pay for and bag up another woman's groceries because she was moving too slow. "There's nothing you could do if you were here sooner."

"Except see Ad and if needed, kick some Bisset butt. They have to be the trouble, right?"

"It's complicated," Iris said. "Text me when you get here. Do you need a ride?"

"No. The traffic will be heavy when the ferry gets in. I'm going to run to the hotel. I need to burn off some energy."

"Okay, I'll see you later then."

"Bye."

Zac set the glasses on the table before sitting down across from her. He rubbed the back of his neck and turned to look out at the ocean. His clean jaw and sharp blade of a nose gave him a gorgeous profile but then everything about him struck the right note for her.

"Wish you were out there?"

He turned back and took a sip of what looked like whiskey. "Yes and no. I mean, my mom would've been alone when she heard the news about my dad today if I hadn't been there."

"That was a shock," Iris said. "I was glad I got to escape."

"I bet."

He didn't say anything, just swallowed his whiskey in one long sip.

"Do you want to talk about it?"

"Which part?"

"Whichever part you want to," she said.

"I'm not sure. This isn't part of the contract."

"So? You said it yourself. We're friends, aren't we?" she asked. She had stopped thinking about the contract when shit had gotten real in the conservatory. It had made her feel very shallow to realize she'd been worried about showing up stag when something like this was going down.

"Are we?"

She wasn't sure if he was being cagey because of what he'd learned about his dad or if he had some beef with her. She knew if it were her, she'd want to fight with someone... probably Thea because she knew that she could say mean things to her sister and, in the end, Thea would forgive her.

"Yes, we are. Listen, I can't begin to imagine what you're feeling but if you need to talk or yell or go sailing or—"

"Have sex?"

Her eyes widened but she nodded. Whatever he needed. She hated to see the people she loved hurt... Wait, did she love him? She wasn't sure if she did because she'd never been in love before, but this felt...well, not like anything she'd experienced before.

"Yes. Even that. Whatever you need. I'm here," she said.

He reached for her hand and laced their fingers together. "I don't know what I need. I guess I'm in shock. I've always known my dad wasn't faithful to my mom. He had a very public affair before Mari was born. But I thought we knew the worst of him. Catting around on Mom while she was pregnant with Logan...that is something I can't forgive."

"You don't have to," Iris said. "You get to decide what you feel about that and if you can't get past it, then that's fine. He's always going to be your father, but you don't have to let him be a part of your life."

Zac nodded. "I know what you are saying but here's the kicker. I want him in my life. I've always worked so hard to make him proud. To prove that I was better than he was. And now, knowing in my heart how petty I want to be about this, I don't think I am any better."

Iris went around to sit next to him at the table. She put her arm around him and her chin on his shoulder. "No one is. That's something I had to figure out the hard way. But no one is better than anybody else. We are all messed up and trying to figure out how to get through each day. Your dad had a shock, as well. He screwed up and probably thought that he had put all of that in the past. And then today his mistakes were front and center for his entire family to see."

"You're right. I know you are," Zac said. He pulled her around onto his lap and just held her in his arms. She knew she should get up, that people would see them, but she didn't want to. She wanted to give as much comfort to this man she loved as she could. And it didn't matter what kind of image they presented to the world.

Nick took Adler to the new home he'd had built for them on Nantucket. She watched him pacing around the living room, that she'd had designed for their future. But as she looked around she saw it was all the things she wanted them to be and maybe not who they really were.

"What are we going to do?" she asked him.

"Do about what—the wedding?"

"Yes." What did he think she was talking about?

"I really don't know. We have all these people coming to Nantucket. If we cancel—"

"Are you thinking about not marrying me?" For the first time she had to face her fears about Nick. He was questioning everything about himself and his life. Maybe he was questioning a future with her, too?

"I don't know," he said, shoving his hands through his hair. "My gut says this isn't going to blow over easily. I want to manage it."

"I get that. Managing the news about your parentage should be the top priority. But are we going to do it as a team?"

He turned on her and she saw anger in his eyes. "Can we have one minute where it's not all about you, Adler? Is that possible?"

She took a deep breath and nodded. She was about to start crying and blinked rapidly to keep the tears from falling. "Take as much time as you need. I'm going to my gran's."

"Run away. That's what you do when life gets too real, isn't it?"

"It's what I do when I'm confronted with a bully who is lashing out because he doesn't want to admit he's hurting," she said. Her voice was low and rough from trying to choke back tears. "Let's have the clambake tonight and tomorrow we can figure out if we should still get married. We have a lot of people coming. Try to remember it's not all about you, either."

Adler left the room, tears streaming down her face. She wished her mom were here so she could talk with her about this. She had no idea how to handle Nick right now.

Was the man she loved gone? Had Nick disappeared when he learned he was August Bisset's biological son?

Fifteen

Iris and Zac ended up taking a lead role in entertaining the guests who were attending the clambake on Thursday evening. The elder Williams and Bisset couples had spent the day with Carlton coming up with the spin on today's revelations in case the story somehow got out to the press.

Iris just stayed by Adler's side and did whatever her friend asked her to do. It was odd to see Adler so fragile because she'd never been like that before. This thing with Nick had rattled her.

It was safe to say the couple hadn't resolved things. They were still going through with planned events but Iris could tell nothing was right.

Nick was drinking a lot; Iris had known him in his frat boy days so that was saying something. Zac was keeping pace with him and she had to say she was both surprised and happy to see that he was a really funny drunk. His brother Logan, who had the fiercest rivalry with Nick in business, had surrounded himself with a group of women that Iris wasn't sure were part of the wedding party. Leo, Zac's younger brother, was keeping an eye on Zac and Nick and running drinks back and forth to them. Nick's brothers, Asher and Noah, were hanging with Leo and Nick's sister Olivia was at Iris's side, helping Adler out.

The food had been prepared by a catering company Adler had hired, which meant there was little for them to do but keep the conversation going and that horrible truth buried.

Iris saw Toby Osborn before Adler did. He still had a full head of hair despite being sixty. He had a mustache and short beard and carried his legendary guitar, Martha Mae. He had his usual entourage with him, including his live-in girlfriend, whom Iris had met before and liked.

As soon as Adler saw her dad, she ran to him and he pushed his guitar around to his back and caught her. Iris knew that Adler had always wished for a more normal upbringing but there was no denying she had been well loved by her father. She was his world.

"What'd I miss?" Quinn asked, coming up beside her and handing her a gin and tonic.

"Nothing. The elders are back at the house having a meeting, Nick's getting drunk and Zac is helping him, and Toby's just arrived."

"Are you dating Zac?"

"That's what you got out of my rundown?" Iris asked.

"Well, I did see it on my newsfeed. He's not your usual type, is he?"

"Uh, no. Graham kind of put me off my usual type."

"Graham was a douche bag," Quinn said.

"Did everyone hate him?" Iris asked.

"Yes," Quinn said. "I'm glad you aren't with him anymore."

She glanced over at Nick and Zac, who were singing along to Sister Hazel's "All For You." She especially loved when they tried to harmonize and neither of them sang a note that was near the other's. Toby set Adler down and went over to the two would-be singers and joined in.

"Oh, my God, they're hilarious," Iris said, grabbing her phone so she could capture the moment. She knew that Nick would want to see this happy moment later, after a day that had been filled with so many ups and downs.

Zac caught her filming and wriggled his eyebrows at her. The next time the chorus came on, he gestured to her as if to say he only wanted to be with her. She knew he was drunk and kidding around but she wanted this to be true.

Adler came up beside her and looped her arm through hers and Quinn took her other arm. After the crazy day they'd had, she was so grateful to have these two women by her side. She wasn't sure that anything was going to come of her and Zac but she'd have this memory to last forever.

And after the way she'd seen the past come back to haunt August and Cora, she wondered if she shouldn't come clean about hiring Zac to be her man for the weekend. She didn't want that to come out at some odd time when they were both older and more established…maybe with other partners.

The thought hurt and dimmed her joy of the moment, but she had to be honest with herself. She loved Zac but that hadn't made her blind to how impossible it was for the two of them.

He was in the spotlight, dancing and singing and loving the attention, and she would never be comfortable out there. She needed her glam squad and her prepared scripts to be comfortable in front of the camera.

She stopped filming the video as the song ended. Toby started singing some of his hits and Adler drifted over to Nick and they walked down the beach. Quinn's phone went off and she turned away to take the call. Iris was left standing by herself. Zac was surrounded by his brothers. She watched him and realized that he always knew how to handle every situation and she envied that.

It was something she'd never been able to find in herself. She could only function with rules. She took a step backward as she realized that she had let herself love Zac because it was safe. She'd let her guard down, thinking her contract and her end date would keep her from getting hurt. Never realizing that letting her guard down was the thing she should have been avoiding.

It wasn't a certain type of man who could hurt her—it was herself. Her own flaws and fears had been driving her to this moment ever since she'd become an adult.

She looked at Adler, trying so hard to find a man who was nothing like her father and then finding out on the eve of her wedding that he had a scandalous secret, even though it was no fault of his own. Then Iris thought of her own secret with Zac, one she was 100 percent responsible for.

There was no way to protect herself from herself. She wished she'd realized this in Boston before she'd walked into that bar and seen that sexy man for the first time. She wished she'd had the strength to know herself and be real about her fear of being alone then. She wished... Hell, it hurt her to her core but she wished she'd never talked to Zac Bisset.

Without saying a word to anyone, she quietly left the party and went back to the hotel.

She was in her bed for a good four hours before she heard Zac in the other room with some other guys. They were laughing and shushing each other and she lay there alone in her bed, realizing that even paying for a man hadn't changed her.

* * *

Zac woke up with a fuzzy mouth on the couch of the suite he'd been sharing with Iris. He had one shoe on and his belt was removed but otherwise he was fully clothed. He blinked, surprised he didn't have a headache. But he'd been very well hydrated the night before. He blinked again, seeing the light through the window, and then Iris sitting in a chair opposite him. She watched him with that prim expression she had when she was in an awkward situation.

He scrubbed his hand over his face, felt the stubble on his jaw and something that might be a bruise later—did he punch Logan last night? Then he forced himself to sit up and tried to smile but the light was really bright and he had to close his eyes for a second.

"If you can manage it, I've put in an order for a bacon, egg and cheese biscuit for you," Iris said.

"You really are an angel. Coffee too?" he asked.

"Coffee too."

He knew he should go and wash up. He'd been in this situation before. Women didn't always respond positively when he came home drunk and passed out on the couch.

He washed his face, brushed his teeth and debated a quick shower. After a whiff of his clothes as he took them off, he decided that there was no debate and spent three minutes under the hot jets of water.

He felt closer to human as he left the bedroom dressed in a pair of basketball shorts and an old America's Cup team T-shirt. His food was on the table under a cloche, along with a cup of coffee and a plate of fresh fruit.

Iris sat at the table, looking so elegant and put together, like a woman with a mission on her mind.

"I'm sorry about last night. I knew Nick needed to drink because I would in his situation. My brothers were being uptight and his were too, so someone had to be the one to break the ice," Zac said.

"That's okay. Honestly, you were so funny and probably exactly what everyone needed," she said.

He opened the cloche and took a bite of the bacon, egg and cheese biscuit, and closed his eyes. It was perfect. Exactly what he needed.

"What about you? I know I wasn't delivering on my duties last night," Zac said.

"About that," Iris said. "I think we can agree that your behavior last night can't be repeated. Starting today, I need you to be everything I asked for in the contract."

"I'll try," he said, taking another bite of the biscuit. Honestly, at this moment, he was only half listening to her. The food was making him feel a lot better.

"You'll do more than try or you will be in breach of our agreement and I will call my father and tell him that I don't think you're a good investment," she said.

That he heard.

He put his biscuit down and his hands on the table next to his plate. "Are you threatening me?"

"I am. I know your family is going through some messy things, but your first priority is the commitment you made to me."

"Other than last night, have I shirked my duties?"

"Last night was the first time you were supposed to be doing your duties in front of other people."

"I sang to you, Iris. Even Toby said that was romantic," Zac said.

"I came home about four hours before you did," Iris pointed out. "You didn't even notice I was gone… Not very romantic."

"Sorry I wasn't paying one hundred percent attention to you," he said. "I already apologized for last night."

"You did and I appreciate it. I'm just saying don't let it happen again."

She stood up and walked past him to go to the bedroom but he stopped her by catching her wrist lightly in his hand. "Are you okay?"

She nodded, tugged her hand free and kept on going.

But he knew she wasn't. He wanted to blame it on his hangover but he knew he was missing something. He'd done something last night that had changed the way that Iris was looking at him. Damn him if he could remember all of the details clearly enough to figure it out.

He finished his biscuit and coffee. He wanted to make this right. He stood up and went to the bedroom door, knocking on it before entering. She was standing in front of her wardrobe when he entered.

"Hey, I'm sorry about last night. Whatever you need today, I'll be there for you. I think we have the scramble golf tournament and you wanted me to pose for some photos, right?"

"Yes. My glam squad will be bringing some clothes for you and I'll text you when I need you. I kind of like the stubble so if you want to leave it for this morning and then shave before tonight's rehearsal dinner—if it's still even on—that would be fine. Did you see Adler last night?"

"I don't remember," he said. "Angel face, I really am sorry. I never meant to drink like that. It's not every day I find out I have another brother."

She nodded. "I know. I'd be a monster not to understand it, and I definitely am not upset that you drank last night."

"Then what are you mad at me about?" he asked. "Don't deny it, you are upset with me."

She shook her head. "I'm upset with myself because I thought you were something that you aren't."

Something he wasn't. He'd been more himself with her

than he'd ever been with anyone else and she still thought he was phoning it in.

He was tired, he knew that, and a wiser man than he would have kept his mouth shut. But hell, no one had ever labeled him the smart Bisset.

"I'm not what you thought?" he asked, approaching her as she turned away from the wardrobe to face him. "Iris, you hired a guy you met in a bar to be your boyfriend for a four-day wedding. What exactly were you expecting?"

"Don't get defensive, I wasn't attacking you," she said, folding her hands neatly in front of her.

And that right there was enough to push him over the edge. He'd seen glimpses of the real woman beneath all the prim and proper behavior but more times than not, this was what he was faced with. Some cardboard cutout of the real woman. No man wanted that. Actually he felt safe in saying that no one wanted to have a relationship with someone who was always hiding behind the perfect smile, clothing and manners.

"I've gone above and beyond for you. I actually like you as a person most of the time, but I can't with this," he said, gesturing to her holding her coffee cup with one hand while smiling serenely at him. "It's not real. I get that we have a contract, but I've never been anyone other than myself with you. Who does that?"

"I do, according to you."

"You can't fight properly. Tell me what's on your mind. Don't worry about hurting my feelings or how it might make you seem human instead of a social media goddess with the great life. Just be you, Iris. Do you even know who you are?"

"Screw you, Zac. That's not a very nice thing to say. Of course, I know who I am," she said.

"That's it. Get mad, girl. Show me what's really bothering you," he said. He wasn't sure where this was going but after last night, learning that most of his life he'd been lied to by his father, he was tired of half-truths. He was no longer interested in playing a part. Any part. He was going to live life on his terms and he wasn't holding back. Iris should do the same.

"What's bothering me?" she said. "I don't think you really care that much, Zac. We both know you're only here until my dad and Collins Combined come through with your funding. Then you are off to train and race for three years. We both know that you are playing a role even though you want to pretend that you're, what, better than me, more honest than me? You're not. You're here dressing in jackets with pocket squares, shaving and trying to fit into a role as much as I am. You're judging me while excusing yourself."

"I didn't say I was disappointed in you," he pointed out.

"Well you didn't have to. I'm disappointed in myself. You know what's the matter this morning? My dad sent over some paperwork for both of us. He has assembled your investors and you will have the money wired into your account on Monday. And I know you'll be out the door. Sure, you'll be sweet and polite about it, but that's it. You'll move on.

"And while I watched you singing and dancing in front of the fire last night, I realized I didn't want you to leave. I didn't want to see you walk out of my life because I'm an effing idiot and fell in love with you. Sure, I knew I shouldn't. Hell, you're not even the kind of man I usually fall for. But you know that perfect image you're so sure I'm hiding behind—well, I wasn't. I was myself. Sorry I'm not more exciting and can't deliver nonstop fun the way you can, but that was me. Guard down and being totally myself."

He was stunned. He was pretty sure in the middle of her rant she'd said she loved him. Iris Collins, the most sophisticated, sexy, sweet, charming, smart woman he'd ever met, loved him. He'd lashed out because he knew he wasn't worthy. Even now he realized he'd let her down. Again.

He should apologize. He knew that. But his brain was working slowly this morning and Iris just shook her head and blinked a lot before she walked out of the hotel suite.

Why was she leaving?

He hadn't had a chance to tell her any of the things he needed to. He ran out after her, but she'd gotten in the elevator and was gone. His gut told him if he let her go, he'd regret this for the rest of his life.

This wasn't a moment where time was going to make things better. She needed him now.

He went to the balcony. They were only on the third floor and he climbed over and lowered himself onto the balcony below and then one more time until he was on the ground floor.

The gravel path was rough on his bare feet, but he made it around to the front of the building just as Iris exited. She had her large black sunglasses on and a sheath dress. He stood there with dirt and rock embedded in the bottom of his feet, looking like a beach bum instead of a Bisset.

He was never going to be the picture-perfect man on her arm, but he knew that no one would love her better or give her more adventure in her life.

Now to somehow show her that.

Sixteen

Iris walked straight past him and he realized that maybe it was better if he just let her go. She was definitely not thinking straight. He knew women tended to get all those romantic feelings during a wedding weekend and Adler and Iris were best friends.

He stood there next to the valet, barefoot and looking like he'd just come off a night of binge drinking, which he had. Watching the woman he loved more than he'd ever thought he could walk away from him was sobering. This was the reality of life with the two of them. They were both busy people and weekends like this would be the best they could hope for.

She deserved more, and in her own words, wanted more. Shouldn't he just let her have it? He watched her get into her sensible car and drive off and then he slowly made his way back into the hotel.

His brother Logan was slinking in, as well. He had his

eyes shielded behind his Ray-Ban Wayfarers and as he saw Zac, he lifted his hand in a weak wave. His brother looked worse than Zac felt, and he wasn't sure how that was possible given that Zac's world was crumbling. Everything he'd ever believed about himself was shattered. He wasn't the man who was looking for another horizon—he had been looking for Iris. No other woman had ever made him feel like he was okay just as he was.

"Dude, you look rough," Zac said. "Where'd you go last night?"

"Took a trip down memory lane and I'm not sure how but we ended up in bed," Logan said. "I think it's going to end up biting me in the ass."

"Her too," Zac said. Logan hadn't always been the type-A, driven COO he was today. Once upon a time he'd been a very competitive kid with a girlfriend who liked to one-up him. Quinn had gone on to take television by storm. She was one of the top producers today. But Logan had caught up and maybe even moved past her, making a name for himself at Bisset Industries. It was interesting to think of the two of them hooking up. And it was just the distraction he needed after Iris walked away looking broken.

"Yeah, I know," Logan said. "What are you doing in the lobby looking like a hobo? If you have even the slightest chance of keeping a woman like Iris Collins, you have to up your game," Logan said. "Come up to my room and I'll get you some decent clothes."

"Thanks, bro," he said, trying to play it cool but knowing he failed when Logan put his hand on his shoulder. Everyone could see that he and Iris weren't meant to be. He should just take the investor money and start focusing on the one area where he was good. Sailing. Captaining a racing team. He could do that.

"You okay?"

"No. I screwed up, Logan. I have no idea how to fix it or if I should even try. I'm hungover. I might still be a little drunk. I've had the kind of morning that Dad should be having but he probably is too coldhearted to realize that everything is slipping out of his grip."

"Z, Dad's not the heartless monster that the media and Carlton play him up to be, you know that. Despite everything else happening right now. What's wrong that you are lashing out?"

He shook his head. He had no idea where to start. "Never mind."

"I'm on your side. I'm always on your side, no matter what happens. Talk to me. If there's one thing I'm good at, it's solving problems," Logan said.

He was good at it. "All right. I agreed to be Iris's plus one this weekend in exchange for her getting some investors for my America's Cup run. We both said it would be temporary, but it didn't feel that way until this morning. Now I don't want to let her go, but even you pointed out that she's too good for me and you hardly ever notice stuff like that."

Logan put his hand on Zac's arm and urged him to move out of the lobby. For the first time, Zac was aware of their surroundings—the fact that it was a crowded lobby and that people had been staring at the two of them.

Damn.

Hell.

He was the biggest asshole on the planet. He'd had blinders on because he wasn't used to anyone caring what he did when he was on land.

"Do you think they heard?"

"I have no idea, but let's get up to my room and figure out what's next," Logan said.

"She'll be ruined by this, Logan. I can't believe I didn't

think before I spoke. She's all about image. I mean that's why we—"

Logan put his hand over Zac's mouth as they got on the elevator. The door closed and Logan dropped his hand. "Paparazzi are all here trying to get the scoop on the latest Bisset scandal. You have to stop talking."

"I know."

Zac didn't say another word until they were down the hall and in his brother's room. "Why aren't you staying at Gran's?"

"I didn't want to make Adler uncomfortable. I've been a douche about Nick and he's her groom. But I do love our cousin. I figured the least I could do was stay out of her way."

"Yeah, that's a good call. Nick's not a bad guy."

"I know. It's just that for as long as I can remember, I've always been trying to beat him. Sometimes I do and other times I don't. I hate losing and he's a Williams, so it makes it harder to let it go," Logan said, tossing his sunglasses on the bed and then looking over at him. "Now about Iris... We need to get ahead of this before it comes out."

"What am I going to do?" Zac asked his brother. "I love her. I was trying to ask you how to win her back, but it seems impossible now, doesn't it?"

"Nothing is impossible. You told me that when we were teenagers. If you were smart enough to realize that back then, you can fix this," Logan said.

Zac wasn't sure his "wisdom" as a teenager was anything more than bravado, and he didn't know how to fix this. But he regretted that he might hurt her and had to try to make things right.

Iris didn't have a destination in mind as she left the hotel behind. She could think of only one person who actually needed her this morning and that was Alder. Sure Iris wanted to escape. She'd never been in love with anyone before and confessing it to Zac and having him just sort of blink at her wasn't the reaction she'd been hoping for. She'd had two breakups fairly close together and honestly she had to say this one was affecting her way worse than the first.

Not that she and Zac had broken up. She started crying as she realized how messed up this truly was. She pulled her car off the road and just sat there for a few minutes, realizing that the only place she wanted to be was off Nantucket. But she couldn't do that to Adler.

She was trapped by her own bad decisions. She almost texted Thea something mean but it wasn't her sister's fault that she'd decided to choose a man to be her fab, fun plus one and Zac Bisset turned out to be the one. She couldn't have predicted it and she couldn't blame it on Thea.

She drove her car back to a public parking lot and left it there, walking toward the beach because going back to the room she was sharing with Zac was completely out of the question. She took her shoes off as soon as she was on the sand. Tendrils of hair started to escape from the chignon she'd put it up in, when she was still trying to pretend that she had it all together. She reached up and took the pins out, knowing that she was done fooling herself.

Since she'd gotten the internship with Leta Veerland, she'd promised herself she wouldn't waste a moment. That she'd craft a life that was successful and leave no room for failure and she'd done that. On every front except on the personal one. But there was no way she was ever going to be successful in a relationship unless she let herself be. The problem with men, and Zac in particular, was that she didn't want to be vulnerable to him. She didn't want him to see that she wasn't that social media person. The one with the fabulous life who made good choices. But until him, she'd never found a way to be comfortable with herself.

Now she had no choice and she was failing.

Big time.

She took a deep breath and tipped her head back, letting the sea air sooth that troubled part of her soul. She'd taken a risk, a real gamble, when she'd approached Zac. And it had given her so much more than she'd expected. She had to let herself have that.

Her phone vibrated but she ignored it. She wasn't going to respond to anything right now. She needed this walk on the beach to gather her thoughts and regain her equilibrium. She knew she was the maid of honor at the wedding and Adler might need her.

Adler. Something had been up with her and Nick last night. Iris pulled out her phone to text Adler and saw on the Find My Friends app that she was on the beach as well. She walked toward her position and found her friend standing on the shore just staring out at the water.

"Hey, Ad," she said, coming up behind her and hugging her. "Everything okay this morning?"

Adler wiped her eyes and immediately Iris knew it wasn't.

"Nick and I had a big fight last night. I'm just not sure if we should cancel everything. He was too hungover this morning to discuss it and said whatever I decided he'd go along with."

That didn't sound like the Nick she knew. "He didn't mean that."

"I'm not so sure. He's reeling from learning that August is his father."

Iris held Adler's hand. "I know, but he loves you."

"He did."

"Stop that. This is just bridal jitters on steroids. He's

not himself because of the news, but I'm sure how he feels about you hasn't changed. Do you want to cancel the wedding?"

Adler hesitated and Iris's heart, already sore and aching, broke for her friend. Men. Love was kicking her ass and now Adler's ass, too.

"I can't cancel it. Everyone is arriving today."

Iris took a deep breath. She completely understood where her friend was coming from. If she cancelled a televised wedding she was going to bring a lot of unwanted attention down on herself and Nick. "If you're not sure about Nick, then you should postpone things. You're going to spend the rest of your life with him."

She nodded. "I hate this. It's like when dad had that affair with that stupid eighteen-year-old. The media isn't going to be kind."

"Are you cancelling things?"

"I need to talk to Nick," she said.

"Okay. Do you want me to go with you?"

"No. I have to do this on my own," she said.

They both went their separate ways, Adler walking up to the house that Nick and she had purchased on the island and Iris walked back to the hotel. She started up the path toward the hotel, stopping at a bench to wipe her feet off and put her shoes back on. She took her phone out and glanced down to see that she'd missed a call from Quinn and one from Zac.

Good.

She wasn't ready to talk to Zac. She had to figure out how to pull herself back from what she'd admitted. From now on, she wasn't going to let her emotions get the better of her.

She texted Quinn and got back a call.

"Hey."

"Where are you?"

"On the beach, fixing to walk back to the hotel. Why?"

"Stay there," Quinn said. "I'm tracking you with the friend app, hold on."

She did as her friend asked, looking up at the sun. "Still there?"

"Yes, what's up? Did the media already start pinging you about Nick?"

"Yes. But that's not all. Something else has come up and it involves you."

"What?"

"Zac blurted out that you paid him to be with you this weekend in the lobby at the hotel. It was overheard by a bunch of reporters and everyone is running with the story."

"What?" Shock warred with anger and betrayal inside of her.

"Yeah, I know. Listen, it gets worse. Someone videoed him saying it on their phone, so everyone has it. There's no denying it," Quinn said.

"What am I going to do? I'm prelaunch on the new couples line. This affects everyone who works for me. My partnership deals," she said, but she stopped talking. Had Zac done it to prove he didn't love her? Had he thought that he needed to make it clear that things between them would end when the wedding weekend was over?

She was horrified and angry. She felt tears burning in her eyes as she fumbled in her bag for her sunglasses and put them on. She wasn't about to let him know how badly he'd hurt her. She texted her team to get another room at the hotel and meet her there in forty-five minutes. She was going to have to go on the offensive to save her business.

Quinn showed up a minute later and sat down next to her on the bench. She looked at her friend and all the betrayal and pain inside of her welled up. Quinn hugged her close.

"He's an idiot."

"He is," Iris agreed. "But I think I might have been the bigger one. I love him, Quinn."

"I know," her friend said. "I could tell last night."

"I'm going to have to spin this," she said.

"I think he cares for you too," Quinn started.

Iris shook her head. "It doesn't matter. We can't be together after this."

She hoped if she said the words out loud enough, her heart would get the message.

Zac didn't have the chance to talk to Iris before the rehearsal where she pretty much ignored him the entire time. Nick and Adler looked fragile and both went their separate ways after they were done. Zac wasn't sure what was going on between the two of them but he wanted to fix things with Iris.

He didn't blame her for ignoring him. Stephan from her team had come to see him and had advised him that he wasn't needed for any promo or to do anything with Iris for the rest of the weekend.

He'd tried to talk to Stephan, but it was clear the other man wasn't having it. He'd left Zac feeling even worse about what had happened. And when he got to his grandmother's house, his entire family was tense. Even Mari, who usually found a way to lighten the mood, looked somber.

They were all gathered in the formal living room when Mari walked over to him and gave him a hug. "I love you, big bro, even though you are totally clueless sometimes."

"I'm not used to having anyone care what I say."

"But you knew she does," Mari said. "I like Iris a lot. I'm surprised at what you said, but I can see how it would be something she'd agree to. She's really smart about her brand and has been careful about how she manages it."

"Yeah, until I majorly messed it up. That wasn't my intent," Zac said. He'd spent all day thinking about the business side of it but he knew that if he'd handled the declaration of love better, they wouldn't be in this situation and she probably wouldn't care because she'd know he was on her side.

"No one thinks you did it intentionally," Mari said. "How are you going to make it up to her?"

He had a few ideas. So far none of them had been that great. He'd hoped he could talk to her. He knew that he was going to have to show her how much she meant to him. Make the big gesture and prove it to the world. His family was all for him doing something with Iris, anything that would take the spotlight off his father and the illegitimate son that no one had known about until yesterday.

Now that the media were beginning to hint they had the scoop on what had transpired at the Bissets' yesterday, Carlton was releasing a statement that had the backing of both the Williams and Bisset families. But no one believed that the scandal would go away that easily.

"I'm hoping that when the time is right…it will come to me."

Mari punched him in the shoulder. "Don't wing this, Zac. If she's important to you, then show her and make an effort."

"I am," he said. He had spent the entire day thinking of all of the things he'd learned about Iris since they'd met. It might not have been a long time but they'd both been real with each other. He was pretty sure he knew her better than anyone else.

He knew how badly he'd hurt her. He had humiliated her

without meaning to and he knew he was going to have to bare his soul in order to have a chance at winning her back.

The rehearsal dinner was being held in the ballroom at his grandmother's house. It had been set with large round tables that would seat eight and a large dance floor in the middle. There was a live band and later on he knew that Toby Osborn was going to perform.

There was media at the event as Adler and Nick's wedding was being filmed and most of the wedding guests were present. He had an idea and knew that if he was going to pull it off, he needed to get to work.

"Bye, kiddo. Wish me luck."

"Good luck," she said as he turned and walked out of the ballroom to find Toby. If there was a man who knew how to survive scandals, it was Adler's father. He didn't need advice because he knew what he needed to do, but he could use some backup.

He found Toby outside smoking a cigarette.

"Hey, I need your help. I'm not any good at this sort of thing and I screwed up royally with Iris."

"After last night? I thought you were going to propose," Toby said.

Drunk Zac had been prepared for that. Unfortunately that wasn't an option until he fixed things with Iris.

"Yes, I really messed up today. I want to do something that will show her what she means to me. Can you help me with some lyrics?" Zac asked. "I want to use the old song 'They Can't Take That Away From Me.' The song means something to us."

Toby listened to everything that Zac had to say and then nodded. "Okay. If that doesn't work, be prepared to grovel."

"I am," Zac said. And he was. He didn't want to lose Iris over this. Not when he'd finally realized that she was the person he wanted to always come home to. The one woman he needed to be his home port.

He told Toby what he wanted to say and the other man wrote it down, wordsmithing it as he went along. When they were done, he handed the paper to Zac who read over the words and hoped that Iris would understand that she was his world. She was the ocean underneath his yacht and he needed her.

He hurried into the ballroom. The band was almost ready to take a break but he asked them if they would stay and play for him while he sang for Iris.

They agreed and Zac took a deep breath.

"We have had an odd request and I hope you won't mind helping this man out by welcoming Zac Bisset to the stage. He has a special song he'd like to perform for Iris Collins."

Seventeen

The last thing Iris was interested in was seeing Zac dressed in a dinner jacket and tie looking way more handsome than someone who'd broken her heart should. She almost got up but Mari came over and put her hand on her shoulder.

"Give him a chance," she said. "If this doesn't make it right, then I'll be surprised."

She thought Mari was giving her brother too much credit but she sat back down and looked up at the stage.

"Thank you for allowing me to take the stage," Zac said. "Many of you may have heard about a pact that Iris and I made for the weekend and I'm sure you've inferred all sorts of things about it. But whatever you've come up with, it's not the truth. I'm sorry, Iris, for not being more careful when I spoke. I'm not used to the spotlight but that's no excuse. You asked me for a favor, which I agreed to and then broke my word. This in no way makes up for it, but I hope it will help you accept my apology. The sentiment is my own, the song is borrowed and the lyrics were tweaked by Toby Osborn."

He turned to the band and they started to play the beginning notes of "They Can't Take That Away From Me." She was flooded with memories of him dancing her around his living room and singing under his breath. That was the moment, she thought, when she'd first let her guard down and started to fall for him.

Zac started to sing in his off-key tone. He was singing the actual words of the song until he got to the chorus. Then she stopped breathing as he sang. Because the chorus was all about her and how he hoped she'd give him another chance.

He ended with, "Please don't take my angel face away."

Her heart was in her throat. Today had been long and she'd been through the wringer. But she'd missed him. Her manager had called and she'd done a live video on her YouTube channel talking honestly to her viewers, and it had resonated. A lot of them had made mistakes and understood how hard it was to find love. It had led to a good discussion, one Iris intended to keep going.

One of the brands she'd partnered with had dropped her but Iris understood they needed someone who was perfect, not human like her.

He stood there on the edge of the risers waiting for her, and she hesitated for a second before she got up and walked over to him. The band started playing one more song as Zac led her to the corner of the ballroom.

"This morning when you said you loved me, it was buried in a bunch of other stuff and my foggy brain was still processing it when you walked out the door. I climbed down to the ground floor to go after you but…there you were, all you, and there I was, sloppy me in bare feet. And we both know you deserve better than that."

"No," she said. She could tell he still had more that he wanted to say but she wasn't going to let him go on believing she wanted more than him. "I think I made you feel like you wouldn't be good enough if you weren't fitting into my image of life, but I like life with you. I like me with you."

"I do too. I honestly am in love with you, but I feel like we could both use some time to believe it," he said. "I'm so sorry I blew our cover. I didn't mean to. For the first time in my life I was on rough seas and had no idea how to navigate myself through it. I realized after I blurted everything out to Logan that you are my keel, angel face. You keep me on course. I didn't know I needed that until we found each other."

"Me too. I love you, Zac. All of you. You embrace life in a way that I have never been comfortable allowing myself to. I guess I thought no one would accept me if I wasn't perfect but you have done that from the beginning."

Everyone applauded as he took her in his arms and kissed her.

A moment later there was a commotion and Iris looked up to see Adler pulling away from Nick and throwing her engagement ring at his feet.

"I can't do this," she said as she ran from the room.

* * * * *

COMING SOON!

We really hope you enjoyed reading this book. If you're looking for more romance, be sure to head to the shops when new books are available on

Thursday 2nd April

To see which titles are coming soon, please visit
millsandboon.co.uk/nextmonth

MILLS & BOON

THE HEART OF ROMANCE

A ROMANCE FOR EVERY KIND OF READER

MODERN

Prepare to be swept off your feet by sophisticated, sexy and seductive heroes, in some of the world's most glamourous and romantic locations, where power and passion collide.
8 stories per month.

HISTORICAL

Escape with historical heroes from time gone by. Whether your passion is for wicked Regency Rakes, muscled Vikings or rugged Highlanders, awaken the romance of the past.
6 stories per month.

MEDICAL

Set your pulse racing with dedicated, delectable doctors in the high-pressure world of medicine, where emotions run high and passion, comfort and love are the best medicine.
6 stories per month.

True Love

Celebrate true love with tender stories of heartfelt romance, from the rush of falling in love to the joy a new baby can bring, and a focus on the emotional heart of a relationship.
8 stories per month.

Desire

Indulge in secrets and scandal, intense drama and plenty of sizzling hot action with powerful and passionate heroes who have it all: wealth, status, good looks…everything but the right woman.
6 stories per month.

HEROES

Experience all the excitement of a gripping thriller, with an intense romance at its heart. Resourceful, true-to-life women and strong, fearless men face danger and desire - a killer combination!
8 stories per month.

DARE

Sensual love stories featuring smart, sassy heroines you'd want as a best friend, and compelling intense heroes who are worthy of them.
4 stories per month.

To see which titles are coming soon, please visit

millsandboon.co.uk/nextmonth

MILLS & BOON

HEROES

At Your Service

Experience all the excitement of a gripping thriller, with an intense romance at its heart. Resourceful, true-to-life women and strong, fearless men face danger and desire - a killer combination!

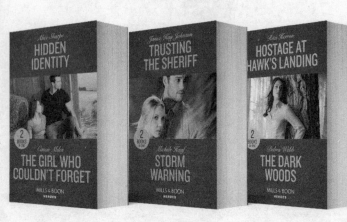

MILLS & BOON

MODERN

Power and Passion

Prepare to be swept off your feet by sophisticated, sexy and seductive heroes, in some of the world's most glamourous and romantic locations, where power and passion collide.